PSYCHOTIC SKANK

ZENA LIVINGSTON

authorHOUSE®

AuthorHouse™
1663 Liberty Drive
Bloomington, IN 47403
www.authorhouse.com
Phone: 1-800-839-8640

This is a work of fiction, all characters are fictitious. Any resemblance to any person living or deceased is coincidental.

Published by AuthorHouse 9/18/2013

ISBN: 978-1-4918-1275-4 (sc)
ISBN: 978-1-4918-1274-7 (hc)
ISBN: 978-1-4918-1276-1 (e)

Library of Congress Control Number: 2013915390

Any people depicted in stock imagery provided by Thinkstock are models, and such images are being used for illustrative purposes only. Certain stock imagery © Thinkstock.

This book is printed on acid-free paper.

Because of the dynamic nature of the Internet, any web addresses or links contained in this book may have changed since publication and may no longer be valid. The views expressed in this work are solely those of the author and do not necessarily reflect the views of the publisher, and the publisher hereby disclaims any responsibility for them.

DEDICATION

This book is dedicated to the most important people in my life: our son Douglas for his constant love and support, his sons Jonathan and Harrison who are just precious, and to Leon, my husband of 51 years, who is always there for me and always encourages and loves me.

A special thank you is given to Doug and Kathy, Margaret and Tom and Carolyn and Ron. They define the word friendship. Thanks to Mary S and Sara J for their help.

CHAPTER ONE

There she is. Jeff could not believe his eyes. It had been years since he last saw her walking away from him and there she was. It was almost as if the years had not passed and it was just yesterday when he and she had been friends. He could not believe that just seeing her lying on the bench in the gym would evoke such emotions within him. He was embarrassed as he felt himself harden and he was also a little ashamed of himself. How could he allow such feelings after all that Vicki did? How could he even look at her without disgust and humiliation? It was at that moment that she sat up from the workout bench and caught his eye. She smiled at him with that slightly whimsical smile she had when she knew the other person's thoughts. It was as though she was saying she knew she could have him again, hurt him again. Jeff's first impulse was to turn and leave but his self-esteem would not allow him to do so.

"Hi, Vicki. Long time no see." he said as he approached the bench where she was sitting. "You don't have to tell me what you've been doing with yourself."

"No need to get nasty. It is none of your business what I have been doing. Just in case you fail to remember, you have no ties on me."

"How is Joseph? He must be getting big. How old is he now?"

"Joseph is fine. In fact he is finishing high school this year and he is already taller than his father and hopefully smarter as well. What about you? Still married; kids?"

'I'd rather not talk about me. Let's just leave it as nice seeing you and call it a day." Jeff said as he turned and walked away from her, though he knew he would never walk away from the memories seeing her had rekindled.

Jeff left the gym and drove his car to the beach. He knew that here he could try to get his thoughts in order and try to understand how Vicki could still create havoc in his head. Jeff knew he could not go home as Stacey would definitely pick up on turmoil in his mind and he was not in the mood to have to start explaining things to her. So, he took the Wantagh Parkway south down to field seven at JonesBeach. At field seven you could sit in your car and actually see the waves hitting the beach. As Jeff sat there, he could hear the sounds of the ocean and it was as if his thoughts were coming rushing back with the same cadence as the waves crashing into the beach.

He first saw Vicki when he was hired as a new lawyer at the firm of Schwartz, Schwartz and Reed in Garden City, New York. She was the receptionist and seemed pleasant enough to the new attorney who was a little nervous presenting himself to his new employers on that first day fifteen years ago. Vicki and he would engage in the usual office small talk whenever he passed her desk on the way in or out of the office. Eventually, he learned she was married and had a young son. Her husband was not doing particularly well in his construction business, so she was forced to go to work and leave Joseph with her mother-in-law.

One day several months after they initially met, Jeff was shocked when he saw Vicki. She had been out on vacation the week before and when she returned to work she had a new nose and enlarged breasts which she was showing off in a rather tight fitting sweater. The change in her appearance was startling.

"What made you decide to do this to yourself?" Jeff could not help himself from asking.

"I've decided to make changes in my life. I threw out George and told him that I want a divorce as soon as possible. I see no reason to continue living with that no good bum. I've met someone else and so the story goes."

"So who is this new guy in your life?"

"Actually, he is not all that new. He is my next door neighbor. His wife is as boring as George and we have a good thing going for us."

"Too bad I am not a divorce attorney. It sounds like your block could keep a guy in business. I'm betting the wife did not see any of this coming her way. That could make for an interesting divorce."

"I told you she was boring. She is Miss prim and proper; the happy little homemaker taking care of the house and the children but forgetting to excite the man. Ironically, I was actually friends with her and she thinks I am her friend. It's a joke but she has no clue what is going on right under her nose. God, Todd and I were actually doing it in their garage while she was inside making dinner."

"Vicki, on a need to know basis, that is more than I need to know."

"Hey, I consider you a friend. I think you should be happy for me that I found someone I could really care about."

"I guess, I am happy for you but a little confused. What about Joseph? How is he going to take it when his father does not come home?"

"Joseph is too young to understand. He will still see George and George's parents; so little will change for him. In fact, I understand that George is living with his parents in their house which is around the corner from mine. So Joseph will see him whenever and George's mother is still going to babysit for me. She is really good with Joseph and he loves her so why not?"

"And Todd- what does he do?"

"He's an electrician and works in the city. It's a union job and he makes good money. Once this is all settled, I will be able to quit my job and we will be more than comfortable living off his income; even if he has to pay that bitch of a wife child support."

"Oh, so he has a kid too?"

"He has three girls. They are good kids but my guess is that they will grow up to be as boring as their mother."

"And this Todd guy wanted you to have all of this cosmetic surgery?'

"I did the surgery for me not for anyone else. My body is a temple and I want it to be worshipped."

"Wow," was Jeff's comment as he turned and walked away shaking his head.

Each day there seemed to be a change in Vicki's demeanor. At first the changes were subtle such as tighter fitting sweaters and shirts. Then Jeff began to notice other changes in her body shape. She was more toned and her ass seemed to stick out and wiggle as she walked. It was almost as if her body was inviting those around her to touch it and invade it. Her flirting also became more and more obvious to all of those around her in the office. The men seemed to love it but the women resented her. She would refer to the women as catty bitches who were just jealous of her.

Jeff could not help himself but to inquire about Todd. He wondered if their relationship was still so hot and heavy.

"Oh Todd, he's crazy about me and will do anything to keep me in his bed. I have to tell you what happened last night. It is truly hilarious. There we were in the hot tub on my back patio. All of a sudden the lights went on and there was Stacey, Todd's wife. She was screaming at us so loud that the neighbors certainly heard it all. All I could do was stand up and show her my naked body. I said, "Bitch try to compare with this!" Man was it hilarious and all Todd could do was laugh and mutter that you could not make up this shit if you wanted to."

"Doesn't it feel awkward? After all he is still married to the other woman and the two of you are carrying on right under her nose?"

"I could not care one little bit. In fact I just used to take and throw her bra off the bed and fuck him into oblivion right there in her bedroom.. It does not matter if she knows or doesn't know. He is mine now and she can just move out and leave us alone. She and those whiney girls of hers are not worth talking about. They are past history and I am the present."

Jeff could just walk away shaking his head and wondering about what he had just heard. It was hard to imagine anyone being so callous and so uncaring about someone else's feelings. He almost felt sorry for Stacey and the girls. They were certainly no match for Vicki. But then again, he had to wonder what type of person this Todd guy really was. Was he just capable of turning away from his family just for a great roll in the hay? Jeff decided on the spot that he was going to stay far away from Vicki and the drama surrounding her. His instincts told him she was trouble with a capital T and he did not want to do anything to jeopardize his position at the firm.

Three weeks passed before he again came face to face with Vicki in the hallway of the office. She was very animated and agitated and he could not help but ask if anything was the matter.

"That wicked bitch. She is accusing me of threatening her and has gotten an order of protection to prevent me from coming anywhere near her or the girls"

"What did you do to justify something like that?"

"I told her what a cunt she was in no uncertain terms"

"Did you threaten her? A court order of protection usually follows a threat of some type."

"No, not really. I just told her to leave us alone and get out of our lives. Todd is finished with her and we want to move in together."

"What about Joseph?"

"Oh, he comes with me wherever I go."

"How does George see all of this?"

"He is too stupid to see anything. He is willing to continue to support Joseph and me. He has promised to keep paying for the Mercedes and the house and anything else that I want as long as he can spend time with Joseph. Of course, he really wants to get back in my pants but I have no interest. He is just so boring- always the same old, same old. It is just hard now with that stupid order of protection. After all Stacey is my next door neighbor and there are only sixty feet separating out property lines. So, if I am at my house and she comes out at the same time as I do, I could get arrested. I am not allowed to be near the girls and that has put a damper on things when Todd wants to see them. It's a stupid mess. Frankly, I am hoping the law firm can help me to resolve this and have the order of protection rescinded. There must be something that you could do?"

"I can ask around and see if there is anything that can be done, but I make no promises. I get the feeling that you are not being totally truthful with me on this one. You had to do something to anger her to the point where she would go to the police to get an order of protection. Were you arrested or anything?"

"Yeah, the bitch accused me of threatening her and actually had me taken to the precinct. But I was not really arrested. They just warned me to not have anything to do with her and to stay away from her and the girls. The guys at the precinct were real nice to me. In fact I invited them back to the house for coffee and cake."

"What type of cake were you serving?"

"Now, now-you don't have to get nasty."

"Is Todd still living next door to you?"

"No, he took a place in the next town so he could get away from Stacey and her constant nagging. He has a real nice place on the water, so that is cool."

"Correct me if I am wrong- the only issue here is your coming and going from your own house. If you see Stacey, you can just ignore her but you cannot maintain the one hundred feet that is part of the order of protection. Am I correct?"

"Yes, that is the issue. I need to stay at my place until Joseph is finished with school as I do not want to upset his schedule. George is okay with it. He has moved in with his mother, he probably never should have left her side in the first place. Joseph and I have the house to ourselves and Todd does not come over. I usually go to his place and I usually do so when Joseph is with his father as I want him to get used to the idea slowly. Eventually I would expect that Joseph and I will move in with Todd but that is not for now."

"I'll look into this whole situation and see what I can do to help you. In the meantime, stay away from Stacey and do not even call her house. You are to have no contact with her in any way or form. Do you understand?"

"I am not an idiot."

"Does she go to the same gym as you do? And what about school? Do her children attend the same school as Joseph?"

"She is too flabby to go to any gym and as for school, her girls go the Catholic school and Joe goes to public school."

"Okay- that solves one set of problems. From what you are saying the only way you and she can come face to face with each other is when you are coming or going from the house or if you should happen to frequent the same supermarket etc. I'll get back to you as soon as I get things sorted out.

And so began my professional relationship with Vicki. I knew from the start it was against firm policy to represent someone from within the firm but I thought the matter was relatively insignificant and that I could clear it up in no time. Here I was on a track to be offered a partnership after only a short time with the firm and I was really proud of my accomplishments. On the other hand, I was intrigued by Vicki and that was definitely clouding my judgment. Part of me just had to keep getting information about her escapades. It was just unbelievable that a woman could be so free and easy. I just had to call Stacey and see if she would speak with me. I was genuinely surprised when Stacey not only agreed to speak with me but suggested that we meet at the local diner where we could talk face to face.

Jeff arrived at the diner early and requested a table in the back of the restaurant. He was sitting there when a very attractive woman came up to the table and identified herself. Somehow, he did not expect someone so well dressed and even sexy. His mental picture was of an overweight, non-sex appealing person; and Stacey was neither. She took her seat and asked what he wanted of her.

"I just want a picture of what is really happening. Vicki has spoken with me and requested that I try to get the order of protection lifted."

"Let me fill you in. There is no way in hell I will allow the order to be lifted. I do not know what you know about this entire horrible situation but I have three young children who have to be protected and shielded from it all."

"I understand your concern. Maybe you can fill me in a little and I will see what I can do to help."

"It's as simple as this. Vicki and I are neighbors and I thought we were friends. That was until I discovered that she and Todd were having an affair right under my nose; right in my house. It was an unbelievable shock to me. I thought Todd and I had a good marriage, that we loved each other. Well, I threw the bum out once I found out and frankly, I want nothing to do with him except that is not possible as the children need their father and he and I will have to have contact with each other until Cathy, she is the youngest, is at least eighteen and that is thirteen years away. However, they do not have to have any contact with Vicki and, as long as the order of protection is place, she cannot be there when Todd sees the girls."

"Why did you get the order? I know the police would not give it just to prevent her from being with the children."

"My guess is that somehow Todd told her that he wanted to get back together with me. It made her totally crazy. It was as if she put my number on fast dial and she kept calling and threatening me and screaming obscenities at me. It was sick and I was trembling. When I stopped answering the phone, she came and started banging on my door. Luckily, or maybe not so lucky, I was alone in the house and I really felt threatened, so I called the police. They found her banging on the front door and screaming on my front stoop and she was arrested. Unfortunately, she was back home in a few hours and the calls began all over again."

"Is Todd coming back?"

"Only to get the rest of his stuff and after that he will never cross my threshold again. They can have each other; they deserve each other. But, if he wants to see his daughters, he has to see them when he is alone or I will have her arrested on the spot. The girls know they are not to be with her, that she is evil, and if she is near them, they are to call me immediately. Janet has a cell phone and she knows how to use it. The girls love their father and I do not want to do anything to spoil that as they really do need him. Right now, they know we cannot be together because he does not love me anymore and he and I no longer want to be together. I've told them that it does not mean that their father does not love them and does not want to be with them but that adults sometimes change and when they change, they want other things and other people in their lives."

"That seems very big of you. Most women are very resentful when this happens and show their resentment even to the children."

"Let's understand something. I am resentful, even hateful but my children come first and will always come first. Poisoning them toward their father is destructive not constructive and someday they will make their own judgment, but they will always see that I did the right thing. That is what is important to me. I will tell you this that if Todd chooses to be with Vicki when he is supposed to be with the girls, I will do everything to stop his visitation and it will be open war. He knows this."

"Your feelings are extremely strong. I just do not understand why Vicki was triggered to make those calls to you."

"She really thought he wanted to come back home and she could not stand it. She is an extremely jealous person and I guess it was an affront to her that he might choose me over her. She collects men. Just look at how she is treating George, who happens to be a really nice person."

"Would you elaborate on that?"

"George really loves her. In fact he and I spoke recently and he would take her back in a heartbeat. He could forgive everything if she were to come back and allow him to move back home. You know she sent him out on an errand and then changed the locks so he could not get back into the house. The guy had to go to his mother's house which is actually around the corner and that is where he is living now. He pays all the bills and he and his mother take care of Joseph whenever Vicki takes off. He even pays for her Mercedes. I don't get it, but that is none of my business. As for Joseph, it is good that his father and grandmother are nearby. The child is so insecure that as soon as he doesn't see his mother for a moment, he begins to panic. This was true even before I knew about Vicki and Todd. I used to see it when I would be there during the good times. The other thing I used to see is that she would kiss the boy in an inappropriate manner. She has a habit of planting very sensual kisses right on his lips. I used to tell her it wasn't right but she would tell me that was nonsense. Nonsense, my eyebrow. I wonder what child protection would say about it. Unfortunately, it would be very hurtful to Joseph if I went there and under the present circumstances, I might be viewed as the scorned woman looking to make trouble. So what's the point! George knows about the kisses and he used to tell her to stop as well. Now that ball is in his court. Me- I just have to protect my kids."

"Have you thought about moving?"

"Yeah. As soon as the divorce is final and the house is totally in my name, I will look to sell it and get as far away as I can. I want to change school districts so that the children can attend public school and will not have see her at their school and I will never have to run into her whether it be at school, or shopping or anything. It should be interesting to see how things run their course. Todd is not a wealthy man. Once he has to pay child support and maintenance as well as paying for a place to live, I cannot imagine there will be anything left over. We'll see how long the princess stays when money is tight. You know she is dollar driven and loves to live the good life. My guess is Todd will rapidly become a thing of the past and she will move on to greener pastures. Maybe then he will appreciate what he had but it is too late to recapture what is lost."

"You are totally different than I expected."

"What did you expect?"

"Well, I could only get an impression from what Vicki said. I expected someone who was a housewife, somewhat uninteresting both physically and mentally."

"Well surprise! The one whose impression is fallacious is Vicki. She is crazy! Look, I hope it has been helpful but I have to get going. The girls will be home from school soon and they cannot come into an empty house. I am sorry I cannot do anything to help you to be her golden knight, but if you were listening you understand my position. Let her have Todd, they deserve each other but keep her away from me and the girls."

With that Stacey stood and left the diner leaving Jeff unsettled to say the least. He really believed everything the woman said and really felt sorry for her on one hand but admired her strength on the other. She was a person of integrity and she really cares about her children. There was little doubt she would go forward with her life.

Jeff went back to the office and made a point to see Vicki. He told her there was nothing he could do regarding the order of protection and that she should stay away and leave Stacey alone unless she wanted to get arrested again.

"You are an idiot. You call yourself a lawyer, you are a nobody. Lawyers are supposed to help people and all you can do is to tell me to stay away. Don't try to help me anymore. Your type of help, I don't need or want."

"That's fine with me. I am an officer of the court and can only tell you that the order of protection is in force and that's it."

With that Jeff turned his back and walked to his office. He knew it would be odd seeing her every day at the reception desk but he also knew that he really believed Stacey and he did not want to get sucked into something that would end up putting egg on his face. Vicki was a user and he had no intention of being added to her list of the used.

CHAPTER TWO

The weeks turned into months but all through that time Jeff kept thinking about Stacey. She was indeed a very interesting woman who impressed him with her morals and the caring she demonstrated toward her children. He kept wanting to get to know her better. He kept thinking that she was a quality person. Finally, he decided to reach out to her and call to invite her out for coffee. She at first was skeptical of his invitation wanting to know what he really wanted and if his invitation was somehow linked to Vicki.

"This has nothing to do with Vicki, I am calling you because I would like to get to know you better. Let's understand something, I do not want you to do anything you do not want to do nor do I want to discuss the Vicki situation any further."

"You do realize I have quite a bit of baggage. I have three children. Not many men want to have anything to do with a woman who has three children. To make matters even more complicated, I am and will always be devoted to my kids. They come first and will always do so in my world. Add to that the scenario of my ex and his lady of the night and you have a genuine soap opera on your hands."

"First of all, I am asking you out for coffee not to go to the marriage bureau for a license. Secondly, I am well aware of your so called baggage and it does not frighten me. If we decide we want to get to know each other better, we can take it step by step. There are no commitments on either part. You are a woman who left a lasting impression on me and I would love to get to know you better."

"I am working during school hours and in the evening I would need to get a sitter unless we arrange to meet on a weekend when Todd has the girls. I've thought about you since we met but I never expected to hear from you on a personal level. It would not have surprised me if you called to represent Vicki but it does shock me that you want to see me personally."

"Try to get a sitter for Saturday if that is a night that you have the girls and let's meet at the same diner at eight. You can call me to confirm once you have the sitter. If that is not good, we can go from there."

"The girls are home this weekend. So I will see what I can do and get back to you. I have your number in my phone. By the way, this is one of the nicest things that has happened to me in a long time. Even if nothing comes of our meeting, it is great to think that a man would find me interesting."

"Don't sell yourself short, you are a very interesting woman and I am sure that I will not be the only man who finds you such. But let's talk more in person. I am looking forward to Saturday, hopefully you can arrange things."

And so began a new chapter in Jeff's life. Stacey proved to be more interesting than he could hope. She had an excitement about life and everything they did together seemed new to both of them. They discovered that they both liked walking on the beach, boating, fishing, being in nature preserves, going to ball games and just being together. Jeff did not go to Stacey's house because neither of them wanted to have Vicki see them together. That seemed unproductive with their relationship in its infancy. Stacey also did not want to introduce the girls yet for the same reason and because she felt it would be confusing to them if the relationship terminated and again someone they potentially cared about would leave their lives. Jeff felt he had no choice but to honor Stacey's wishes and in some ways he actually respected her for shielding the girls. From his point of view, he wanted more from the relationship after each time they were together and the more they saw each other the more he wanted to be with her. He began to feel that he had actually met his soul mate and that they were totally in sync. The only question in his mind was what would happen when the children were introduced into the mix. After all, he had no experience with kids and while he always thought he would like to have children one day, having three all at once and three that had issues and habits already formed was another question. No matter how hard Stacey has tried to keep the girls on a positive road, they were affected by their parents' split and they did not understand why their parents could not get back together. From what Stacey had told him it was obvious that Todd was blaming her in front of the children as the reason for the split. She did tell the girls that their father had found someone new but they could not relate to that as they were not seeing Vicki as part of his life and therefore, they believed Todd when he told them that she asked him to leave. To Stacey, the girls were just too young to be told the details of the split and she wanted them to only know that their parents could not get along any longer and that they no longer loved each other and they wanted to go their separate ways. Now if she introduced Jeff into the mess, it would further cement the idea that she was to blame for everything. For her that notion was a difficult one and she was not ready to shoulder the complications. Hopefully, Todd would soon stop poisoning the girls with misinformation and start to realize there was no possibility of reconciliation. Stacey could only imagine that he was feeling the pinch of paying maintenance and child support as well as indulging Vicki's expensive tastes.

For now, Jeff had to be content with things as they were. He saw Stacey on the weekends that the girls were with Todd. During those times, they would be together at his apartment, They were sure Vicki was watching Stacey's comings and goings especially since she was at her house on the weekends that Todd saw the girls.

The days and evenings Jeff and Stacey spent together were exciting beyond expectation. As they developed a physical relationship, their closeness and their desires to satisfy each other added to their attractions for each other. She was everything he could want in a woman and he was the man she had always hoped to be with. They both knew that they wanted more, they wanted to be together without restriction and they wanted to share their daily lives together. Just how to achieve the next step, remained an unanswered question.

Ironically, it was Vicki who solved their dilemma. One evening they were having dinner in a local restaurant when she walked in accompanied by a man neither of them knew. She actually saw them before they saw her but everyone in the restaurant heard her yelling at them. It was amazing how sick she was that she actually believed they had violated her by being together. She accused Stacey of being a whore and yelled at Jeff for being unfaithful to her. To say that everyone in the restaurant was amazed at the verbal attack is an understatement and all Jeff and Stacey could do was to ask her to leave them alone.

"Our being together is none of your business. We have nothing to be ashamed of so why are you yelling at us. And by the way who is he? Aren't you supposed to be in love with Todd or have you forgotten about him? Just go away and leave us alone. You are a person who brings turmoil wherever you go. We are not interested in your drama. Who you are with and what you do is none of our business so just go away before we call the police, just in case you have forgotten about the order of protection that is still in effect."

Jeff seemed to take the wind out of Vicki's sails with that comment and she turned and stormed out of the restaurant. However, they both knew they would have to explain things to the children as they were sure Vicki would somehow turn things around and recount the story with a negative twist when she told Todd about their meeting and that he in turn would use this information against Stacey when he spoke with the children. They decided there and then that they would introduce the children to Jeff and explain their relationship and how their relationship started after their father had moved out of the house. After that it would be up to Jeff to either win over the girls or, as much as they would hate it, they would have to stop seeing each other as it would not be possible to go any further with the relationship. Once again, Vicki had manipulated Stacey's life but hopefully, this time a positive outcome would be effected.

As they got up to pay their check, all Jeff could do was to apologize to the waitress whose face told him that she felt sorry for them even without understanding the relationships involved. Everyone in the restaurant seemed to detect that a crazy person had been in their midst.

It is truly amazing how resilient children really are. When Stacey and Jeff sat down with the girls they actually were excited to be included especially when Stacey told them that they would be going to Six Flags over the next weekend and that they were planning to make it a really fun time, Cathy, the youngest, only wanted to know if they were all getting married. A question that made everyone smile.

"Maybe someday we will all get married. Right now we all have to get to know each other and make sure we all care about each other." Stacey said.

"You know you can never be our Dad" was Janet's comment.

"I have no intention of replacing your Dad. He is your father and your mother and I want you to have a great time with him and to love him. I only want a chance to be part of your life and for all of us to be able to have fun together and to enjoy each other. Your mother is a special person and she and I want to be together and for you to feel good being with us."

"Were you together before our Dad left?"

"Your mother and I did not even know each other before your Dad left. When we met he was already out of your mother's life and I have never met your Dad."

"My Daddy says that Mommy was in love with someone else and that is why he had to leave," said Kristine, the middle child.

"There was no one in my life when your dad left. He left because he no longer loves me and I no longer love him. That sometimes happens with adults. It does not mean that either of us feels any differently towards you but it does mean we can no longer live together. Why we no longer love each other is not a question that has to or can be answered right now. I think it is enough to say that your dad and I grew apart, we have different interests and different desires for our lives and whether or not Jeff is a part of my life, your dad will never again be a part of my life.'

"Daddy says he still loves you and wants to come back home."

"That can never happen. He made choices and sometimes when we make choices we cannot change them later. This is one time he cannot change his choices. No matter how much I love all of you, I cannot and will not live with a man whom I do not love and I do not love your dad. You are too young to understand that I cannot give up my morals just because of you and I would never expect you to give up your life for me when you are older. I will always be here for you and you will always be a part of my life going forward. I will not exclude you for anyone so never worry about that."

"How do you feel, Jeff?" This came as a rather surprising question from the twelve year old Janet and Jeff had to swallow hard to hide his surprise.

"When I first met your mom, she told me that she came with her girls as a package. If I wanted to be with her, I have to be with all of you and I accepted her terms. We have to get to know each other but if you girls are anything like your mom, I am sure I will grow to love you. Look, I do not have any kids, so I am sure there is a whole lot I have to learn about kids. But I am willing."

With that the girls got up, gave their mom and Jeff a hug and declared it was time to get going.

"You said we could go to the beach today. Let's go, and remember we will hold you to your promise to take us to Six Flags. That sounds like real fun."

And so began Jeff's first family outing. At the end of the day he was surprised at how tired he was but he had to admit he had a great time. It was fun watching the girls make castles in the sand and he helped drag the water for the mote and enjoyed being incorporated into their world. They seemed like easy children to be with even when they started whining because they too were tired. But the greatest joy was watching Stacey enjoy having them all together. She was willing to take a backward position and allow him to develop his own relationship with the girls but her pleasure was evident. For Jeff the day was a feel good experience and it was great having their relationship out in the open.

When Jeff arrived home that night his telephone answering machine was blinking rapidly. He started listening to his messages and was appalled as he listened to Vicki verbally assaulting him with rapid fire insults, curses and inane remarks. It was almost as though she believed she was talking to a live person and waiting for a reply. When the reply did not come, she became more infuriated and the cursing escalated to a level that would make even the most hardened football player blush. All Jeff could think was that it was obvious that Stacey felt threatened after her episode with the cursing on the telephone and that it confirmed all that Stacey said about Vicki being unbalanced and at times dangerous. Jeff pressed the save button after each message and knew he would record them just in case he ever needed an example of how insane she really was.

The next morning when he came to the office, he ran right into Vicki in the hallway even though he purposely avoided the front desk. It was like running into a lioness in heat.

"You bastard, you fucking bastard, how could you fuck that bitch? If you want a real woman let me know and I will show you what a real woman can do but no, you go to that fucking bitch and fuck her right in my backyard."

"What are talking about? Who I see and what I do is none of your business. Stacey and I are special friends and we do not know where the relationship will go but wherever it goes, it is none of your business. You have no right to try to control who I see and what I do. You and I have only a professional relationship here at the office. We have never had anything more. All I did was to try to help you regarding the order of protection and you act as if you and I are lovers and you have been jilted. This is nuts."

"If you did not try to help me, all to no avail, I might add, you would not even know that bitch and her slimy kids."

"You have a point there. When I first met Stacey, I was impressed at what a lady she is. That is what initially attracted me to her. Now that I know her even better, she continues to impress me while you impress me as a nut. And talk about being a lady- who was that dude you were with Saturday night? I know Todd was with the girls."

That dude, as you call him, is a friend. He has deep pockets and a wife who is a moron. He'll do anything for me. See this Yurman bracelet, he bought it. He knows how to treat a woman."

"How do you explain him to Todd? He is not a guy who likes to share from everything I've heard about him."

"What he doesn't know, doesn't hurt him. Remember he is taken up with those kids and I can't be there when they are, I have enough time to do my thing. We'll see what happens if Joe actually leaves his stupid wife. He wants me and Joseph to move in with him and believe me, I am tempted. He can afford to give us the life I want. I would even be able to stop working in the hell hole. He promises we could travel and do all sorts of things. Todd can't afford to leave Massapequa. His idea of an exciting evening is a roll in the hay and then spending the rest of the night in front of the idiot tube. That just does not do it for me."

"I am glad you feel some allegiance to the guy. After all you wrecked his marriage and he did give up a whole lot just to be with you."

"Yeah, Mr. Preacher Man, you go on telling me about morals while you are fucking his wife."

"Wrong again, she is no longer his wife. They are actually divorced now so he has no ties on her. Besides, she did not leave him for me, he left her for you."

'Yeah, well, a girl gots to do what a girl gots to do. I am not getting any younger and I need the best deal I can get. Now I have someone who has the dollars to go with the cock and he can afford to pay off his stupid wife and still be able to take care of me. What a change that would be!"

"Vicki, you are a piece of work. I really think it would be better for the both of us if we stop talking to each other about things that are not related to this office. I really do not want to know your business nor do I want you to know my business. Just leave me alone and you go about your life and I will go about mine."

"You can't mean that. We're friends!"

"I can mean that and I do mean that. We are not friends, we are business associates. You are the receptionist here and I am hoping to become a partner in this firm. For my professional well being, I need to sever any relationship you think we have and I hope you will respect my wishes. I believe in a policy of live and let live but if you force me to go further with my complaint that you are harassing me, it could have bad ramifications for you. Do you understand me?"

"You are a prick, a real class one prick. Rest assured I will get the last word and I will see you buried. No man ever tells me to take a walk."

With that she stormed away and Jeff knew this probably would not be the end of it but he really did not care. He saw her for the sick person she really was and he no longer cared what happened to her. It was laughable, but he actually felt sorry for this new guy in her life. She was about to break up his life and to take advantage of him just as she did to Todd. He also knew he would have to speak to the partners of the firm and try to get her replaced if she did not quit soon. Having her at the office could only prove problematic for everyone. But he knew he had to wait until the time was right to do this.

CHAPTER THREE

S tacey and Jeff's relationship was amazing. They enjoyed the same things such as spending the day at the Metropolitan Museum of Art, going to the Broadway theater, walking on the beach and doing nothing at all. There was a comfort level in just being together that Jeff had never experienced before. Hours could pass and it would seem like minutes. On the weekends when the girls were with Todd, they would spend the nights together. It was wonderful to explore each other's body and find new ways to effect pleasure. Stacey had a way of making it seem as if each time was the first time. Jeff could not believe how exciting she was. It was even better that she felt the same way.

When they were with the girls, they planned things that were more child oriented. The girls really loved the Children's Museum and the Museum of Science. Trips to the Natural Museum of History and the Metropolitan Museum of Art's Egyptian exhibit were all exciting to the kids and fun for Stacey and Jeff as well. The biggest difference came after dark. Jeff would return to his apartment as they both felt it was wrong to show the girls that they were sleeping in the same bed while they were not married.

Their main problems came when the girls would come home from Todd with their heads filled with negative thoughts. Todd was trying his best to turn them away from Jeff by telling them that he was preventing reconciliation between Stacey and him.

"Let's understand something once and for all, your father and I are done," Stacey told them one Sunday after their return. "Your father seems to be giving you the wrong impression. He was the one who left. He was the one who was involved with Vicki. He chose Vicki over me. When he left, I did not even know Jeff. Now he is acting like the scorned person."

"He says he wants to come home." Janet answered.

"He will never be a part of my life again. Regardless of what happens between Jeff and me, your father and I are done, done. In order to have a relationship with someone, there has to be trust and love. Your father lost my trust and love."

"Daddy says you will give us up as well."

"Your father is completely wrong about that. You, girls, have always come first and will always come first. The love a mother has for her children is different than that a woman has for a man. Nothing can ever come between our love. Understand that and don't let your father put crazy ideas in your heads. Maybe he is sorry for what he lost, but once lost, it can never be rekindled. I would rather be alone for a lifetime than spend one day with him."

"Do you hate him?"

"Hate is a harsh word. He hurt me especially when I found out he was involved with my friend. I felt betrayed but as long as he and I have to make decisions for your welfare, I can tolerate that much contact with him and if I hated him I could not even tolerate that. I think we have said enough about this. The way you should look at the whole situation is that you have two homes and in each there is someone who loves you and you are important to both of us."

"What about Jeff and Vicki?"

"Jeff really cares about the three of you. He wants to be a part of your lives and he wants you to be a part of his. As for Vicki, she cannot be a part of your lives. She said some pretty crazy things and I cannot forgive her. As part of the divorce, the judge has ruled that she cannot be with you. So your father has to choose if he wants to be with her or with you."

"Joseph says his mom is a good person."

"I am glad he feels that way. That is their business and has nothing to do with me. I would not want to see Joseph hurt in any way. Now, enough is enough. Let's make dinner and get ready for school tomorrow."

That night after the children were asleep and Jeff had left, Stacey called Todd's house. When he answered she asked if he were alone.

"I'm alone, what do you want."

"You have to stop filling the girls' heads with nonsense. You know there is no chance of reconciliation for us so stop telling them that you want to come back and I will not let you. You made your choice, now live with it. Filling their heads with the impossible is wrong. They are too young to really understand and I don't want to have to keep trying to explain things to them. You have to stop trying to poison their minds and if you don't you will leave me no choice but to return to court and to try to have your visitation limited to being supervised by a court guardian. Telling the children that I will abandon them is a horrible thing to do when you were the one who abandoned us. Get your act together or you will lose your daughters."

"Stacey, I know now that I made a mistake."

"It's too little too late. Some mistakes cannot be wiped away with I'm sorry. Obviously, I think you made the wrong choice but it was your choice to make and now you have to move on."

'Is there any way for you to forgive me?"

"You are not listening. I'll say it again-NO."

"You know I am having trouble making ends meet with the child support and maintenance payments."

"Maybe you should stop buying your girlfriend all those expensive gifts. Every time I see her, and I cannot help but do so, she is sporting a new designer bag and enough jewelry to make sure she calls attention to herself."

"She buys those things for herself."

"If you believe that, you are a bigger fool than I thought you to be. Be careful, your pussy cat is on the prowl. I see her going out all decked out when you have the girls and she had better not be going to your house. Look, she is your problem, not mine as long as she is nowhere near our children. You have to find a way to keep your mouth buttoned around the girls because you and I will not be having this conversation again except in front of a judge. And just for the record, I did record the conversation I had with the girls in case I have to present it in court. Am I making myself understood?'

"Ok, ok, enough. I will try my best."

"Try harder than that. Your best is never good enough."

With that she hung up the phone and sat there trying to understand why she had even attempted to reason with him. She probably should have just taken the matter to court and let the judge decide but here she was, again, trying to be the nice person. The only reason he wants to get back together is for financial purposes. Screw him. Let him pay through the nose. He deserves to suffer for what he did. As she sat there in the dark, she kept wondering how she could have been so blind for so long. Todd was always selfish and she chose to ignore it rather than make a stink. She probably should have left him long before Cathy was born. After that she felt trapped what with three young children. She even questioned if Vicki was his first extra-marital affair.

"There are questions for which there are no answers," she said out loud as she walked away from the phone and went up to her bedroom knowing that her conversation with Todd would probably not solve anything but she had to admit she enjoyed throwing out the information about Vicki. That should really make him crazy, if he were listening.

CHAPTER FOUR

Todd could not get his conversation with Stacey off his mind. He kept replaying it in his head and the one thing that kept coming back was her remark about Vicki. Was she just being a bitch and saying something bitchy to get back at him or was there an element of truth in her remark? Todd kept thinking about the calls from Vicki when she could not come over to be with him because she had Joseph and there was no one to watch him. Was she telling him the truth or was she really out with someone else? She did have some really nice new clothes and that Yurman bracelet had to cost a pretty penny. It was unlike her to buy those things for herself and he, unfortunately, really did not have the extra money to spend. He kept thinking that Joseph was the perfect excuse and it would not be unlike her to hide behind her son. She was good at playing the part of the dedicated mother but in reality she was always ready to dump him on George or George's mother.

Todd decided that he would have to find out the truth for himself even if it meant following her to see what that truth really was. He also decided that there was no point in talking to Vicki and tipping his hand.

The first thing he decided to do was to get a list of her incoming and outgoing telephone calls. This would not be that hard to do as his cousin worked at Verizon and had always said that she could get such information. Maybe, that information would clear up things and he could just go on with his life but in his heart of hearts he felt he would find out things he really did not want to know. He had been noticing that even when they were together, she would talk on her cell phone while she was in the bathroom and then would tell him she had to leave to get Joseph.

He was amazed that one remark could make him think of so many things so quickly. Of course, he was not so stupid as to think that Stacey had any other intent in making the remark, but he just had to keep at it until he knew the truth. He would hate to lose Vicki for any reason. She was a real hot cat in bed and with her he did things he never would have imagined doing with anyone. She could make a man feel unbelievable and she did it with such little effort and made him feel like she really cared just about him. After all, she did leave her husband to be with him. But she never wanted to bring Joseph into the relationship. She would always say that she did not want to confuse the kid and that until they decided to get married, she felt it was better that Joseph spend time with his father when they were together. Now he wondered if the real reason was that she feared the boy would say something that would expose her lies. He could not and would not allow her to make a fool out of him. He gave up his financial security and his family for her.

He was so tormented, that he decided to call Vicki even though it was late and tomorrow was a working day. He called but the call went directly to voice mail. Now he was troubled because why would her phone be turned off? They often spoke well into the night on nights they could not be together. With that he got his car keys and decided to drive by her house. He had to know if she were home or not. Since she did not have a garage, he knew that her car would be in the driveway if indeed she were home. There was no car in the driveway when he passed the house so he decided to park up the street and wait. Hours passed and though he would doze off, he would awaken every so often to check the driveway only to find it still empty. He again tried to call her, but again the call went directly to voice mail. With each passing hour, his anger intensified. He had to know the truth and he had to make her come back to him and to him alone.

Finally about three in the morning he heard a car approaching. He watched her pull into her driveway and walk into the house. If she noticed his car parked up the street, she gave no indication of it. He watched as the lights went on in the various rooms and then he decided to call just to talk to her. This time the call did not go to voice mail and when she answered she seemed surprised to hear from him.

"Why are you calling me at this hour? I've been asleep for hours. Don't you know you could wake up Joseph?"

"I decided I missed you and just wanted to hear your voice. I know it's late but I did try to call you earlier and I even left a couple of messages."

"I have a really bad headache, so I went to bed early and decided to turn off the phone. I just got up and went to the bathroom and I noticed the phone was off, so I put it back on. Look I am beat and I have to go to work in just a few hours. I'll see you at your place tonight and we can make up for you being lonely."

"That's a deal, See you tonight around seven."

He waited until the lights went off in her bedroom before he started his car to drive home. All the way home he could not stop shaking. She was lying and he knew it but now he had to find out who she was with before he could do anything about it. He knew he would make that person's life intolerable and in the end he would have Vicki all to himself.

The next evening Todd stood at the window waiting for Vicki to come. He watched as she stepped out of her truck. It was amazing how sculptured her calf muscles were and when she did that little wiggle to straighten her shirt, her ass looked so perfectly rounded and firm that he could feel himself harden from just watching her. He literally ran down the stairs to open the front door to let her in. He knew there would be no small talk and he could not wait to take her and in some ways even vent his anger by intensifying the act as though to show his dominance over her. There was no doubt that she enjoyed rough sex and responded to him with her own vengeance. Todd completely lost all sense of time and place and it was as though someone shot him when he heard her saying she had to go and get Joseph.

"I just don't understand. Joseph can stay with George and I am sure George will make sure he gets to school on time tomorrow. It has been too long since we spent the night together."

"Yeah, you don't understand. I am still Joseph's mother and I did promise him I would be there to put him to bed tonight."

"You make it sound like you haven't been there lately. After all I did not see you all weekend. Weren't you with Joseph then?"

"Of course I was. But he likes it when I put him to bed and he prefers to sleep at home in his own bed."

"I thought he loves being with George and staying at his place. I don't know but this sounds fishy."

"You are nuts. You are letting your imagination take over. Remember he is only a kid and right now he wants his mother to be there when he goes to sleep. It's as simple as all of that."

"Do what you have to do. When will I see you next?"

"I know I have to work overtime tomorrow as the firm is having all sorts of meetings and they want me there to greet everyone and keep things running smoothly. So I guess we can steal a few hours on Wednesday, if that works for you."

"Can I call you on your cell tomorrow? You know how much I miss you when we are not together."

"You can try but during the meeting and all, I probably will not be able to answer the phone. The partners do not like cell phones to ring when important things are going on. I will try to call you if I get a break."

Todd wanted to say that he didn't believe a word of what she was saying but decided to let things go until he had the proof he needed with which to confront her and confront her he would. He was sure something was going on behind his back. He could almost smell another man on her as he fucked her. This was going to be interesting and he knew he would do whatever he had to do to find out the truth and to stop her from seeing whomever she was seeing. She was certainly worth the fight, he thought, as he watched her dress in the most seductive manner anyone could dress. She made sure to show off every part of her perfect body as she slipped into her clothes. Even though he knew the breasts were enhanced, he could not help but to admire them as though they were a work of art. In fact every part of her was a work of art and spoke well for the hours she spent in the gym perfecting them.

When Vicki left he again called his cousin to remind her that he needed the call history.

"Look, things like this cannot be rushed. I am not allowed to get this type of information and it takes a little fanagaling to get it. I have my sources and they have promised they will have the information some time this week."

"Great, I really need it and I do appreciate your help."

"I'll call you just as soon as I have the information in hand and we can decide how you will get it. I don't want to mail it or fax it to you, so I guess you will have to pick it up at my place."

"That's not an issue. I can come to your apartment or we can meet for coffee at the diner. Whatever is best for you."

"I don't know what you are looking for but remember, you have to lose the information or I could lose my job and that would not be pretty."

"I promise there will be no connection possible between the information and you. I just need to know who she is calling and receiving calls from. Once I have that, I promise to destroy the list so no one will ever know how I got the information."

"You are really crazy about this woman. I just hope she doesn't destroy you. I do not trust her for one minute. To me she is trouble with a capital T. Just look how she ruined your marriage and the job she did on Stacey and the kids. Wasn't she Stacey's friend?"

"It was probably over between me and Stacey even before Vicki came on the scene. After all, if I were happy, I would not have wanted to get involved with her in the first place. Understand this, Stacey is a nice woman but boring as hell. She was boring, the marriage was boring and the sex, when there was sex, was boring. I am too young to live in boredom."

"So this is better? Now you are crazy for a woman you admit you cannot trust. It does not sound like that is much of a relationship."

"Stop preaching to the pews, the choir has left. Just please help me by getting the information I need and after that we can have this discussion again. Maybe I am all wrong, we don't know for sure."

"When it smells bad, it tastes bad and it is bad. Don't forget that for a moment and don't forget she left her husband for you and now what makes you think you can hold her?"

'We'll know soon enough. Call me when you have the phone list."

With that Todd hung up but he could not get Margie's words out of his mind. She always has had a way of seeing things clearly and it was clear that she did not trust Vicki even though she barely knew her. He thought they had met once or twice at barbeques at his place but that would be the extent of her involvement with Vicki. He could only imagine that Stacey had given Marge an earful about the breakup. She and Stacey had always been close. It was more like they were cousins than cousins in law.

Todd went down to the kitchen to fix himself some soup and a roll. He smiled as he thought of his mother who always said that the bums in the Bowery could exist on just soup, and here he was having just soup, of course for different reasons. As he sat there eating his dinner, he thought back to the previous few hours. It was amazing how excellent Vicki was with oral sex. She could make him come just by using her tongue. But she did brag about being a three way broad, and he did make sure he had all three ways. He could feel himself getting hard just by thinking about their encounter and he decided to call her just to hear her voice and maybe do some phone sex, if Joseph was already in bed. The call went immediately to voice mail and he sat there wondering why she would turn off her phone. He then called the land line, but there, too, he got voice mail. He slammed down the receiver without leaving a message, and got dressed and drove to her house only to find her car gone and all the lights out.

"What a fucking liar" he said out loud. He could not imagine how she could leave his bed and go to another man while using her son as an alibi. He knew if he saw her at that moment, he probably would be unable to control himself. Now more than ever, he needed to find out the truth and find out the truth he would. With that thought he put his car into gear and went back home to a night that he knew would be restless, if not sleepless.

CHAPTER FIVE

It took Marge several weeks before she finally called Todd. "Don't ask me any questions. Let's just meet for coffee at the diner at seven this evening," Marge said and quickly hung up the phone before Todd could say anything more. Of course Todd had every intension of meeting her at the diner. But he was a little confused by her cloak and dagger approach.

"Why the hush, hush on the phone earlier?"

"You have to be more stupid than I even thought. There are eyes and ears everywhere and what we are doing is illegal. You must never discuss this with anyone, and we can never discuss it over the phone. Do you understand?'

"Yeah, I get the picture but I would never have thought that someone could be listening to my conversations on my phone."

"Get with it! Cell phones are anything but secure and you never know what, if anything, someone wants to get on you; especially when you have done something illegal."

"You are making more of this than is necessary. How would anyone know we have the phone records, and if they were to know we have them, how would they be able to connect us?"

"That's just the point. I don't want any of this getting back to me. Let's face it, I doubt you are just going to sit on the information. I know you better than that. You want this for a purpose and my guess is the result will be some sort of fireworks. Just do not get me connected to any of it. Do we understand each other?"

"I got the message. Now let me see the phone list."

"I have it in a sealed envelope. Don't open it here. Make sure you are home before you open the envelope."

"Okay; now give to me."

"I will but let's order some coffee first so it does not look as though this is an unusual meeting."

"More cloak and dagger, but okay. Do you want anything with your coffee?"

"Just coffee would be fine. By the way, have you heard from your mother lately? I hear she is having a grand old time down in Florida."

"We talk at least once a week. She seems to be really enjoying her retirement and her community has a lot of women her age who are also single, so they all get together and raise hell."

"I am glad to hear that; she really deserves to enjoy herself now. Her life with your father was never really easy."

"He was a rather difficult dude, but there is no denying that he loved her. Too bad he did not live to retire with her. That might have been interesting."

"Well, I have to get going. Please be careful how you use that information in the envelope. I would hate to see you get into serious trouble with it. In fact, I could not forgive myself if you do."

"Don't worry so much. I promise I will not do anything we both might regret. Take care of yourself and keep in touch. It has been great seeing you."

With that Marge got up, kissed Todd on the cheek and left the diner. Todd was close behind her after paying the bill. He could hardly wait to get home and look at the phone records. This could prove to be a long but interesting evening.

The first thing Todd noticed when he looked at the list of calls was that there were over two thousand five hundred minutes used. He shook his head and wondered how anyone who was working could possibly talk on the phone that much in one month. He immediately recognized several numbers as being those that belonged to George, himself, Vicki's mother, and several friends whom he had met and whose numbers had been on his own phone from when Vicki was staying at his house. But, there were several numbers that were certainly not familiar and did appear with tremendous frequency. He blocked his own number and called the number that appeared the most. He was not surprised that a man answered. Now the challenge was to get a name and address that went with the number. A reverse search on the internet did not yield any information, so Todd could only assume it was a cell phone number that she was calling. He decided that it was time to get help from a private investigator whom he knew from having done electrical work at his home. The guy had given Todd his card and told him if he could ever be of any help on anything, just to call him. Todd knew he was going down a complicated path, but he felt he did not have any choices, he had to know who Vicki was screwing and he had to try to get her back, no matter what.

It did not take Al, the private investigator long to get a name and address for the phone number. He had not asked any questions when Todd had called and he made it clear that he did not want to know where the number had come from.

"The guy's name is Joseph Gordon and he lives up in Brookville, in a real fancy neighborhood. The guy obviously has some real bucks."

"Can you get any more information about him? Has he needed an attorney for any reason?"

"What's your connection with this dude?"

"He is screwing my girlfriend and I don't particularly like it."

"And, if I give you the information, what are you going to do about it? I really do not want to get involved in a lovers triangle."

"I am not about to hurt the guy or anything like that. I just want to make her life a little difficult by confronting them and it would probably be helpful, if I have a little dirt on him. That way I can make him see the light more easily. Don't worry, I'll do nothing that can come back and bite you in the ass."

"Okay, give me a little time and I'll see what I can get. I just hope this chick is worth all of this effort. What makes you believe that she will come back to you if this guy breaks off the relationship?"

"She cannot be alone. She needs a man, and I am willing to wait to get her back. Yeah - she is really worth the effort. Believe me!"

"Whoa – it is amazing what a guy will think up when he is using his other head! I'll be in touch. At least this is getting interesting."

It took a little over a week before Al called to set up another meeting. They arranged to get together at Todd's house that evening right after work.

"What do have for me?"

"Like I told you last time – This dude is a rich guy who works on Wall Street. He has a history of extra martial involvements, most of them never lasted as long as this one. He has the perfect setup with a fifty foot Post harbored in Greenport which his wife rarely goes to, so it is his personal playground. His wife ignores his cheats as long as he continues to provide her with the lifestyle she has gotten used to and as long as he makes the necessary appearances at the country club and school functions. This time is different. She is really pissed; she's pregnant with their third kid. There she is stuck at home with two young kids and a third on the way and there he is flagrantly showing off his new toy all over town. I heard she really lost it when she got a peek at his credit card and saw large charges at Gross Jewelers in Garden City and at Nordstroms. I don't know how the guy could be so stupid as to leave the bill around unless he is trying to get her to leave him so that he could marry Miss Sex Appeal."

"That could be difficult as Vicki is still married to George who refuses to give her a divorce on religious grounds. The guy is a devout Catholic or, at least, his mother is, and divorce is totally out the question."

"Well, it sure looks to me as though those two are planning to take up permanent residency together. She has even been seen bringing her kid to the boat."

"Really, I am sure that would not go over well with George. He has always been pretty emphatic about keeping Joseph away from here whenever Vicki came over. He wants the boy sheltered and probably is trying in his own way to protect Vicki's image. That guy really loves her and would take her back in a second."

"She really keeps her castaways on the hook."

"I am telling you she is something special. I have never known a woman like her. She can make you feel like you are on another planet and no matter what is happening, you forget all about it when you're with her. Sex with her is truly out of this world. She can do things that other women would never consider doing and she does them as though it is no big deal."

"Spare me the details!"

"Do you have any info as to how she met this guy Gordon?"

"Word has it that he is a client at Schwartz and Schwartz. But, I have not been able to get any details as to why except that it has to do with some type of security fraud and the Feds are involved."

"The Feds- that's big time. This guy must have some really big troubles. I am surprised he can devote so much time to Vicki."

"It would seem to me that he is compounding his troubles. But he has to be some kind of a cad to do this to his wife what with her being pregnant and all. Theirs is a long term marriage and she stands to walk away with a fortune if they were to divorce. She'd get the house, and half of everything he has and no judge is going to have sympathy for him."

"Any idea as to his net worth?"

"Not really, but the guy has a big house in Brookville on a couple of acres, a G class Mercedes, a S500 Mercedes and a Bentley along with the yacht. Not too shabby. He is some type of money manager and pulls a really big yearly income. Guys like him are good for a couple of million a year."

"Whoa – Vicki found herself a real live one this time. I always knew she was looking for the money and the good life, but I never thought she would completely prostitute herself for it."

"It looks like you are in no position to compete on this level."

"But I can give her other things she really needs."

"How do you know that this guy, Gordon, can't give her those things as well. Money can make a guy even more sexually satisfying.

Let's face facts. This guy has been around and he has had many women in his time; he knows what he is doing."

"We need to know more about his problems with the Feds. Maybe we can make matters worse for him if he persists with seeing Vicki. No one wants to really fight the federal government and maybe even face jail time. There is no way little Miss Vicki would be willing to wait for Prince Charming to get out of jail."

"I doubt if his problems are that big judging by the attorney he has chosen. Schwartz and Schwartz are not known for representing clients in serious cases with the Feds. They are more known as attorneys for tax offenses and stuff like that."

"People go to jail for tax offenses."

"Yeah, but most often it is a fine and repayment of back taxes, and that's it. Anyway, look, I did my part and I got you all the info I can get. Leave me out of this from now on. You are playing in dangerous waters and I don't want to be dragged down with you. In my opinion, you should just forget about lovely Vicki, and go on with your life. There are other dames out there and one hole is just like another. This Vicki person has no staying power especially with a poor schmuck like you. Here you are burdened with child support and maintenance. You can't afford someone with her tastes and needs. Get reality into your head before you need a lawyer."

"You don't understand. I left my wife and kids for her and she promised to be with me through thick and thin. I love her and need her."

"Through thick and thin, but not through poverty. Get with it! It seems to me she likes the conquest but lacks staying power. Look, in reality, she is doing the same thing to Gordon as she did to you. She is taking him away from his wife and kids. The only difference is that he has more money."

"Do you have Gordon's address, phone numbers for his office and the name of the boat?"

"I wrote all the information down for you and you have his cell number. Good-bye."

"Thanks for everything. I'll let you know how things work out."

"Don't bother. I really would like it if you were to lose my number. I think you are big trouble about to erupt and I don't want any part of it."

With that Al left Todd to his own thoughts.

The first plan that Todd came up with was to write Vicki a letter which he decided he would hand deliver to the boat in Greenport when she and Gordon were there. In the letter he would explain his relationship with Vicki and would detail how she would receive calls from Gordon while she was in bed with him. It was almost funny how he thought she was talking to Joseph, her son, when indeed she was arranging to meet Joseph Gordon. Todd was sure that he would affect their relationship once Gordon realized that she was unfaithful to both of them. He would get a more accurate picture of Vicki. Todd felt sure that would start the fireworks.

Next, he decided to let George know that Vicki was taking their son with her to the boat. The one thing he knew was that Vicki did not want to lose custody of Joseph. Having evidence that she was taking the boy to sexual rendezvous' could give George the ammunition needed to get full custody of the boy. Also her behavior and the fact that she was away from the boy so often would also help George in his case. It was indeed strange that it could be possible that he and George could help each other. War does make for strange bedfellows. Needless to say, he was going to let Vicki know exactly what he was telling George and he was sure that would make her crazy.

Todd waited for a day that he was sure Vicki was at the boat. He drove past her house and saw that her car was not in the driveway and then he went out to Greenport where her car was in the parking lot. He casually walked down the dock and saw "The Escape" in its slip. The boat looked like no one was on board as he walked past it several times. He then decided to go aboard and knock on the closed door to the salon. The man who came to the door looked disheveled as though he had hurriedly dressed. Todd handed him the letter he was carrying and then called out Vicki's name in hopes of seeing her, but there was no response.

"I thought you should know that Vicki and I are a couple. Also let her know that I plan to help George get full custody of their son on grounds that she is an unfit mother," Todd said as he turned and got off the boat. He was actually enjoying the moment and the look on Gordon's face was enough to make him smile. He could only imagine Vicki's reaction. It was too bad he could not stay to hear the fireworks.

When Gordon brought the letter into the salon and began reading it aloud, Vicki was shocked and kept telling him "That's a lie. Why would I want to be with an electrician? He is just a poor sole who is stalking me and has been doing so for some time. I didn't want to worry you with this and I believe he is harmless but he is a stalker none the less."

"You know you can never really know what a stalker will do. Look he found you here. Who knows what he'll do? And how does he know about Joseph being here and about George? I am confused?"

"Obviously, he has been following me for some time."

"Yeah – next he will probably go to my wife and make trouble there. That could be really interesting now. It is the last thing I need at this moment. Can you imagine the sympathy she'll get what with her being so very pregnant?"

"Look. Joe, I am really sorry about this. I have no control over it. Maybe I can get to talk to him and make him see how wrong he is."

"Talk to him? Are you saying you know who he is?"

"Actually, I do know who he is. He was my neighbor before he left his wife and moved out. He always had a thing for me and imagined that we could be a couple."

"He does have some accurate information in this letter. Is there any truth to his claims that you left his bed to come to mine?"

"Don't be ridiculous. He's a poor slob with dreams that he could have me, and all he wants to do is to ruin our relationship. Let me go and talk to him. I am sure I can get him to listen to me and prevent him from going to your wife; not that I would be unhappy if your wife left you and we could be together all the time."

"The timing is not right. I have to keep things together until she has this kid or she could wipe me out and you know that."

"But you do want to be with me all the time, right?"

"Hell, you know I am crazy about you! It's just that now you have me doubting things. You have to tell me the truth. Were you involved with this guy? You know I have ways of finding out the truth."

"We were involved when he left his wife, but that was a long time ago, long before I met you. I would never be with anyone but you, you are the greatest." With that said, she reached down and pulled his cock out of his pants and started to fondle him until he became hard. She then put her lips around his member and listened as he groaned with pleasure. All the time she was thinking about Todd and how she could make things better. She had to make him understand that he was the past and her future was now with Joe and she certainly did not want to have any problems with George or to risk losing custody of Joseph. What a mess!

"You can't tell me you want to give this up."

"I want you all the time. I think about you constantly. There is no denying that. I have never enjoyed sex as much as I do with you. You can make a man feel things he never imagined possible."

"So, why would you even consider giving me up?"

"I find it hard to think of you with some other man, in his bed, doing things to him like you do to me. It is also impossible for me to accept that you are a liar and that you come to my bed right after being in his."

"I would never do things like that. He is the liar not I."

"Prove it!"

"How could I possibly prove or disprove something when there are no witnesses. It's his word against mine and you should accept mine as he is a crazy man. Besides, you are in no position to be jealous of me. You go from my bed back to your wife's. I cannot deal with that. I need a man who is faithful to me; who does not treat me like a whore. That is what you are doing. You are treating me like a whore, trying to keep me on the side while you live your life with Adrienne."

"I've told you many times that I cannot leave Adrienne now. God, she's about to have my kid!"

"What about me? What am I supposed to do?"

"We've had this discussion hundreds of times. I told you I was prepared to set you and Joseph up in a really nice house and to make sure you have everything you need."

"You want me to be a kept woman and you think I would bring my son into such a relationship? That's nuts! George would never stand for something like that. I would lose custody of my son!"

"Take it or leave it. It's up to you. This is all I can offer. I cannot afford to leave Adrienne especially now with the baby and this stupid tax case pending. Even if I could, now is not the time for you to make demands of me; what with your lover coming here. You are in no position to demand fidelity or anything else."

"You'll miss me! You'll see. You'll come running back." Vicki yelled as she grabbed her purse and ran off the boat.

Once in the car, Vicki started shaking. She knew she let the situation get out of control. And now she just might have lost everything. Joe was her way out of her stupid job. Had she gotten him to marry her, she would have had it all, money, position, the nice house, the good car – all of it. Now what would she have? A stupid electrician who could afford Burger King. Before she knew what she was doing she found herself on the cell phone screaming at Todd, "You fucking, stupid bastard. How could you do this to me? You're crazy if for one minute you think you will ever get me back." The tirade continued until Todd hung up the phone only to have her call back and continue yelling obscenities at him and at Stacey. Todd repeatedly hung up the receiver only to have Vicki call back in speed dial fashion. He finally just put the receiver down and walked away from the phone knowing that there would be no reasoning with her, she had crossed the line to insanity. He had seen this before and knew eventually she would calm down and come crawling back to him. It amazed him that she could drive while she was in such an uncontrolled state. Eventually the phone went dead and he thought it was over for now.

Vicki was so enraged as she drove down her block that she could not stop herself. She went directly to Stacey's house and starting banging on her door screaming obscenities. Stacey refused to open the door and yelled at her to leave or she would call the police. This further enraged Vicki who then proceeded to threaten to kill Stacey because she was ruining her life. All the neighbors could not avoid hearing what was going on and no one was surprised when the patrol car arrived to find Vicki still banging on the front door.

"Calm down, young lady."

"Don't tell me to calm down. That bitch has ruined my life and she will pay for it."

'You are violating the order of protection that is still in effect. Do you realize that?"

"Order of protection –fat stuff. That bitch has to pay for what she has done."

"You are under arrest. Come with me, we are going to the station house now."

"You're arresting me? You had better speak to Sergeant Brown before you arrest me."

"I will not speak to anyone. If you continue to refuse to get into the squad car, I will increase the charges to resisting arrest. Are you hearing me?"

"We'll see about that." Just then Stacey opened her door and Vicki lunged at her with such force that the officer was almost knocked over when he tried to step between the two women.

"Officer, get this crazy woman off my property now. She has totally upset my children and she is out of her mind. I will come to the station house and press charges whenever you need me to do so."

With that the officer took Vicki, who was still screaming every curse word imaginable, forcibly to the patrol car. The officer was also shaken; he had been involved in many domestic disputes but had never seen one quite like this. There was a woman who was fashionably dressed and obviously quite beautiful behaving like a person totally out of her mind. All he could wonder was what had triggered her behavior?

Stacey immediately called Jeff to tell him what had happened. She was petrified that Vicki would be released from jail and come back. Who could know what she was capable of doing?

"Just stay put; I am on my way over and you and the girls will stay at my place tonight. Don't open you door to anyone until I get there."

"Thanks."

Stacey's next call was to Todd. He had to know what had happened and how his whore had upset his children. Even if he did not care about her, he did love the girls.

"I don't understand why she took it out on you. You have nothing to do with this mess," Todd replied. "Look Stacey, I am really sorry you were dragged into this; she's just out of her mind."

"Well, maybe, some time in jail will get her back into her mind. I don't care. Just keep her away from us. Am I making myself clear?"

"Clear as a bell - but I am not responsible for her actions. I did nothing to bring this on to you."

"I very much doubt that statement. My guess is that you did something to really piss her off and she took it out on me. Somehow every time there is something going on between the two of you, I'm the one who gets hurt. Remember there is a court order in effect that she is not to be anywhere near the girls. Don't violate that order or I will make sure that you don't get the children. Understand?"

"Understood - with that the line went dead and Todd could only stand there contemplating what to do next. Obviously, he would have to get Vicki out of jail but he decided to wait a little while and let her cool off before going to the station house. In her present state of mind, there was little anyone could do to calm her down. He needed her to know that she did not belong with some rich NorthShore guy and that her place was with him. After all, Gordon was not going to be the one to get her out of this mess. "I guess my little letter had the desired effect," he said feeling rather proud of himself.

Stacey was still visibly shaken when Jeff arrived. She told him everything that happened and shook her head, "I had no way to see this coming. All of a sudden there she was banging at my door. My guess is that Todd had something to do with this, but I don't know or care what."

"Whoa- that's tough. The only long-term solution I can see is to get you and the girls away from here. You don't need to see her coming and going and she should not know any of your business."

"I have been thinking of moving but I wanted the girls to finish the school year and very honestly, I don't know what our relationship is going to be, so I didn't want to commit to a new house and all."

"Those are good points and I agree. Personally, I want us to be together all the time. I was only waiting for you to be ready to make such a commitment and for the girls to also be ready. Now is not the moment for that discussion. Let's deal with the immediate problem. Go and pack some things for yourself and the girls and let's go to my place. Vicki will not bother you there and it is not all that far to drive to get the girls to school."

"Thanks for coming and for taking care of us. I am sorry we are such a burden."

"You could never be a burden to me. Now get moving. We don't know how long they will hold her at the precinct. I really do believe she has something going with Sergeant Brown. They were real close last time she was arrested and she did get off real easy then."

"You can't mean that. That is horrible. It completely destroys my trust in the police. If she is not held at least overnight, what is the purpose in having an order of protection?"

"Orders of protection are all too common these days and they are often not enforced. We all know of killings that have taken place while there is an order of protection out."

"Now you are really scaring me."

"You should be scared. You are dealing with an obviously crazy person. No one knows what she is capable of doing when she perceives that she has been wronged."

While Jeff and Stacey were having this conversation, Vicki was at the police station waiting to be booked. She was still screaming obscenities when she arrived so the booking officer made her sit on a bench and promptly handcuffed her to it.

"Young lady, and I use that term loosely, get control of yourself before you make matters infinitely worse," he said as she tried to kick him in the shins.

"Get Sergeant Brown down here now. He'll get things under control and get me out of her," Vicki yelled at the top of her lungs.

"How do you know Sergeant Brown?"

"That's none of your business. Just tell him that I am here and tell him I need his help, NOW."

"Okay, I'll see if he's in the building."

"If you need to, call him at home. Just get him down here."

It was not too long before there was a hush in the room as a rather large man entered and walked over to the bench where Vicki was still sitting handcuffed to its arm. There was no smile and his eyes showed how angered he was but his voice remained calm.

"You crazy cunt! What do you think you're doing? You're letting everyone in this station house know that there is something going on between us. They're thinking you bribed me with sex. That's really great for my career. You are a real low-class whore. I don't get it."

"I need you to get me out of here. Do you understand that?"

"I understand that you would like my help but telling everyone that I am having an affair with you is not a way to make me want to help you. Before we go any further with this situation, I need you to calm down and try to rationally tell me what happened that made the officers arrest you in the first place."

"All I did was yell at that bitch Stacey because she is ruining my life. She is constantly watching my comings and goings, and telling that no good ex-husband of hers what I am doing and when I'm doing it. If she would mind her own business, none of this would have happened. I've lost Joe because of her and now Todd is threatening to go to George and tell him I'm an unfit mother so I could lose Joseph. My life is falling apart because of her."

"This is far too complicated for me to absorb. You were involved with that guy, Todd, the last time I saw you here. Isn't that correct?"

"He's just a loser. Now that he has to pay maintenance and child support, he has no money to do anything. What do I need with a poor electrician? I want someone like Joe Gordon who can give me the world, take me to good places, and buy me beautiful things. That's what I need."

"Let me see if I have this somewhat straight. You think Stacey put her husband up to ruining your affair with this Gordon guy?"

"Yeah – she's jealous of me. Always has been."

"One little thing that seems to have slipped your mind. She has an order of protection to prevent you from having any contact with her. That order is still in effect and you definitely violated it today. I am not the one to help you. You need an attorney, and I would suggest you call one right away, or you will be spending the night in jail."

"I don't have an attorney and I really don't want the firm I work for involved in this. That could cost me my job which I really need now that Joe has taken a powder."

"What about that guy Jeff who tried to help you last time you were here?"

"He has a thing going with Stacey. I doubt if he would be willing to help me especially since she's the one pressing the charges."

"Oh my, you do live in a tangled web. My only suggestion is that you call that guy Todd and see if he has the name of someone who could help you, or call that Gordon guy."

"Joe uses the firm I work for when he needs a lawyer, so that would not work. Why can't you help me? Last time you just signed off on everything, and I left."

"Last time you didn't make it look like we were involved with each other. Now if I were to just sign off on everything, as you put it, it would trigger an internal investigation. Personally, I don't need or want that headache and I don't need or want to get involved with the likes of you. You are trouble."

"Could you at least call Todd for me? He's pretty mad at me and I'm not sure he will help me either."

"That much I'll do, out of the goodness of my heart. What's his number? Just do me one favor from here on out. Forget my name. I want nothing more to do with you. Someday you'll learn that you cannot use your body to get what you want." With that the sergeant turned and walked away leaving Vicki sitting there with her mouth hanging open. She knew that if Todd was not willing to help her, she would have to call George and that would definitely complicate matters even more. She could only imagine how he was going to react when he hears about what happened. George was such a good schmuck who still would do anything for her except if he perceives it as hurting Joseph. Having his mother arrested right on his own block would embarrass the kid especially now that he seems so insecure and afraid every time she is out of his sight. With that thought in mind, Vicki put her head in her lap and began to sob knowing that she had really screwed up this time. She could not bear to think of losing Joseph.

"God, George could still be the most powerful force in my life. He controls everything because he controls Joseph. How ironic life can be! This has been a truly crazy day, one minute I had everything going for me and now I stand the chance to lose everything that matters," she thought as she sat there crying.

She had no idea as to how long she was sitting there crying but suddenly she became aware of two pant legs standing in front of her. She looked up and saw Todd standing there kind of smiling down at her; it was that smile that says, "I got you good."

"Are you just going to stand there and gloat or are you going to help me get out of here?"

"I called my attorney and he is here trying to get them to release you in my custody as long as I promise not to let you anywhere near Stacey or the girls. That will allow you to go home with me tonight. But you'll still have to appear in court and then the judge will decide what to do with you. He thinks he'll be able to get you off with a possible fine and a severe scolding but if you do anything like this again, they'll throw the book at you. Am I making myself perfectly clear?"

"Clear enough even for a dumbbell like me. I just lost it and I was so mad at you that I took it out on Stacey. You know you were a real bastard coming on to Joe like that."

"You had better stop calling me names if you want my help. You need me more than I need you."

"I get the picture."

"You had better keep that picture. You belong with me; never forget that."

It wasn't long before one of the officers appeared with some papers for them both to sign. The handcuffs were released and Vicki was told she could go to Todd's house. She was cautioned to stay far away from Stacey and the girls and reminded that if she violated the order of protection again, there would be no getting out of jail.

CHAPTER SIX

L ife was amazing for Todd when Vicki came back. She even cooked dinners and cleaned the house so that it looked better than ever before. So that they could spend even more time together, Vicki started bringing Joseph over after school and he would stay the night. It was fun having a child in the house and Todd started going to his soccer games and even helped him with his homework. In some ways this helped fill the void of not having his girls there, but in other ways it made him miss them even more. On nights when Joseph was not there, Todd never knew what he would come home to. One night he opened the door to find Vicki in a maid's apron minus any underwear. What a glorious sight she was and, needless to say, dinner was rather postponed that evening. Life with Vicki was sheer sexual excitement as she knew no bounds and was willing to try anything

On the days when Todd was to pick up the girls, things would get touchy. Vicki greatly resented that she and Joseph had to leave what she now came to consider as her house. If Joseph was scheduled to see George on the same day, Vicki was even more upset because she had to be alone and had to fear going back to her own house because Stacey was still next door and any contact would be considered a violation of the order of protection. It was a mess that had no resolution especially since Todd was not willing to give up his time with his children.

"You're too selfish for words," Vicki yelled at him. "You expect me to go and sit in that house and do nothing but play with myself while you have fun with your children."

"You know the situation. I have no control over it. You created the situation as it now is. I don't understand what you want me to do. I cannot and will not give up my daughters completely, if that is what you want."

"I want you to make that shithead of a wife of yours understand that we are a couple and she cannot dictate where I have to be and when I have to be there."

"She is not the one setting the rules. There is a court order in effect and that includes the children. Maybe had you not been so crazy and made the threats you made, things could be different. But they are what they are and you know it. She is afraid of you and afraid that you will take out your hatred of her on the children."

"I would never do anything to hurt the girls."

"I know that and you know that but you were thinking about them the night you went there like a crazy person. You scared them and they are still frightened to be near you."

"And you have done nothing to change that."

"What do you want me to do? Do you want me to tell them you are a wonderful person who never loses her temper? I doubt I could do that with a straight face."

"You're still a whimp with no backbone. You are content to be controlled by Stacey and if not by her by your mother."

"How did my mother get sucked into this conversation?"

'I see how you have to call her with every decision and get her permission before you do anything."

"If that were true, you would still be in jail. My mother does not approve of our relationship and she despises how you treated Stacey even before your temper tantrum. To her marriage is a scared entity and it is wrong to violate the marriage vows."

"So--- She is probably a cold bitch who doesn't know how to satisfy a man and only a schmuck like your father would stay with her all these years."

"I don't know anything about my parents' sex life and neither do you but I do know they love each other and have done everything possible to make each other happy through the years. Not that that is something you would know about."

"I know how to make a man happy and you know that and you seem to enjoy that as well. Go fuck your high and mighty mother and while you're at it, fuck Stacey as well." With that Vicki grabbed her bag and left the house with Todd wondering where she was going and what she would do. He even considered calling Stacey to give her the heads up that Vicki was on the war path once again but decided against it. Why make matters worse? After all he would have the children with him and chances were that Stacey would be with Jeff anyway. He only hoped he could make it a fun day for the girls. Somehow, Vicki could always cast a dark cloud over his mood whenever he had them and he was sure it showed.

Stacey and Jeff dropped the girls off exactly on time. Todd truly believed they insisted coming to his house to drop the children off so that they could be sure Vicki was indeed gone. The children really seemed excited to him and they were even happier when Todd told them they were all going to the Children's Museum and then out for Sushi, which was their favorite type of food. And so the day passed without incident and, of course, Vicki refused to answer her phone when Todd called but that was to be expected. When Todd brought the girls home the next day, Vicki's car was parked in her driveway so he was relieved to know that she was probably home. He was sure he would hear from her in a day or two and if he didn't he would have to take further action; though he was not sure what action he would or could take.

It was late that evening when Todd heard the key in the front door. He made believe he was asleep but could not prevent himself from getting hard as Vicki slipped into his bed and snuggled up against his back.

"Welcome home," Todd said trying to keep his voice even. "What did you do these past two days?"

"You very well know what I did; I cleaned the fucking house. How was your time with the girls?"

"They're great kids but now we can forget about them and concentrate on us. Is Joseph here?"

"He's with his Dad, but he'll be here after school tomorrow."

"Great- so tonight is the night we can make as much noise as we wish! Let's not waste any time," and with that life resumed with each doubting the current arrangement could prevail for any protracted time. Todd knew Vicki was not about to give up and would do anything to alienate him from his parents and make him give up his children. Vicki knew she had to get her way with Todd or there could be no way for her to stay with him. She also had to make him understand that he needed to make more money if he expected to keep her interested in him. She knew she was not about to spend the rest of her life with a poor electrician who was constantly sending her away but since there was no one else in her life right now, Todd would do; he was a pretty good lay, if nothing else.

It was obvious that Vicki had a need to discredit Stacey, and it was equally important to her that Todd side with her against Stacey. Everyday, she harped on the fact that Stacey was taking too much money in support and maintenance payments.

"You do know that if she lives with a man, you no longer have to pay her maintenance?" She told Todd one day after work. "I know this for a fact because I asked one of the matrimonial attorneys at the firm. He said that all you have to do is prove she is cohabiting with someone and any court will allow you stop paying maintenance. I bet she and Jeff are basically living together and, knowing her, she is keeping it a secret from you. Just think what we could do with that money!"

"I know for a fact that she and Jeff are maintaining separate residences. The girls keep telling me how much they like him and hoped he and Stacey could be a real couple. Knowing Stacey, she wants to be extra sure especially since what happened to her because of us."

"We have to figure out a way to decrease the money you give her. That is plain as day."

"You know, I am getting tired of you harping on Stacey and the money I give her. Stacey deserves to have a proper home for my children. We were married for over ten years and it was not her fault that things worked out as they did."

"It was her fault. If she was a proper and exciting wife you would never have strayed in the first place. She drove you away with her complacency. I could never understand how you could be married to little miss perfect housewife."

"There is no denying that she could never compete with you in certain areas. You literally blow her away," Todd said with a broad smile on his face as he took Vicki into his arms and started stroking her breasts. And so ended another tiresome conversation which Todd knew would be resumed shortly. Deep in his heart, he knew he would never challenge Stacey about the money in the settlement, but he also knew it would be a relief if she were to marry Jeff and end the maintenance portion of the package. He also knew that he would not be able to keep Vicki happy without having more money to spend on her extravagant tastes. For that reason he was looking into moonlighting work. Side jobs pay well and usually pay in cash so they are a win - win situation. The only negative was that he would have to work evenings and weekends and that would leave Vicki on her own and give her time to wander once again. Trust was not a word that describes Vicki nor was fidelity in her vocabulary. He figured he had until the court hearings came about to enjoy Vicki. After that, if she got the charges dismissed, she would be up to her old games again. Vicki loved the chase for a new man especially if he was in another relationship. Once she had him just where she wanted him to be, she would lose interest and he would be there waiting for her to come back; and come back she would.

At the office Vicki was definitely much more demur. Her main goal was to stay under the office radar and to hopefully keep her legal problems from becoming office knowledge. In order to accomplish this she had to keep her distance from Jeff who seemed to want to maintain his own space as well. The only real problem she had was when Joe Gordon came to the office on his own legal business. He never failed to stop at Vicki's desk and exchange remarks.

"I really miss you baby. Don't you want to be with me as well," he said.

"Joe, you know how I feel. I will not compete with your wife. If you want me, leave her. If you want to stay with that cow, leave me out of it."

"You know I cannot just up and leave her especially now that the baby is here."

"Why? I thought you had always said that you had to wait for the kid to be born."

"I know, I know. But things are a little rocky with the case and I don't want to shake the boat; so to speak. Although, I wouldn't mind really shaking the boat with you."

"Yeah, yeah. All you want is good lay and then you'll be off to the little woman with the screaming kids. I'll tell you what, you can dream about me when you fuck your wife and maybe that will help you get hard."

"Man, you are one tough broad."

"Tough, maybe, but sexy for sure. I think you are getting late for your appointment with your lawyer and he charges from the appointed time; so you had better get going."

"I'll see you on the way out."

"Don't count on it."

When Joe left, she sat there for a few minutes trying to compose herself. She really did not miss him because as a lover he was clumsy and rather selfish but man did she miss his money. "Oh well, there will be someone else soon that will be as good a lover as Todd and as rich as Joe. "But first things first," was her next thought as reality came into focus. She had to get the charges dismissed or everything could blow up, her job, her custody of Joseph, even her support from George. The money he gave her was a real help; he was just one good slob.

Of course, eventually she would have to deal with Jeff. He seemed to be advancing in the firm and if he ever got to be in a decision making position, her job could and would be in jeopardy. She could not be sure he could keep his personal life out of the picture and his allegiance to Stacey could really hurt her future at the firm. Up to now he seemed to want to keep his personal life completely separate from his office life and rarely talked to anyone at the firm about anything other than legal matters. But he was well liked and the senior partners were noticing him more and more. It was obvious that a partnership offer was in the near future. There was no chance she could make a play for him as he had already made it obvious that he wanted nothing to do with her and wasn't interested in even maintaining any degree of friendship. It was hard to believe that he could prefer that bitch Stacey to her; but that was his choice. In time, she was sure she would be able to get her revenge. Tincture of time had to be her motto.

Jeff on his part knew he had a formidable adversary in Vicki. He had no doubt that she would do anything to get back at him for siding with Stacey and there was no doubt that she was ruthless. He tried to keep his distance even coming and going through the back door of the office so that he could avoid the reception desk. But it seemed ridiculous to him that a mere receptionist could create such havoc for him. He even considered leaving the firm but that seemed rather self-defeating as he was starting to get recognized for his work. His immediate superior even told him that the partners were exceptionally pleased with him. He could only hope that things would settle down and the Vicki situation would vanish, one way or the other. In the meantime, he planned to keep his ears opened to other positions as he knew he would be more comfortable without Vicki in his daily life. Otherwise, his life was near perfect. The time he spent with Stacey was idyllic and they were actually starting to feel like a real family when they had the girls with them.

As Vicki's first court appearance drew near, her level of agitation greatly increased. She feared that one of the attorneys from the firm might see her in court as she had to lie to them and claim she was sick and could not come to work. There was always the possibility that her case would not go well and she could even have to serve time though she honestly doubted that. Then, there was George who was actually making noises about getting full custody of Joseph if the case went against Vicki and he could use it to prove she was indeed an unfit mother. She knew for sure she could not stand losing Joseph. The only person who remained firmly in her corner was Todd who kept telling her that her lawyer was really excellent and she had nothing to worry about. He was sure the charges would be dismissed and then they could go on with their lives like the whole thing never happened. But there was always that little voice in the back of her head saying "What if?" and it was driving her crazy.

The day of the hearing finally came and Vicki dressed in her most conservative clothes. She wanted to make a really good impression in front of the judge who, she was told, was a woman. Her lawyer had warned her that it was not particularly good for her case that the judge was a woman as you never know how her history might influence another female. Unfortunately, there was nothing he could do to get a change of venue, so they had to do whatever they could to make sure the judge would not be prejudiced against her. To say that Vicki was actually shaking when her attorney met her outside the courtroom was an understatement.

"Calm down. Nothing is going to happen today. I am going to ask for an extension because I do not like the assistant district attorney assigned to your case. She is a real hard assed bitch who thinks she is about to make a real name for herself on your case."

"How can we get rid of her?"

"Assistant DA's change all the time. Just cool it and let me do the talking."

"Don't worry about that counselor. The ball is totally in your court. It's just that I really want this thing over and done with"

"I know that and believe me I am working on it. I have different approaches in the fire."

"You do realize that every time I have to come here I am putting my job in jeopardy. All I need is for one of the attorneys from the firm to see me and it's curtains."

"There are other jobs. It is not like you are doing something so special that you could not do the same thing elsewhere."

"What are you suggesting?"

"Let's see how this plays out and then we'll talk about it further. All I am saying right now is that it might be in your best interests to start looking elsewhere for a job and leave this whole mess behind you."

"Am I detecting some type of deal going on behind my back?"

"It's too soon to talk about it. I am just thinking out loud."

"I bet this has something to do with lover boy, Jeff."

"I can assure you that he has nothing to do with this conversation. All I am prepared to say is that I am thinking out loud and maybe things can really work out well for you."

"You know I would do anything to have the stupid charges dropped so that George would not have any ammunition to use against me in a custody fight."

"Now you are using your head. Just hang in there and don't do anything or talk to anyone unless I tell you to. Am I making myself clear?"

"Let's just say I find another job; should I take it?"

"Not yet. Do nothing and talk to no one unless I tell you to do so. Clear?"

"Clear as day."

As Vicki sat in the courtroom all she could think was that her attorney was trying to get some type of a deal with Stacey to have her drop the charges. It would be really great if that were to happen. "Hell, I could easily get another job with another law firm and it would probably be better if I did not have to see Jeff or Joe ever again,' Vicki thought to herself. "After all, where am I going at Schwartz and Schwartz? The partners are really old gezzers who have shown no interest in me except as some lowly receptionist and the clients are real boring. If I stay there, I could be stuck in this hell hole of a life forever."

It did not take long for Larry to turn and look at Vicki and indicate they were leaving the courtroom.

"What happened?"

"It went just as I planned. We've been granted an extension on the grounds that I am preparing some new evidence in the case and the case has been remanded for one month. Hopefully, I can get this whole thing resolved by then and you can go on with your life."

"Larry, if you can pull this off, you're a genius."

"If I can pull this off, you would have to work very hard to stay out of trouble because the next time you open your big mouth without thinking, there will be no getting you out of trouble. Comprendo?"

"Comprendo!"

With that they left the courthouse by the side door to minimize Vicki's exposure and then attorney and client each went their separate ways. Vicki left thinking Larry was wonderful and a real genius who was going to make all things right for her. Larry left wondering why he got such crazy clients and questioning himself if he was doing the right thing.

The meeting with Stacey was scheduled for 2 pm the next day. At precisely 1:55 his secretary announced that Mrs. Moreno was there to see him. When the door opened, Larry was shocked to see the woman standing in front of him. She was extremely beautiful in a sophisticated way. Her attire, while business like, was completely updated and most becoming and her manner was completely self-assured as she approached his desk. All he could think was how any man could leave this woman for someone like Vicki was unthinkable.

"Good afternoon, Mr. Kessler, and thank you for seeing me."

"Mrs. Moreno, it is I who should thank you for coming in today. I really appreciate it that you are taking the time to meet with me."

"Please call me Stacey.'

"Absolutely, and please call me Larry. I much prefer that."

"I think we both know why I am here so I would prefer to cut to the chase. I want to propose a settlement that I think would be beneficial to your client and to me. I want Vicki to leave Schwartz and Schwartz immediately."

"May I ask you why?"

"It is rather simple. Jeff works there and he has a promising career which I think is in jeopardy as long as Vicki remains with the firm. You see, I met Jeff through Vicki when she first tried to terrorize me. He was the one who came and asked me not to press charges against her. I agreed and he and I started a friendship which has grown. It is just another thing that feeds Vicki's resentment and her jealousy. Needless to say, Jeff no longer wants to befriend her and that makes it difficult for him at the office. He does everything to avoid passing the reception desk. But I think this is not enough for Vicki. She will try to sabotage his career and that would be horrible."

"I can understand your concern. What else would you want Vicki to do to drop the charges against her?"

"Basically, I want her to be forbidden to have any contact with me or the girls. The order of protection is to be in place indefinitely. If she were to be at Todd's house when the children are there, I would want his visitation rights to be terminated and for him to only have supervised visits with the children. In reality, I want Vicki to leave us completely alone and not to interfere with my life or with Jeff's."

"That all sounds very reasonable but I am not sure the court will grant an indefinite order of protection as that carries some very serious implications. She could be in violation with the order if she is at the same school activity as you or in the same supermarket at the same time."

"I don't care about that type of contact. I only care about her coming to my house or calling my home in the insane way that has happened in the past. I do not want her to terrorize my children or myself. If she were to do these things I would want her prosecuted to the fullest extent of the law."

"You do understand that in regard to the order, that has to be left up to a judge as neither of us would trust Vicki if she were to promise to never infringe on your privacy again. But assuming we can get such an order, is there anything else you want before you would consider dropping the charges?"

"Yes, I do not want Jeff to know about our conversation. He would be furious if he knew what I am doing."

"You love this man very much. That is obvious."

"Does it show so clearly?"

"Knowing how much you dislike and at times fear Vicki, it is quite obvious that you want to right the situation for Jeff's sake and I admire that."

"Let me know if she accepts the deal and if you can arrange things with the court and then we can proceed. Thank you for your time Larry. I will look forward to hearing from you shortly." With that Stacey rose and extended her hand to Larry who felt a need to hold it just a little longer than usual.

When she left his office all Larry could think was that she was one hell of a woman. "This Jeff character is one lucky man," Larry said out loud as he dialed the number of a judge whom he knew well and who he thought could arrange the extension of the order. If he could clear that hurdle, he was sure he could get Vicki to agree to the other demands in exchange for the dropping of all charges against her. Hopefully once the case was completed, he too could wash his hands of Vicki and all the drama that seemed to follow her everywhere she went.

The judge felt he could have an Order of Protection drawn up that would exclude casual contact and just cover Stacey for an intrusion into her private being or that of her children. If the two women were to be at the same school function or supermarket, it would be assumed they would ignore each other and continue about their own business. The next call was to Vicki, "I think we may be able to get all the charges dropped against you."

"Yeah- what do I have to do- eat shit and die?"

"Let's discuss this in person in my office tomorrow."

"You know I have to work tomorrow."

"We'll meet here at 5:30 and it should only take a few minutes."

"See you tomorrow."

Hanging up the phone, all Larry could think was "Ever the lady!"

The meeting the following day went as well as Larry could expect. Vicki readily agreed to the terms presented though she was a little sarcastic when it came to leaving the firm and quickly came to the conclusion that Stacey was trying to protect Jeff.

"Look, Vicki, this has nothing to do with Jeff directly. It is just that you are creating an uncomfortable work environment and we both know that is accurate."

"Look, it is a shitty job with no future for me so I really don't give a darn about leaving it. I was even thinking of doing so before you suggested it the other day in court because I see it as a dead end. The guys I meet are all losers and the pay stinks."

"So, am I to assume you will agree to all the terms and that you will not drag Jeff into this discussion?"

'Yeah- just get it done. I'll do whatever the bitch wants. It's got to be better than facing those charges and risking losing custody of my Joseph."

"So I can tell Stacey you are giving your notice tomorrow?"

"How many times do I have to say the same thing? Yeah- tell her that. By the way, do you need a really good receptionist?"

"I never mix business with pleasure."

"I could make sure you have a lot of pleasure."

"Laughing, Larry stood up to end the meeting. "Just call me when you have stopped working at Schwartz and Schwartz and I'll take the matter from there. Hopefully, this whole mess will be cleared up in a few weeks and everyone will be able to get on with their lives."

"But I'll still need a job. Remember that bitch, Stacey, takes all of Todd's money."

"I'm sure you'll get another position in no time at all especially if you do not have a record or charges pending against you. Call me."

With that Vicki swaggered out of the office and slammed the door behind her as though to say," She won this round but I'm not done."

CHAPTER SEVEN

O n the way home Vicki had all she could do to control herself.
Her first instinct was to call Stacey and scream at her for
trying to manage her life. But a little voice in her head kept
telling her that was indeed the wrong thing to do. In her heart of
hearts she knew she would really piss Stacey off and the only result
would be that the charges against her would not be dropped. For once
in her life she knew she had to listen to the voice of reason and not
the voice of anger. She then tried to call Todd so she could vent her
frustration and scream at him while she was driving; but Todd was
not home and though she did scream into the answering machine,
she had little satisfaction. She then called George to demand that she
have Joseph this evening but he too was not at home and he did not
answer his cell. This meant that he was probably at Joseph's hockey
game and did not hear his cell phone. Todd was another matter; he
always answered his cell; always at least until now and Vicki was so
enraged she could feel herself shaking as she drove to Todd's house.

The house was dark as she drove into the driveway and Todd's
car was nowhere to be seen. Vicki let herself into the house with her
key and immediately saw the note taped to the table by the door.
Todd's mother had suffered a massive stroke and he was at the ER at
WinthropHospital. The note told her not to come to the hospital as
only family would be allowed in so there was no point in her coming
especially since she could not stand his mother and vice versa.

"Whoa- that really puts me in my place!" Vicki said out loud as all she could think of was that Todd had once again put his mother before her and didn't care about the crisis she was having.

"That bastard! How can he expect us to have a relationship when he can just exclude me as if I am a piece of garbage," Vicki again yelled out loud despite the fact that no one was there to hear or care. With that she ran upstairs and opened the closet taking out the most provocative dress.

"I'll show him that I will not be treated this way," she said as she changed and redid her makeup.

Leaving the house with the lights all ablaze, Vicki drove without an immediate plan as to where she was going. She knew one thing- she was going and she was going to have a good time despite everything. She drove like someone on automatic pilot and before she knew it she was getting out of the car at Jesse's Roadhouse on Merrick Road. There were quite a few cars parked outside the tavern and she knew that meant there would be music and drinks. It was a good feeling to see the men's heads turn as she walked into the bar and took a seat at the end of the bar. It wasn't long before a voice behind her was asking her if she wanted a drink and when she turned and saw a handsome guy had made the offer, she quickly responded.

Charlie was a nice enough guy who worked on Wall Street. They sat together and talked about their lives and their challenges. The drinks helped make conversation easy and before long they felt as though they had known each other for years not hours. Since the Gateway Motel was just blocks away, they decided to go there and really get to know each other.

That night Vicki knew no inhibition and Charlie could not believe how lucky he was. She made him experience sex as he had never before done so. Every sensual part of his body was titillated and when he climaxed it was as though he had never before climaxed with such intensity. Finally he could take no more and he actually begged her to stop as he was totally exhausted and the entire bed was just drenched with his sweat. Vicki just laughed.

"I thought you were a young stud but you are more like an old man."

"And you are one sexual bitch. I wonder if any man could keep up with you. Do you ever stop without the guy begging for mercy?"

There was no reply. Vicki just took her clothes and walked into the bathroom. Moments later Charlie could hear the shower running as he fell into an exhausted post coital sleep. He never heard Vicki leave the room and in the morning he realized he did not even know her last name or phone number; not that it would matter as he knew he would never see her again. One thing for sure, he would always remember his night with the sex machine.

Once in the car, Vicki turned her phone back on expecting to retrieve her messages. Before she could dial her own number, the phone rang and Vicki immediately knew it was Todd. Composing herself, she answered knowing he would be demanding to know where she was and what she was doing.

"Hello," was all that Vicki could think to say as she heard his angry voice on the other end.

"Where the hell have you been? I've been trying to reach you for hours?"

"I met some friends and we went out for drinks and to have some fun. You were not there for me when I needed you."

"You selfish bitch. I told you my mother had a stroke and that I was at the hospital with my father. It was an emergency and there were no choices."

"You always put her before me and somehow whenever I need you, she has some sort of emergency that takes you away."

"Yeah- she had a stroke just to spite you. Do you know how ridiculous that sounds? We are still not sure she is going to make it and all you can think about is yourself."

"She hates me and the feeling is reciprocated and you know that. All I know is that it took every ounce of self-control for me not to call that wife of yours and tell her off after my meeting with Kessler and you were not there to help me."

"I sincerely hope you did not call Stacey."

"No I did not. Instead I called some friends because I felt I could not be alone. Not that you care."

"Oh, Vicki you know I care, it was just bad timing. I needed to be with my Dad. He is all broken up and doesn't know what he'll do if anything happens to my mother."

"Don't worry about her. She is too mean a bitch to die. I can guarantee that."

"It will be even worse if she is left paralyzed or unable to speak. I don't know how my father could manage."

"We could not be that lucky that she would be unable to speak."

"Look, let's stop this. I hate it when you are mean and miserable. Why don't you come over here and we can be together for a little while before I have to go back to the hospital."

"Call a whore and let her come over to give you some sleeping meds. I'm too tired and I really want to just go home to bed. Besides I really don't want to see you right now. In case you don't get it, I am still mad."

"Come here. I promise I'll let you go to sleep and not bother you. At least if you are here we can talk about your meeting in the morning and you will not be alone for the rest of the night. Remember, I love you and I did stand up to my mother when I left Stacey for you. In case you forget that minor fact."

"I'll think about it and call you back if I decide to come over." With that Vicki closed the phone and thought about shutting it off again. she really did not want to go to her empty house but she was a little afraid that despite her shower, Todd would still be able to smell the other man on her and that would not be good.

As she drove to her house and saw the darkness that surrounded it, she knew she could not stay there. She ran in and used some feminine deodorant and quickly left for Todd's house. As she got into her car, she saw a light go on in Stacey's house and she quickly gunned her engine to make sure she left before doing anything stupid.

Todd was fully alert the minute he heard the key in the door. In his heart, he knew Vicki would be there before the night was over and he knew he would not question her as to her whereabouts or activities of the night. There was no point in questions because all he would get were lies that could complicate their relationship. Vicki was who she was and there was nothing anyone could do. He could never hope for fidelity, and all he really wanted was for her to always return to him. He also knew that she would claim to be too tired for sex and that was a confirmation that she had spent the evening in someone else's bed. He knew that in the morning she would do everything possible to make up for the night's misadventures. As Vicki slipped into the bed net to him and coddled up to him, Todd could feel his excitement as he stroked her hair and smelled the unfamiliar shampoo on it. His sex kitten had returned and that was all that mattered for now.

The next morning started with the first rays of the sun. Todd awoke to being sucked by Vicki in a way that made all negative thoughts evaporate. She knew how to give oral sex better than anyone could ever imagine. Sometimes that all was he needed to climax and Vicki knew it and used it when she had to leave at a set time. Today was one of those times as she had to get to the office and submit her resignation. Then she would have to start looking for another job. This time she was definite that the job would have to be with a younger firm where greater opportunities would exist for her. In no way did she want to waste her life with this poor electrician who would always be devoted to his mother and ex-wife.

Word traveled quickly on the information highway at Schwartz and Schwartz. Everyone was surprised that Vicki had resigned and no one was more surprised than Jeff. As soon as he heard the news he could not help but think that Stacey had something to do with the situation.

"Vicki just resigned from the firm. Please tell me that you are not at the heart of her decision," Jeff said as soon as he called Stacey.

"I can't tell you that. I can tell you that a deal was made with her attorney. I agreed to drop the charges as long as I have an order of protection for myself and the girls and as part of the deal she was to resign so she would not be in your face on a daily basis."

"I told you I could take care of myself as far as she was concerned."

"I know you did. It is just that I think she is such a dangerous person and she would do anything to hurt me. That would include sabotaging your opportunities at the firm especially if we were to marry or even move in together."

"But that would help her as Todd would not have to pay maintenance and there would be more money available for her."

"Yes, but our happiness would be a thorn in her side. She would always resent that you chose me over her and that is something she cannot accept."

"Conquest is something that she feeds upon. It seems as though she is happiest when she can destroy a relationship. I know that is what she tried to do with Joe Gordon and she certainly succeeded in your situation."

"And she would love to do it again, especially to me. She hates it that I am happy."

"I guess you are right. It's just that it would hurt me if the word were to get out that you had a part in her resignation, and that you did it for me."

"Part of the deal is that she cannot drag you into this in any way. You cannot be part of the reason she is leaving and you cannot even know the underlying reason. If it were to come out, the deal is off and the case against Vicki will go to court. Even Vicki is smart enough to know that I mean business and will do whatever I have to do to protect my own interests. She also knows that a conviction would help George to get full custody of Joseph and that, above all, is a controlling factor."

"Man, am I glad I am on your good side. I would hate to have to fight with you."

"The only fight we can have is to determine who loves who more."

"I love you, see you tonight."

"See you then and I love you too," Stacey said as she hung up the phone feeling really good about the way things worked out. Having Vicki out of any part of her life was a good thing and it was even better not having to worry about what she might do to hurt Jeff.

CHAPTER EIGHT

That night after work Jeff could hardly wait to see Stacey. Unfortunately, he had promised to meet some guys from his old fraternity for drinks. It was too late to cancel so he decided to go to the Marriot to meet then, have a quick drink and leave to see Stacey. When he walked into the cocktail bar, everyone was there and it was really great seeing the old college friends. Some of the guys were in for just a few days and most of the others worked on Wall Street so this was an unusual opportunity to get together. The first person Jeff saw was Chuck.

"Man, it's been too long guy," he said as Chuck gave him a big bear hug.

"We have to do this more often."

"Yeah and I am anxious for you to meet Stacey."

"Stacey? Who is Stacey?"

"She's one hell of a woman and the way things look, we are a serious couple."

"Talking about one hell of a woman-you should meet the dame I met last night at Jesse's Roadhouse."

"What the hell were you doing at the Roadhouse. Isn't that a little out of your way?"

"I happened to be in Merrick seeing a client and decided to stop there for a drink. At the bar there was this gorgeous woman sitting all by herself. I could not help myself and I went over to her. One thing lead to another and before I knew it we were at a place called the Gateway. Man, I never had sex like that before and I very much doubt I ever will again."

"And what did she look like?"

"Petite, dark hair, a pair of headlights and an ass that was solid and rounded like a basketball."

"And a name of Vicki?"

"Man-how the hell did you know?"

"It's too long a story but take my advice, stay away from her. She is trouble with a capital T."

"Don't you worry. I have no choice. She left without giving me her last name or phone number and I doubt she took mine either. It almost seemed like it was an act of revenge and I was the lucky participant."

"You might be right about that. Now tell me what else is new and exciting?"

"Man, life on The Street is difficult and the tension is enough to make everyone pop Tums by the dozens. Are you a partner yet at your firm?"

"Not yet but it appears I am on the right track. Listen, man, I really have to get back to my special lady. Why don't we go out to dinner and really catch up?" With that Jeff started making the rounds with the other guys and they all promised to see each other more frequently. They were really a great bunch of guys who had all taken different paths after college. Now it would only be possible to have real friendships if the significant others got along.

On the way to Stacey's house later that evening, Jeff decided not to share the Vicki escapade as there was nothing to gain by adding salt to a wound. He just wondered where Todd was that evening and why the prowling cat had to lick her wounds elsewhere. She was really one piece of work.

CHAPTER NINE

I t did not take long for Vicki to find new employment. Bergman and Bergman was a firm with just two partners, Jason Bergman and Evan Bergman. They were brothers with Jason being married with two children and Evan being single. Most of the legal work done at the firm involved wills, real estate closings, pension management and some personal injury cases. Not the most exciting types of legal work but relatively profitable. Their receptionist left to have a baby and did not intend to return at the end of her maternity leave, so the position appeared to have some stability for Vicki. The firm was located in Garden City which was a plus as it did not present a difficult commute and Vicki could easily get to Joseph in an emergency, a situation she expressed to Jason during the interview. She emphasized the fact that she was a single mother and while she had excellent child-care support, she needed to be available in an emergency though to date it had never happened that she was called away from work. Jason seemed to accept the arrangement and even liked the idea that she was a single mother as that might make her an even better employee as she needed the income. He also liked the idea that she did not bargain for a higher salary than the one he offered. Her only comment was that he would see that she is worth every penny being offered and more. And so it was decided that she would start the next day since she was not obligated to give Schwartz and Schwartz any time after having resigned. They had a firm policy that once an employee resigned, he or she was finished at their firm; no lame ducks at Schwartz and Schwartz.

When Vicki appeared for work the next day she was dressed rather conservatively, especially for her, and she felt that she fit in immediately. The new telephone system was not a challenge and being that there were only two partners, it was not hard to learn the layout of the office. Calls either came in for the partners or one of the associates or the paralegals so she had no problem learning the extensions and common sense along with her previous experience, helped her to know what calls had to be put through immediately and which calls should be taken as a message to be dealt with later.

Jason seemed to take the lead in training Vicki. He appeared to be the more business oriented of the two brothers and seemed to want to make this known to Vicki from the beginning. Evan, on the other hand, was the more likeable of the two. He had a real sense of humor and a twinkle in his eyes that told Vicki he was fun to be around and did not take himself so seriously. He also seemed to be the busier of the two brothers. He received many more calls from clients than did Jason. It almost appeared that he was given more cases by Jason and that Jason took more time off using the excuse that he had a family and Evan did not. Whatever their arrangement was it was not Vicki's business but she knew that in time, she would find out more about the workings of the firm and the personal side of it.

After work, Vicki went straight to Todd's often taking Joseph there with her. Things were going well for them as a couple especially since Todd's mother had recovered and was on her way back to Florida to complete her rehabilitation. This freed Todd to spend the evenings with Vicki and even go to Joseph's hockey games, an activity he genuinely enjoyed. For him, it was great having a child in the house and Joseph was an exceptionally nice kid who was well-mannered and respectful. It was interesting that he and Joseph seemed to get along really well. Joseph was comfortable with Todd as he had always been when they were neighbors and Todd made it a point not to ask the boy questions about his father or any other subject that could make him nervous. Todd knew how it felt to be in the question peppermill as that was always the way he felt after he spent time with his girls. And therein lay the problem with his and Vicki's relationship. She continued to resent his spending time with the girls and always made him feel insecure about their relationship whenever he did so. He knew she hated to be alone and if his visitation worked out to be the same as George's, she would be alone and who knew what she did then.

The other problem was money. Vicki was making enough to take care of her own needs and with Todd moonlighting he was bringing home enough for them to be able to enjoy some of the luxuries that she needed to keep her happy. Dinners at the best sushi restaurants and gifts of name brand clothing and handbags brought great rewards to Todd. Whenever he brought home an expensive gift, he knew that night the sex would be extra special and he usually planned it so that Joseph would be with his father on those nights. Vicki never ceased to amaze him as to how well she could suck him and how expertly she could touch him and excite him so that he would feel as though he was going to burst. She knew just how long to prolong the foreplay so that the experience would be intensified. She seemed to get great satisfaction out of driving him crazy and she did not demand much in return. Todd often tried to attempt to arouse her but more often than not she would take his hand away or reject his attempts at oral sex. She had to be in control and there was no doubt about it.

At work, Vicki was all business. She made it clear to both Jason and Evan that she was an asset to the firm. She had an unique ability to greet clients and make them feel comfortable while they waited for their appointments and she handled the more difficult clients in a way that made them more amenable when they actually saw the attorneys.

"I always say that the first impression a client gets is from the receptionist. If that initial contact is positive, the rest of the meeting is usually positive," Jason said one afternoon shortly after Vicki had started at the firm. "You have helped make some of our most difficult clients easier for us to handle and we thank you for that."

"I told you you would appreciate me. I know how to handle

people though I can honestly say I tend to handle men better than women."

"I wonder why that is," Jason replied with just a hint of a smile as he turned and walked away leaving Vicki to wonder what his marriage really was like and if she could encourage him to pay real attention to her.

"That might be real cool," Vicki said to herself as she smiled at the thought of the chase that could lie ahead. "This is a guy with real money and the fact that he is married would make it even better," she thought. Vicki loved getting a man away from his wife; the challenge made the victory all the sweeter.

CHAPTER TEN

For Todd it was dejavu as he watched Vicki's dress change from conservative business, to provocative business, to sheer sexy. He knew that she was up to something and that something would definitely impact on their relationship. It would not be long before she would be calling him and telling him that she had to stay with Joseph and then the lies would just compound from there. Todd knew he would never be able to satisfy Vicki's thirst for all the things real money could buy and yet he knew he would always be there for her to help pick up the pieces when the new relationship fell apart. He also knew he would be there to help in the dissolution of any relationship she might have. He could always find the Achilles heel of the new guy in town. His was a waiting game and he was content to wait for the prize at the end; a prize worth waiting for.

And so- Todd was not surprised one morning when Vicki told him that she would be going back to her house that night as George had some business meeting and she had to be there for Joseph.

"Why don't you just bring Joseph here? He loves fishing in the canal and we could even take him for a boat ride."

"Joseph has a hockey game and after that he'll first have to do his homework and study for a big test tomorrow. It would be better for him to be at the house where all his books are. If George did not have to be away, it would not be an issue. George has actually been staying with Joseph at my place as he also feels it is better for the child to have one place to call home even if we alternate being there with him."

"But you have not been alternating at all. You usually bring Joseph here and he seems to love it here."

"Not on nights before a big test. You know that you tend to get him all excited and distracted from what he has to do and tonight is not a night to distract him."

"Now you are accusing me of not being good for Joseph?"

"Don't be ridiculous. You are very good for the boy and he really does have feelings for you. I guess that next to his father, you are the most positive male image in his life. And, I might add, I really appreciate you spending time with him. It has really helped ease the pain for him that my no longer being with George has caused. Let's not argue about things. It is only one night and I promise I will be here waiting for you to come home from work tomorrow night. I'll even cook you dinner."

"I don't need you to cook dinner. I need you to stir other things for me."

"I'll be here to do that as well. Sometimes it is good to take a little rest; it makes everything function that much better."

"I thought I have been functioning just fine. You seem to really enjoy our time together."

"Look, this is getting ridiculous. I am not going to be here tonight but I will be here tomorrow night and that is that. When you want to be with your children, you don't hesitate to exclude me and tonight I want to be with my son. Get that through you thick head and stop acting like a jealous husband. It is what it is!"

With that Vicki grabbed her sweater and handbag and went to her car. She knew Todd did not believe her and did not trust her. She also knew that she had to be careful or that guinea would do something to screw things up for her. If only she could create a stable relationship with someone then she could finally break away from Todd once and for all. "He's a dead end even if he is a good fuck," Vicki said out loud as if hearing the words could give her the courage to really break away.

Once at the office, Vicki was all smiles. No one there would ever guess she had been arguing with her boyfriend that morning. For that matter, no one there even knew she had a boyfriend and that was a good thing for her especially now that she was sure Jason was going to ask her out for a drink after work. Jason had been showing some serious attention to Vicki for the past two weeks and she could see him sweat a little when he looked down her low cut sweaters. He just had to get in there and that was obvious. She wondered how he would be in bed. He was not too bad looking for a slightly balding guy and he did seem to keep in good shape especially for a married guy. Most importantly, he did have some serious bucks which sweetened the package considerably.

Jason was all smiles when he came over to Vicki's desk that morning. No one else was around and that was helping Vicki who was sure Jason would be somewhat inhibited in front of the other staff members.

"Do you put out?" he asked with a broad smile on his face.

"Do you put in?" was Vicki's reply and they both broke out in laughter.

"I have never heard that answer before."

"There are a lot of firsts around me and that was only the beginning."

"Seriously, how about a drink tonight after work?"

"I've been waiting for the invitation. Where would you like to meet?"

"I have a suite at the Garden City Hotel. We could meet there and they are rather discrete. All you need to do is to go to the concierge and he will give you a key to the suite if you get there before I do."

"Hey, I don't want you to get the wrong idea about me. I am not a one night stand."

"Believe me I realize that. It's just that I am married and I really don't want my wife knowing I am meeting someone for a drink after work. There is no reason to stir that pot. It's bad enough that you work here and I know I should not be meeting an employee, even if it's only for a drink and some conversation."

"Oh, so you don't like to mix work with pleasure."

"You could say that. I very much doubt that Evan would approve of my even having a drink with you."

"What he doesn't know won't hurt him. I'll be at the Garden City Hotel by 5:30 and if you are not there by 5:45, I will assume your stupid concerns won out and you are not coming. After all, I would not want you to do anything you are afraid of doing. Just know this could be the most exciting drink of your life."

With that Vicki turned away from Jason so he could not see the smile on her face and pretended to get busy with the work at hand. She just knew he would be at the hotel long before she arrived and she also knew she would make the adventure worth his while. Who knew where it could lead. Obviously, he was not madly in love with his overweight wife or he would never have started flirting with her in the first place. It always amazed her how these women who are married to affluent men could let themselves go because they think they are so secure in their marriages just because they have the guy's kids. Those husbands were the easiest picking for her and she really enjoyed winning them over and taking them away from "the little woman at home."

Promptly at 5:30 that evening Vicki's heels clicked as she walked across the lobby of the Garden City Hotel. She was aware that heads turned as she passed and that helped confirm the fact that she really looked good in her tight fitting shirt and low cut sweater.

"Mr. Bergman is in suite 401 and told me to tell you to just come right up," the concierge said as she approached his desk. That bothered Vicki a little and she wondered if she did look too much like a hooker and maybe it was a little too obvious.

"Thank you," was her only reply as she turned toward the elevator knowing she would have to again change her image somewhat if she wanted respect not only from strangers but from Jason or any other man with whom she were to be involved.

As she stepped out of the elevator, the door to suite 401 opened.

"You know I am not a stupid hooker," were the first words out of her mouth as Jason stood there smiling.

"Why would you say such a thing?"

"How about- the concierge guy knowing whom I was going to see without me having to say a word to him?"

"That is simple to explain. I told him one of the most beautiful women he has ever seen was coming to meet with me and that he should just tell her to come directly up here."

"Yeah-sure. All it did was make me feel cheap."

"How can I make that up to you? I really don't want to spoil our time together ."

"Let's have that drink and maybe I will relax after that."

Jason served the champagne and strawberries in the beautiful Waterford glasses and they both slipped into a conversation of small talk. Jason told Vicki he had the suite for out-of-town clients and that he had never met another woman there in all the years he had had it.

"It is really exciting to see you in such a beautiful surrounding. At the office, I never really realized how beautiful you are."

"That's because you never really look at me, you are too busy looking down my sweater."

"You make me sound like a lecherous man."

"All men are lecherous. It is only a matter of degree."

"What degree am I?"

"I don't know yet." With that Vicki put her hand over his cock and could feel him harden as she gently stroked him. One thing led to another and before long they were both naked and heading for the bedroom where Vicki took total control of the situation. She knew just how to excite Jason but to keep him there until he all but yelled for mercy. When she finally let him come, it was as though he exploded and all energy was drained from his body. That was when she started oral sex and she was determined to excite him all over again only this time he would have to try to arouse her and give her pleasure as well. By the time she was finished with him, he was as limp as a wet noodle and too drained to even speak.

"I told you, you would have an experience you would not forget. Did I keep my promise?"

"All I can say is Whoa! Having been married for so many years, I had forgotten how exciting sex can be. At home it is one, two, three and over."

"My sympathy to you and to all the other jerks who stay married to women who do not try to really please them."

"There are not too many women like you. You are one exciting bitch and really know how to touch a guy and make him feel like something unbelievable. You were right, I will never forget this business drink."

"Who knows, maybe we'll do it again sometime. Right now I have to get going. I have to pick up my kid."

"I didn't know you have a child."

"Yeah- I sure do. I told you I am a single mom when you hired me. Joseph is with my ex right now but I promised to get home in time to tuck him in for the night."

"Does your ex live with you and the kid?"

"Of course not. He lives a couple of houses away with his mother and both he and his mother are really good about watching Joseph for me."

With that, Vicki got up and went into the bathroom to shower. She could not help but notice that everything a person could need was right there in front of her. From the look of the place, it seemed obvious that it was used regularly for intimate meetings despite what Jason had claimed.

"If he lied about that, he probably will lie about everything," Vicki thought to herself as she got dressed and came to the conclusion that he probably was not the right guy for her. The whole experience was one that did not satisfy her and she really did not like the feeling that she was a whore. She wanted a guy who would want her all to himself and be willing to give her whatever it would take to get her all to himself. Jason was a little too slick and she felt he would just use her until he tired of her and then he would creep back into his wife's bed as though nothing had happened. Besides, he was a selfish lover and really did nothing to satisfy her. "This dude is one waste of my time," Vicki half said out loud as she exited the bathroom and gathered her stuff to leave.

"When will I see you again?"

"I'll see you at the office tomorrow," Vicki said with a big smile on her face as she left the suite.

That night when Vicki got back to her house and finally tucked Joseph into bed for the night, she realized how dirty she really felt. A one night stand with one's boss was not a way to advance and knowing that the relationship was totally one-sided really upset her. She really wanted a long term relationship with a guy with money who could afford to buy her the things she wanted. In no way did she want to be someone's play toy to be used and discarded and that is what she knew she would be for Jason. No matter how good the sex was, Jason would stay with his fat wife because that was politically correct and that would not hinder his professional position or his bank account.

As she put her head down on her pillow in her empty bed, she was sorry that she had not gone directly to Todd's house. At least he really loved her even if he could not afford her and he was an unselfish lover who always wanted to please her.

"Oh well, everyone makes mistakes and I certainly made one today."

CHAPTER ELEVEN

The gloom of the rainy morning matched Vicki's mood. The rain pelting the windows seemed to echo throughout the empty house. Joseph was having breakfast with his father, a tradition that started right after their separation but this morning it really irritated Vicki who did not want to be alone. It all added to her feelings that she had made a dreadful mistake. There was no way she could justify her actions. Making it so easy for Jason only made him feel that she was a play thing, to be used at his whim and not to be taken seriously. In reality it was no loss to her as he was a very selfish lover who could never satisfy her needs but nevertheless it was a mistake and it could jeopardize her job.

"Oh well, jobs can be replaced," she said out loud as she finished her black coffee and decided to prepare for work. Vicki immediately decided to wear her most conservative suit. She knew she would look business-like and that would probably deliver her message without her having to say a word. She carefully applied her makeup as it was important to her to look especially pretty and not to show she had any concerns about anything that had happened. In her heart she wanted Jason to know it was his loss and not hers.

Jason also came to work with an all business attitude. He acted as though nothing had happened the night before and he barely spoke to Vicki except when it was absolutely necessary. There was none of the usual banter or jokes and definitely no sexual innuendos which had become customary especially during the times the other employees were not around such as early in the morning or at lunch time. It was clear to Vicki that he was not going to be a problem to her and that he, too, felt it had been a mistake. In some ways she was relieved but in others she wanted some form of revenge. No man just used her and discarded her; it just did not happen that way.

"I will find a way to make him pay for the way he treated me. Time- all in good time," she said to herself as she gathered her things at the end of the day and left the office to go to Todd's house. As she drove to Todd's house she kept comparing him to a really comfortable pair a jeans; they fit really well but definitely were not exciting to wear. That was Todd. As a lover he was more than adequate as he always tried to make sure she was satisfied and usually did so rather well but there was no excitement, no real bells and whistles, everything was rather predictable. However, he would do if it weren't for the money problems and all the crazy restrictions imposed by that bitch of a ex-wife.

"He sure beats being alone even if I have to do the dishes," Vicki said out loud as if hearing it made it more convincing for her. "Who knows, maybe we will actually see the bitch married to that jerk, Jeff, and then at least, it will be the end of the maintenance payments."

Vicki was rather surprised to see Todd's car in the driveway as she drove up to the house. It was rather unusual that he got home before her.

"What a surprise!" Vicki said as she entered the house through the unlocked door.

"I worked on the Island today so I was able to get here and actually start dinner. How does fluke fried in Panko sound to you?"

"Good but I was hoping for a first course of cock."

"I'll change the menu without hesitation."

With that they both started undressing on the way to the bedroom. There was an urgency on Vicki's part to show Todd she was really hot for him so that maybe, just maybe, he would believe she really had to work late the night before going home to be with Joseph and he would not give her the twenty questions as to her whereabouts.

He was not a fool and she definitely was not in the mood to create the usual lies.

And so, once again, Vicki fell into a pattern of fidelity. She was at Todd's house every evening and often Joseph actually came with her so that they could all go to his hockey game. Todd was loving life even though he knew that it would not last indefinitely but for now the good wine, great sex and the semblance of a real family were enough to make him feel contented for the moment and it was in the moment that he lived; the future was too far away and the past had no relevancy. That was how life with Vicki was and always would be.

Vicki, herself, was amazed at how contented she was being with Todd and Joseph. She almost felt whole again, for the first time since life was turned upside down by her leaving George for Todd. It was fun presenting herself as part of a real family and she even spoke of having her mother come and stay with them for a long weekend. After all, Joseph had not seen his grandmother in several years.

The only time she reared her back up was when Todd suggested that his mother come and spend time with them. There was no way Vicki was going to allow that critical woman into her space even though Todd kept assuring her that his mother was really happy for them and wanted to see them make a life together. What Vicki really feared was that Greta, Todd's mother, would somehow see through her and alert Todd to some of Vicki's true goals. Things were good for now, why risk it was the way Vicki was thinking. Todd sensed her apprehension and decided not to press the issue for much the same reasons as Vicki had; why risk it! It was all too easy to cause Vicki to slip over the edge and go on the prowl again for better pastures. So Todd put his mother on the back burner along with any discussions about Stacey or money.

The only real conflict that he could not put there was regarding his daughters. On those weekends when the girls came to stay with him, they did arrange to have Joseph stay with Vicki so that she was not alone. Todd even tried to convince her that it was good for her to give Joseph some one-on-one attention which the boy obviously craved. That was all he could do because Stacey remained firm on her demand that Vicki be nowhere near the girls; so if he wanted to spend time with them, Vicki had to leave or he had to go somewhere with them. They did enjoy the weekend they spent in Montauk. They stayed at the Snug Harbor Motel and actually went fishing on Lazy Bones, one of the fluke fishing boats that go out for a half day. It was amazing to watch the girls handle a rod and reel and actually catch fish. Todd smiled every time he thought of how excited the girls were when they had a keeper and how proud they were taking it to the Wok and Roll restaurant in town where they actually ate their own fluke. Of course he never discussed the trip with Vicki but he did consider doing it again with her and Joseph. There was a special magic about Montauk and he hoped Vicki would feel the magic and really enjoy the experience.

Todd figured he could work his mother into one of the weekend when he had the girls. He could even take them to Florida to see her. She would gladly pay the airfare and that way she could see her granddaughters without Vicki being involved. Since she lived in Ocala she was only two hours away from Orlando. They could actually fly into Orlando and she could meet them there and they could all go to Disney World or Discovery Cove. It could be a trip that would make everyone happy except for Vicki and that was why Todd was holding off making the plans. He again feared it would upset her enough that she would dump Joseph on George and do something crazy which could ultimately jeopardize their relationship, yet again. He could not help but wonder if he would ever get tired of worrying about Vicki having a relationship with someone else. In his heart he knew his feelings were a recipe for disaster but he could not help himself. He knew he was addicted to her and would do just about anything to keep her in his life and more importantly in his bed.

Vicki for her part remained somewhat subdued especially at the office. She kept her ears opened to learn whatever was the current topic of the gossip train especially if she felt the information might be helpful for her to find a way to punish Jason for what she perceived as disrespecting her. It absolutely infuriated her that he seemed to not notice her at all. Instead he seemed to be directing his attention to one of the secretaries who was extremely flattered to be the recipient of his overtures. Vicki wondered if she had spent time in the Garden City Hotel and knew if the time was well spent, it would not be long before madam secretary was promoted and given a real raise. Now if she had way to prove the course of events, it might make for some interesting action with the Labor Board or the Law Grievance Committee. The other girls in the office all seemed to have the same thoughts as she did and all were equally annoyed by the favoritism being shown to Jason's new love interest, Donna. Interesting enough word had it that Donna was actually married and had two young children.

It did not take long for Vicki's suspicions to become reality. One month later, Donna was promoted to be Jason's personal assistant and Vicki was sure that office work was not the only activity taking place behind Jason's closed door. Jason and Donna went to lunch together, left the office at the same time in the evening and she even did his personal shopping buying gifts for his wife and children. Vicki just knew that Jason's wife would love to learn about how her new fur coat was purchased and just how many real business meetings Jason had in the course of a week.

"I just have to wait for the right moment and then Michelle will receive an anonymous note detailing Jason's activities," Vicki said half out loud and half to herself. A big smile crossed her face as she started to hatch her plan. She knew it would be double fun to create havoc in both Jason's and Donna's marriages and she would be in a position to watch the fireworks without anyone knowing her role in it all.

"If you want to play, you have to pay," Vicki thought and she was sure both Jason and Donna would have pay once the truth became public knowledge. Even Evan, who up to now seemed oblivious to his brother's actions would have to take notice especially since Donna did have a rather sordid past. She had a child as a teenager and claimed that she was married at the time and left the child's father just two weeks after the marriage ceremony took place. That child was now a teenage himself and it did not take much nosing around to find out that he was involved in drugs and hung with a pretty tough crowd.

Donna's current husband was in debt up to his eyeballs. It was quite obvious that they lived far above their incomes and he, much like Todd, would do anything and buy anything to try to make Donna happy. What gratitude did she display? It was amazing that when Vicki went to a deli in Donna's neighborhood and told them that she worked with Donna, she was shocked to hear the counterman refer to Donna as the "Whore of the neighborhood." It seemed that everyone knew her.

As for Jason, Vicki doubted that he could afford to leave Michelle. Theirs was a long term marriage with three kids involved. Jason would have to pay support and maintenance in some pretty hefty sums. The law firm was doing well but Vicki doubted he could afford to maintain his life style, buy Donna all the stuff she wanted and still pay Michelle who probably would also get the house in any divorce suit. Jason really loved his money and Vicki doubted he would be willing to sacrifice it even for Donna.

"This could really be interesting," Vicki thought as she decided to keep gathering information before putting her plan into action. She had to find a way to benefit from all of this and not just by getting the satisfaction that her havoc could create. She decided to remain under the radar as Donna quickly began assuming the role of the office manager. If anyone complained, that person was quickly discharged and replaced with someone loyal to Donna. Jason seemed to ignore the power struggle in office and Vicki could only assume he was getting what he wanted. Word actually had that Donna's salary was over the six figure mark and that was pretty amazing for someone without even a basic college education.

The only person who, at times, seemed annoyed was Evan. He refused to be told what to do and refused to have his immediate staff placed under Donna's control. His secretary and paralegal were immune to Donna's edicts and he insisted on maintaining that status. When Donna complained to Jason, she was told that Evan was an equal partner and had the right to manage his staff his way.

"But Joan and Debbie are stupid and really do not get their work done efficiently. I know I could make them more productive and really save the firm money."

"Donna, leave it alone. You have enough to do to manage the rest of the staff and while Evan appears to be complacent and easily influenced, he really is not. We have a good thing going here. Let's just enjoy it and leave him out of it. I really don't need him getting upset and going to Michelle. That could blow up everything."

"Are you that afraid of that bitch of a wife of yours?"

"Donna, how many times are we going to have the same conversation? I cannot afford to divorce Michelle, and you know that."

"I have a thought that could help alleviate that problem."

"What are you talking about?"

"I know this firm manages the pensions of some very wealthy clients. We could just invest and divert some of the profits and no one need know about it"

"That's not legal. I would lose my license if it ever became known that our firm was doing anything like that."

"We would not be keeping the money, just using it to make a little extra. Once we build up a little nest egg, we would be able to use our own money. As long as the clients make a profit, they will never know we are using a small portion of their money and we will replace the principal."

"Look, you and I know there are no guarantees when it comes to investing. We could lose all the money and then what would we do?"

"I've been studying day trading and have even dabbled in it. It requires that I watch the market closely, but by doing that, I minimize my losses. I've made some nice money and I do have the time. Who knows maybe I could get enough that we could actually change our lives for good and leave the two losers we are married to."

"I don't know. I doubt it could be worth the risks. Evan is pretty smart and if he ever found out we were doing something like that, he would be the first to blow the whistle on us."

"Maybe we could even cut him in."

"No fucking way! My brother has always been Mr. Goody two shoes. There is no way he would ever consider such a hairbrained scheme. He has the idea that this firm was started by our father and he has to continue our father's standards and ethics."

"We definitely could bypass Evan especially now that his staff is separated from ours. I do not even see them socializing during lunch or after work. Joan and Debbie stay to themselves as though they work in a different office than the rest of the staff. Were they ever a part of the general work population before I took over the office management?"

"I don't really know. I never paid any attention to who was friendly with whom. All I ever cared about was that the work got done on schedule."

"Think about my proposition."

"I'll do that. Now how about a little action for the old Peter?"

"Am I to understand that you want me to suck you right here in the office?"

"Yeah, it is not the first time we've done that and it wouldn't be the last time either. You got me all excited talking about your illegal plan."

"Then you will consider it?"

"Let's take care of the immediate task and I will think about the rest of the conversation."

It was right about that moment that Vicki walked past Jason's office door. She could not help but smile at the thought of what type of business was being conducted behind the closed door. She had seen Donna enter the office so she knew Jason was not in there by himself. Besides, Jason usually kept his door opened while he was working so he could see what was going on in the office.

"Boy, would I like to a fly on the wall in there," she said to herself as she continued down the hall toward Evan's office. She had a message for him which she decided to personally deliver. She knew she looked really good that day and hoped he might notice her. After all he was single and though it was rumored that he had a long term girlfriend, obviously, that relationship was going nowhere quickly.

Vicki had seen his girlfriend when she stopped by the office to meet him for lunch, and she was nothing special. He definitely deserved someone more interesting and she could just be that person. Who knows but if she could develop a relationship with Evan, she could be on equal ground with that bitch, Donna, and then things could really get interesting. She was smarter than Donna and probably more cunning. And even more importantly, she could get a life away from her pathetic electrician and the constant worries about money that came with him.

CHAPTER TWELVE

I t did not take Donna long to start the computer and start scanning the various accounts of the clients with the largest balances. In her mind, she was sure they were too busy making new money to keep a close watch on the accounts managed by the firm. Even so, her plan was to withdraw a small amount and keep it out for a few days and then replace it. She needed to have the actual funds in order to open an account initially and once she started making money, she would be able to use that money to make more money so she would not even have to withdraw any from the clients. It all seemed too easy no to pursue it. Jason had been day trading for some time and she was sure she could persuade him to be a good teacher especially if their time was well spent. He actually seemed to enjoy explaining things to her and making himself seem even more important. She felt confident to start putting her plan into action. Of course, she would not tell Jason about it until after she was successful. There was no doubt in her mind that he would force her to stop if he were to know about it. After all he had not given approval to her scheme when she first presented it to him.

The first account she chose to go into was the one belonging to a Samuel Rodgers, a man heavily invested in oil. He had not made a withdrawal in several years so obviously he did not need the money. The recent increases in oil prices had yielded a healthy profit and Donna figured he would not miss one thousand dollars even if she had to hold it for a week. With the push of one button, one thousand dollars was transferred to a holding account she had just created in a fictitious name. And so it went until she had ten thousand dollars in the holding account. Once the money cleared she planned to go on line and purchase her choices through her Schwab account. All she needed was a few good choices to double her money and hopefully accrue enough extra cash to cover her taxes and brokerage fees. If things were to go south, she knew Jason would loan her ten thousand dollars in a heartbeat. For him that was chump change and a mere blow job would be enough to secure the loan which most likely would never have to be repaid.

"Yeah, I could get the money from him with no questions asked but then it would never really be mine and mine alone," Donna said to herself. It was if hearing the words reinforced her plan and her need to accumulate some real cash in her own name.

"Money has little meaning to those have it but for the rest of us who have to scrape for a living, it has real meaning. For me, it is the path to independence," she thought to herself as she got up from the computer and decided to check on the staff so things would seem to be normal in the office. She really wanted to see what that bitch, Vicki was doing. Vicki was definitely getting too nosey and trying to do things that had nothing to do with her receptionist duties. Donna had already decided that with the first real evidence, she would recommend that Vicki get her ass canned.

Donna was really surprised to see Vicki coming out of Evan's office.

"What are you doing in Evan's office?"

"I had a message that seemed important, so I decided to bring it to him personally to make sure he had it in a timely fashion. Did I do something wrong?

"Who is covering the reception desk?

"Jane said it was not a problem for her to cover it for the few minutes I would be gone. Why am I getting the interrogation?"

"I was just curious. We cannot have the reception desk left with no one covering it."

"You know I would never do that."

With that, Donna turned her back on Vicki and marched into Jason's office closing the door behind her. Vicki just stood there wondering what in world Donna could be doing in there. It seemed as though she was spending her entire day either closeted in Jason's office, usually with him in there as well or in her own office with the door closed. Vicki knew she had to find out what they could be doing as she was sure it was not something to benefit the firm or Evan in any way. The question was how she going to find out. It was not her place to enter Jason's office even if she has a message for him. All of his messages were to be e-mailed to him. With that her thoughts raced to the telephone system. Was there a way to monitor outgoing calls? She had to find out if it was going to possible.

Donna, on the other hand, was using her time to watch Jason who was even more active as a day-trader now than he had been previously. He was much too advanced to copy but she felt she could learn how he made choices of what to buy and what to sell .She knew she could not understand futures and the concepts of selling short or long. She did not have the funds to do that and she could not keep the money out of the accounts too long or she would be risking being found out. She knew she had to concentrate on penny stocks and needed Jason's input to choose the best ones. How easy it would be if she could just ask him for his picks but she knew she could not do that as he would want to know where the money was coming from. He knew she did not have the personal resources to play in the market. She also knew he would not be suspicious of her spending time with him; he really enjoyed her time and attention especially when they were to steal a few minutes of physical contact. One thing Donna knew for sure, she had to make wise choices this first time or there would be no next time. If she lost the money she was investing, she knew it would be hard to get it back into the accounts before the end of the month and she could risk being found out. Then she could lose everything; her job, her relationship with Jason; her home and her reputation, for whatever that was worth.

The three days it took for the money to clear at the brokerage house seemed to evaporate before her. Donna knew the time was ready for her first investments and she chose three stocks that Jason was dealing. The stock she chose were low costs ones that moved frequently during the trading day. She bought them on pull-backs and watched them closely so that she could sell as soon as they went up a few points. Since the buying and selling at the discount brokerage firm did not cost but twelve dollars each time, she was able to afford buying and selling the same stocks over a two day period and was able to accrue some profits. At the end of the week, she was able to return the funds to the clients' accounts and she had a little nest egg in her brokerage account. Once her money increased enough, she would be able to buy and sell for the entire week and not have to wait the three days for the funds to clear. That would allow her more time to make more money. It truly amazed her how fast the day passed while she was doing the trading. She barely saw anyone in office during those two days and even Jason was questioning her that Friday afternoon as to why he had not seen her. Donna knew that could be a problem and wondered how she could correct things. Obviously she needed to be in front of the computer to make her plan work but she still needed to give Jason attention. The other aspects of her job could take care of themselves but Jason was the key to it all. Her initial decision was to talk to him about giving her some money to invest because she was really interested in the day trading and wanted to do it on her own. That way she could trade his money and the funds she was acquiring from the clients' accounts and he would understand why she was spending so much time in her office.

"I do not have a problem giving you some money to play with," Jason said as they were having drinks together that Friday afternoon. "Why can't we do the buying and selling together. That way we can spend the time together and you can still do your own thing."

"You are not getting it. I want to do it all on my own. If we are together, you would not be able to keep your advice to yourself, and you know it."

"I probably agree with you, but I miss being with you during the day. You are the only bright spot in my life and we both know that I have to go home to that miserable wife of mine and those screaming children."

"We could arrange to have important business meetings in the evening so we could really be together. Just think how happy I could make you with a few hours at the Garden City Hotel."

"That does sound wonderful. What about your kids?"

"Don't worry about them. My mother will take care of them. She is very proud of me and wants me to succeed at this job so she will do anything to help me and Pat and Tommy love to be with her. She spoils them to death and they love every minute of it."

"Just like I love every minute I can spend with you. You are a very talented lady and you really know how to please me."

"You are easy to please especially since I really love you and wish we could be together all the time."

"Let's not go there. You know it is impossible for me to leave Michelle. She would take me to the cleaners and back and it would destroy everything I have worked so hard for. It's not that I do not love you. I do! It's just that we have to be realistic. As long as I continue to give her everything she wants, she really does not care about what I am doing, so we can have time together as long as we are discrete. I have enough money to keep you happy as well- fear not."

"It's not quite that simple. I want to be married to you and have the home and the family and all those things. I do not want to be a 'kept woman' and you know that."

"You are not a 'kept woman'. You work and earn a damn good salary and I can perform all the husbandry duties so shut up and let's get over to the hotel so I can show you how well I can perform."

"So, I take it you are ok with me doing my own day trading-right?"

"Whatever you want baby as long as we get to spend time together. I'll call Michelle now and meet you at the hotel in ten minutes."

"I'll be there." Donna said with a broad smile on her face. She knew that fussing about being a kept woman would make him give in on anything she wanted. He was really too easy to read but his money made him extra special to be with and she did at times enjoy the sex.

CHAPTER THIRTEEN

All day Vicki sat at her desk trying to figure out how she could get Evan to meet her after work. She thought about coming right out and asking him but she was afraid of being rejected and jeopardizing her job. She finally decided to wait until he was about to leave and plan on getting into the elevator with him. Then it would be easy to suggest going for a drink. She was sure she was reading him correctly and that he was indeed attracted to her.

Her plan went up in smoke rather rapidly when Roberta walked into the office at two forty five.

"Hi, I am here to meet Evan Bergman. Can you let him know that I am here a little early?" Roberta said.

"Who may I say is here?"

"Oh, I am sorry. I did not realize that you are new. I am a good friend of Mr. Bergman's so if you just tell him that Roberta is here, he will know who I am."

"Of course," Vicki replied thinking to herself "What a bitch. She is so stuck up that it is a miracle that she can see her feet." With that Evan walked into the reception area and he and Roberta went back to his office together leaving Vicki to try to gather her thoughts as she listened to the receding clicks of Roberta's heels.

"Having sex with that bitch must be like have it with a mannequin," Vicki muttered to herself making sure no one was within ear range. "All I need is an opportunity to show him how a real woman does it and that Roberta bitch will be a thing of the past," she thought. However, that did take care of the immediate situation. She did not know where she was going to go after work. Joseph was to be with his father, so there was no reason for her to go home. She thought about the Roadside Café but decided it was too early to hook up and, in reality, she was too tired for that type of a night.

"I guess it is good old reliable Todd," she said to herself as she called his cell to find out his plans, not that he ever had any plans when she wanted to come over. Of course, this night was not going to be any different. Todd was definitely excited to hear her voice and he told her he would be home in an hour with Chinese food in tow.

"Shit, it is like we are an old married couple- Chinese food and a quick roll in the hay then TV and sleep. How boring can it be?"

"Don't worry, beautiful, I guarantee it will not be boring. It feels like ages since we have had a night alone and I can't wait to get my hands on your pretty ass."

"Ok tiger but don't forget the wine. You know that always relaxes me and helps put me in the right mood."

"Wine it is- and I know it has to be red and a Cab."

"You got it!"

"See you soon. I will be leaving at five promptly tonight so don't keep me waiting too long."

"The girls will not here this weekend, so we have the entire weekend to be together."

Poor, pathetic Todd. He was such a good schlep that even she felt sorry for him.

"But a woman has to do what she has to do," she said half out loud but it did not matter as there was no one around to hear her. No way could she spend the rest of her life with a poor electrician who has to make child support for what seems like forever and who has his three brats to entertain without her being able to be there. That remains the second most miserable aspect of our relationship. I have to go and hide whenever those brats come over and he just does not understand how that makes me feel. If I were to marry him, not that I ever would, I would still have to leave when the brats come.

It makes me feel like a whore," Vicki said to herself as she gathered her things and prepared to leave the firm. Interestingly that neither Evan nor Roberta had left the building. For a moment she debated with herself if she should go back to his office to say good night but decided against it.

"If I catch them fucking, it does nothing for me except jeopardize my job. Let the little bitch enjoy herself, I'll have my chance soon and I will make sure she is completely out of the picture."

That night all during the foreplay with Todd, Vicki kept thinking about how she could get into the inner circle with Evan. The only thought that kept coming back was that she had to get something on Donna, then she could bring her findings to Evan. Evan was sure to listen to her if she really had some proof. She was sure that Donna was up to something but the proof aspect was the difficult part of the plan. Tincture of time was her thought as she faked her organism to make Todd feel good about all of his efforts.

The weekend passed as though it was a blur. Todd kept questioning Vicki as to why she seemed so preoccupied and finally she told him about her observations at work.

"You know you are going into a dangerous place." Todd said.

"Why would it be dangerous? The worst thing is that I loss this worthless job. So what; there are other receptionist jobs out there. I really have nothing to lose and if I am right, I can have a lot to gain. Evan is not involved with Donna at all. He would appreciate knowing if she and Jason are doing something wrong. After all, he is a partner and his reputation is at stake as well as the firm's."

"The whistle blower always gets caught in the middle."

"Right now, I have nothing to blow my whistle about except a feeling and you know my feelings are usually right."

"Believe me, I know about your feelings. I also have a feeling that you want more than a pat on the back if you go to Evan."

"You can bet your ass on that. Of course, I want more than a pat on the back. I want the bitch's job and I want to earn what she is earning for doing nothing at all. Everyone does her job and all she does is go around ordering the rest of us to do this and that while she goes into Jason's office and blows him. Now is that a job or is it a job?"

"So now you want to blow Jason?"

"I never said that! Besides I would never want to have anything to do with that horrible, disgusting man. He is a womanizer with no balls at all. He'll never leave that demanding bitch he is married to because it would cost him too much money. That's why I know Donna is up to something. She would never stay with a guy who wouldn't marry her and give her the position she wants. It is not in her pattern to be a kept woman, so you know she is blowing him and whatever else she does, because she has something else to gain."

"And you know all of this- because?"

"Because I am a woman and I can read her like a book. That poor schmuck she is married to means about a much to her as dog shit means to the sidewalk. She has already used up all of his money and then some and I hear he is in debt up to his ears. He is not the first guy she has taken for all he is worth. I hear that is her modus opperandi. The word is that she was married before him and the guy ended up bankrupt and she just moved on with her Gueci bags and shoes and her fur coats. That schmuck is still paying child support for her oldest son who is about eighteen now and the kid is not even his."

"Doesn't she have children with current husband?"

"Yeah- she has two young kids who are rather cute. They did come to office once. Man, did the bitch play mother of the year that day. I still can't figure out why the big show but no one was fooled. Everyone at the office knows she just leaves the kids with the nanny and goes off to do her own thing."

"Vicki, if I were you, I would be careful. Remember you are not lily white when it comes to being mother of the year."

"At least I leave my kid with his father. He and his buddy have a real good time together and Joseph knows I love him. So maybe I am not the perfect mother but I do my best. Let's not waste any more time on this. We cannot solve anything by talking about it endlessly. When I have more facts, I promise I will run them past you," Vicki said as she started stroking his crotch to see if she could get a rise out of him. She knew it would not take long as he was always ready and willing for action; that was what was good about Todd, he was her ever ready bunny.

CHAPTER FOURTEEN

The weekend passed much too quickly for Todd. He could not believe how wonderful it was to have had Vicki all to himself for three nights and two whole days. It was so different being with her without Joseph or any other distractions. But reality was about to set in as the new work week was to begin. He watched her dress and it seemed that she was being exceptionally fastidious about her appearance. She definitely chose an outfit that showed off her curves to their maximum and he was having a real hard time keeping his hands off her as she stood before the mirror turning so she could get a good look at herself.

As Vicki pulled away Todd could not help but think that she was once again up to something. What that something was remained to be determined. He very much doubted that Vicki had any interest in Jason. After all, he was married and would not leave his wife because it would cost him too much money. Top that off by the fact that he was obviously involved with Donna and it seemed safe to assume that Vicki would not want to waste her time on him. Now Evan was a totally different story. True he was involved in a relationship but that would only make him more appealing to Vicki. She would consider it a conquest to get him to end his relationship with his current girlfriend, and establish one with her.

"It has to be Evan that she is after," Todd said aloud. "He would be the one to give her wealth and, most importantly, status. This is going to be interesting to watch, and I'll be waiting to foil the whole thing. That bitch will be coming back to me regardless of whom she is fucking."

For Vicki, the trip to the office was one of liberation. It was the first time she had been alone all weekend and felt really good to be away from Todd and his watchful eyes. She could not help but think he was aware that she was looking elsewhere, and she knew in her heart that she had better be careful or he would ruin everything for her just as he had in the past. How she would ever make him understand that she had outgrown him and needed much more than he could ever provide was a nagging question for which she had no answer.

"He'll just have to get used to the idea that he does not own me," she said to herself as she opened her car window and allowed the wind to rush through her hair as a further sign of her freedom. "No man will ever own me!"

The office was particularly quiet when Vicki entered the suite. The door to Donna's office was closed as was the one to Jason's office. She had to wonder if they were there as it was too early for them to be in the office. She wondered if she should check to see who was actually in the office but decided she really did not care, and it would serve no useful function for her to expose herself to either of them. In her heart she knew she would find out what they were up to but that was not going to happen by knocking on either of their office's door; she would have to find another way to get the information and find it she would.

Vicki did walk back to Evan's office only to find that door open so he was obviously not in the office. To Vicki this was a good thing as she would be able to greet him when he came to work and she knew she would find a topic to engage him in conversation.

"I can make his head spin and he'll do anything I want once I get him into my bed," she said to herself. "I am sure he has never experienced the type of sex I can bring to the negotiating table. That Roberta is no match for me." With that thought, Vicki returned to the reception desk with a smile on her face that radiated happiness.

In her mind a plan was about to be hatched and she was sure she would finally have it all.

"If all else fails, all I have to do is get the goods on Donna and Jordan and if anything is being done that is on the shady side and involves the practice, Evan will indebted to me. I will make the most of his indebtedness and that is for sure."

Evan arrived at the office just a little after nine that morning. He looked tired and Vicki could not contain herself as she inquired about his weekend.

"Did you have a nice weekend?"

"Yes, thank you. It was rather pleasant especially since we spent it in the Hamptons at a friend's house. What a view he has of the ocean right from his back patio!"

"I've never been out there but it is a place I have always wanted to visit. Who knows- maybe someday I will be able to spend some time out there."

"You should plan on it. It is a great place to take your son. There is so much to do and there are always kids around. Most of the kids spend the entire day on the beach and when they get back to the room at night, the parents say they are so tired that they happily go to sleep."

"That sounds perfect. Did Roberta go out with you?"

"Funny you should ask. Actually she elected to stay in the City. She had a ton of work to do and she could not afford to give up the days. The weekends are the busiest time for the real estate agents and what with the housing market being depressed, she cannot miss an opportunity to close a deal."

"Well- maybe you should consider taking someone else with you the next time you have an opportunity to go to the Hamptons."

"Would you know who might be interested in spend a weekend with a boring lawyer?"

"One never knows especially when that boring lawyer may not be boring after all."

"It almost sounds as though I am being propositioned."

"Could be! One should never look a gift horse in the mouth."

"I'll keep that in mind. Are there any messages for me?"

"There is nothing here but should one come in, you can be sure I'll get it right to you."

With that Evan turned his back on Vicki and started down the corridor to his office. Half way there he could not help but replay the conversation in his mind. She was propositioning him and the thought crossed his mind that maybe it would be interesting to take her up on it. She was one sexy bitch. That was not something you could say about Roberta with whom sex was totally orchestrated with no deviation allowed.

"When you talk of boring, you have to be talking about sex with Roberta," he thought to himself. "Of course, an affair within the office could present its own set of problems. But then again, my brother has been doing it and he is married. It is amazing that no one has told Michelle about what is going on between Jason and Donna. Oh well- we'll just have see how this whole situation develops."

While Evan was walking away, Vicki was thinking, "He is interested! This could be fun." At that she knew she would be finding reasons to go into his office during the day. She could not imagine that he could resist her once he really got to see her as a woman not as a receptionist.

Donna did not emerge from her office until 12 o'clock and when did she looked drawn and almost haggard. To Vicki it was obvious that she had been on the computer for hours but the question remained as to what she was doing. Vicki was certain that whatever she was doing had nothing to do with the day to day operation of the firm nor did it have anything to do with her usual activities. Donna rarely worked on her computer and when she did so it was usually to surf the net for bargains and things to buy for herself and her kids. She was not doing that this morning as when she did, she would be eager to share her bargains with anyone who would listen.

"Do you need help with anything?" Vicki asked as Donna passed by the reception desk.

"No thanks. I have a meeting with Jason and I would appreciate it if we are not disturbed for anything."

"No problem. If something comes in, I will just keep it for you or Jason. How long should I tell the party it will be before they can expect a return call?"

"Just tell them that we will call them back as soon as possible. We are in a meeting with a client and cannot be disturbed. Am I making myself understood?"

"Loud and clear."

"I don't need your sarcasm."

"I am not being sarcastic. All I am doing is my job as per your instructions. You always tell me to get an estimated time to give a client."

"Let's just drop this. I will call anyone back just as soon as I can. That's all you need to know."

With that Donna turned her back on Vicki and marched into Jason's office closing the door loudly behind her. It was all Vicki could do not to go into Donna's office and try to see what she was up to by checking her computer for sites entered. She would have to wait until she was sure that Donna and Jason were out of the building before trying to check the computer but she also knew that her curiosity was definitely heightened by the way Donna was behaving. It was so out of character for her to work for hours alone in her office and for her to leave the other employees alone.

"Something is up but what is it?" Vicki asked herself. She even thought about going to Evan with her suspicions but it was too premature to do that, so she decided to wait and watch.

It was not long before both Jason and Donna emerged from his office and walked past the reception desk.

"Hold any messages until we return, we're going to lunch," Donna barked at Vicki and she swung her handbag over her shoulder and strolled out the door toward the elevator.

Vicki sat at her desk and watched as the elevator descended to the first floor. She then continued to watch the indicator to make sure no one was coming back upstairs. When enough time had passed, Vicki could not contain herself any longer; she went into Donna's office making sure she had messages to put on the desk should she be questioned as to why she was there. It was not a difficult task to get into the computer as everyone knew everyone else's password. Upon check Donna's internet access, Vicki saw she had been on line with an internet brokerage house. Vicki then tried to access the company files but a special password was needed, and that she did not have. She was just about to leave when she noticed that Donna had a list of the employee's pension accounts on her desk.

"That is very curious," Vicki thought to herself. This was not the start of the year and why would Donna need the pension account information when she had nothing to do with making deposits or monitoring the accounts.

"I am going to go to Evan with this. Maybe he can see if there was any activity in these accounts," she said almost aloud. With that she returned to her desk and checked all messages. It would never due to allow her job to slip, she thought to herself. She then proceeded to go to Evan's office.

"I would like to speak to you in confidence, if I may," she said as she entered his office.

"Of course, please come in and sit down."

"I have no proof but I suspect that Donna is up to something that may involve the firm. She has been spending an inordinate amount of time locked in her office alone, and that is very much out of character for her. When I put her messages on her desk just before, I saw she had the list of the pension accounts for the entire firm on her desk. I thought you might want to check the pension accounts just to be sure there is nothing wrong going on."

"Why would you think there is something going awry?"

"Call it woman's intuition. It just doesn't smell right to me and when it doesn't smell right it is usually rotten."

"Pardon me for asking- I do not understand why you are coming to me with this?"

"Everyone in the office knows that Jason has a thing going on with Donna. There is no point going to him and if I were stupid enough to do so, it would probably mean I would lose my job. You, on the other hand, have a reputation for being straight and ethical. If there is something wrong happening, you would want to know about it before the firm suffers an embarrassment."

"What is in this for you?"

"Nothing. I just care about the firm and about you in particular. I admire you and I would love to get to know you better."

"Rumor has it you are not shy?"

"Some rumors are more believable than others. Shy has never been part of my personality. Let's not get ahead of ourselves on this one. I really think you have to look into what Donna may or may not be doing and make sure she is not doing anything that can affect the firm. I just want you to know that I will do whatever you want or need me to do."

"I take it you are not overly fond of Donna."

"No one who works here likes her. She is two faced and can be really cutting."

"What do the employees say about her and Jason?"

"Everyone knows they have long lunches at the Garden City Hotel and it is not all business. But then again, your brother is quite the lady's man in his own eyes. He even hit on me but he can never be man enough for me."

"Interesting!"

"Maybe, you should leave this nest of yours and see what is going on for yourself. You are the work horse of this firm and I wonder if you are appreciated."

With that Vicki stood up and turned her back on Evan making sure he noticed how her rear end swayed as she walked out of the office. She was sure she had peaked his interest if not for her but for what could be going on in the firm. Hopefully they would have to have more meetings and who could know where that could go.

Vicki returned to her desk and resumed working as though nothing had transpired. It was three hours before Donna and Jason returned but that was nothing unusual for them.

"Any messages for me?" Donna asked as Vicki prepared to hand over the messages she had previously carried into Donna's office.

After all there was no need to arouse any suspicions by leaving them on her desk.

Donna took the messages without so much as an acknowledgement. Vicki got the message that she was dismissed without having to have a word pass between them.

"She is really one solid bitch," Vicki thought to herself. "She really thinks she is hot but she cannot even hold a candle to me. In time I will really show her up. Just wait!"

CHAPTER FIFTEEN

E van could not believe the reaction Vicki stirred in him as he watched her leave his office. He had never experienced getting hard just watching someone walk away from him. The way she walked and the way her ass moved was unbelievable. Everyone in the office had rumored that she was a sex machine and now he too would never doubt it. For Evan it was totally amazing that someone could stir such feelings in him when Roberta could barely arouse his interest. Sex with Roberta had become routine and uninteresting and that was probably why he did not want to commit to marriage. He almost had to laugh to himself while these thoughts were drifting through his mind. Here he was in a long-term relationship with a very respectable woman who could be a professional asset to him and what was he thinking? He was thinking "how exciting it would be to be involved with someone like Vicki."

"I wonder how many men have had the same thought I am having and how many have actually carry out their thought," he said aloud within the confines of his office. "I doubt I could ever bring myself to get involved with her, but it would be interesting."

With that his thoughts changed their path and he started thinking about what Vicki had said. He had to wonder if a third party could actually get access to the pension accounts. After all, only he and Jason were trustees and there were passwords and all necessary to access the account information.

"Could Jason be so pussy whipped that he would give Donna his passwords?" Evan thought out loud doubting every thought. After all, Jason was a person with integrity when he came to his professional behavior even if he definitely lacked it in his personal life. Being a lawyer would make him fear doing anything illegal as the courts would inflict a much more serious punishment to any lawyer found guilty of any illegal activity.

"Now the question is, what do I do and how do I find out what is going on here?" Evan asked himself.

The first thing he did was to go to his computer and see if he could detect any untoward activity in the pension accounts. It was then that he was shocked to find out that his password did not open the account ledger. A call to bookkeeping revealed nothing to shed any light on the situation as no one was aware of any password changes but that was of little help as no one in bookkeeping has access to the passwords and no one there could see the account ledger. The only activity bookkeeping had was to make contributions after the actuaries made the determinations as to how much was to be deposited in each account and when the deposits were to be made.

Evan then called the pension attorney under whom the actuaries worked.

"Jack, it's good to talk to you." Evan said trying to sound casual and unconcerned.

"It's always good to hear from you. How are things going at the firm?

"It's been busy but rather routine."

"Yeah, I've been hearing reports that Jason has been extra busy lately."

"Really, I am surprised that you would be hearing such reports."

"Too many people see him at the Garden City Hotel to be able to call him discreet. Personally, I am surprised he hasn't had to contact a divorce attorney by now."

"Michelle will never file for divorce. She has it too good and she knows it. As long as he pays the bills and makes the occasional appearance at one of her charity events, the marriage stays on relatively solid grounds."

"I assume the other woman is also married."

"Yeah- married with two young kids to boot. Her husband is said to be a really nice guy but the big bucks are not there. From what I am hearing, he will not divorce her for the same reasons that Michelle stays with Jason. Donna pays the bills and he also remains hopeful that she will stop straying for the sake of the children."

"Rumor has it that she works for your firm. How is that going?"

"So far, she is doing her job and the firm has not been impacted by it except for now. If the rumors are so widespread, they will have a negative impact on the firm. I was not aware that their actions were public knowledge."

Hey- the Mineola legal community is like a small town, you sneeze at one end and someone on the other end of town gets a cold. It is just the way things are. Now tell me about you. Are you getting ready to make that girl of yours a respectable woman?"

"Roberta is a great person but I am just not ready for the big plunge. I really want marriage to be a one-time experience and I need to be extra sure before I go there."

"Have you ever thought you could loss her while you are trying to decide?"

"So be it. If she were to leave the relationship, it would just prove it was not right."

"That damn biological clock that women constantly hear ticking is a power force to reckoned with ."

"Ok, I get the message but that is not why I am calling you. I would appreciate it if we could meet for lunch tomorrow somewhere we can talk privately."

"How about The Riverbay at one. Michael, the head waiter, will give us a table away from everyone and you will be able to bare your soul."

"See you at one at The Riverbay and thanks."

Hanging up the phone, Evan was even more conflicted than before. He could not imagine how he would talk to Jason about the rumors circulating and how he would be able to express his fears that Donna was putting the firm in jeopardy.

"It's probably best to wait until all the facts are on the table before going to Jason," Evan thought. He also considered getting to know Vicki better since she was obviously the one who could see what was going on and could report to him. If he did not read her incorrectly, she would be interested in forming a relationship with him.

"That, too, will have to wait until after the meeting with Jack. Hopefully Jack will be able to clear some of the mud and things will be put back into place without having to go any further," Evan thought as he gathered his paperwork and stuffed everything into his briefcase. He was going home before anything else could go wrong.

That night he slept very little. It was really bothering him that he could not get access to the pension ledgers and for him it was a trigger that something was going on that was definitely not kosher and his brother was probably involved in it in one way or another. Just how deeply did things go and how illegal were they? These were questions that nagged Evan all night. He kept thinking that here he was at a good point in his life; the firm was on solid ground; he was involved in a relationship that while it lacked excitement, it was stable; things were generally good between him and his crazy brother but he could ignore Jason's shortcomings and discretions as long as the firm was not affected. Could everything be shattered because a receptionist had come to him with her suspicions? What were Vicki's motives for coming to him? Did she really just have the good of the firm at heart or did she want to upset the apple cart and get Donna fired and maybe take Donna's place. Was Vicki trying to get him interested in her? After all if one brother was involved with an employee, why could the other brother not do the same? Now for another big dilemma, would he want to get involved with Vicki? No doubt about it, she was one sexy broad but she was not a class act, like Roberta, he could never take her to social functions or introduce her to his clients. Everything about her yelled sex and everyone would know that was the reason he was involved with her. A little voice within him kept saying, "Not a bad reason."

Evan was so happy to see the first rays of daylight that he literally jumped out of bed. He felt like he had been tortured all night and knew he had to find answers to some of his questions and find them quickly. No matter what, the integrity of the firm had to be protected.

Evan arrived at the office before he thought anyone else would be there. He was genuinely surprised to see Vicki sitting at her desk and he was amazed at how beautiful she looked. To himself he wondered if she was really as beautiful as he thought or if it was her sexuality that he was admiring.

"My lord, you are here early," she said as he walked through the door.

"I have a lot on my mind and since I wasn't sleeping anyway, I thought I would get an early start. Why are you here so early?"

"I am always here by 7:45 as the madam wants someone here to field any calls than might come in though they never do until 8:30. It's a good time for me to read the paper and have an extra cup of coffee before anyone else arrives and I kind of enjoy the quiet time."

"Sorry to interrupt you. I will be going to a business luncheon around 11:30 and would appreciate it if you were to take any messages that come in as my clients are used to me eating at my desk."

"No problem that is what I am paid to do."

"Oh, by the way, could you also let me know what Donna is doing today? I am real curious about what she does behind that closed door."

"I can only tell you what I see and that is not much. She is either behind her closed door or Jason's. I really would rather not attempt to spy on her when she is not here as there are too many eyes in this place and I am sure she will find out if I go poking around."

"I agree. I really do not want you to do anything like that. Just keep your eyes and ears open. By the way, I really appreciate the information you brought to me yesterday. I still do not know what it means but I will try to get to the bottom of it."

"There are other things you can get to the bottom of around here," she replied with a twinkle in her eye that left no doubt as to what bottom she was referring to.

"Is that an invitation?"

"Consider it what you wish. My only comment is that one never knows what is out there if he is afraid to venture to new experiences."

"Venturing in an office relationship has its problems and it has always been something I strongly disapprove of."

"Disapprove all you want but no one need to ever know as we could and would be more discreet than your brother and his playmate."

"Do you want to be a playmate?"

"I have too much self-respect for that. If I wanted that dubious status I could have had it a long time ago. But I am not one to put the cart before the horse so to speak. Something has to start somewhere."

"Aren't you in a long term relationship?"

"Oh, you mean my electrician? He can never be the man of my future. He is stuck in alimony and child support and is as boring as can be imagined. I almost feel sorry for the poor schmuck because his life is such a mess. But talking about long-term relationships- what is the story with you and Roberta?"

"We are a long-term relationship and everyone keeps telling me she is the perfect wife for an attorney. She is classy and poised and really knows how to handle herself in professional settings."

"Man- you could hire a secretary for that. Is she any good at the important things?"

"She is adequate."

"Adequate is like saying the medicine is bitter. Adequate is boring and boring gets more boring as time passes. You need to see and feel what not boring is really like."

"Are you saying you can show me that?"

"You bet your pants I can and when I am finished with you, you will never want to go back to adequate."

"Is this an invitation?"

"Classify it as you wish." With that she got up and purposely walked away from him so he would get a good look at how her ass swayed as she walked. She knew he had noticed her walk yesterday as she left his office and this was just to reaffirm it. He was interested but was he able to act on his desires? That was the big question. He could be the answer to all of her problems. He was single, rich and properly connected. She was sure that once she had him under her spell, it would be an easy ride to the top of the ladder and she could have it all. Probably the best way to get to him was by getting the dirt on Donna and Jason.

Evan walked to his office amazed at the hardness he felt. That had never happened to him before and he kept thinking that if talking to her and watching her walk could do that to him what would she do if he gave her the chance? He was actually sweating thinking about it but he had to put the thoughts aside as he had things to do and answers to find. At 8:30 he put a call into the broker who managed the pension accounts and asked about the password changes.

"Evan I thought that Jason had told you about it. We had a security breach here at the firm and had the password changed as a way of protecting the accounts."

"Are Jason and I the only trustees on the account?"

"Absolutely, that cannot be changed unless the pension attorneys change it."

"Well, I guess Jason just forgot to tell me the password. Can you give it to me now?"

"Sorry but I do not have access to it. Once it is changed only the trustees know the actual password. The fastest way for you to get it is to ask Jason."

"Don't you think it would be better if we each had our own password?"

"I never thought about it but I guess that would be a good idea."

"Can you set up a password for me that is unique to me?"

"Let me find out. I do not know if I can do that without Jason logging on with the established password."

"I would rather not bother him with this issue. He is under a lot of pressure right now and rather busy."

"Let me ask the tech guys and I'll get back to you in a few."

"A few what- hours, minutes, days-"

"Am I detecting some urgency in this situation?"

"Let's just say I want to be able to see the pension accounts and the sooner the better and I really do not want to make this part of the office gossip."

'Are you referring to Donna?"

"How does her name come into this conversation?"

"She has been calling on Jason's behalf lately and asking a whole lot of questions. She is even the person who has authorized some of the deposits. I am under the impression that she is Jason's personal secretary and is taking over some of his responsibilities in regard to the superficial management of the pension accounts."

"I am one of the trustees. Don't you think you should have discussed this with me prior to accepting any instructions from her or giving her any information?"

"Now that you say that, I have to agree. It is just that Jason had told me that he and she had a special relationship and that he trusted her implicitly."

"That just does not float my boat. I strongly suggest that you arrange for me to have my own password immediately as I want to see what is really going on with the pension accounts and I do not want to alert Jason or Donna before I get a good look see. Am I making myself clear?"

"Definitely, but do you really think your brother would be doing anything illegal with the pension accounts?"

"Look, John, I am not making any accusations but we both know that men do strange things when they think with the wrong head. It is not a secret around here that Jason is having an affair with Donna."

"Jason has always had affairs but he has never allowed that to interfere with his integrity when it comes to the well being of the firm."

"Fine and hopefully this time will be no different but I still have to know for sure. If you value this account, and you should, you will make sure I have access to the accounts before this day is over. I think I am making myself perfectly clear."

"Man, I hope you are dead wrong. You realize that if you find something, it could have a horribly negative impact on your firm and your relationship with your brother."

"Sticking my head in the sand could have a horribly negative impact on the firm. As for my brother, I am tired of his crap. He should keep his pants on while he is at work and concentrate on business and not his cock. His wife may be willing to ignore all his antics but I am getting tired of it all."

"I hear you loud and clear and I'll call you back just as soon as I get in touch with the tech guys."

"I hope you will keep this conversation confidential."

"Of course, there is no reason for me to do anything differently. As far as I am concerned, you are just an interested trustee and you have every right to be one. There is no way I want to be in the middle between you and your brother; he can be very difficult to deal with."

"Speak to you soon and thanks."

Hanging up the phone, Evan could only wonder how many people with whom they had dealings considered Jason difficult. He had always ignored his actions because he was so bright and seemed to bring money to the firm from everywhere he went. Jason was so good at generating the dollars but now did he need more because of his high maintenance mistress? The Gucci shoes and handbags and the flowing mink coat had to come from somewhere and that somewhere was definitely not her salary or from her husband. Rumor had it the poor schmuck was barely making a living in his chiropractic office. Then there was Michelle. She was also high maintenance as was the Garden City Hotel condo. It was totally conceivable that Jason was digging a hole that even his salary could not fill.

Evan's next thought was to check the salary records for the firm. He wanted to know who was getting what. A simple call to the payroll office would answer his questions and put his thoughts to rest. Little did he expect to find that payroll was no longer handled at the firm but farmed out to a payroll management concern and there too, he did not have access to the password needed to secure any information. Now the bells were sounding in his head and he began to fear the worst possible scenario. Was he working so hard just to help support Jason's life style? Was Jason stealing from the firm? Evan knew he had to get answers and get them he would. But he also knew he could not tip his hand and let Jason or Donna suspect that he was looking into matters; he had to get his information behind their backs or he would never get it at all. One thing he was beginning to realize was that he needed an ally and the only person he could think of to fill that role was Vicki. She was in the middle of things by virtue of her position and she could see what was going on without anyone else knowing she was doing so.

"It would not be hard to start a relationship with her and Lord knows, it could even be enjoyable," Evan said to himself as he started making a list of things he had to investigate. The pension plan, the management of the clients' pension accounts, the salary issues, Donna's real responsibilities and Jason's client base and billable hours were all on the list. The next list was for the questions he wanted Jack to answer. How could someone manipulate the pension accounts and what should he look for? Jack would know better than anyone else as he was the one who decided who should get what pension contribution each year and he was also the one to defend the plan should it come under scrutiny by the IRS. Pension audits were anything but unusual and experience with that aspect would give someone experience to answer his questions. Jack was a really smart man and Evan always respected his opinions.

"Man, how I wish I could discuss this with dad right now. He would be able to give me good advice. He was always so honorable and so respected," Evan said half out loud and half to himself as he picked up the picture of his father that he had always kept in his office as a reminder of the need to always be honorable and to treat people as he would want to be treated himself. Dad would never get involved with someone in the office but then again he and Mom have an unusual relationship; they actually love each other. Probably neither ever cheated on the other during their years of marriage.

Dad would probably be furious at me for getting involved with Vicki. But a guy has to do what he has to do," Evan again muttered. "At least I have no wife and probably Roberta will never need to know. Maybe when I have all the answers I will be able to take it all to Dad and lay it out on the table but not now. He deserves his peace and it is wrong to worry him without firm grounds."

It was lunch time before Evan even knew it and Vicki was calling him to remind him of his luncheon appointment.

"Thanks a million. I have no idea as to where the morning went. Is Jason here?"

"Yeah- he and Donna are closeted in his office and I have been told to hold their calls."

"If he asks where I am, please just tell him I had a luncheon appointment but do not give him any other information."

"Don't worry. I understand."

"By the way, do you think we could go for a drink after work today?"

"That would be great. I will look forward to it."

That was much easier than I would have thought, Evan thought as he reached for his coat and prepared to leave for his meeting with Jack.

Jack Weiss' relationship with Evan had evolved from strictly business to professional friendship. He had first been introduced to the firm by Evan's father and he was responsible for maintaining the pension plan's paperwork and deciding the contribution that had to be made for each participant and overseeing the pension accounts entrusted to the firm by their various clients. With Jack there was no cutting of corners, all T's were crossed and all I's were dotted and that was the way their father wanted it and the way Jason and Evan had continued to do things since taking over the management of the firm after their father's retirement.

Jack, as usual, was early and already seated when Evan arrived at The Riverbay. They greeted each other first with a handshake and then with a hug.

"It's great to see you. Usually we wait to meet until after the first of the year," Jack said. "How are you and how are things going at the firm?"

"I am fine and things appear to be doing well at the firm but I wanted to meet with you because I have some concerns about the pension plan. It appears that the password for access to the plan's information at the brokerage house has been changed and I am closed out."

"That cannot be. Both you and Jason are the trustees and you both have a fiduciary responsibility to oversee the plan and its investments. Failure to do so could lead to legal actions against you should a plan member challenge the investments or management of the plan. Let me make it clear to you, you are covered by the insurance that you renew through my firm."

"I understand and that is what I told Merrill Lynch this morning. They are in the process of getting me my own password."

"Wouldn't it be easier to just ask Jason for the password?"

"At this point, I would rather not involve Jason in any of this. If there is some hanky panky going on, he could be involved and I think I need the facts before I confront him. He is in over his head with this woman he is involved with and she is his 'personal secretary.' She should not have any access to the pension account and yet she had paperwork regarding them on her desk. I think that is rather suspicious and that is how I came to find out about the password being changed."

"Am I hearing you correctly; you think she has somehow penetrated the accounts?"

"That is what I want to find out. The brokerage house said that she has been authorizing deposits for our clients as well. John said that Jason gave authorization for her to do so. That is something I do not understand. If she has done anything with the accounts, then we need to determine if Jason is involved or even knows about her activities. I would like to believe that he had no knowledge about any of this but if I go to him, he will probably alert Donna."

"You have to be careful not to make any false accusations. That could lead to legal actions and even worse the end of any relationship with your brother let alone damage the firm."

"I understand all of that but I cannot sit back and allow them or her to run wild. That too will damage the firm and leave me open to legal ramifications."

"There we are in complete agreement. Let me recommend that should you find anything that is suspicious, call Jeff Adler. He is a young lawyer with Schwartz and Schwartz here in Garden City. He is bright and articulate and he does their work with corporate associations and partnerships. From what I am hearing he is about to be offered a partnership with that firm which is something to say for a young guy."

"That is an expensive firm."

"I know but if you are put in that position, you do need the best. Jeff has a reputation of not lawyering up so he charges for his time and his time alone. I am sure that should you need him, he would extend professional courtesy as well, especially if he knows I referred you to him."

"Thanks. I definitely will keep his name in mind. Hopefully, I will not need him. Now, how do I go about looking for tampering in the pension accounts?"

"There should not be withdrawals or transfers from one account to another. Any fees must be posted as such and can be checked with Merrill. I would look at each account, no matter how small the account is, and see if there are any transfers or withdrawals. This has to be done on a day to day basis. If a withdrawal is made in the middle of the month and then paid back before the statement comes out, it may not be easily recognized on the statement as the end amounts in the account would be correct and the small loss of interest would not be something that would scream at you. Does Merrill give you the daily activity in their statements?"

"I really do not know as I have never had to look at them that closely. If it is not on the regular statement, I am sure I can request an accounting of the daily activity from John."

"Will John blow the whistle on this and give Jason a heads up?"

"I spoke to John this morning and explained it all to him and he promises to keep it confidential. He actually understands that any false accusations will have a permanent damaging effect on the firm and he does not want to do anything that would hurt the involved parties."

"Sounds like a smart man."

"Is there anything else I should look at?"

"I think you have enough to start with and depending on what you find we will discuss this further as needed. Let's hope that this is all for nothing and that your suspicions are without grounds."

"I hope so too. But you and I both know that where there is smoke, there is fire. My brother is living high and spending wildly and I do not know how he can do it all, even on his salary."

"Just do me one favor. Keep an open mind and do not allow your prejudice to influence your fact findings."

"I understand what you are saying. Now let's enjoy this wonderful sesame grilled tuna."

With that the two men started eating and talking about Jack's family and their upcoming plans for a vacation in the Caribbean. Of course the topic of Roberta came up but Evan quickly dismissed it saying he was just not ready for a commitment especially with all that was on his mind at the firm.

Lunch ended and Evan got up to leave with no check ever coming to the table.

"I get it! You gave Michael the credit card on the way in, didn't you?"

"What else should I do? Here you are giving up your time to help me. There is no way I wanted to have the usual fight over the bill. Thanks again for your help and I promise to keep you informed."

"Hopefully, the next time we speak, you will tell me your fears are groundless. Remember, keep an open mind."

With that the two men left the restaurant to find that the valet already had their cars at the door. That was what Evan liked about The Riverbay; they knew how to cater to the busy professional.

It did not take long to get back to the office and when he did, he was greeted by Vicki. He went to his office and closed the door before calling her, but just as he picked up the phone, she came bustling into the office. She handed him a sealed envelope.

"I believe this is what you are waiting for," she said as she handed him the envelope.

"Thank you for sealing it."

"What I lack in formal education, I make up in life experience. Believe me, I know there are all too many eyes and ears in this place."

"It is really important that no one knows that I contacted the brokerage house or that you brought your doubts to me. It could jeopardize the very foundation of the firm."

"Worry not. My lips are sealed and hopefully all this cloak and dagger is for nothing."

'Thanks again and are we still on for drinks after work?"

"I am looking forward to it. Where do you want to meet?"

"How about Morton's? They have a real nice bar and it is never particularly crowded. We could even get a bite to eat, if that fits into your time schedule."

"Sounds great. Don't worry about my time schedule. Joseph is with his father tonight and I am free as a bird."

"Joseph?'

"Didn't you know I have a nine year old son?"

"Yes, now I do remember you saying you are a single Mom."

"I have the best of both worlds. My ex is very available and just loves being with Joseph. We have a very good relationship regarding shared custody. If George needs to go somewhere then I make myself available and vice versa. Besides that Joseph is a real nice kid and is no trouble whatsoever."

"I will meet you at the restaurant at six."

"Great, see you then," Vicki said as she turned her back and made sure that Evan was watching her leave. She just knew he had to admire the way her ass swayed and the way her small waist showed up as she walked. She had practiced her walk to make sure it said "I am one sexy lady."

Vicki was right; Evan could not help but notice the way she walked and could not help but wonder how she would move during sex. Her raw sexuality was something he had never experienced with Roberta who was always the paramount lady.

"This could be interesting," he said out loud as he opened the envelope to read the message inside it. It was simple, John had a new password prepared. All he needed to do was to call and things would be put into place. Looking at his watch, he realized he needed to make that call soon if he wanted to have things ready for the morning when he actually planned to spend some time going over the pension accounts.

"Hi, John please."

"One moment Evan, I know he is waiting for your call."

"John, I truly hope that you have not discussed this with your secretary or anyone else in the firm."

"Fear not. All I told Nicole is that I wanted to speak to you when you called so she would put your call right through. I realize this is a sensitive issue and you have my complete confidence."

"How do I get a new password?"

"Just give me at least six characters including two numerals and I will get it established for you. You probably will not be able to get in until the morning as it takes some time for our system to be set."

"That's fine with me. What will happen to the password that Jason is using?"

"For now I would suggest that we leave it active so he can get into the accounts without knowing that anything has been changed."

"That is exactly what I was hoping for. If anything is going on, I want it to continue so that we can see a pattern and I definitely do not want to scare him off."

"Just be sure you can remember the password we are setting up as I will not record it anywhere here."

"That's fine. Make it BIGFISH 22."

"Consider it done. Just one request. Please keep me in the loop."

"No problem. All you need to do is to make sure I can see the day to day events in the accounts"

"That is a given. Do you want me to e-mail directions on accessing the day to day events?"

"That sounds like a plan, you do have my private e-mail, don't you?"

"Yep. I have it right here in my blackberry. If there is anything else you need, just call. I will even put my home number and cell in the e-mail so you can reach me after hours if you need to."

"Thanks, you've been great and I will not forget this."

"Good luck and hopefully you will find nothing."

"Thanks again."

Hanging up the phone, Evan just sat at his desk thinking. After checking the pension accounts, he obviously has to check the clients' accounts.

"One thing at a time," he said shocking himself with the sound of his own voice.

There were a few other messages that needed to be attended to before the end of the day and Evan quickly dispatched them. Most were simple confirmations of appointments for the following day and one was from a client with some innane questions, but all the same he did deserve a response.

It was truly amazing how fast five o'clock came. Some days the minutes on the clock just seemed to pass at a snail's pace but today was not one of those days. Evan knew he could easily stay at the office well past eight but he was committed to meeting Vicki so he left promptly at five thirty. She had already left the building when he passed the reception desk. He did look into Jason's office to say goodbye but that too was empty. It did seem strange that Jason would make no attempt to say goodbye to him.

It took only twenty minutes to get from Garden City to Morton's even during the rush hour. Walking into the restaurant, he could not even see the bar; a good thing considering he did not want to have anyone he really knew see him out with someone other than Roberta. At first he felt his heart drop as he entered the bar because Vicki was nowhere in sight but as he walked further into the room, he caught a glance of her sitting at a small table around the back of the main bar.

"I thought you would prefer this table," she said as he approached. "It gives us a little privacy which is always a nice thing the first time two people get together."

"You do use your life experiences well."

"I told you so," she said smiling brightly knowing exactly what he was thinking without him having to say another word.

Their meeting for cocktails lasted over four hours during which conversation just seemed to flow without effort. Evan was amazed at what a good listener Vicki was and found himself opening up to her with so little effort. Vicki, for her part, just kept thinking how easy this was going to be. Here was a guy who never knew anyone like her and she was sure she could get him just where she wanted him to be. He could be her passport away from her poor electrician and the boring life they had established. Roberta, she was sure, would prove to be no match for her and once she got him into her bed; he would be completely hooked. Tonight was but step one and she knew she had to play her cards right and not rush him into the next step or she could scare him off.

At ten o'clock, Evan seemed to just realize that they had been sitting in the bar for such a long time and had not even ordered dinner.

"I bet you are as hungry as I am. How about we order a steak before we call it a night?"

"Sounds like a call to me. Can they serve it here?"

"I am sure they will serve us right here." With that he signaled the waiter who promptly brought the menu and serving cart to the table. They politely listened to the description of each cut of beef being offered before placing their orders and felt like giddy teenagers as the waiter left.

"This place must be used to people monopolizing a table for hours on end."

"Fear not, we'll pay for the privilege. We've already had two bottles of wine and now with dinner, a family of four could eat for a month with what the bill is going to be."

"I am always suspect when the lady's menu has no prices. I read that as expensive."

"I don't know about you, but I have enjoyed the evening immensely so it is worth every penny."

"Thanks Evan. I feel the same and hopefully we can do this again real soon."

"I don't see why not. But let's continue to enjoy this evening. The food is not even here yet."

Dinner was served and Evan was amazed as he watched Vicki eat. She even did that in a sexy way and she made him feel as if he was the center of her world. Every time he spoke, it was as though she gave him her undivided attention. He was almost sorry when dinner was over and they left the restaurant to go their separate ways.

That night Evan could not sleep. He just could not turn off his mind. Thoughts about the pension situation at the office and how he would go about investigating it troubled him deeply. He feared that it would come down to one brother against the other something that would break his parents' hearts. He also could not stop thinking about Vicki. It was amazing how comfortable he was in her company. They could just sit and talk the evening away; no awkward silences, no hesitations about saying the wrong thing. He never really felt that way with Roberta. With her it was always essential to say the right thing and do the right thing. He could not deny that he was curious about sex with Vicki. If she was so free and easy to be with and to talk to, how would she be in bed? There was no dispute that she just radiated sex.

By four in the morning, Evan just gave up attempting to sleep and went into the shower. He decided he would access the pension accounts from home so he could look them over in privacy. Hours passed before he realized that he should have left for the office, but he could not leave the computer; so he called Vicki and told her he would be in late and if anyone needed him to please call him at home.

"What do you mean that you'll be in late. You are late and Jason has been asking for you."

"Put me through to him."

"I will, but am I going to see you later."

"Right now, I really don't know. Let me call you as the day goes by. Now let me speak to Jason."

"Evan, where are you? This is so unlike you to be late and not let anyone know," Jason said with concern in his voice.

"Actually, I decided to work from home today as I have a big case presentation pending and need some uninterrupted time. Is everything ok?"

"Yeah, I was just worried about you."

"Don't worry. If you need me for anything, I am home and will be here for the next few hours."

With that Evan hung up the phone not wanting any more questions about the case he was supposedly working on. One thing he knew for sure; he was a horrible liar and the only thing that could happen if he continued to engage in conversation with Jason was that he would trip himself up. One thing he now knew for sure; this was not going to be an easy project. He had worked for three hours and had just finished his own account. There were multiple entries with funds going in and out but all were legitimate and made by John or one of his associates. He doubted he would find any irregularities in Jason's or Donna's accounts as it was unlikely they would steal from themselves. But he knew he would go over those accounts before going on as he was never one to overlook the obvious or take anything for granted.

By five that afternoon, he had finished the three accounts and had found nothing to hang his hat on. He could not help but notice that Jason's account seemed to be more actively monitored than his but that did not surprise him. Jason, after all was into day trading and was probably doing it with his pension money as well as his private funds. Under their pension laws, this was within the parameters of the regulations. It also did not surprise him that Jason had never included him when he made the different decisions. Evan knew he was too conservative to risk his pension funds and he would never want to have to day trade.

"Each to his own," he said as he stood and walked away from the computer for the first time in hours. Picking up the phone, he called the office to check on things.

"Glad to hear your voice," Vicki said without sarcasm.

"It's been a long day and I am beat."

"How about I bring some dinner to your place?"

"I am really exhausted."

"You still have to eat. My guess is that you skipped lunch without even realizing it."

"How do you know that?"

"Again, what I lack in formal education, I make up with life experiences. I'll see you in an hour. Is there anything special you would like for dinner?"

"Anything will do and thanks. It is really kind of you to go out of your way like this."

"No sweat- see you soon."

Evan decided a quick shower was just what he needed to revive himself before Vicki came. He was pleasantly surprised at how refreshed he was once he put on new clothes and dried his hair. He finished dressing and primping with just minutes to spare before the doorbell rang. There she was carrying a bag of food and dressed in a trench coat and wearing the most beautiful high-heel boots.

"Don't just stand there with your mouth open. Where's the kitchen?"

With that Evan realized he was just standing there silently admiring what he was seeing. He quickly closed the door and led the way to the kitchen. Once there Vicki put the packages down on the table and before Evan could offer to take her coat, she opened it and allowed it to fall to the floor revealing that all she was wearing under it was a garter belt attached to stocking knit stockings and those gorgeous high heel boots. Evan knew he was staring but could think of nothing to say as he felt himself harden.

"I thought you needed a lift after the day you just had and I can see I achieved what I set out to do," she said smiling from ear to ear. With that she came over to him and whispered, "Shall we find the bedroom or do you like to do it right here in the kitchen. Either way is just fine with me," as she reached down and took his hand and placed it on her breast.

Later Evan would try to remember what happened next but he could only remember the extreme pleasure he felt. He never exploded like he did that evening and she kept making him come over and over again until he wanted to cry out for mercy. Evan had never been with any woman as uninhibited as Vicki or as talented in pleasuring a man as she. She was a whole new experience and he instantly knew he would have to have it again and again. Sex with Roberta was like kindergarten and this was on a graduate level. Roberta would never go down on him the way Vicki did over and over again arousing him more and more and over and over again. They started in the kitchen and ended up in the bedroom and Evan had no idea as to how they got there nor did he care.

When he finally was so limp that even her efforts failed to arouse him, she consented to getting something to eat.

"Let's eat the food I actually did bring and who knows what we'll do for dessert."

"How about sleep? You exhausted me!"

"We'll have to see about that."

CHAPTER SIXTEEN

When Evan woke up the next morning, he knew by the silence that he was alone in the house. He went down to the kitchen expecting to see a note on the table; there was none. The only remnant of the happenings of the night before was a carefully folded towel in the bathroom. He was surprised that he did not even hear the shower running.

"Oh well, there is no denying she is one very different woman!" he said out loud realizing that she probably left right after he fell asleep. He knew it would be interesting to find out why and where she went; but that would have to wait. Now was the time to concentrate on the matters at hand. He knew that once he got to the office he would continue exploring the pension accounts hoping to find nothing and wondering what he would do if there actually are irregularities.

"One step at a time," he muttered as he stepped into the shower.

It was exactly 8:30 am when Evan walked into the office and he was surprised to see Vicki already at her desk.

"Interesting seeing you in a place like this," he said with a big smile on his face.

"Yeah- a girl has to make a living. Sorry about the disappearing act but you were gone and I wanted to be home to have breakfast with Joseph. It is our tradition to have breakfast together after he spends the night with his father. "

"I would really prefer we talk about private things in private. There are entirely too many ears in this place and I, for one, like to keep my private life completely separated from the office world."

"I understand. It is just that I know for a fact that no one else is here. You can trust me to honor your feelings."

"I will be in my office and would prefer not to be interrupted except for something really urgent."

"Do you want me to tell Jason that?"

"No need to initiate anything with Jason. If he wants me just buzz me and same goes for Donna. But, please buzz me in advance. I do not want anyone barging into my office."

"Does that include me?"

"Yes."

With that Jason turned his back on Vicki and walked to his office closing the door behind. In his heart he knew that despite what happened last night, he was going to keep his professional relationship with her exactly that. He hated the way Jason and Donna conducted themselves in the office and he definitely did not want to follow suit. In his heart of hearts, he felt that any relationship with Vicki would be short term as she was not the type of woman he wanted at his side at professional events. No matter how she did herself up, she always radiates sexuality. Roberta on the other hand, was perfect for professional events and extremely boring in the bedroom. Who knows, maybe there is actually someone out there who combines the best qualities of the two.

"Now that's an interesting thought," he muttered smiling to himself at the thought.

Evan wasted little more time thinking about his personal life and he started to review the pension accounts of his larger clients. He had eliminated Jason's account, his own and even Donna's yesterday. Now he was going to branch out and he was relatively sure that if there were any irregularities it would be in the larger accounts which were not monitored on a day to day basis. These accounts relied on the firm to manage them and the principals were most often uninterested in the day to day activities.

The first two accounts were clean and it wasn't until two in the afternoon that he saw some strange activities in two account of Lester Gordon, the head of Gordon Pharmaceuticals. There were two definite withdrawals for five thousand dollars each and they were followed by deposits in the same amounts several days later. No holdings were purchased or sold; it was just a movement of cash and no memos were imputed to explain the withdrawals and deposits. Evan made a hard copy of the transactions and decided not to say anything to anyone until the other accounts were reviewed. Now he was sure he had made the right decision to review the accounts with large cash holdings first and that was exactly what he proceeded to do. By five o'clock he had found three more accounts with similar withdrawals and deposits. Interestingly they were done on the same day. Now he needed to know where the money went. He could not find any transfer orders so it looked like the withdrawals were straight cash withdrawals making them harder to trace. The deposits were also straight cash. It actually looked like someone had taken thirty thousand dollars, used it for whatever purpose and then returned the money.

"Someone is making interest free loans for his or her own reasons," he said out loud as though to make himself believe the supposition. "but why?"

Evan could not believe that Jason would do such a stupid thing. Even if he really did not believe anyone would check, thirty thousand dollars was petty cash for him. If he were going to do anything like this, it would have to be for bigger bucks than that. Now Donna was another story. Thirty thousand dollars was big money to her; but how could she have access to the pension accounts? Could it possibly be that Jason is so stupid that he could share such valuable information with her? That was totally unbelievable but not impossible. After all she was in his office every day, sometimes all day.

With that Evan decided that the next step was to check with the brokerage firm and see who authorized the withdrawals. That should be easy now that he had the exact dates and amounts. He knew he would have to wait until the morning because their computers were shut down after five and it was almost six as Evan grabbed his briefcase and started out the door.

He was surprised to see Vicki still at her desk as he walked toward the elevator.

"What are you doing here so late?"

"I thought I would wait for you, just in case you needed something. Everyone else has left."

"You should leave as well. After all, you need to spend some time with that son of yours, don't you?"

"He is with his dad. Joseph has a hockey game and it is their tradition to go to the games together. I really hate hockey, so it is cool with me. Do you want to grab a drink together?"

"Not tonight. I have a prior commitment. See you in the morning."

"Have fun with Roberta. Just remember she cannot ring your bell like I can."

"You have a good evening as well," he said as the elevator doors opened. One thing he felt really good about as he descended in the elevator was that he had a special lock installed on his office door and only he had the key. Even the cleaning people could not get into his office if he locked the door and he had done so tonight.

"I don't know why but I definitely have the feeling that the first thing Vicki was going to do now that the office is empty is to try to get into my office," he said to himself as he strolled to his car. That was another thing about Vicki, she was a hard woman to trust. Her leaving his place the way she did really alerted him and he wondered if anything she said was the truth. It would be interesting to know where she went and when but that was an investigation that would have to wait until his current concerns were satisfied. "One thing at a time," he thought as the Mercedes started and he pulled out of the garage.

Evan did call Roberta on his way home but he failed to make any attempt to see her. He explained that there were some problems at the office that were taking up most of his time and he was really exhausted. They left it that they would speak the next day and hopefully see each other then. Their call ended with the usual declarations of love which only made Evan feel guilty and somewhat dirty. Roberta was such an understanding and trusting person and here he was, a cheat and a cad.

"It's amazing how complicated life can get and how quickly it can get there," he thought as he pulled into his driveway and let himself into his silent house. It was only then that he realized he had not even spoken to Jason for the past few days. He did not know if Jason had been in the office at all. With that, he decided to call Jason on his cell just to see how he was. Long ago, Evan made it a practice to use only Jason's cell so he would not have to lie to Michelle if Jason were not home.

Jason answered on the second ring and seemed surprised that Evan was actually calling him.

"Where have you been? I haven't seen you in days. Donna said you were locked in your office all day today."

"I've been buried under a big project but it is starting to come together. I was just wondering how you are and what's up with you."

"With me it is the same old, same old. Can I do anything to help you with your project?"

"Not necessary. How are Michelle and the kids?"

"All's well. In fact we are just about ready to start out for dinner. Do you want to join us?"

"Nah- I'm too tired. I'll just grab some leftovers and I'll see you tomorrow. Enjoy dinner and love to Michelle and the kids."

"Will do. See you tomorrow."

Interesting- Evan thought as he hung up. Jason was actually going to dinner with his family and not with Donna. He was so slick; he knew just how to balance his lives. Evan knew he could never manage to maintain a marriage and a side affair. He would probably call one woman by the other's name; it was just too complicated for him.

He was startled when the silence was pierced by the ringing of the doorbell. Opening the door, he was even more surprised to see Vicki standing there.

"Aren't you going to invite me in?"

"Don't you believe in calling before coming?" he said as she aggressively entered the house.

"No need to call. I knew you would be alone tonight."

"Now how could you know that?"

"Call it woman's intuition. I even brought dinner because I know you have nothing in this house to eat."

"I cannot deny this is making me very uncomfortable. What would you have done if Roberta were here?"

"I would have said that you forgot something at the office and I thought you might need the information. You need not worry; I wasn't born yesterday and I know you need time to come to the realization that you and I belong together."

"Oh, so now you are making plans for the future?"

"I know how to make a man happy and you need to be made happy. Believe me, you will never forget me and you will always want to be with me. That's a fact and the sooner you come to realize it, the better."

"I am not used to anyone making decisions for me and I am not comfortable with you making the plans."

"You'll get used to the idea. Now let's eat some food and then I promise I will make you a believer," she said as she walked into the kitchen making sure she was in front of him so he could see her ass sway as if it was inviting him to grab her.

Dinner was accompanied by inane conversation. The sex that followed was anything but inane. Sex came all too easy for her and inhibition was not part of her being. Other women would be disgusted by some of the acts that she did without flinching and she knew just how to make a man come over and over again until he cried out for mercy. But before he would allow himself to fall asleep, Evan had to ask, "Are you leaving or will you be here in the morning?"

"Don't expect me to be here. Joseph does not know that I will not be there in the morning since I did not know I would be staying here. I need to be home in the morning to have breakfast with him. Next time, I promise, I will make other arrangements if I know for sure we are going to be together. Don't worry, I'll lock the door behind me."

With that Evan fell asleep as he knew there was no logical comeback to what she was saying and he was not entirely sure he cared if she was being truthful or not. She was one hell of a woman and he was enjoying the moment and even he knew you should live in the moment from time to time.

The next morning Evan awoke and knew he was a man with a purpose. He was going to get answers to his questions today and that was that. A quick shower and a cup of coffee and then he called Jim at the brokerage house by eight. Jim was usually at his desk that early so he could get his thoughts together before the market opened at nine thirty. After the usual greetings, Evan quickly got down to business.

"Here are the account numbers and the dates when I saw withdrawals. Now I need you to run all the other accounts through your computers to see if there are more transactions of a similar nature. None of our pension accounts should have any withdrawals made against them. Now that I found several, I want you to find all the transactions and present me with a detailed list and documentation as to who authorized these transactions."

"That should not be a problem. When do you want the information?"

"Yesterday would have been fine but I guess I'll settle for this afternoon, but no later. We are a big account and I do not care if you have to take your entire staff off their other projects to complete this. Am I making myself clear?"

'Absolutely clear. I understand your concern and want you to know you have my complete cooperation. I really hate to believe that someone is manipulating the pension accounts in any way. It is very interesting that on the accounts you have given me there are deductions and deposits that correlate. It is almost as though someone used the money for a short time and replaced it."

"That is exactly what I believe is happening. Once I have conclusive proof, I will have to go further to see what was done with the funds and why. For now, we have to have step one answered. By the way, do any of our employees have private accounts with your firm?"

"The only private accounts that I am aware of are yours and Jason's. I will double check if any of the pension accounts are tied to private accounts if you would like me to."

"While you are doing that see if Donna has a private account."

"That is not a problem but you do realize that I cannot give you any information regarding the private account's activities without the account owner's permission."

"No problem. I do not want you to divulge any information that would be a breach of confidentiality. Look we'll talk later when you have the information I need. I will want any information sent directly to my personal e-mail not to the office's fax or e-mail."

"I understand and I'll get it to you as soon as humanly possible."

"Thanks. Speak with you later," Evan concluded and raced upstairs to finish dressing. Before he left, he did change the sheets on his bed, just in case he decided to see Roberta this evening. It would not be good if she were to get suspicious as he had too much going on to start a new problem.

The office was quiet when Evan arrived but Vicki was seated at the reception desk looking as fresh as ever.

"Good morning, nice seeing you in a place like this," Evan said as he approached the desk realizing that he had greeted her in precisely the same way yesterday morning.

"You're here bright and early."

"I have a busy day planned. Please let me know when Jason comes in as I have a few things to go over with him."

"No problem. Do you want coffee or anything?"

"No thank you. I'll be in my office."

It was really hard for Evan to keeps the conversation on a business-like level. What he really wanted to know was if she had breakfast with Joseph; but that was not for here and now. Now he had to get things done. Too many days had passed without getting his regular work done and things were really piling up. His desk, for one, was a mass of clutter, something that was totally out of character for him. So he decided that while he was waiting to hear from Jim or to have Jason come to the office, he would clear his desk and try to get some order in his life. Once the clutter was cleared, he was able to get his priorities in order and he started calling clients who had to have return calls. It was kind of fun to be working on the clock again and seeing his billable hours accrue. It was also good to get his mind on other things except the pension situation and Vicki though every time he heard her voice announce a call he was surprised to feel himself become aroused. It was rapidly becoming clear to him that her time at the firm was growing short regardless of what happened between them personally. He knew he was incapable of a dual relationship as it was all too distracting for him.

It was almost twelve before Jim called to tell him that the list was complete.

"There are about twenty withdrawals and about fifteen matching deposits from the different pension accounts. Some accounts have more than one set of withdrawals and deposits and some have very recent withdrawals and no matching deposits. All the deposits were authorized by a single letter signed by Jason stating that withdrawals can be made if the proper identification code is presented and it was presented prior to each withdrawal."

"Will you e-mail the list to me and a copy of the authorization letter?"

"Absolutely. I just want you to know that our firm has done nothing improper. We do have authorization."

"I do understand and I am in no way implying that your firm has done anything improper or illegal."

"I am glad you understand. I will scan in the authorization letter and e-mail everything to you within the next thirty minutes. Let me know when you receive the e-mail."

"Will do and thanks."

Hanging up, Evan needed a few minutes to get his thoughts

together. He decided that he really did not want to confront Jason alone. He could see where that would lead to a big showdown and nothing productive could be achieved. With that thought in place, he decided to call Jeff Adler, the attorney Jack had recommended. Hopefully he would have some ideas as to how to handle this whole situation.It was meaningless to know what Jason was doing with the money. It was wrong, if not illegal, for him to use pension funds that did not belong to him regardless of the fact that he had replaced most of the money taken. The why's and how's seemed irrelevant especially since it was hard to believe that Jason needed such small amounts of money when his salary was exceeding half a million dollars a year. One thing was sure, Evan was hell bent on stopping this mess and clearing it up before the entire firm was sucked into it and he wanted to go about it properly and with someone who was not personally involved. The other thing that was clear to him was that he did not want to bring his father into the mix. His father was always such an honorable man and Evan was certain that there was no way he would condone any shady practices by either of his sons. He had built the practice up from nothing and had turned it over to his sons just two years ago so that he could retire and enjoy his remaining years. He sometimes still came to the office when he was bored and would kibitz with the staff all of whom respected and admired him. Evan felt it would break his father's heart if the boys split or if there was friction between them.

With that thought in mind, Evan called Jeff and arranged a meeting for the following morning. He decided it would be best to meet at his office just in case Jeff needed any additional information but he set the time for nine as he was relatively sure Jason would not be in that early. After all it was past twelve today and Jason still had not graced the office with his presence. Then again, neither had Donna come in so Evan did not need to give it much thought as to what Jason was doing.

The e-mail arrived just as Jim had promised and the authorization letter did indeed have Jason's signature on it. However, it seemed strange that a blanket authorization would be issued. The firm had always had a policy to authorize each transaction individually. When Evan called Jim to ask if he had any conversations with Jason regarding the blanket authorization, Jim denied having spoken with Jason about anything in the past few months.

"You know that at the mid-year there is little to be done with the pensions and these do not require day to day management, so I would have no reason to speak with Jason. His personal account has also been exceptionally quiet for the past several months. I have not had any investments that I would recommend, so I have not called him or you."

"Thanks, I was just curious as it seems so out of character for him to issue a blanket authorization."

With that, Evan could not help but wonder if Donna was at the bottom of this situation. After all she was Jason's personal assistant. How often had he been handed a pile of papers to sign by his assistant an how often did he not take the time to read each paper carefully before signing it? Evan knew he trusted his assistant implicitly and knew she had gone over all the documents before presenting them to him. Could Jason trust Donna in the same way and could she have used that trust to slip an authorization in among the papers he signed? In fairness to Jason, it was totally possible that was precisely what had been done. Why she would do such a thing was another question but Evan could only guess that she might need money and was using the withdrawals to make money on the side. If that were the case, the picture could be even more complicated. No one could anticipate how Jason would take this entire mess and Evan knew for sure that he needed to bring all the possibilities to Jeff's attention and consideration before discussing any of it with Jason.

It was after one when Jason finally came into the office and Vicki called Evan to let him know. Evan did bring some routine office matters to discuss with Jason and did his very best not to comment on the late arrival or the fact that their high-paid office manager still had not come in. Despite all that was on his mind, Evan maintained a cordial demeanor during his meeting with Jason and they were able to settle many open matters so that the business of the firm could go forward.

Evan really did have to bite his tongue as he left Jason's office and saw Donna waltz into the office as though she owned the place. Once the other things were settled, Evan was certain he was going to take that bitch on and if she were to remain in their employ, she would have to do something other than fuck his brother. For now he kept thinking to the cadence of her heels "Now is not the time; now is not the time."

It seemed like minutes had passed when indeed it had been hours and it was time to go home. Evan made it a point to let Vicki know he was leaving and to tell Roberta, if she called, that he would meet her at Bryant and Cooper as they had discussed. He knew he was taking the chicken way out but he definitely did not want Vicki to appear at his doorstep tonight and he did not want to engage in any personal conversation with her while they were in the office. "So be it!" he thought, "she's a big girl and she will get the message."

Dinner with Roberta was an easy time. As usual Evan had no problem keeping conversation going and she was such a bright woman, it was easy to get her thoughts and she did have a way of making him see things more clearly. Before he knew it, he found himself telling her about the situation at the office.

"This just does not make sense to me," she said. "Jason does not need small amounts of money. If he were going to use other people's money, he would use large amounts not a couple of thousand dollars here and there. To me, it looks like you have to look elsewhere. I would even wager it that Jason knows nothing about all of this."

"That's what I am thinking but I do have to go to him first and enlist his help in getting to the bottom of this situation. If I had to make a guess, I would guess that Donna is the culprit. She is in an awkward position. I know her marriage is not going well. Her relationship with my brother has no future as he will never leave Michelle."

"Why do you say that? Men have been known to do strange things when they think with the wrong head."

"Jason is too cheap. It would cost him a fortune in child support and maintenance. He has no need to leave; he just does whatever he wants whenever he wants to do it. Michelle is happy just as long as he makes the necessary appearances at the country club and gives her whatever money she wants. "

"I don't understand that type of relationship. Maybe, I am a little old fashioned; but if I knew my husband was fooling around on the side, I'd kick him out without hesitation. I expect the same fidelity as I give and if he did not want to be with me, he could just leave."

"Things are not always that simple. They do have a special needs child. Roseann is extremely hyperactive and does need special intervention both at school and after school. That is expensive. Also, Michelle has a lifestyle that she could never maintain as a single parent and I think she likes the way she is living. She probably cares about that more than she loves Jason. I always felt she married him not because she was madly in love with him but because he offered the life she wanted. Maybe, she is just as happy that he goes elsewhere for physical satisfaction."

"That may all be true but we are off the topic. If Donna is your primary suspect, why and what is she doing?"

"My guess is that she is creating a nest-egg for herself. I know that she has had a lot of interest in Jason's day trading. My guess is that she is using the money from the accounts to finance her own day trades and that she is replacing the money as soon as she makes a hit. I would think that she would never expect anyone to go over the accounts with a fine tooth comb and she probably thinks she can get away with it."

"How did she get authorization to withdraw the money?"

"Jim at the brokerage house faxed over the letter authorizing the trades. It was too open-ended and he is upset that it escaped scrutiny but was signed by Jason. If I had to guess, Donna gave Jason a stack of papers to sign and he never really read what he was signing. He has no reason not to trust her."

"Very interesting! Now that you have all of this figured out, what are you going to do?"

"I called Jeff Adler to come in tomorrow to meet with me. I want him to go to Jason with me."

"I like that idea. It would be better to have a non-biased person there to mediate the discussion. We both know Jason can be rather hot-headed. Let me just throw one more thought into the pot. You have a new receptionist. Could she have access to the accounts?"

"Why do you bring her into this discussion?"

"Call it woman's intuition. I do not trust her. There is just something about that woman that I do not like or trust. She is after you, or have you failed to notice?"

"Why would she want me?"

"Oh, come on. You are a prize catch for someone like her. You're single, rich and influential. You can give her social acceptance, as well as money and status. You are the perfect piece to complete her puzzle and she really wants to get you in her pants."

"Whoa- so this is what woman's intuition is all about. You scare me."

"No reason to scare you, just keep your eyes and ears open. She is no miss sweety pie."

"Ok but she has no access to the pension information and she is not Jason's substitute secretary. So how could she get something signed without his being aware of it?"

"Sherlock, I have no clue. But you can bet that Donna will bring her into the mix if you point a finger at Donna. There is no love lost between those two women, of that I am sure."

"You get all of this just by visiting the office for a few minutes. You are unreal."

"Vicki is very easy to read. If I were you, I would do a real careful background check on that chick. My guess is that you will find many skeletons in her closet. In fact I'll go far enough to suggest that Donna already did the check and has it set up in such a way that Vicki will take the fall if anyone comes after her with this pension mess."

"That is some web your spider is weaving."

"Just don't be naïve. Those two women are trouble with a capital T. They each have their own agenda."

"Enough office talk; let's enjoy dinner. I promise I will let you know what comes down tomorrow after I meet with Jeff. "

"You can't make up this shit."

Before he knew it, dessert was being served. He had to wonder if Roberta was going to suggest that he come to her place and then he was wondering if he could get himself together. She had really touched a nerve with her comments about Vicki and he was feeling more than a little guilty about his evenings with her in his bed. One thing he knew for sure, he would never be able to fool Roberta and he really had to come to terms with that. If he were to continue seeing Roberta, he would have to be faithful or she would certainly find out about any infidelity.

Roberta broke into his thoughts almost like she knew where his head was.

"I think you have a really big day ahead of you tomorrow. So let's call it an early night. Hopefully, you'll be able to get some sleep tonight. You are going to need it tomorrow."

"Thanks for understanding. You are right; I haven't been able to get a decent night's sleep since all this crap began. Talking to you has been helpful and I really appreciate your insights."

"I'm here for you. Just make sure you have your head together before you go to Jason. The firm is more important than this petty nonsense."

"I agree with you but the firm is at jeopardy for doing illegal withdrawals from the pension accounts. Our fiduciary responsibility cannot and must not be violated."

"I understand. Just let Jeff lead the way with it."

With that they left the restaurant. Evan waited while the valet brought Roberta's car to the front door and he gently kissed her good night. Watching her drive away, he could only think she was one hell of a woman and friend even if she was boring as hell in bed. He wondered if he were man enough to be able to stay with her on her terms. He would have to do so if their relationship were to go forward, Vicki had definitely cast some doubts if he could really be happy with Roberta and gave him something to think about.

But then, there was Vicki. Could Roberta be right about her? Could she be the one manipulating the accounts? They always say to look toward the messenger and it was Vicki who first alerted him to the possible situation. He kept wondering how she could have known that there was tampering with the pension accounts. If she were not the person doing the manipulation, then she definitely had to spy on Donna. Either way, she was a sneak, just as Roberta had intimated.

"Man, can women smell out the negative in other women," he said out loud to himself. All the time he was really thinking "Did Roberta have a suspicion about him and Vicki?" He was sure that was the reason for the fidelity talk and it made him even more uneasy. Evan kept thinking, "Am I that transparent or is it that Roberta just has a sixth sense about these things?"

Needless to say, Evan had a long night ahead of him. He had more questions than answers and was constantly thinking about the possibilities at the office and his own personal mess. He knew the office situation would be taken care of one way or another. Once he exposed the situation, he was sure it would stop even if he could not prove who was doing it. He now had two prime suspects, and, of course, that did complicate things. In his mind he was still leaning towards Donna because her access to information was much greater than Vicki's. In his mind, Vicki was probably guilty of going into Donna's office after she had left for the day and snooping around; maybe even going through Donna's desk and possibly even going through Jason's. If that proves to be the case, he knew he would want to terminate Vicki immediately. Evan was certain he could never trust her and he would always be concerned that she would acquire information that could put a client in jeopardy. Who could say what she could do with privileged information?

Then there was the personal side. He could not deny that sex with Vicki was exciting and different. He had never known a woman like her and probably would never know another one. But, and there was a big BUT; she was not the woman who could stand at his side at different functions. She looked the part of a whore and his associates would so identify her. Roberta had made that patently clear to him and he knew that he did not need her to do so as he knew it himself. When Vicki walked, her body swayed and yelled sex. Everything about her from her enlarged breasts to her pumped up lips told the world what she wanted to do and he was relatively sure that she would have sex with whomever she felt could help advance her position. Evan knew his social circle would never accept her and he would be the laughing stock of the country club if he appeared with her on his arm.

"So, ok, I have to end the personal relationship with her," he said out loud in the empty house; his words echoing back at him. "What do I do at work?" Shaking his head, he knew he had to end the work relationship as well. Having her in the office could only sabotage him and possibly the entire firm. "Whoa, what a stupid web this dumb spider has woven," he said as he glanced at the clock seeing it was only two in the morning. He had three more hours before he could even think to start his day. Sleep was not going to come and give him any comfort so he continued to toss and turn until he finally put CNN on and allowed the monotone to make him drowsy.

CHAPTER SEVENTEEN

The television was still playing when the alarm startled him. A quick shower was all he needed to feel alert but he did grab a cup of strong black coffee just to complete the wake up process. Opening the front door, Evan was shocked to see a man standing next to his car in the driveway.

"May I help you?"

"I'm, Todd. Hasn't Vicki told you about me?"

"Todd, I do not mean to offend you, but I have no idea about what you are talking about?"

"Look, Vicki and I have a long term relationship and I don't need you coming between us."

"I still am not getting it."

"Look, I know Vicki was here and spent part of the night here with you. Very honestly I know you two did not sit around talking the evening away, so let's not make up stories here. I just want you to know that when she left your bed, she came to mine and she will always come to mine. Am I making myself patently clear? If she told you she had to get home to have breakfast with her kid, she was lying; she had breakfast with me after she fucked my brains out. Are you getting it?"

"I'm hearing you loud and clear and all I can think is that she has one hell of a lot of stamina."

"Look, I know what she is and who she is and I have to accept her as she is. Believe me, she will treat you just like she treats me if you continue to have a relationship with her. She is incapable of staying with one man. She likes to get the guy, especially if he is in a relationship with another woman, fuck him until he thinks he can never live without her and then leave him for her next victim. I left my wife and children for her so I know how she operates first hand. I also know I don't have enough money to keep her happy. Between my maintenance payments and the child support, it is hard to make ends meet especially since Vicki likes the expensive stuff. Yurman this and Gucci that and the next thing I know is that my credit card bill is too high to be paid off without incurring interest charges and so it goes from one month to the next. I am in a hole and I have to get out of it, so off she went and she jumped right into your bed hoping to get whatever she wants from you. You are perfect; nice looking, rich and most likely in a long-term relationship. Do I have it right?"

"No matter what, you'd take her back?"

"Call me a schmuck, but I love her despite it all and I know she really loves me. No matter what, she will always come back to me and the other guy ends up the schmuck."

"Look, I really have an important meeting at the office and I have to go. Obviously, you are hurting or you would not be here and for that I am sorry. If you want to continue this conversation, it will have to be at another time." With that Evan opened his car door and stepped into the BMW knowing he never wanted to see this man again.

"Leave her alone or I will be back" Todd yelled as the BMW backed out of the driveway, his voice making Evan shiver as if a blast of coldness had just entered the car.

As Todd's image faded away, Evan kept hearing his words. It was rapidly becoming clear that Vicki was leaving his bed not to be home for her child but to go to Todd. How had he found out who she was seeing or where he lived, were questions that for now had to remain unanswered. One thing that was blatantly clear was that Vicki was not a person to be trusted and Evan was certain that he would not only terminate their personal relationship but also her relationship with the firm. When and how he would do the latter would have to remain to be seen after his meeting today with Jeff Adler. Their personal relationship had already ended with Todd's appearance. No more lies, no more sneaking around, no more great sex. Evan shivered hoping to shake off the coldness that still remained. He knew that his decision was correct and the only right thing for him to do. What repercussions would develop, would develop. He knew he had no choices and with that resolve he parked his car in his parking space and entered the office. He had to acknowledge Vicki who was sitting at her reception desk looking absolutely beautiful and giving no indication that she had any knowledge of Todd's visit.

"Good morning. I am expecting an appointment to arrive at nine. Please just show him in when he comes," Evan said as he rushed past her desk.

"Who are you expecting?"

"It really doesn't matter, does it? We do not have many appointments who come in that early."

Vicki shook her head and wondered to herself why he was being so secretive. Looking at her watch, she knew it would only be a few minutes before she would know with whom the appointment was and would also probably know the whys and wherefores.

Jeff Adler was rushing as usual to the nine o'clock appointment. No matter how much time he always allowed, he always found himself rushing at the last minute. Something always came up to divert his attention and this morning was not different. Stacey had called as he was approaching Evan's building to tell him that Todd was once again late with the monthly support. Not that this was unusual but it always got Stacey hot under the collar because she so resented his spending money on Vicki and his not caring about his own daughters. Jeff kept telling her not to let it bother her so much. Soon they would be married and he could easily support the girls and they would not need Todd's money.

"That's not the point and you know it. He should take care of his daughters. When we are married, his money can be put into an account for their college, I do not care but he has to keep sending it or I will take his ass to Family Court."

"There is nothing worse than a woman scorned!"

"I agree. His leaving me was the best thing that could have happened to me. After all it was because of him that we met but I still cannot help hating him and her. I know these child support payments are a drain on his resources and that gives me infinite pleasure. Who knows, maybe that bitch is already looking for greener pastures. Wouldn't that be a kick in the head if he were left with no one?"

"Have you vented enough? I really have a meeting that is now becoming late. Can we discuss this later?"

"No need. Thanks for letting me vent. Every time he pulls this nonsense, it makes me crazy. I really can't help it."

"I understand and put this issue in the 'time of the month' category. Just remember I love you and whatever he does or does not do is not important to us."

"I know you are right. He just infuriates me and I hate his being able to be with the girls."

"Remember, no matter what, he is still their father and until they no longer want to see him, you cannot say or do anything that interferes with their seeing their father. It you speak against him to them, you just drive them closer to him. That is human nature."

"I know you're right. It's just so hard."

"Let me go or I am going to be really late and that's no way to start with a new client."

"Love you"

"Love you too." With that the call disconnected and Jeff pulled into the first parking space he saw. There always was a little apprehension and excitement when he was meeting a new client for the first time. This time those feelings were enhanced because he knew of Evan's firm's reputation and wondered why Evan would want to meet with someone from Schwartz and Schwartz.

As the elevator doors opened and Jeff saw Vicki sitting at the reception desk, he felt his mouth drop to his knees. She was the last person on earth that he expected to see and from her reaction, it was obvious that she never expected to see him either.

"Fancy seeing you in a place like this," she said forcing a smile.

"I didn't know you worked here."

"A girl has to earn a living and your firm fired me. Remember? Are you still with Miss boring bitch?"

"I have no idea of whom you are asking about. Besides, I am not here to chat with you. I have an appointment with Evan. Is he in?"

"He said for you to go directly to his office. It's the third door down the corridor. Just remember that if life is boring, I know how to spice it up."

"I am sure you would love to do just that especially if you could hurt someone else in the process. I guess you will never change."

With that Jeff turned his back on Vicki and walked down the corridor towards Evan's office knowing that somehow she was in the center of any problem he was having. Havoc and Vicki seemed to go together no matter where or when.

The door to the office was open, and when Jeff raised his hand to knock, he heard Evan asking him to enter.

"I'm Jeff Adler from Schwartz and Schwartz."

"I'm Evan. Glad to meet you but I must say you look like you've seen a ghost."

"On the ride over here I was wondering why you would want someone from my firm to meet with you. Then I saw your receptionist and all I can think is that is trouble with a capital T."

"You know Vicki?"

"She worked at our firm until she got involved with one of the partners and then tried to get me into her pants. The whole scene was not a pretty one and she had to resign her position. Did you see her resume before you hired her?"

"Actually I did not hire her. Our office manager does the hiring and the firing. She has been here for over a year now."

"I bet she has tried to get you and your brother into her pants."

Evan's lack of a fast answer was enough for Jeff to draw his own impression.

"If this meeting is about Vicki, count me out. I cannot and will not be involved with anything that centers about her."

"This is not about Vicki though she did bring the problem to my attention. Jack says you are the best to advise me and I would appreciate you hearing me out before you decide whether or not to take the case."

"I'll listen but before I do so I just want to give you some free advice. Zip your pants and keep them zippered around that bitch or she will castrate you one way or another."

"Fear not. I met Todd early this morning and there is no way I want to get suckered into the mess any deeper than I am already in it. That guy gave me the chills."

"Smart man. Now fill me in as to why I am here."

With that Evan called the front desk to make sure Vicki was indeed there and told her to hold his calls. He then proceeded to tell Jeff the entire story from start to present.

"Is there any way Vicki could have access to the pension information?"

"No and I very much doubt that Jason would have signed anything she presented to him. Vicki just picked up on the activities and brought it to my attention that Jason and Donna were spending a great deal of time together behind closed doors and that Donna had pension information on her desk."

"Doesn't that seem somewhat stupid to you?"

"I've thought about that but maybe she just feels so secure that she did not think about leaving the pension information around. After all I have no reason to go into her office. My question is if Jason is involved in this or if it is just Donna. To me it seems as though the amounts are too small for Jason to be involved. My guess is that Donna is building a nest egg for herself and using our clients' money to do so. My bet is that Jason does not know anything about it. I cannot imagine he would be stupid enough to risk everything for such small returns. If Jason were doing something it would be more like Madoff 's Ponzi scheme."

"How do you explain the letter of authorization?"

"That could have been given to Jason along with other documents to sign and he could have been distracted into signing it. Donna and he have been involved for a long time now and the office is often their playground."

"Let me get this straight. He's involved with the office manager and you're involved with the receptionist."

"Not quite in the same way or intensity. There is no denying that this is a mess. I have never really been involved with the pensions or the management of the accounts. Jason always looked after those clients and we left the day to day management to the people at Merrill. I really need advice as to how to handle this situation so we protect the firm and our clients."

"How much of this does Miss Vicki know?"

"I told you what she knows and I have not discussed it with her since she first came to me with the information. Why do you ask?"

"Her knowing anything immediately puts the firm at risk. She will not hesitate to go public with any information at her disposal and she is not above blackmailing you."

"I was not looking at her as the problem. I was more concerned with how Jason would take the information and how he would react."

"My guess is that initially he would protect Donna if this is her work alone. In time, I would guess he would think about the firm but that depends on how deep he is into this Donna woman. The other possibility is that you will have a cat fight here between Donna and Vicki and that cannot end pleasantly. In short, you have a total mess on your hands and the future of this firm will be decided on how you address the situation. I, for one, would need time to think about it. I am also worried that my being involved could add fuel to the fire because Vicki does not have any good feelings towards me or my firm."

"Would you have someone else to recommend."

"Let me think about it all and we will talk in a few days. My initial recommendation is that any further meetings have to be away from here so that Vicki does not know about them and for god's sake," stay away from her. Do not discuss anything with her or ask her for any help in any way. If she comes to your door, and come she will, do not answer. If she calls do not respond. Every time you speak to that woman, you are putting another nail in your firm's coffin. Am I making myself clear?"

"You are." With that Jeff rose taking his briefcase in hand. In his heart he did not want to be involved in the mess but he found the story interesting and had to admit to himself he was curious about its outcome.

"I'll call your cell and if you have anything you want or can add, please call me. My cell's number is on my card so you can reach me anytime."

"Thanks for coming. I'll show you out so there will be no need for you to talk to Vicki. I really wish I could just terminate her right now."

'Don't do anything until we think about it and come up with a plan of action. You might actually need her testimony if things really go south."

"I hear you."

The two men walked to the elevator both trying not to make eye contact with Vicki. Evan stood and watched the elevator descend before turning to face her.

"Is he a friend of yours?"

"He's a business associate. Do you know him?"

"I worked for his firm before coming here. Didn't he tell you that?"

"Come to think about it, he might have mentioned that in passing. Please excuse me, but I have some calls that have to be made."

"Here are the calls that came in during your meeting."

"Thanks."

"Do you want me to let you know when Jason comes in?"

"Don't worry about it. I'll call him on his cell."

Once back in the safety of his own office, Evan wanted to punch the wall. How could he have been so stupid to get involved with someone in his employ? Stupid was not a good word for it. The only saving grace was that he had not confided in her. He could only imagine how he would feel if he had done so.

Evan did his best to avoid Vicki for the remainder of the day. It was almost easy to do so; all he had to do was to stay in his office with the door locked. In that way he not only avoided Vicki, but Jason and Donna as well. After taking care of the issues confronting the firm, he continued to examine the pension accounts and the list provided by Merrill. He was somewhat surprised at the small withdrawals and matching deposits in several of the larger accounts for which the firm acted as custodian. The most interesting finding was that the money was always repaid within a few days and the movements never occurred at or around the time the statements were generated. It probably would never come under anyone's radar because the accounts were large enough that small amounts being missing for several days would not really affect the bottom line. On the other hand, the small amounts were adding up and it was obvious to Evan that someone was accruing a nice nest egg using the funds entrusted to the firm. He knew that Jason was involved with day trading as he always bragged about the large amounts of money he made. Of course, if he lost money, he never discussed it with anyone; much like a gambler who always tells of his winnings but never of his loses.

But, and the but remained in Evan's mind, Jason would be doing it on a much larger scale. He would never be interested in getting tens of thousands of dollars when he could have hundreds of thousands. Now Donna was another story. She loved to gamble. For her it was the ultimate excitement to play at the blackjack table or to spin the wheel of fortune on the one hundred dollar slot machine. Winning was the ultimate orgasm. He could just imagine how exciting she would find it to day-trade with other people's money. The big question remained as to how she handled it if her trades went south. Where would the money come from to replace the lost amounts or did she just take more from another account so she could pay back the first one and keep going much like Madoff did with the investments he embezzled. That was exactly what Evan imagined was going on. He felt reasonably sure that it was Donna moving the money around and that, in all likelihood, Jason did not have any knowledge about it. Somehow she had gotten him to sign the authorization and to give her the access code for the accounts. Why he would do such a stupid thing was beyond Evan's imagination.

The next question had to be how did Vicki fit into the whole mess? Obviously she was snooping around Donna's office and had seen things that were carelessly left around. There was absolutely no denying she was one smart bitch and, according to Jeff, one dangerous person if she could get anything on an individual or the firm. Having met her electrician, Evan was sure that Vicki would stop at nothing to get whatever she wanted whether that be money, status or even publicity. Controlling her and minimizing her damage to the firm would require professional help and probably, some big bucks. Evan was not sure that Jeff would be the person to help with Vicki. He seemed somewhat afraid of her and what she might say or do. It was quite obvious that Jeff and Vicki had an unpleasant history.

"Man this is one fucking spider web," Evan said out loud as he shook his head and wondered what the next step would be. One thing was for sure; the work day was over faster than ever before. Evan reached for the phone and called Roberta because he knew he needed someone to steady him and he had to with someone with whom he could talk. As always, she was ready and available to meet him for dinner.

"I'm not in the mood for a big dinner. Why don't we meet at the Seven Seas Diner. I'm sure we could get a booth and be able to talk," she suggested. "Afterwards, we could come back to my place for a nightcap."

"Sounds great to me. Especially the part of going back to your place. Don't I still have a change of clothes there or do I have to stop at my place first?"

"Silly, you know we always have clothes at each other's houses. It will be great to spend the night together."

"Meet you at six," he said as he hung up the phone knowing he was taking the chicken way out. If he did not go home to his place, Vicki could not get to him especially if he turned off his cell and there was no way he could have another confrontation with the electrician. Right now he needed time to plan a course of action because any mistakes could be and would be costly. Hopefully by tomorrow Jeff will have come up with some plan as to how to approach Jason; that is if Jeff wants to be dragged into this at all. If Jeff refuses to help, the only other person Evan could call upon would be his father. Right now that was not an option if it could be avoided.

CHAPTER EIGHTEEN

Once again Evan left the office being careful to lock his door. He was shocked to see Vicki still sitting at the reception desk as he pressed the elevator button.

"Hey, handsome. Want some company tonight?"

"Actually I am busy tonight."

"Not so fast buster. What did that bastard Jeff tell you?"

"I don't know what you are talking about."

"You have been avoiding me all day. Remember, I wasn't born yesterday."

"Look, Vicki, my meeting with Jeff is none of your business and has nothing to do with you."

"Then why the cold shoulder?"

"To be blatantly honest, I am totally uncomfortable with having an office affair and I do not want to continue seeing you outside of the work environment."

"No one bushes me off like that."

"Everything happens for the first time and I guess this is a first then."

"Something had to have happened. You were really enjoying yourself."

"Look, Vicki, you are a sexy woman. There is no denying that. You know how to reduce a man to putty and the time we spent together was rather interesting. Please accept it that I cannot continue having a relationship with you. It is me, not you or not anyone else."

"Do you want me to quit this stinking job so you do not have some stupid conflicting challenge?"

"If you want to quit, please be assured I will make sure you have an excellent reference. But, get it through your head, we're through. You have to go back to your electrician and I have to go back to my life."

"Don't tell me that Todd paid you a visit with his absurd lies."

"Actually that was the way my day began and I don't need it or want it."

"He's a nobody with no life. He had been stalking me for a long time. You have to believe me that I have nothing to do with him. He's a liar."

"If he is stalking you, call the police. There are laws against such behavior. He is not the reason for my decision. My feelings are my feelings and when I am uncomfortable, I cannot continue doing something that makes me uncomfortable. Being with you makes me uncomfortable and that is that."

"You'll be sorry. I am not a disposable item."

"No one said you are disposable. People have affairs all the time and they end when they have to end. That's it in a nutshell. I am ending our personal relationship and if you want to end the professional relationship, I understand and I will do whatever I can to help you find new employment."

"That almost sounds like I am being fired. How would you like it if I were to go to your beloved brother and tell him about us and the information I gave you?"

"You can do whatever you want to do. I very much doubt that Jason gives on once of caring about whom I fuck and he certainly cannot say anything about an office affair. As for the other matter, he and I have already discussed it and we are working on it together."

"I don't believe you for one minute."

"That is irrelevant."

"You are such a fool. Don't you know that you and I could have had it all. We could have taken over control of this firm and we could have cut Jason and that bitch out like you cut out a cancer. Neither of them do anything to bring money into this place. You are the work horse and the schmuck. Now you split your billable hours with him while he sits in his office day trading or fucking the witch."

"Enough! I have had enough of all of this." With that he turned his back on Vicki so he could not see how red in the face she was or how she was shaking with fury. Her whole plan to establish a relationship with Evan was about to walk out on her. She knew he was not only leaving the room but leaving her life as well. There she was, once again, left with nothing. That bastard Jeff had to have given Evan a strong warning because there is no way Evan would have done what he just did. He was too soft and even too stupid to see through her on his own. The other problem was Todd. Vicki could not put it past him to have confronted Evan. He probably followed her when she went to Evan's house. She could put nothing past him. If he kept her dependent, he knew he would keep her in his bed and that was all that was important to him.

"That poor, pathetic idiot, I can do anything and he comes running back like a lame dog," she said to herself and she grabbed her bag and rang for the elevator. She was sure that if she went home to Todd, he would be there for her as always with no questions asked. She still had to give it one more try to get Evan back. With that thought, she dialed his number and when he picked up she screamed, "You just can't walk out on me like that. What do you think I am, a common whore?"

"Look, Vicki, it is over. It was a mistake to have ever started a relationship, no matter how short it was, with someone in the office. We are not right for each other and I have no intention of continuing any relationship with you either privately or in the office."

"Now you are firing me to boot!"

"You could say that. I really think it would be best if you find other employment."

"You ass, I have information that can really hurt your precious firm and I will not hesitate to use it."

"You do whatever you want with whatever you want to use. I will not be blackmailed. Am I making myself clear?"

"You fucking ass- you think you can just use me and throw me away like a piece of garbage!"

"Goodbye- this conversation is over. Please do not call me again." With that he disconnected the call inhaling deeply as if to try to get fresh air into his system to replace the disgust he was feeling with himself.

It was not long before the psycho dialing started. Evan would answer the call only to hear Vicki continuing to scream obscenities. Finally when he realized there was no making her listen to any reason, he shut off his cell phone knowing he was dealing with a truly crazy person. Now he was really looking forward to being with Roberta and he only hoped he could stop shaking before he arrived at the diner.

It was not a surprise that she was sitting in a booth at the back of the diner when he arrived. The smile that greeted him immediately put him at ease.

"I tried to call you to let you where I was sitting, but your phone was off. Is anything the matter?"

"It is a long story" and with that he started telling her everything that was going on in his life. He did not know why he had such a need to confess but he did and as he kept talking, he kept feeling better about himself and everything else. In his heart he was sure Roberta would understand but he could not be sure she would forgive him and yet he knew that if he did not tell her everything, he would forever live under a cloud and the rain could come down at any moment and destroy him.

"Now you know everything and please also know how sorry I am about the entire situation. I never wanted to hurt you and I truly feel I always want to be totally honest with you. The more I was away from you, the more I realized what a special person you are and the more I realized you are the person I really want to be with."

"I can't say I am not hurt that you would see someone else

especially someone like that. I always felt she was up to no good and I never trusted her."

"You were right on all counts. I realize now that she was trying to use me for her own benefit but the question remains that I do not know how Donna could have been involved with the pension accounts. Jason would never sign anything she brought to him with reading it and without the signed authorization, she could not have manipulated the accounts."

"That is something you will have to find out for yourself. Have you actually seen the signature on the authorization?"

"Jim faxed it over to me and I would swear that it is Jason's."

"Speak to him before this goes any further."

"That is exactly what Jeff and I are planning to do tomorrow. However, that is the business side of things and it is really not as important to me as our relationship is. Can you ever forgive me?"

"Time can heal many wounds. You are very special to me and I cannot throw away our years together like it is garbage. I guess what I need to know is if I can trust you going forward. I am not a woman who can share her man with another woman and I do not want to be in a relationship where I cannot trust the man I am with. Our lives are very complicated and we both have to stay away from each other for periods of time. I need to know that there are no one night stands when we are apart. Am I making myself clear?"

"You are and I totally understand what you are saying. If this whole experience has taught me anything, it has shown me how much I love you and how much I need to be with you and you alone. I know trust is a foundation for a real relationship, and I want to regain your trust and never lose it again."

"If we are to continue as a couple, we need to marry and start our family. My biological clock is ticking rather loudly of late and I really want to have children, a house, and all the accouterments of a happy life. Can we have that?"

"I know we can."

"I also do not want to think that I do not measure up to her in the bedroom. I know I am a little inhibited and I cannot stand to think you will be bored with me after the wild sex you had with her."

"Worry not. I would never trade one minute with you for any time with her or anyone like her ever again. She is crazy and her lack of inhibition is just another symptom of her insanity."

"I really believe that you could have never told me about your sexual relationship with that bitch and the fact that you did tell me, makes me want to believe you totally. Loving someone requires forgiving that person as well. Now let's stop talking about it and let's think about ways we can enjoy being together and starting over. I love you, you stupid fool."

"I love you too and I really feel that I do not deserve to have anyone as beautiful and understanding as you to share my life." With that he reached across that table and took both of Roberta's hands and just held them with tears streaming down his face.

Evan had no clue as to how long they just sat there, but finally a waiter came to ask if they were ready to order. They both felt as though they were snapped back to reality and realized they had taken up the table for far longer than they should have. Even though they both really did not feel like eating, they ordered knowing that they were expected to do so.

While Evan and Roberta were at the diner, Vicki was almost totally out of control. She had no idea as to how many messages she had left on Evan's cell phone and his home number as well. She just kept repeatedly calling and screaming obscenities and demanding that he be with her. In between those demands there were calls threatening him with sexual abuse and threatening to have him arrested for abusing her and threatening her. During one call she even threatened to have an Order of Protection issued against him. At one point she screamed into the phone," You know the cops do not take kindly to issues of domestic dispute and I will tell them that we are living together and you threatened me. I have friends at the precinct and they will believe me regardless of what you say." It was at that point that she realized she was screaming into an answering machine and no response was going to be forthcoming. Her frustration was at such a level that she really did not know what to do with herself. She knew she could go to Todd's but she also knew she was shaking too badly and there was no way she wanted to give him the satisfaction that he had ended another relationship for her. Once again he had stolen the golden goose right out of her arms and had ruined her life. At that moment she hated him as much as she hated Evan and all the other rich men who used her and discarded her as if she was garbage. She knew she deserved better than a poor electrician with mountains of debt. He had certainly misrepresented himself when they first became involved. He had promised her the sky and moon and everything on earth. What did she get? She had to work to support herself and she ended up with a life where she had to leave the house when his ratty kids came and she was always second fiddle to them and that horrible ex-wife of his to whom he had to pay almost every penny he made. It just wasn't fair that that bitch probably had a cleaning lady and she had to clean the house after those spoiled brats left.

Vicki worked herself up so much that she started calling Todd and yelling at him for ruining her life. He, of course, continued to answer his phone and continued to try to calm her down. This was not the first time he had heard the vengeance in her voice and he knew it would not be the last time either.

"Vicki, you know I love you. Just come home and I will help you to calm down. You belong here with me. I understand you and I forgive you. We belong together."

"Don't give me that shit! I don't belong with a poor electrician. I deserve to be with someone who can take care of me and give me the things that can make me happy.'

"Baby, I make you happy and you know it. Now come home!" With that Todd hung up the phone knowing she would either just call back or eventually wander back to his bed before the night was over. She would always have other relationships but she would always come home to him. That was just the way things were.

Vicki just looked at the phone with disgust. Even she knew there was no point in calling anyone as no one was going to help her but herself. Before going home, she decided she needed a real man. Vicki stopped in the ladies' room to refresh her makeup before getting into her car and driving to the Marriot where she was sure she could pick up some action before going to Todd. She needed a real fuck not some limp guy with a short member like Evan or some pansy like Todd. The pickings at the Marriot were always good and convenient. After all, most of the guys there already had rooms

When she walked into the Marriot's bar she was disappointed to see how few people were there. There were a couple of kids from Hofstra and several couples along with one old geezer who probably could not get it up even with the help of Viagra.

"Today is really my lucky day," she said to herself as she approached the bar and ordered a double martini. At least she could have a strong drink if nothing else. The old guy looked up and told the bartender to put her drink on his tab for which Vicki thanked him but decided not to waste her time. Right then she did not need to fuck someone, she needed someone to fuck her and he was not the man to do it.

The drink helped calm her down and she even considered having a second but then thought better of it. After all, her luck was not good and the last thing she wanted was a DWI on her way back to Todd's. He was right, of course, there was no other place for her to go and right now, no other man who wanted her.

As Vicki got into her car, she decided there was one more call she had to make. She remembered Jeff's number and waiting for the call to connect, she could feel her rage for him increasing. When the call went to voice mail, she could not help herself but to let the obscenities flow. She actually felt better when the call disconnected but she still needed to let Jeff know personally how much she hated him and Stacey. No matter what she does or where she goes, they always interfere in her life. With that thought in her mind, Vicki hit the recall button on her phone and this time Jeff answered the call. He waited while a stream of vulgarities came over the line. When Vicki finally stopped screaming at him, Jeff told her," You must realize that this call is being tape recorded as was the last message you left on voice mail. Secondly, you have to stop calling me. There is a law against harassment and you are harassing me."

"Don't you threaten me with calling the police. Remember I have friends there. You fucking putz."

"Just in case you have forgotten I am an attorney and I know the law so consider this fair warning. I will call the police and have you arrested for harassment, so stop calling me. I have nothing to do with anything that is happening in your life nor do I want anything to do with you."

"You said something to Evan during your meeting today. You screwed me, you bastard."

"You were not the topic of my meeting with Evan. In fact I had no idea you worked there until I saw you at the reception desk. My meeting with Evan is none of your concern."

"You and that bitch Stacey just have to ruin everything for me."

'Vicki, we want nothing to do with you and do not care what you do or where you do it. Just leave us alone." With that Jeff hung up the phone and shut off the power. Any more calls would have to go directly to voice mail as he had no more patience for Vicki's nonsense. It was amazing to him that she had not changed at all. He could still remember her psycho dialing from before and he still remembered how upsetting it used to be. There was a time he would actually try to calm her down but the end result was that she fed off of his efforts and just kept cursing and yelling.

Todd was waiting at the window knowing that Vicki would eventually come home. It was too early when he saw hecar pull into the driveway so he knew that she had failed to hook up with anyone and when he saw her eyes were bulging out of her head, he knew she was far from having calmed down. He decided to pretend that he was asleep because he did not have the energy to be engaged by her. When she entered the house and saw him asleep on the couch, she stormed into the bedroom and slammed the door. She was ready for a fight and was somewhat disappointed when Todd did not wake up.

There were pills to help her sleep and this was a perfect time to take two. She decided she really needed to sleep and that in the morning she would have to address her situation. Now she was not only out of a relationship that could have given her everything she could ever want, but she was also out of a job. Once again she was being forced to start all over.

CHAPTER NINETEEN

E van and Roberta left the diner and he walked her to her car
not knowing if she was going to invite him back to her place
or not. She had every reason to want to be alone and yet he
really wanted to be with her, to let her know that she was the one
he wanted to spend the rest of his life with, and to let her know he
would never again betray her trust.

"Are you coming to my place?" she said as she adjusted her seat
belt.

"I was hoping you would ask me to come. There is no place on
earth I would rather be."

"Meet you there," she said as her window went up and she shifted
into drive leaving him standing there watching her departure.

It was strange driving to Roberta's condo. At first Evan felt
uncomfortable and then tranquility set in. He was sure he was doing
the right thing. Psycho sex was something he could never forget
but he knew it was something he could not take as a long term
relationship. He needed stability and someone who really cared about
him. He needed a companion who made a good impression on the
professional people in his life; that person could never be someone
like Vicki who people viewed as a whore and rightfully so. Roberta,
on the other hand, was someone stable, personable and confident in
her own right. She could handle even awkward situations. She was
perceived as someone who could and would take care of herself and

did not need a man to solve her problems. He wondered if she would ever be willing to try new things in the sex department. It would be great if she could relax and experiment along with him. That could be something to work on once their relationship returned to a more firm footing and, if it proved that she was unwilling, he would be satisfied with whatever they had together. He knew that for a fact and knew that he would never again allow himself to stray as he could never be responsible for hurting her again. He was lucky she was willing to take him back now and he was sure that should anything like this ever happen again, she would send him packing for good.

On his way to the condo, he checked his phone for messages and found the mailbox full of screaming messages from Vicki. He decided to keep them all and knew that once he was in the office in the morning he would download all the messages to prove harassment should he ever have to build a case against her. He was amazed at the language and rapidity of the calls. She would scream into the phone until the time ran out and then call back within seconds and continue screaming. Obviously, this was not the first time Vicki had ever behaved in such a manner and probably it would not be the last time either. It amazed him that he did not see how unbalanced she really was before they became involved and then he even failed to realize it initially. He concluded that he was really a bad judge of character especially where women were concerned.

"I guess there is some truth to the saying that men sometimes think with the wrong head," he said out loud to himself as he shut the phone and turned off the car in almost one motion. As he was about to ring the doorbell, Roberta opened the door and greeted him with a big smile telling him he was home.

Theirs was a quiet night. They simply lay in each other's arms and held each other all night. There was no wild sex and no need for any; theirs was a love between two people who deeply cared for each other and that was all that was important.

The next morning, Evan was up at the crack of dawn. He just had to get to the office before anyone else. There was no way he wanted Vicki there by herself, and he had to get the locks changed so she could not get access to the office in the future. Jeff was to come by ten and he had arranged a meeting with Jason for shortly thereafter. It would not be an issue to explain to Jason that he no longer wanted Vicki in the office in any capacity. They had always understood each other where the staff was concerned. Of course, it could be a bigger issue if Donna proves to be involved in the pension mess; but one thing at a time.

Leaving Roberta proved to be the hardest part of the morning. Evan really did not want to leave her but he knew he had to do what he had to do and for now the firm had to become front and center in his thoughts. The firm had to be protected from the psycho and the thief and he hoped he could affect the protection without getting his father involved. Dad really deserved his retirement and his peace of mind. To pull him into the mess at hand would be wrong and selfish.

It was eerie walking into the empty office. Evan could not remember the last time he had been the first to arrive. He knew one of the secretaries would be able to fill in at the reception desk until they hired a replacement, so that would not be a problem: but all the same it seemed extremely strange. Unlocking his office held no surprises for Evan. Everything was exactly as he had left it the night before. Even the cleaning people lacked access to his office when it was locked. Evan quickly went about arranging his paperwork for the meetings ahead. On top of the pile he placed the signed authorization allowing for the transferring of the funds from the pension accounts. That would be the first order of business that he, Jeff and Jason would have to discuss. Next he had the itemization of the accounts that had money transfers within the past six months. For all accounts and purposes, all the funds removed appeared to have been replaced except for some really recent transactions. Evan planned to lay his chips on the table, so to speak, and to see where they fell at the end of the day. No matter what, he was happy that Jeff was going to be there, if to act as a mediator if nothing else. Jeff's presence would prevent a screaming match from developing between the two brothers. If that were to happen, nothing could be achieved.

Next on the list, were instructions for his secretary to call the locksmith to change all the locks, and to change the telephone codes and the computer access codes. There was no way he could permit Vicki to get to any information and since he had no idea of what information she possessed, he had to take no chances and change everything. "This list can be done by 9:30," he said out loud as he put it on his personal secretary's desk.

He then wandered into Donna's office. Why he was doing that, he had no idea; it was just curiosity. He often wondered what she was doing when she was in her office. What she did when she was in Jason's office was not a question. Her office was extremely neat and it appeared obvious to him that she did not want any eyes prying on her work. Every paper was put away and the place practically appeared to be uninhabited.

He then went into Jason's office which was a room in turmoil. There were papers stacked everywhere and Evan could not believe anyone could ever find anything in the colossal mess. Jason always worked in a messy environment and that was why it had always been so important that they work on different projects as they really could not work together effectively. Evan would have to always be cleaning up for Jason and nothing could ever get done. It was amazing how things had not changed.

The next order of business was coffee. It had been years since Evan had been the one to start the coffee in the morning but there are some things that are not forgotten, and making coffee was one of those things. There was the individual coffee maker but today, Evan knew, was a day for a big pot and that was what he was going to make. Before long everyone would be wanting a cup of brew and having it ready would facilitate things.

Just as the coffee was finishing being brewed, the secretarial staff started arriving. At first the women seemed surprised that no one was at reception but no one wanted to ask any questions and they all seemed to accept that changes were coming down and some of them actually seemed pleased that Vicki was not there. It quickly became obvious to Evan that she was not well received by the other women and it was more than their being catty. Women can be so much smarter than men when it comes to dealing with other women. Anyway, there was no time to think about that any longer. Evan decided to solve the problem of the missing receptionist by having Joanie sit at reception. She presented herself in a very professional manner and knew how to answer and field calls for the firm. Evan could not help but think she would be a good permanent replacement and he decided he would recommend that to Jason later.

Barbara, his secretary, was already busy on the phone taking care of Evan's list. He was grateful that she did not ask any questions and just accepted the tasks at hand. She was a very smart woman who probably had an inkling that something was going on between him and Vicki. She probably decided it was not her business in the first place and she would not want to get involved in something that was none of her concern. Barbara was a no nonsense person who did her job and did not engage in office gossip; that was something Evan always liked about her.

Promptly at ten, Jeff arrived and Joanie announced him to Evan. Jeff did not seem surprised to see the change at the reception desk.

"I guessed that Vicki would not be here today. My cell phone buzzed for hours last night and I finally had to threaten to call the police and have her arrested for harassment."

"You mean she called you too? I don't get it."

"Don't be naïve. She is sure that I told you about her and that I suggested that you get rid of her. There is no love lost between Vicki and me. Remember my fiancé is her electrician's ex- wife. Vicki hates Stacey and views her as the cause of all of her problems."

"It is truly amazing how much turmoil one woman can effect. She is really nuts and last night's phone messages prove that to me."

"Nuts and dangerous. She can be very vindictive. Believe me you have not heard the last from her."

"I already downloaded all of the messages she left on my voice mail last night and I plan to keep them. They show a very disturbed mind."

"Good move. I just hope she does not bring sexual harassment charges against you and Jason. She is capable of something like that."

"We will deal with that if and when it happens. There is absolutely nothing I can do about it right now and we do have other issues at hand. I did change the locks and all the access codes so she no longer has any way to get information about the firm."

"Good thinking. Now when do you expect Jason?"

"He should be here momentarily."

It seemed like only moments before the door to Evan's office opened and Jason came in with a look of real concern on his face.

"Jason, this is Jeff Adler from Schwartz and Schwartz. I asked him to join us as a consultant."

"Nice to meet you, Jeff. I have to say you two look like SS officers. What is going on here?"

"There are several issues we have to discuss."

"Let me guess, this has something to do with that bitch who was sitting reception just yesterday. Where is she anyway?"

"Vicki is no longer in our employ. This is not really about her directly and the issues surrounding her are much less important than the other issues at hand. You and I can resolve the Vicki matter later."

"Ok so what are the issues at hand?"

Jeff reached over and touched Evan to stop him from speaking any further. Jeff wanted to be the one to present the matter to Jason as he really thought he could be less emotional. He proceeded to explain what Evan had discovered in the various pension accounts and then he showed Jason the authorization that was used to move the money out of the accounts.

"I know nothing about this. I never authorized the withdrawal of any of our clients' money and I am beginning to resent the accusation."

"We are not accusing you of anything. Both Evan and I believe that this authorization was acquired without your knowledge. What we need to find out is who is doing the withdrawals and where is the money going."

"I don't see how Vicki could be doing something like that. She did not have access to clients' account information."

"We agree with that. This is above Vicki's security clearance. However," Evan continued "she was the person who first alerted me to the situation. She claimed she was in Donna's office and saw account ledgers that were opened and on Donna's desk."

"That is absurd. Why would Donna be fooling around with the accounts? She has everything she wants and needs. There is no reason for her do something like this and jeopardize the firm."

"She is the logical person to suspect. She has access to you and you trust her. I am sure she gives you papers to sign all the time and you probably do not really read each one. Is that not accurate?"

"Of course. She is my personal assistant and she does handle quite a bit of the routine work that goes over my desk just as Barbara does for Evan."

"So, it would be possible for her to have passed this authorization to you without you knowing its intent?"

"Possible yes, probably no. She knows better than to do something like that. Donna is a smart woman and she would not want to lose her job and ruin her reputation in this way. I also cannot believe you would put me in this position. Donna really cares about me personally and I cannot believe she would want to hurt me."

"Look, Jason, there is over twenty thousand dollars that has been moved from the various accounts. To you that is not a lot of money but to someone in Donna's position, it is a nest egg and if it could continue the proceeds could have been much greater. I know her husband has not been doing well financially and let's be honest, here, you are not leaving Michelle to marry Donna. That is a pipe dream of hers" Evan said trying to keep his emotions in check.

"Evan, do you have any proof that Donna is involved in this or is it all supposition?"

"All I have proof of is the movement of the money. Sums were withdrawn from several accounts and then several days later the same amount was replaced. Where the money went after it was withdrawn and where the return fund came from is not something I can see from our records. So I have no proof as to who is doing the moving but I do have guesses. If you were doing something like this, the amounts would be much greater as this is penny stuff to you so I am assuming that you have no knowledge of any of this. Vicki would have been capable of doing something like this but she did not have security access. That kind of leaves Donna. As office manager, she has the security access and she has your trust."

"I hear you. I just do not want to think this way."

'Jason," Jeff interrupted, "we have to think every way possible. If this matter were to be released to the press, you could have a Madoff situation right here. That is where Vicki could become a problem as she is crazy enough to bring the press into this if we do not get it cleared up quickly and steal her thunder."

"Why would she want to do that?"

"Vicki is consumed with jealousy. I would guess she made moves on both of you hoping to entangle one or both of you. Am I wrong?"

"No you are not wrong. She did come on to me and even met me at the Garden City Hotel once. She was not my type so I blew her off. Don't tell me that she then went after Mr. Goody Two Shoes here?"

"Jay, stop. There is no point in your getting nasty towards me," Evan said in an authoritative manner.

"Ok- next question. Jeff how do you know so much about Vicki?"

"She broke up my fiancé's marriage while she was working at Schwartz and Schwartz and it was not a pretty picture. I met Stacey after the whole thing had gone down but the negative feelings remained. It basically came down to either she had to leave the firm or I was going to leave as there was no way I could work anywhere near her. She is vicious, cunning and hateful."

"And she left her position here because?"

"Because I will not continue to have anything to do with her," Evan replied. I told her I would not see her privately and she went basically crazy. Yesterday some weirdo came to my house in the morning and threatened me if I were to continue having any type of relationship with Vicki."

"That had to be Todd, the guy she lives with. She can shit in his face and he just cleans it off and goes on as though nothing had happened. He is the guy Stacey was married to and they were all neighbors before Vicki set out to get Todd. Believe it or not, she thought he was a better provider than her husband was and that he could give her all the things she wants. That did not work out for her either. Todd is strapped with child support and maintenance. The worse his financial picture is, the crazier Vicki is. You guys had to look like the golden goose to her."

"It sounds like she has the motive."

"No doubt about that but motive without means does not a deed make. She is not the one moving the money," Jeff said with conviction. "If Vicki were taking the money, she would not be putting it back into the accounts. I really do not think she is smart enough to do that."

"So, you are saying that you suspect Donna?"

"I do not know this Donna person. But it is clear that she has access and possible motive and from what I hear, she is pretty smart as well."

"Obviously, we cannot walk into her office and start questioning her until we have more than supposition. How do you guys want to handle this mess?"

"Right now, Evan has spoken with the people at Merrill and they are aware of the authorization problem and will not allow any further withdrawals without prior approval from the both of you. So whoever has been doing the withdrawing will be alerted to a problem the next time an attempt is made to withdraw funds. There are some accounts that are currently owed money but deposits do not need prior authorization unless we can change that as well."

"I would imagine we could do just that. Jim and John have always been very good working with us and if we were to require prior authorization for deposits, the person involved would really get nervous. How much money still has to be replaced according to your figures?"

"About another ten thousand dollars. I would have to keep going through every account but that is the figure I came up with for now," Evan replied.

"Ten thousand is not the end of the world for the firm. We can replace that money ourselves if need be."

"That's obvious. But-"

"No buts- I agree we need to get to the bottom of this and let the chips fall where they may," Jason replied. "It's just that I am having problems accepting that Donna could be involved in something like this."

"Is there anyone else you can think of who could be involved?" Evan asked.

"Logic says no and obviously you both have had more time to think about this than I have and you are also unable to come up with an alternative person."

"We both eliminated you immediately. The amounts were too small for you to bother with or for you to risk it all for."

"Thanks. I am glad that you are not accusing me of being a thief. I guess I am just being thought of as a fool."

"No one in this room is casting any stones. We have all made mistakes and been fools who at times have allowed ourselves to be controlled by the wrong head. You and Donna have had a thing going on for quite a while and I have been surprised that it did not all blow up in your face before this. After all Michelle is no fool."

"Michelle really does not care what I do on the side as long as she has the amenities of marriage. There are actually times that I think she is grateful that I have action on the side. Of course that could all change if there were to be a scandal. Michelle would not enjoy being the brunt of the country club gossip."

"And so the web thickens," Evan commented.

"Don't you have some issues here as well? Roberta is not going to be happy to learn that her lover boy has been dipping into another ink well."

"Roberta and I discussed it all last night. She knows everything that has happened and we have decided to put it behind us and go forward. She is one hell of a person and I realize how lucky I am to have her."

"Does she know about the pension money?"

"That is not her business at this juncture. All she knows is that I have some concerns and that we have to resolve some issues between you and me. I see no point in bringing her into the firm's business."

"Thank you little brother. I was starting to worry."

"Look," Jeff quickly interjected, "let's leave your personal crap out of this for now. Let's devise a plan of action and let's see if we can get to the bottom of the important issue before we are all sucked into it any further. I am in favor of putting a preauthorization on all deposits and withdrawals and have that go into effect immediately. We might be able to smoke out the culprit rather quickly that way and once we know for sure who it is, we can decide on a proper course of action. No one in this room can discuss any of our conversation with anyone else. The next thing is that the accountants have to be called in to go through all the pension accounts and determine exactly which were violated and get an exact amount that is currently missing from each account. Do you have accountants that you can trust to do this?"

"I called the accounting firm and the actuaries and they will be here right after lunch today." Evan replied.

"Am I being naïve or wouldn't that further alert the person moving the money?"

"Bob and Jack are regulars at the office. We can circulate a statement that they are coming for a regular review and not make a big deal of it. Or I can bring the information to them and have them work at their offices. Whatever you think."

"I personally like that idea better" Jason replied. "If this proves to be that Donna is involved, I need to know and need to have proof positive."

"What will you do?" Jeff asked.

"Right now I really don't know. Part of me would want to punish the person responsible no matter who that person might be. The other part of me wants to protect the firm and to try to keep this mess as quiet as possible."

"The later would seem like a better choice to me. The integrity of your firm is your most important asset and that has to be protected. All firms are being placed in a suspicious situation ever since Madoff ripped off his clients. This mess is small potatoes compared to him but the papers would enjoy it none the less. Then of course, your clients would lose confidence."

"Jeff, thank you so much for coming and for your advice," Evan said as he stood indicating the meeting was over.

"Yeah, thanks for everything, I think," Jason said as he too prepared to leave Evan's office wondering what the day ahead would bring.

Jason wasn't in his office but a very few minutes when the door burst open and Donna was standing in front of him, her face bright red. There was no denying she was close to being in a rage and Jason just stood there trying not to laugh at her.

"What the hell is going on here? I come in this morning and Joanie is sitting at reception, Vicki is nowhere to be found and you are locked in Evan's office. Am I not the office manager and doesn't someone have to let me know when there is a meeting and when there are changes in the staff?"

"Calm down; you are out of control."

"Don't tell me to calm down; tell me what's going on."

"Vicki did not show up at work this morning so we put Joanie at reception until we can find a suitable replacement. There was no need to call you as it was a simple matter. What is your problem with it?"

"Do you know what happened?"

"She made a move on Evan and he does not want anything to do with her. She is one sick puppy and we are better off without her being here. If you think you have to hire someone, call the agency and start the interview process. Her's is not a position that should be hard to fill."

"Now what about that secret meeting? I hear there was a lawyer present from another firm."

"It was not a secret meeting but one that Evan and I wish to keep confidential. It does not affect you; so let it be."

"As the office manager, everything that goes on here affects me and I need to know about everything or I cannot do my job."

"Since when is doing your job so important? I thought you primary job was to make me happy and right now you are not doing that at all."

"Don't be ridiculous. You know I take my job here seriously and I think I do it rather well. But I cannot help but feel that something is going down behind my back and I don't like that one bit."

"It's such a pretty back," Jason said trying to relieve the pressure in the room, but Donna would have no part in that. She simply turned her back on him and stormed out of his office slamming the door behind her. Her demeanor was telling him that she suspected she had been found out and that Evan and Jeff were right in considering her the primary suspect. But why would she steal from the clients? He would have given her twenty thousand dollars if she needed money.

With that thought in mind, Jason opened his computer screen and the screen immediately went to his day trading site.

"Oh, my God," he said out loud. "Donna wanted to become a day trader and I taught her how to do it." It immediately became clear that she was day trading using the client's money as bankroll and then replacing the withdrawals once she had acquired enough profit."That stupid bitch! In her mind she was not stealing; she was borrowing and no one was to get hurt." It was then that Jason remembered their conversation about using the pension funds to finance day trades. He clearly remembered telling her that was not a possibility but obviously she had failed to listen.

"Proof, I need proof," he said as he picked up the phone to dial Charles Schwab, the brokerage house that Donna always referred to when she talked about stocks. Luckily he knew Dan Drake, one of the vice presidents over there and it did not take long to have his call transferred.

"Hi, Dan, it's Jason. I need your help with a little situation we are having over here. Can I speak with you under the confidentiality umbrella?"

"Of course. If there is anything I can do to help, you know I am here for you."

"Great. There is actually something you can do. Donna Dimeno works here as the office manager. I believe you know her."

"I sure do. She is one pretty woman."

"Yeah, well- I need to know if she has been placing day trades with your firm."

"I know she has an account with us but I do not have any information as to the activity in the account. Give me a little while and I will look into it for you. Can I reach you at the office?

"Call my cell. Do you have the number?"

"I do. Speak to you soon."

"Thanks, I really appreciate you looking into this for me."

It wasn't long after that call that Jason's door again flew open and Donna stormed into the office.

"Mr. Cohen wants to make a deposit into his pension account and I cannot get it done. Jim is telling me that I have to have you do the deposit. What's going on here? I have never needed any preauth for making deposits."

"Oh, I neglected to tell you we are having some issues with the pension accounts and right now any deposits and, of course, withdrawals need preauth. Do you have a problem with that?"

"What kind of problem are you having?"

At that moment, Jason had had enough. He was getting tired of playing footsie.

"It seems that someone has been using our client's pension funds for his or her own gain. We have a record of various withdrawals and deposits from several different accounts and it has been going on for a while."

"Do you think that Vicki could have gained access to the accounts?"

"That is highly unlikely since she did not have the necessary security codes. Interesting enough, it was Vicki who first brought this to Evan's attention; so I really doubt she was personally profiting from it."

"Then who?"

"You tell me."

"I don't like the way you are making that sound. Don't tell me you think I would do anything that stupid."

"Would you?"

"Look, Jason, I don't like your tone; not one little bit. You sound like a pompous ass and you are insulting to boot."

"You asked and I am telling you what the problem is. Now I need answers; it's that simple."

"What about Mr. Cohen's deposit?"

"Leave the information with me and I will see to it that it is done before the day is over. Is there anything else you need?"

"A new guy!"

With that she again turned and walked out of his office again slamming the door behind her. This time Jason was sure everyone in the office noticed but he really didn't care. He had given her an opportunity to come clean, so to speak, and to tell him what she was doing. Instead, she tried to insinuate that it was Vicki and not she who was manipulating the accounts. Did she really think he was that stupid? Man, how long had he been walking around with his head up his ass? Donna and Vicki are of the same ilk; both whores who use their bodies to get what they want; both with wants that exceed any realistic expectations; both are women who will do anything and use anybody for their own personal gain.

"And I really cared about that bitch. I even thought about leaving Michelle for her and trying to make a life with her. Other than a good lay; she is nothing but a bitch," he said out loud as if hearing the words could make him feel better about himself. "Never again; never again will there be any type of office romance tolerated in this firm. That's for sure!"

Now he began to wonder about the deposit. Was Mr. Cohen really making a new deposit or was his account one of the ones that was tampered with? A quick call to Evan could answer the question without going any further as Evan had a relatively recent list of accounts waiting for money to be returned.

"Hey, Ev, Donna just came in with a request to make a deposit into Mr. Cohen's account. She was really annoyed that she could not do it without preauth and I told her we were having a problem with the pension accounts. I wanted to give her an opportunity to fess up but she did not do so. Please check your list and let me know if Cohen is one of the accounts you are watching."

"Actually his account is down five thousand dollars and he usually only makes new deposits at the end of the month. I would guess the deposit is a pay back."

"Great! I have a call into Dan Drake at Schwab and he is checking to see the activity in Donna's account there. I hate to think about it but she has been overly interested in my day trading for some time now and my guess is that is what she is doing with the money."

"What will you do if it is Donna for sure?"

"One step at a time. The firm comes first- have no fears about that and we will lean on Jeff for help. She is my problem. I will take responsibility for it and I will deal with it. Rest assured, there will never be another office romance with me in the middle of things and hopefully, you also feel the same way."

"I am done. From now on I plan on being committed to Roberta and I will be a one woman man. This whole mess has proven that psycho sex is not worth anything."

"I am glad for you. Unfortunately, Michelle will not be that understanding once this gets out, if it gets out. She will be embarrassed at the country club and that is an arch no no. In my house there is going to be hell to pay. I am also wondering if there is not some leverage with Donna's husband being drawn into this mess. He can't be too happy about having a wife who is fooling around."

"It would be a real kick in the head if she loses out on it all- you, her husband, the money, the job- all of it."

"Right now I would love to see that happen. The bitch deserves it."

'Try to keep cool and try not to talk to her about this mess anymore. We do not need you tipping our position."

"Do you want me to authorize the deposit?"

"I would just make sure it is all properly recorded for now."

After that conversation, the two brothers separated and each became engrossed in his own thoughts and tasks. The hours sped by, and before either Jason or Evan was aware of the time, the staff came to each of them to say good night. No one asked any questions though it was obvious to Evan that everyone was wondering what had happened to Vicki and their curiosity was heightened by the fact that Donna left the office early without saying anything to anyone. Evan became aware of her absence about two o'clock that afternoon and when he questioned Jason, he was surprised that Jason was totally unaware that she had left the office. One thing the brothers knew for sure was that they had not heard the last of either Vicki or Donna.

CHAPTER TWENTY

Donna was furious when she left the office. There was no way she was going to be discarded as though she was a piece of garbage. Jason's insinuation that she had done something illegal had made her lose it big time. He should have stood behind her and stood up for her.

"How dare he side with that super righteous brother of his?" she said out loud as though saying it would change it. "That bastard was all sweet and honey when I sucked his cock. I'll make him pay for the way he is treating me."

With that she picked up her cell phone and called Vicki.

"What the hell happened to you?" she said as Vicki answered.

"I quit. There is no way I want to work at your illustrious firm. It's not worth my time and energy. Why are you calling me? I would have thought you would have figured that much out for yourself."

"I am calling you because I do not think you are being treated fairly and I think you and I should get together and try to help each other out."

"Wait a minute. Are you saying you were fired too?"

"I wasn't fired but I am being treated like garbage and I do not like that- not one little bit."

"Oh, so you know they know about you taking the money from the pension accounts."

"How do you know about that?"

"You were not as careful as you think you were. You left papers around and one conclusion led to another. No offense, but you are not as smart as you think."

"So you are the bitch who spilled the information. What did you think you would get out of it?"

"Oh come on- you know I wanted to get Evan. He was an easy target and if things went the way I wanted, I could have had it all-money, position- all of it."

"Evan has no balls."

"Actually he surprised me. He has more integrity than I gave him credit for having. I really thought if I fucked him into oblivion, he would cave and leave that stuck up bitch. Then along came Jeff Adler and everything got shot to hell."

"I still think that if we work together we can come out of this winners."

"I don't see myself winning. I see myself stuck with my electrician and being doomed to a life that I hate. I think you want me to help you and that is really strange since you are the paramount user. I think it is best for both of us for you to leave me alone." With that Vicki hung up the phone.

No sooner than Vicki stopped shaking did the phone ring again. Seeing it was Lisa, she thought not to answer it but when she did not answer, it was only minutes before the ringing started anew.

"Leave me alone," she shouted into the receiver when she finally picked it up.

"Before you make your decision final, meet me and let's talk face to face."

"I am too upset right now to meet anyone anywhere."

"Let's meet tomorrow morning. We can meet in the parking lot at Gilgo Beach. That way there are no ears or eyes and we can talk. How about ten o'clock."

"If I am there, I am there. Just stop calling me."

As she hung up, it seemed really strange to Vicki that she could be annoyed by the phone when it was a weapon she had used so many times. One thing she knew and that was that she did not want to lose it and have Todd come home to find her in a rage. Right now she really needed him and she needed to control herself. She also needed to not allow Donna to use her as she knew for sure Donna would only call her if it were to be for her own benefit. There was no way that Donna cared one bit about her nor would she do anything to help anyone but herself.

"That bitch just wants to use me," she yelled out loud.

The next morning, Vicki was surprised to find herself driving along Ocean Parkway. As she came off the Wantagh Parkway and passed field seven at Jones Beach, she almost decided to turn around at the next turn around. Something kept her going toward Gilgo Beach. She was not sure what that something was; curiosity, a desire for revenge or just a need to look Donna in the eye and tell her to go to hell. It was not long before she passed the entrance to Gilgo which was on the west bound side of the road. She went on to the turn around and moments later she was entering the parking field which was deserted expect for Donna"sSL convertible. Man how she always hated that car and its symbol that the Bitch was something special; something above everyone else even though she really could not afford the car. To Vicki the car just yelled whore as she was sure Jason was paying for it.

"At least she is smart enough to get a guy with money while I have my electrician." Vicki said to herself. She pulled up next to the SL and watched as Donna got out of the car.

"I thought you would be here," Donna said in her usual know-it-all manner.

"I came to listen."

"Look, I am ok that you were the one who blew the whistle on my gig. I can't say I blame you. You probably thought it would give you an in with that prick, Evan."

"I already told you that I gave the information to Evan. I am done and I am not admitting or denying anything. Understand that. Nor do I care what you have done or are about to do. I am finished with that firm and all the farts who work there. In my opinion, there is not a real man among them."

"Yeah, well money talks and bull shit walks. Don't bullshit me. If you could have gotten Evan under your wing, you would have done so in a heartbeat. You are no better than I am. You would fuck the devil if you thought it could help you."

"You can't blame a girl for trying. I am not going to stand here and deny that I wanted to have a relationship with Evan. What's so wrong with that? The guy is single, has money to burn and we could have continued to have some fun if that bastard Jeff had not come along and spoiled it for me."

"Who is that guy Jeff anyway?"

"He's a partner at the firm where I used to work. Now he's shacked up with Todd's ex and he has it in for me. That bitch filled his head with all kinds of lies about me and how I ruined her marriage etc, etc."

"Is that all?"

"Well, I did try to come on to him. I thought it would be interesting if I ruined it for that bitch a second time and besides, he has more dough than my electrician. But that is all past history now. What do you want from me?"

"I am thinking we could have an interesting sexual harassment situation. You and I could claim that we were sexually harassed and believed we had to be intimate with those bastards in order to keep our jobs."

"And you believe we could float that?"

"If we both claim harassment then there is a chance we could get a pay-off. I really believe neither Evan nor Jason would want the charges to become public knowledge and they would make a settlement before the charges could be heard in court."

"I am not interested in doing anything for a few hundred dollars."

"We would not settle for that kind of dough."

"Who would handle this type of thing for us?"

"Don't worry about that. I have attorney friends who would do it for us. No problem."

"Yeah, and they would get the money and we would end up holding their dicks."

"Maybe, maybe not. The main thing is that we would make the brothers' lives miserable and we would have some satisfaction."

"I can't help but think you are using me as a chip to help yourself. I know you were manipulating the pension funds and that is a criminal offense. My gut says you will sell me straight down the river and use any charges I bring along with you as a negotiation tool. Frankly, I am not interested in being used by you and I do not trust you for one minute."

With that Vicki turned her back on Donna and got back into her car. She could see the rage on Donna's face and her face was telling Vicki that she was right on as to Donna's plan. Opening her window, she yelled out, "You are one queen size bitch and while I may not have the highest morals, I will not be used by the likes of you." The window went back up so she could not hear the curses Donna was yelling and she quickly drove out of the parking lot heading back to Todd's house. Job hunting would have to wait until tomorrow as she knew she was far too upset to be able to successfully control herself. But before she could stop herself, she was calling Evan's cell phone. When he answered, she started screaming at him,

"Don't you dare hang up on me, you, bastard. I have some interesting information for you and your dear brother and you had better hear me out."

'What is it that you want? I told you I do not want any more contact with you, ever."

"I just want you to know that I just left Donna and she wants me to go in with her and have sexual harassment charges made against you and your beloved brother."

"And you are telling me this out of the goodness of your heart…"

"I am telling you this because I do not want to be used by that bitch but she has her fangs out."

"I guess, I should say thank you for the information."

"Despite what you think, I am not all that bad. Just remember I am the one who brought the information about her using the pension money to you. You do owe me."

"What do I owe you?"

"I'll think about it and you do the same," and with that Vicki broke the connection. She was sure Evan really understood from where she was coming and that an offer would be forthcoming; if for nothing else but to keep her quiet about the pension funds being violated. If that information were to be made public, all confidence in their beloved firm would be lost.

"Hell, I don't need that wicked bitch. I'll get a settlement all on my own terms," she said out loud with a big smile across her face.

Donna, on the other hand, was beside herself as she left the parking lot. She could not believe how poorly the meeting had gone and how much she had underestimated Vicki. She had been sure that Vicki would take the bait and not see what her ulterior motive was. Now she was going to have to find a way to save her ass and not lose her nest egg in the process or face criminal charges. Jason could be very vengeful.

CHAPTER TWENTY ONE

The two brothers called a meeting right after Evan received the call form Vicki. Evan told Jason exactly what the conversation was and the veiled threat in it. They both knew that an offer would have to be made to her if they were going to salvage the firm's reputation. Now they were worried about Donna and the damage she could bring. Jeff was called immediately and when he heard about the latest developments, he suggested that they all take some time to think about things before taking any actions.

"You are in a delicate position. Paying her off puts you in the position of being blackmailed again in the future. Knowing her as I do, I am sure she will stop at nothing to get what she wants and to hurt you in the process. And then you have the other one out there. She too is a danger to you personally and professionally."

"You are making it sound like there is no way to salvage the situation."

"I don't mean to sound that way. I am really just thinking out loud. We have to wait and see at this point. My advice, at this moment, is to do nothing and let's think about and discuss every option before doing anything. I will talk it over with some of the people here at our firm. I am sure they will help us come up with some solutions."

"One more thing," Evan said, "One of our larger pension clients called this morning. He was questioning the withdrawals and deposits he sees on his statement. How would you suggest we handle his call?"

"Whoa- that did not take long to happen."

"Statements went out on the first of the month. Most of our clients probably never look at their statement but Mr. Gordon sure as hell did."

"I would like to think about just how to answer him with the least amount of damage. Give me a little while and I'll call you back."

"Please do not take too long. The man does deserve a call back."

"I'll call you back within the hour. I just like to think things out before putting my foot in my mouth."

"Fine- we'll speak again within the hour."

With that both brothers stood looking at each other, neither knowing what to say to comfort the other. The web was definitely getting larger by the minute.

"Have you had a chance to determine how much is missing from the accounts? Yesterday, you said you thought it was about ten thousand dollars," Jason asked Evan.

"Merrill is still checking all the accounts. They are running a report on all withdrawals from all the pension accounts and then they will run one showing matching deposits. It is going to take a few days before we know for sure."

'Like I said yesterday, the firm can handle covering even twenty. So let's hope that is all. I do believe she can be made to make restitution."

"One step at a time- just like Jeff said. We are not doing anything right now."

"I know one thing for sure," Evan said with a strong sense of conviction in his voice, "I am dead set against giving that bitch any monetary settlement. She cannot be trusted and her word is shit. If we were to give her money, it would be gone in a flash and she will be right back on our doorstep demanding more."

"I hear you loud and clear. Maybe Jeff could draft some type of agreement that would prevent her returning and demanding more."

"Agreements only work with honorable people. She does not

qualify under that category. Let's be accurate, here. This is a woman who uses her pussy as well as other parts of her anatomy to get what she wants. She really does not differ from a common street whore. Her word or acceptance of any agreement has as much value as dog's doo."

"I hear you loud and clear and don't think for a second that I think Donna is any better. That bitch had me just where she wanted me. I was even thinking of leaving Michelle and moving in with her. She kept telling me that I am her soul mate and that she would always be there for me, no matter what."

"Well 'no matter what' has come and she looks to have taken off. I would have thought she would have left town by now; so I am a little surprised to hear she is still around."

"You have to remember she does have two young children. I cannot imagine she would take off without them."

"Oh, so now she is mother of the year!"

"I wouldn't say that; but I do think she cares about the kids. I know for a fact that she does not trust her husband's judgment when it comes to them. He is somewhat of an air head and into things like motorcycles."

"Sound great for those kids; one parent an air head and one a thief."

"Look, we are not going to accomplish anything here except to say horrible things about two women who took advantage of us. Let's try to get some work done while we wait for Jeff to call. At least that way we can have some billable hours for today," Jason said and he started gathering up the papers he had brought into the meeting.

"Good thought. I am with you on that. I'll call you as soon as Jeff calls and we can conference the call," Evan said wondering to himself just how successful he could be in dealing with the other matters at hand. He felt as though his head was about to come off and all he really wanted to do was kick himself for ever allowing himself to succumb to Vicki.

CHAPTER TWENTY TWO

J eff was good to his word and did call in just about one hour.

"Look, there is no way around this situation with the pension accounts but to become proactive and notify the clients that their accounts were violated and that you are taking all the necessary steps to insure restitution and to prevent any future violations. That way you take the lead and remove the possibility of blackmail. Our pension people said you should also notify the SEC and Merrill Lynch, which I am assuming they already know."

"I did speak with our account representative at Merrill; but I do not know that he has informed anyone else," Evan interjected.

"Well, it is time to write a formal notice and while you are at it, put in writing what new safeguards are in place to prevent anyone in the future from getting a letter of authorization signed by omission. You will need to be very specific as that letter may have to stand up in a courtroom."

"We'll draft the letter and e-mail it to you for your consideration."

"No problem. Now to deal with the women. I would tell Vicki that you have notified your clients and the regulatory personnel, so there is no need for her to threaten you. However, and this is solely up to you, I would offer some type of settlement as a good will gesture." Money is her driving interest and if you give her something, maybe she will just go away and leave you to live your lives. Trust me, I know how vicious she can be and when she gets on a tear, there is no stopping her. Hell, Stacey had to take out an order of protection to insure that the children are not exposed to her vengeance."

"How much would you suggest we offer her?"

"Well, I think if you offer too little you will infuriate her and actually make matters worse. My guess is that an offer of ten would probably appease her and she'll crawl away to contaminate someone else's life."

"That's a lot of money and since I feel totally responsible for creating the problem with her, I am prepared to pay that out of my personal funds and not the firm's," Evan replied with basically no emotion.

"Look, Ev, no one here is casting any stones. We'll worry about where the money comes from in due time. For now let's just get Jeff's ideas as to how to handle Donna whom I view as a greater problem," Jason said.

"Donna is rather easy to deal with. She did something totally illegal and you can press charges against her. In the current climate, thanks to Mr. Madoff, I would guess she would be convicted and have to face prison time. If she is nearly as smart as you say she is, she will be happy to just go away if you agree to not press charges. Who knows, she might even be willing to make restitution if she is allowed to retain her profits. Do you know the status of her brokerage account?"

"It would take a subpoena to get that information and we then have to press charges. All I was told is that she does have an active account at Charles Schwab and there has been active trading in the account. Even that much information was only given as a personal favor."

"That could be enough to use as a bargaining tool. She obviously knows she is in legal trouble and if she does pursue a sexual harassment charge, you will counter with exposing her activity; so, it should be rather simple to effect a deal with her. Let her keep her profits and end all ties with her."

"Fear not- all other ties have been completely severed."

"Well, she could still go to your wife and expose your infidelity."

"Too late, I told Michelle all about it last night. She really surprised me with her attitude. Michelle told me she knew all about the Garden City Hotel apartment and the fact that I was having an affair. It seems that one of her friends works there. To Michelle, all that really matters is that it is over and I have promised never to stray again. She is actually willing to forgive and forget. We'll see how long that attitude lasts. I would imagine the first time she does not get her way with something, she will throw the entire mess up into my face. But that's my problem and I will have to live with it. At least I removed that form of blackmail from Donna's repertoire."

"What about you, Evan?"

"I also told Roberta all about my involvement with Vicki. Of course it was a little different in that we are not even engaged but she took the conversation well and has proved herself to me. She is one hell of a lady and I really respect her."

"Ok, so you both came clean and cleared the air, so to speak. Now neither of the women would benefit from threatening you in that avenue. Of course, knowing Vicki, she is capable of telling Roberta that you said horrible things about her. It doesn't matter if what she says is true or not, she can be very convincing."

"Roberta and I did discuss just that and she told me that she would not entertain any conversations with Vicki. I believe her."

"Good. Hopefully Michelle will stand as firm if Donna contacts her."

"Hopefully. I would not want to see her hurt any further; she's been put through enough."

"Ok, so get yourselves to work on the letter we discussed and compose one to your clients as well. As for Mr. Gordon, I would call him and explain what happened. Hopefully your personal attention will satisfy him."

"I'll do that as soon as we get off the phone. He and I have a personal relationship that goes way back to when I first joined the firm and our father was his advisor," Jason said hoping he was correct.

When Jason went back to his office, he closed the door and put his head down on the desk. He had a headache beyond description and wanted only to have it all go away. It's amazing how fast everything unraveled right before his eyes. Life had been fun for quite awhile. Donna was definitely an interesting sex partner and her lack of inhibitions was exciting and challenging. There was definite excitement to having sex right here in the office; it made the work day far more interesting.

"Man, what a fool I was," Jason said out loud, "to have trusted someone like that with confidential company information. What was I thinking?" With that he slammed the desk almost injuring his hand. It is always hardest to accept when you know you are responsible for a bad situation. He taught the bitch how to day trade and he exposed the clients' account information to her. "Stupid is as stupid does," he said as he picked up the phone and started to dial Mr. Gordon's number. There was no way to predict how Mr. Gordon was going to take the news but Jason knew for sure, he had to swallow the bitter pill sooner or later and sooner was better.

When Mr. Gordon answered the phone himself, Jason spent little time going directly to the conversation at hand. He explained how the account had been violated and by whom and why. There was silence on the other end and the lack of questions puzzled Jason. He finished the explanation with the pledge to make restitution and the promise that procedures were being placed to prevent something like this from ever happening again.

"I appreciate your honesty. My one question is what would have happened if I did not discover the withdrawals?"

"Actually we discovered the situation prior to your call and were investigating it with the help of an outside law firm. We are in the process of finding out the exact amounts involved and the various accounts affected and all the information will be available to us within the next few days. Letters and calls are going out to all the accounts affected but since we have always had a special relationship, I wanted to call you immediately. My hope is that you will accept my apology and understand that we will do everything possible to protect your accounts going forward and to respect your privacy. The person who did this was a trusted employee who violated our trust."

"Are you going to press charges?"

"That measure is under consideration at this time. The pressing matter is to determine the scope of the situation and to make sure all restitution is made."

"Jason, pardon me, but am I wrong to detect that you and she had a special relationship?"

"She was the office manager and my personal assistant and in that capacity, you could say, we had a special relationship. Also in that capacity she was privy to the confidential information which she used for her own personal benefit."

"How will you protect the accounts going forward?"

"Only Evan and I will have the information regarding the accounts and the passwords to access them. All the passwords have been changed already. None of the support staff will be able to access any account information or process any orders."

"What would happen if there is a common accident and neither you nor Evan is able to function?"

"That is a really good question. We are putting into effect, immediately, a policy whereby each client has support people at Merrill Lynch. You will have your own password and be able to obtain account information directly from Merrill should you so desire. We will still manage your account and personally direct Merrill as to buys and sells but you can make your own decisions should you so decide."

"If I wanted to make my own decisions, I would have been doing so long before this. I do not have the time or energy to monitor the market but I like the concept that I can contact someone directly should I need or want to do so."

"That's the whole idea behind this. I just hope you can accept my apology and that we can continue our professional relationship going forward. You are a very valued client."

"Let's have a meeting once you have all the information in place. I would like a review of my accounts and some idea of the performance history."

"No problem. Just give me a week or so to stabilize things here and Evan and I will be happy to meet with you and discuss the past year and our plans for the upcoming year. This is a volatile market and we respect your desire for conservative and safe investments."

"I do find it interesting that this person was able to make so much money in such a short time."

"Day trading can do that but you can also lose so much in such a short time. It is not an investment strategy we would ever recommend for a pension account especially for someone your age. If you were to lose big time, recouping your money could take too long. You have to remember you are near the age of having to take the required minimum distributions. These are things we will discuss when we have our meeting. We will also discuss the various tax-saving investments we have in mind for you when you are required to take the RMD. Don't worry we have your money covered."

"Thanks for the call, Jason. I am going to look forward to our meeting and good luck resolving your firm's mess. I do understand it is always hardest to accept when someone you trust disappoints you."

"You are so right about that but it is a learning experience and we have been well educated by this entire episode."

"Good luck to you and we will speak really soon."

"Absolutely and thank you for taking my call."

Mr. Gordon needed one more call to be made. He placed a call to Evan whom he regarded more like a son than an advisor. He, after all, had watched Evan grow up and he so reminded him of Evan's Dad with whom he had always had a trusted relationship and friendship. He had kept Evan's personal telephone number which he now used as he did not want to go through the firm's telephone system.

"Evan, it's Lester Gordon. I hope you do not mind my calling you directly."

"I never mind speaking with you Mr. Gordon. Has my brother called you yet?"

"Actually I just got off the phone with him but I have a need to speak with you as well. Please level with me. How extensive is this mess that you are finding the firm in?"

"It is not extensive. Several of the pension accounts were tampered with but most have had all the funds re-deposited. There are small amounts of money still due some clients and we are prepared to make restitution immediately. That is not the issue. We are very upset that this could have happened in the first place and we have created new safe guards to prevent anything like this from ever happening again."

"Does your father know anything about this mess?"

"No- we are trying to handle this without him having to be involved. You know what an honorable man he is and how much this would hurt him."

"I definitely agree with that. I do get the feeling that there was some hanky panky involved here."

"There was and that too has been addressed and the situation corrected. I sincerely hope you will allow us to retain your accounts."

"Jason suggested a meeting to go over the management of my funds and that is something I definitely would like."

"I think you will be very pleased with the way things have been handled for you. In my review of the accounts you are up over nine percent which is rather remarkable considering the current market. We have out-performed the S&P and that is with placing you in conservative positions. I guarantee that your account will be personally managed by myself and Jason going forward."

"That makes me feel a little better. I really do not have the time to think about buying and selling my holdings; that is why I have been willing to pay your management fees right along. I need to know that Jason has his head on straight and that he is thinking with the right head. Do I make myself clear?"

"Perfectly clear and have no fear. Both of us have our heads on completely straight and we are dedicated to this firm and our clients. That is something I promise to you on my father's honor."

"Good, I will look forward to our meeting."

"Just give us a few weeks to finish straightening everything out and to compile all the data and then we can schedule the meeting at your convenience."

"A few weeks. Does that mean two, three or more weeks?"

"I or Jason will be in touch with you at the end of next week to schedule the meeting. We can meet the following week as I am sure everything will be back to normal by then."

"Good, I will look forward to seeing you and thanks for speaking with me."

"Thank you for giving me the chance to do so. You are and always will be a most important and respected client."

"Speak to you soon."

As Evan hung up the telephone, he felt as though all the air had been sucked out of his body. Lester Gordon was no fool and he had immediately seen through Jason. How many other clients would also see that there was misconduct on their parts that allowed for the breach? He was beginning to wonder if he had to go to his father and let him know what was happening. It would be terrible if Dad found out from someone else. After all, the legal community of Garden City was small and always enjoyed gossip. "Man, this mess just keeps getting more and more complicated," Evan said out loud as if hearing the words would make it seem less impacting.

His next call was to Jason who listened silently while Evan told him of his latest concern.

"Man, I feel like a little boy who has to tell Daddy he did something wrong and then wait for the hammer to fall," Jason said.

"I guess I feel the same way. In my heart I really think it would be best for Dad to hear about this mess from us and not from one of his cronies. I am also beginning to think that it would not be all bad to have dad field some of the calls from the older accounts. After all it was he who had the relationship with these people long before we came into the picture."

"Now, you not only want to tell Dad, you want his help as well."

"It's just a thought. He probably would welcome something to do and thinking he is helping the firm would really give him a purpose. He is one of the most respected people in this legal community."

"I was really hoping we could get through this without his knowing or his help."

"The Lester Gordons of this world just love to air the dirty laundry and gossip has a way of spreading faster than the speed of sound."

"I guess you are right. If he hears about this mess from someone else, it will definitely be worse. How do you propose we tell him?"

"Let's stop by their house on the way home tonight and lay our cards on the table."

"All the cards?"

"Absolutely. We need him to know everything otherwise none of this makes sense. You would never have allowed someone to get access to the accounts if you were not emotionally involved with that person. Neither of us would be worrying about sexual harassment if we did not have affairs. We're both equally at fault for this mess."

"It is big of you to take the blame, after all Vicki really did nothing to hurt the firm yet."

"The operative word is "yet." We cannot forget for one moment that she is crazy and could do anything to hurt us. If she and Donna join forces, they could create havoc."

"All things taken into account, I still appreciate that you are not putting me out there to take all the blame. What time do you want to leave to stop by the folks' house?"

"Soon, let's get there before dinner. I have plans to meet Roberta for dinner and I really do not want to disappoint her."

"I can be ready in ten minutes."

"Me too. Meet you at the reception desk in ten. I'll call the house to let them know we are coming."

"What reason will you give?"

"Just that we want to discuss something with dad and to get his opinion. That should do it." With that they both hung up and Evan sat looking at the phone for a few minutes before placing the call to his parents' home. There was no doubt that Dad would be suspicious as it was totally out of character for them to stop by without previous plans. Be it as it would. There was no doubt in his mind that this was not only the correct thing to do; it was the only thing to do.

Arriving at the house and walking up the front walk made Evan and Jason feel like two kids going to the principal's office knowing you were guilty of the infraction and wondering what the punishment would be. Their mother opened the door before either of them could ring the bell. Behind her stood their father who was still a dominant figure despite his age.

"Ok, let's bypass the pleasantries and let's hear why the two of you are here," their father said in an all too authoritative tone.

"May we come in and sit down?"

"Oh, this is going to be a long story?"

"Kinda"

With that the boys walked into the den and sat on the couch while their father took his favorite reclining chair and their mother rushed to the kitchen to prepare some drinks and snacks. Jason proceeded to tell his father everything that had happened and Evan filled in the details of his own misconduct.

Dave Bergman listened carefully and without comment as the story unraveled and only started speaking once the boys completely stopped.

"It seems to me you created a mess and that we have to do whatever is necessary to make things right and restore confidence in the firm. When will you have a complete a list of the accounts affected?"

"That will be available tomorrow as will be the details of which accounts still need restitution."

"I want to see the complete list and I will be prepared to come in and call those accounts with whom I had a relationship. I think it will be helpful for the people to know that I am giving my word that things will be corrected. I am also assuming that both of the women involved no longer are in your employ or your beds."

"I really think that Donna will not pursue a course to make trouble for the firm as she is well aware that we could press charges against her for stealing the money and since the amount exceeds twenty thousand dollars, she could be facing some pretty long prison time if we press charges," Jason countered.

"What about the other bimbo?"

"She is a loose cannon. She gained nothing and came up empty handed from this whole mess. Unfortunately she does have suspicions about the pension accounts but she does not know the particulars. Jeff Adler knows her and says she is a nut case. He also knows that Larry Kessler has been involved with her in the past and he thinks he can enlist Larry to help to try to control her this time."

"I know Larry well. I can talk to him, if need be. To me it sounds like some money might help to make her go away."

"Jeff said the same thing. He just wants to be sure that any offer is properly presented so as not to further infuriate her."

"I agree with that. Now have you two straightened out your personal lives?"

"All is cool. Both Michelle and Roberta know what happened and surprisingly they are willing to forgive us."

"Is Jack Weiss on board?"

"He knows all about this mess and is standing by should we need him. Evan actually met with him when he first became aware of the withdrawals."

"At least he was thinking with the right head that time."

"Dad, neither of us is proud of ourselves and we really wanted to handle this without dragging you into it but we felt that it would be much worse if you heard of this mess from someone else. If you want to help, we would appreciate whatever you can do."

"Of course, I want to help. No matter what, you are both my sons and your mother and I are always going to be there to support you even if you do stupid things. On a professional level, I do not want to see our firm's name dragged through any scandal and I really think that if we combine our efforts we can prevent that from happening. It is not like either of you tampered with the accounts and you are obviously prepared to make restitution so there will be no financial hardship for any of our clients. If Madoff had not been in the news, this probably would have just been able to be swept away more quickly. I'll be at the office in the morning. Just give me a desk with a phone and the list of involved clients and I'll start doing damage control."

With that both Evan and Jason stood and hugged their father knowing that the family would always stand together no matter what. Dave Bergman was always one tough cookie and while he may have slowed down some with age, his toughness was still apparent. Everyone who knew him professionally and personally always respected him and now that respect would be a valuable tool once more for the firm he so loved.

As they walked to their cars, both Jason and Evan knew they had probably just had the hardest meeting in their lives. Somehow disappointing their father was even worse that disappointing Michelle and Roberta. Yet, they knew they had done the correct thing and in the end their family would be stronger for the challenges ahead.

CHAPTER TWENTY THREE

There was an absolute hush in the office when Dave Bergman walked in the following morning. If anyone had doubted there was a problem at the firm, his presence removed any doubt. Yet his being there was a comfort to the employees who had had the privilege of working under him prior to his retirement. Dave was not a very large man but he still casted a huge shadow. He was confidence personified and no one, even those who had never worked under him, could or would question his authority. It was just like the old days, as he went to each employee and greeted her as though she were a personal friend. He was such a nice man that everyone would always go the extra mile to help him.

Dave went straight to Evan's office knowing he would have the most complete list of violated accounts. "Just give me the list and a computer and I will get going on making the calls," he said not bothering with any small talk.

"Are you going to call everyone, even those accounts where restitution has been made?"

"You bet I am. Full disclosure is the only way to put this mess behind us. Those with whom I have dealt will understand and I am sure we can restore their confidence. The newer accounts would be better having you or Jason make the calls as they probably never heard about me. I'll keep a list. Now where can I do this without being in anyone's way?"

"You can work in Donna's office. It is quiet and no one will be able to overhear your conversations."

"That brings us to another issue that you and Jason have to inform the staff. By now, rumors are probably flying all over the place and I am sure what they imagine is worse than what is actually happening."

"As soon as Jason gets in, we'll call a staff meeting. That should not take long, once he gets here."

"I see. Little has changed with him. He was never one to get in early or to stay late."

"Dad, Jason gets his work out and that is all that matters. I am here usually before the rest of the staff so if there is a problem, I can handle it."

"I guess I am just a little annoyed that he would allow someone to use him in this way. I thought about it all night and I cannot come to grips with it all."

"He trusted her. Right or wrong, he had no reason to doubt her loyalty. After all she was making good money and he was extremely generous with her."

"Had your flu flu not come to you with this whole thing, I would imagine it could have gone on for a very long time without any of you ever being aware of it."

"Probably not. Lester Gordon came upon the withdrawals and deposits on his own. He would have called and opened the pandora's box. I really think she was trying to use accounts where she felt the people were too busy or too preoccupied to really check their statements. Using Lester's account was a major mistake. She had no way to know how exact he is."

"What is that person like?"

"Fairly good looking, very sexy and someone who knows how to take command. She was actually a good office manager."

"Why do you think she did what she did?"

"Quite simply put- Jason would not divorce Michelle and marry her. He and I spoke about it and he felt he could not afford to go ahead and divorce Michelle as theirs is a long term marriage and he really did not want to do so. Donna was a play thing to have on the side. That was what made her exciting."

"And you?"

"I was the paramount fool. I dabbled in something that was not for me though I can truthfully say that psycho sex was rather interesting."

"I am shocked."

"Dad, in all your years did you ever think of wandering? Weren't you ever bored?"

"I might have had thoughts but I never acted on any of them. I think you have to realize that there are women out there who pry on wealthy men. They know all the tricks and can make you feel like you are something special when all they really want is your wallet."

"That is so true of Vicki. I was her ticket to bigger and better things and that was all she really cared about."

"Where are things with that nut case?"

"Jeff threatened to have harassment charges leveled if she did not stop calling and screaming at all of us. He knows what buttons to push with her as he had the displeasure of dealing with her in the past. I know he is having her personal attorney contact her to defuse the situation. Jeff feels that some monetary settlement might make her go away."

"Who is her attorney?"

"Larry Kessler. I do not know him but Jeff says he is a straight guy."

"Are you prepared to make a settlement?"

"No problem. Of course, we will discuss it before anything is finalized. I value your opinion."

"And the other whore?"

"Jeff again thinks we can get her to go away as well. What she did was illegal and if we press charges, she could have to serve time. She was banking on the fact that Jason would not tell Michelle everything but he has. Now the clients are also going to be informed so that is not something she can hold over us. Jeff thinks, and I agree, we are holding the cards with her. Even a sexual harassment charge would be difficult for her to make stand up in court. We did not fire either of them, They walked out and abandoned their positions. What they did sexually was of their own free will and Jason can prove that she willingly met him at the Garden City Hotel. Theirs was a long standing relationship. As for Vicki, she and I never did anything here at the office and I never went to her place. She always came to my house and often did so uninvited."

"That could be your word against hers."

"Tom, at Morton's knows she met me there and actually arrived before I did. That does not sound like someone being forced to do something. Forget about her; she is not worth you thinking about her. I am sure Jeff and Larry will work it out to make her go away."

"I will leave that end of this mess up to you. Now I am going to make the calls. If you need me, you know where I am."

"Thanks Dad. If anyone can help with the clients, it's you."

As Dave walked down the hall to Donna's old office, he was amazed at how busy it seemed. The telephones were ringing constantly and the junior associates all seemed to be occupied. The firm had definitely grown since he retired and it was a good feeling to see it even under these circumstances. He felt more exhilarated and alive than he had felt in what seemed like ages. Just smelling the smells and being in the midst of the activity was wonderful. He realized how much he missed this part of his life.

By lunchtime, Dave had completed a good portion of the calls and things seemed to be going extremely well. Most of the clients said they had no knowledge there had been any tampering of their accounts but were grateful for the information. Just knowing the firm was being proactive gave most people confidence. Dave even called some of the newer accounts and he was equally well received by them. As he stood and walked out to the reception area, he was amazed at how tired he felt. It had been a long time since he had talked so much and while it was stimulating, it was also tiring. The rest of the calls would have to wait for tomorrow. With that thought, he said goodbye to the staff.

CHAPTER TWENTY FOUR

While things seemed to be coming together at the Bergman firm, this was not the case for Donna. Her life was spinning out of control and she felt there was nothing she could do about it. Tom was threatening to throw her out of the house. He knew all about her affair with Jason and even had gone so far as to contact the concierge at the Garden City Hotel who confirmed that he knew Donna and had seen her at the hotel many times. To say this infuriated her was an understatement. Part of going to an exclusive hotel was to protect their identity and now this man had completely revealed her personal information. She was tempted to go to the hotel management and complain but that would have to wait until after she dealt with the problems at hand.

She also knew she could not afford to maintain her lifestyle without a job. Her personal stash of money would not last but a month what with the car payments, the nanny and the mortgage. Tom really could not afford it all either on his salary. Getting a new job was yet another problem. Jobs were few and hard to find in the recession that was gripping the nation and the meager money that unemployment paid would do little to help her. She felt relatively confident that Jason and Evan would give her a decent reference if she were to agree to make restitution but one never knows for sure especially after she so successfully screwed up. And then there was Vicki.

Vicki had to be the source who told Tom about her affair. He would never have known about the Garden City Hotel if someone hadn't told him nor would he have been smart enough to conclude that she and Jason had a thing going on. She had been extremely careful not to give him anything to be suspicious of. He was always happy to have her pay attention to him and to have her leave him alone to tinker with his motorcycles and cars. As long as she came to his bed, her time during the day was never questioned.

"That bitch had to have called him and told him what was going on," Donna said out loud as she picked up the phone and dialed Vicki's number. The phone was answered on the second ring and Donna did not wait for any exchange of pleasantries.

"You fucking bitch! Why did you call my husband?"

"Who said I called him?"

"Don't bother lying to me. You are the only one who could have done this. I just don't understand why you would want to screw up my entire life. What's in it for you?" With that she heard a laugh on the other end of the line and then the receiver was slammed down. She was tempted to call right back but decided there was no point in psycho calling as she knew the truth and there was nothing to gain by confronting her again. Vicki knew she knew and one thing was for sure, she would get back at her one way or another. Right now getting back at Vicki was less important than trying to salvage her marriage which she needed to do until she could figure out another way to maintain her lifestyle. She had never seen Tom so angry and hurt.

"I guess he is more a man than I figured," she said. "But does he really have the balls to throw us out or to leave me and his kids?" One thing she knew for sure was that Tom loved his two kids. For him the sun and moon rose on those children and Donna felt relatively sure that she could use them to get him to soften his position and maybe even forgive her. After all, she was not the first woman to have an office related affair and if she could convince him that she did it to better her position in the firm and to make more money maybe, just maybe, he would temper his stand. She could even say that Jason forced her into the affair.

Then there was another problem. Several weeks ago she felt a lump in her breast. At first she thought the implant had hardened and that was what she was feeling. Then she thought it was related to her cycle and that it would disappear after her period. None of the above was the reason. Yesterday she went for a mammography and the radiologist confirmed she had a suspicious lump and recommended a biopsy. As if she did not have enough trouble. She was scheduled for the biopsy tomorrow and if the results revealed that she has breast cancer, she did not know how she would be able to even pay for the treatments since the firm provided her with health insurance and she would never be able to afford the Cobra payments especially if Tom were to leave. He did not have health insurance at his job. The whole thing was too scary to deal with. One thing for sure, Donna knew she was not prepared to just give up without a fight. She kept wondering how she could get Jason to continue paying her health insurance at least until she had another job with benefits.

"Life sucks when you are in a position of need. When you have control, it is a totally different story."

With that she decided to call Jason on his private line.

"How dare you call me?" was his opening line as he picked up the phone.

"I need your help." With that she poured out her entire tale of woe, somewhat surprised that he did not hang up the phone while she was midway through.

"Look, I truly feel sorry for you. No one should have to face a battle with cancer and have all the other shit going on. You made your own bed and now you expect me to help you when you did such horrible things to our firm and hurt me personally."

"I know what I did was wrong. Please believe me that I expected to return all the money to all the accounts. It was horrible what I did and I have no excuses. It still remains that I did care about you and you and I had a good thing going until I screwed it up."

"Donna what we had is over and done. There is absolutely no going back."

"I don't expect that. I just need some help so I can conquer this cancer thing and move on with my life. Tom is threatening to throw me out because of our affair and I do not have enough money to live on. Besides he does not have any health insurance with his job and we cannot afford the cobra payments. So you see I am stuck between a hard place and a nail."

"How did Tom find out about us?"

"Vicki-"

"She is really one piece of work. At least I told Michelle myself so I took that pleasure away from the bitch."

"I am sure that had I told Tom, the end result would not have been different. His manhood has been violated and his ego is hurt that I would have an affair."

"I cannot help you with that."

"I know, I know."

"What do you want me to do?"

"I need help with the health insurance. If it is what I think it is, I will be facing radiation, chemo and even a possible mastectomy and reconstruction. It is not going to be fun and it will be hard for me to hold a new job because of the time it takes for the treatments and if my appearance is altered by losing my hair or whatever. Jason, you are the only person I can ask for help. I know I have no right to do so but I am desperate. I do not want to die."

"Donna, to be blatantly truthful, I do not trust you for one minute."

"I will do anything you want me to do. I will sign any papers you want and promising anything you want me to promise."

"Let me discuss this with Jeff, my attorney and get back to you."

"Assure him I am not looking to make any more trouble for any of you. I want this behind me as much as you do."

"Donna, if I were to refuse what would you do?"

"Look, Jason, there is no veiled threat here. If you refuse, I will probably not be able to get treatment. That is the end of it. I am asking you for help out of the goodness of your heart and not because I would take any actions against you or the firm if you refuse."

"Interesting. Vicki had called here telling us that you wanted her to file sexual harassment charges."

"She is a liar and a vindictive person. There is no basis for any sexual harassment on my part. You and I had an adult consensual affair with no strings attached. Personally I am grateful if you do not file charges against me for my actions. What I did taking the funds was wrong, no if ands about it."

"Why would she call here?"

"She views herself as the innocent victim of this whole mess. She wants to get back at me because she probably feels it was my fault that she lost her job."

"She has a point there."

"Look, the fact that she called Tom and told him all about us and the Garden City Hotel is enough. She just wants to make trouble and hurt me. She even gave him the name of the concierge who told Tom about us."

"That surprises me."

"What surprises you? The fact that she told Tom or the fact that the concierge confirmed it?"

"The later. I always thought that part of the job was for the concierge to be discreet. I am sorry he made your life more complicated."

"It no longer matters. Just know what you are dealing with when you talk about Vicki. She is one bitch."

"I got it loud and clear. Let me talk this over with Evan and Jeff and I will get back to you. If it means anything, I am sorry you are having the health problems."

"Thanks, that is all I can ask." With that the connection was broken and Donna realized she was crying. How she hated begging for help but there was no choice.

That night Tom did not come home nor did he answer his cell phone. Donna could only think that he went to his parents' house but she would not call there under any circumstance. She and they had been on the outs for years and it was quite obvious that they did not want to have anything to do with each other. How it all started seemed too distant a memory but they had always made it clear that they did not trust or like her. For the first few years they tolerated her especially after the children were born because they wanted to see the grandchildren. Recently they had even arranged to have Tom bring the children to them so they could avoid seeing her. Even the children knew about the estrangement but they seemed to accept it without questions.

When the kids came home from school, Donna attempted to act as though nothing was wrong. Tommy seemed to question why she was home but easily accepted that she was looking for a new and better job. Patricia, on the other hand, was delighted to spend time with her mother and told her that she hoped it would be a long time before she had a new job. Children always have a way of seeing things the way they want it to be. Interestingly, no questions were asked when Tom did not come home around his usual time. This made Donna wonder about how often he did not come home when she was at work and where was he going. Maybe he was not the innocent he presented himself to be.

The next day proved to be a nightmare for Donna. Her worse fears were confirmed. The biopsy procedure was barbaric as the doctor used a syringe that felt like a drill to pull the tissue out of her breast. They said it would be a few days before they had the report back from the lab but her surgeon called her later that afternoon to tell her the biopsy was positive and she needed to schedule surgery as soon as possible. Of course, as part of the procedure, they would remove the implant.

"Great! Now I am going to be a lopsided freak."

"Right now we have to think about the problem at hand and address the cancer," was the only answer.

"Let me call you back once I get my head together."

Somehow hearing the word "cancer" and knowing it was applied to her was a chilling experience. No one knows how to react and everyone has fear when they know it is for real. The one thing she knew for sure was that there was no point in asking "Why me?" Living on Long Island, made breast cancer a reality for all too many woman and even some men. Everyone wondered if it was the water, the above ground power lines, the recycling plant, or the general air pollution. Everyone wondered but no answers were forthcoming. Some people blamed lifestyle and diet. Donna did not smoke, eat meat nor was she overweight. She did not have a family history of the disease. All of these thoughts rushed through her mind as she sat looking at the phone and wondering if Jason was going to help her.

Her first call was to Tom. When he answered his cell phone she simply told him the diagnosis.

"I am going to need your help. Please come home tonight so we can discuss all of this."

"Where is your lover boy?"

"I told you that is over. There is nothing to gain by bringing it up. If I could change history, I would. I am truly sorry I hurt you and I do want to make amends to you for the sake of the children if not for us."

"Now you are Mother Theresa."

"Tom, please stop this. I need your help."

"I'll think about it." With that the line went dead and Donna could only stand there and shake her head.

"If that bastard had cancer, I would help him no matter what."

Her next call was to Jason.

"The test came back positive," was all she said. She heard him say he was sorry before she hung up and allowed the tears to overtake her.

All Donna could think is "cancer" is a word that brings a chill when uttered. No one really believes that it will strike; even smokers believe they will escape the revenges of their habit as cancer hits other people, not them.

"I have no choices; I have to deal no matter what comes my way," Donna said out loud as if uttering the words would reinforce her conviction. Being forty one and having two young children made accepting the treatment protocols essential even if it meant losing her hair and not having her implants. Somehow she was having trouble thinking about a mastectomy but there was a little inner voice urging her to take that course of action. A mastectomy would mean reconstruction and her physical appearance would not be affected. There was also the chance she would not have to have radiation or chemo, but only a chance and that would not be known until after the lymph nodes were analyzed. A lumpectomy would almost certainly mean radiation and chemo. The question of the implant being reinserted was a definite question and without it her appearance would be altered dramatically.

"Shit- I could be stuck with Tom forever. No guy wants a woman with a bad medical history and especially one who is lopsided," she yelled out and hearing the words almost made her laugh as she visualized herself standing naked in front of a mirror. It would be horrifying if she went the lumpectomy route.

Getting herself together, she went about making sure her health insurance was still in effect. Even though she was no longer employed, she knew she had the option to take Cobra and now that was no longer an option but a necessity. Tom did not have health insurance benefits, so even if they stayed together, she needed her health insurance. She promptly made the calls to the insurance agent and had the Cobra forms sent over to her. What she needed to know was if she had to take the Cobra for everyone who had been insured or if she could just continue coverage for herself. Cobra was going to be expensive. It was her understanding that she and she alone could elect to have Cobra coverage. That would kinda put the ball in Tom's court. If he wants health insurance for himself and the kids, he would have to stay with her and be nice; that could be a good bargaining point. The other problem is that in order to be able to get Cobra the qualifying event cannot be discharge for misconduct. If Jason claims she quit because of misconduct, she would not be able to get cobra. If he were to press charges, she would not be able to get cobra.

"Man, I could be totally at his mercy!"

While Donna was thinking about her choices, Jason was also thinking about the situation. There was no way he wanted anything really bad to happen to her. They had a wonderful relationship and he always really enjoyed the sex. Yeah, she took advantage of her position and did some really bad things but she did not deserve to die. He knew for sure he would help her pay for health insurance and make sure she had everything she needed to help her through the crisis. Now he needed to convince Evan about doing the "right thing." After all, pressing charges against Donna would not benefit the firm in any way. If anything, the potential publicity would be harmful. If they allow her to claim she left for personal reasons, she would be eligible for Cobra and that would be no skin off their backs. They could even get her to sign an agreement that she would be willing to testify on their behalves should there be a sexual harassment case.

His first call was to Jeff. He explained the entire situation and when he was finished, Jeff felt there was some merit in his decisions. Jeff even offered to draw up an agreement for Donna to sign regarding any potential actions against the firm, whether that be sexual harassment or a claim made by one of the account holders for the violation of his account. Donna would have to take total responsibility should such a claim be made.

"People sue for the most ridiculous reasons and we never know where a suit can originate. We have to protect the firm and since she does not have any remarkable assets, it would be no skin off her back to take responsibility."

"I know she would be willing to do so. Of course, that still leaves Vicki and there is no controlling that bitch."

"One problem at a time. I am going to draw up the agreement. Do you want to discuss this with Evan or would you prefer me to do it?"

"I would love to take the chicken way out, but I guess it would only be right for me to go to him with the proposal. We do need to work together."

"I agree. Let me know what he says. In the meantime, I will start putting things down on paper."

"Thanks for the understanding."

"No problem. I actually respect your decision and it is probably best for the firm to prevent any more publicity about this matter." With that they hung up leaving Jason to muster up the courage to approach Evan.

The conversation with Evan went much better than Jason could have hoped for. Evan also did not want any unnecessary publicity and he too felt it would be worthless to press charges against Donna or to deny her the opportunity to get Cobra. He also liked the idea that she would testify should there be sexual harassment charges and that she would take total responsibility should a claim be made against the firm.

"Now the question is, who would be paying the Cobra costs?" Evan asked.

"Not the firm. Our policy requires that anyone insured under our plan must be actively working at the firm. Obviously, she is no longer in our employ not will she ever again be employed by us. If she really cannot afford the coverage, if that no good husband of hers does not or cannot help her, it would be up to me personally to pay her portion of the policy."

"That is really big of you, brother."

"I would have a really hard time to completely turn my back on her now that she needs help. We had an interesting relationship."

"If I were you, I would not let anyone know what you are thinking."

"Fear not. This is between you and me. The only other person I discussed this with is Jeff because I did not want to do anything that could have negative effects for the firm."

"Jeff is on board?"

"It was he who suggested the signed agreement as a condition. He too feels that it is important to prevent any negative publicity etc."

"Just make sure you have the signed agreement before you go any further. Once she has what she wants, she may not be so willing to sign any statements."

"I definitely agree. Thank you for understanding my position."

"You are a schmuck but a good schmuck."

"And if you had to solve this problem?"

"I would be a schmuck too. You would have to be a real hard ass to turn your back on someone with cancer who really needs the help. You do believe her?"

"I have no doubt she is telling me the truth."

"I am with you on this. Do whatever you need to do."

"Thanks."

Jason decided not to call Donna immediately. He wanted to give Jeff time to draw up the statement and he wanted her to have some time to think about her situation. He did contact Kathy at the insurance agency and she gave him the Cobra costs for Donna alone. There was no way he was going to pay for the kids or for Tom. That no-good bastard would have to take some responsibility for himself and his kids.

CHAPTER TWENTY FIVE

For two days and two nights Donna did not hear from Tom. She had never felt so alone in her life. Even Tommy and Patty stayed away from her as if they knew something bad was happening. On the third night, Tom walked into the house and behaved as though nothing out of the ordinary was going on.

"Where have you been?"

"Interesting, you want me to account for my whereabouts when you never feel you have to do so."

"You are right. I have no right to question you. It is just that I was concerned."

"How nice of you."

"Look, Tom, I do not want to fight with you. There are things we need to discuss and to decide. That's all."

"I am sure there are. First, I want to spend some time with my kids. After they go to bed, you can discuss whatever you want to discuss."

"Oh my god, you are Father of the Year!"

"And you are Mother Theresa! Look, give me a break. I know where you are going and I know I am trapped by your cancer just as much as you are trapped by it. If I walk out on you now, I am the bad guy despite all the justification I might have. I do not have to like you or respect you; I just need to be here and I will do so on my terms."

"What does that mean?"

"It means I will do whatever I have to do to help you through this thing. After it is over, we'll see where we are as a couple and go from there. That's all I can do for you and personally I think it is more than you deserve. In the meantime, I want to spend time with the kids and I would appreciate it if you would leave us alone to enjoy our time together."

"That's fair and I do appreciate the support," Donna said with tears streaming down her face.

"Don't turn on the tear thing with me. I know you are one tough bitch. You probably could do it all on your own but I do not need the vicious rumors that would bring."

"You are wrong there. This is once I cannot go it alone. I need you."

"What about your friend, Jason? Do you need him too?"

"That's over and you know it. I made a mistake, several mistakes, and I regret it now. There is no taking it back."

"Yeah, I bet you called him too and he turned you down."

"I did not call him and if I were to do so, I bet he would not turn me down. He has his faults and he is angry at me, but he is not someone who would purposely hurt me."

"Oh- so he is mister goody-goody and I am the bastard."

"I am not saying that. It is just that he and I are over and done with and it was a mistake so it is time to move on. "

"Moving on means coming back to me."

"You could say that. It really means I am sorry I hurt you and I would like another chance to make things right between us. We have two great kids and they deserve a stable family. I really want us to be that for them."

"I know. We will be a stable family until you are well and able to go back on the prowl to find another schmuck with deep pockets to give you the things you want. I just want to know who is going to pay for that Mercedes of yours? It is definitely beyond my budget."

"I'll sell it and get something more reasonable. It is not an issue."

"You do that."

"We also have to budget in health insurance. We really need that now."

"You mean lover boy is not going to pay your health insurance."

"If I am not working at the firm, I cannot be covered under their insurance. It is just that simple."

"Isn't there something called Cobra?"

"Yes, but is expensive. The rates are higher than the group rates."

"Well, you had better get this Cobra thing. My job does not have any benefits and I cannot pay for your treatments and shit."

"How can we pay for Cobra?"

"My guess is that we will have to get rid of the nanny and you will actually have to play mommy until you get another job."

"I hate to lose Yvonne. She is so good with the children."

"And so expensive. That is your choice. I had just better never discover that your lover boy is paying your expenses for anything. I know you all too well. You are not above making him feel guilty and taking his money. In fact, I would not be too surprised to find out he already turned you down."

"I just told you I have not spoken to him. None of this is his business."

"Work it out however you want to. Just leave me alone." With that he turned his back on her leaving Donna with an empty hole in the pit of her stomach. How she ever married such a bastard was beyond her. He wasn't even a good lay. Everything is always about him: his satisfaction, his needs, his reputation. It would have given her tremendous satisfaction to tell him to "fuck off" but she really needed him now. There was no way she could support the house, the kids and take care of herself.

"Someday, I'll make sure he gets what he really deserves.... someday," she said half out loud.

The next morning Jason called and explained his and the firm's position. He told her he took the liberty to have a statement drawn up assuring the firm that she would testify on their behalf in any suit that could arise even a sexual harassment issue.

"You know I have no way to control what Vicki does or doesn't do?'

"We are well aware of that. In fact we would prefer that you have no contact with her. But you did have the means and the ways to observe her while she worked here and you do know she was never sexually harassed by anyone at the firm."

"Including Evan?"

"Most assuredly so. Evan never made promises depending on sexual favors and you know that for a fact. You also know, for a fact, that Vicki was the one who initiated the relationship. She even went after me because she felt she could use sex to get things she wanted."

"She made passes at you?"

"Hell, yes. She even met me at the apartment once."

"There is no end to what that bitch would do."

"It's all spilled milk now. The issue is if you sign the agreement, I will personally pay your Cobra premium but just yours. Your husband will have to pay his and the kids'."

"This almost sounds like blackmail."

"Consider it whatever you wish. I am trying to help you. I know money is tight and you really need the insurance. Because I feel sorry this has happened, I am willing to not press any charges against you so you have a clean record with no professional misconduct and I am willing to help you pay for the insurance. If signing the statement is a big deal to you, we can just forget about the whole thing."

"So, if I do not sign that thing, you will withdraw your offer?"

"I am not making an offer that is dependent on anything."

"I get it! How would I get the statement?"

"I could mail it to you house."

"That would never work out. Tom must never know we've even spoken to each other."

"Ok- I could leave it for you at the front desk of the hotel and you could pick it up. I really do not want you to come to the office. The only other suggestion I have is for you to meet Jeff some place and sign it right in front of him. That might be the best solution."

"I could meet him at the diner on Northern Boulevard right off of Lakeville Road. I really do not want to go to the hotel."

"If you do not hear from me, he will meet you there tomorrow at one o'clock. I will give him the forms for Cobra and a check for this month's premium. After this I will have the money deposited into your bank account at Citibank."

"That works. Thanks for the help. I really do appreciate it."

"Good luck to you. If anyone can beat this thing, you can. Of that I am sure."

In her heart, Donna knew this was the last time she would ever hear Jason's voice. She would miss him in an odd way but then again they say, all good things come to an end. At least he was willing to help her and not to damage her reputation permanently. That says a lot for the man. He wasn't even asking her to repay the outstanding money. She was sure she would have to return it all. Now, at least, she had some emergency funds and that was a good thing.

CHAPTER TWENTY SIX

Todd was never happier. Vicki was being little miss homemaker and even bringing Joseph over to spend the night several times a week. It was so much fun going to hockey games and hearing a child's voice in the house. The only cloud was this intensified his missing his girls. Visitation was becoming a constant hassle what with having to make Vicki leave and fitting the girls' activities into his schedule. He had actually missed some weekends with them because it was just easier to stay away. Everyone had told him that it gets harder and more complicated as the children get older and are involved in more activities. He just never realized how painful it would be not to see his children and he often wondered if the sacrifice was worth it. A little voice in his head often told him he was a fool to leave Stacey for Vicki and to give up his children and the financial security he had. He knew there was no point to having the thoughts because there was no going back to his old life. At least the bed he made for himself had excitement in it but even he was getting tired of Vicki's wandering. In his heart he knew he was getting close to telling her to get lost permanently if she again picked up with another guy and again made him look the fool. He also knew that it was only a matter of time before she would go off with another guy but for now he was enjoying the moment. In fact he was so enjoying it that he decided to surprise Vicki with a cruise in the Caribbean. He had some money saved up and he was able to get a really good deal on a seven day cruise out of Fort Lauderdale. It would be perfect, seven days together in the warm Caribbean with nothing else to do but fuck.

When Todd first gave Vicki the tickets, she thought it was some kind of a joke. How could he afford such a vacation? She knew she was in no position to contribute to it; what with her not having a job or even a job prospect.

"This is nuts. I am not working and money is tight," she said.

"I think it would be good for us to reconnect and reestablish our relationship away from here and all the problems. We will have a week with no interruptions, no children, no job searches. It will be really good for the both of us. We have been through a really trying time."

"I know I made mistakes and believe me I will not make them again. I really love you and I know you are the right man for me. I cannot tell you how sorry I am that I caused you any grief."

"Let's not talk about the past. It is over and done with. I know you were influenced by Donna."

"That bitch really set me up. It is amazing how she wanted to blame everything on me when she was the one taking the money."

"Can we drop this discussion here? There is really no point in rehashing everything. Donna was not to blame for you taking up with Evan and we both know that. Vicki, you and I both know that you were after his money and position and you used your body to try to get it. I just want you to understand that I am not stupid and I am tired of being made a fool of by you. If you want to stay with me, you have to stay with me and stop running off with every guy with loaded pockets."

"Are you giving me an ultimatum?"

"You bet I am doing just that. I love you and no woman has ever been so sexy with me. You are dynamite not only in the bedroom but just having you around the house. I just can't take it any longer. I don't want to worry about where you are or who you are with. I cannot and will not continue to pick up the pieces and put you back together after you blow up another relationship. You must understand I have some pride."

"I know you are right. I also know this is where I belong. I love you."

"Well, what do you think about the cruise?"

"I think it will be a blast and I cannot believe you are doing this for me. I know money is tight."

"Let me worry about the money. All you need to think about is packing and being prepared to enjoy ourselves."

"I'll make it a trip you will never forget."

"Just keep remembering our conversation. There are too many cute guys on board a cruise ship and I don't want any of them dipping into my ink well."

"Fear not. The only one dipping will be you."

With that she rushed over to him and started fondling him. He just knew the vacation was going to be perfect as he felt her pull his pants down and take him into her educated mouth.

Vicki was so excited about the trip; it became all she could think or talk about. First she had to consider what clothing to take. The object was to get everything into one bag; an impossible task considering she needed two formal outfits, poolside outfits and informal wear. She really wanted to be the best dressed and sexiest woman on board the Crown Princess. That would be her way of saying thank you for the trip.

Making arrangements for Joseph was not a problem. George was more than happy to have him for the week. His mother was prepared to be there when Joseph came home from school; so that was covered as well. Recently George was seeing less of the boy than he had as Vicki was actually spending time with Joseph. It was interesting but the child seemed so afraid that his mother would disappear that whenever she was not in his sight he seemed to panic. Even Todd noticed that odd behavior and was making an effort to make the child feel more secure. They had a buddy system and would report to each other whenever Vicki was out of sight. It was becoming a game that Vicki did not like one single bit.

With her excitement about the trip, Vicki placed any efforts to secure new employment on hold. There was no point in looking if she had to tell a perspective employer that she needed a week off even before she could start. Even though the job market was tight, Vicki did remain optimistic that she would find something shortly. Her only hope was that Evan and Jason would not ruin it for her by giving her a bad reference. In her heart she did not fear that would be the case. Larry had assured her they would not interfere with her securing employment as long as she did not cause any more trouble for the Bergmans. That was really the main reason she did not want to get involved with that bitch Donna. There was nothing to gain from initiating a sexual harassment suit that Larry really believed she could lose. All that would result would be further damage to her reputation. The Garden City crowd was a tight one and any word of a harassment issue would mean disaster. Larry kept telling her that Evan and Jason would not want to bad mouth her because if they did so it would only place more negative attention on their firm. Vicki knew in her heart that she should listen to the voice of reason. Larry had always given her excellent advice and he did so without any real personal gain. He never even acknowledged her sexual advancements and often did not even charge for his time. When Vicki questioned him about this all he would say is "I find you an interesting character. I never know what you will do next."

The other loose end was Donna. Vicki knew she wanted nothing to do with her. Donna was a user and abuser who would only befriend you if she could gain from the friendship. Otherwise she really did not care about anybody or anything. Vicki knew she had her own faults and that she was not a candidate for "mother of the year," but at least she was honest about herself. That was more than could be said about Donna. She was not a person to take responsibility for her actions and she definitely had delusions when it came to her morals. She viewed herself as being better than Vicki when in reality she was just as much a whore as Vicki, just as much a cheat and much more a thief. The best Vicki could do was to concentrate on the trip and forget about any extraneous matters. Somehow things would just have to resolve themselves or she would deal with them when she came back.

The day to leave finally came and Vicki could hardly contain her excitement as the limo pulled up to the house to take them to the airport.

"I did not know you had a limo coming. I thought we would drive to the airport and park in the long term parking lot."

"I would do that if I could find the long term lot at JFK but somehow I can never find it. Also I did price it out and the cost is not that much more to go in style and have no hassle. Besides, Baby, you deserve the best."

"I just know this is going to be a great trip. I am already loving it."

The flight to Fort Lauderdale on Jet Blue was non-remarkable. Todd had even booked the extra leg room seats so they could board early and have room for the carry on stuff she was making him drag. Once in Lauderdale the transfer to the ship was effortless and Vicki was hanging on Todd's neck for the welcome aboard picture. The only thing she got upset about was the fact that their names appeared individually outside the cabin for all to see that they were not a married couple.

"Get over it. This is an international trip and the names have to be the same as on our passports. If you ever get divorced, we will be able to get hitched. You do remember that little problem of yours."

"Right now it works in our favor for me to still be married to George. Let's face it. I doubt he would be as generous as he is if we were to be divorced. It's almost like he still thinks there is a chance I will come back to him."

"Realism has never been one of his strong points."

"Don't I know it."

Vicki could not hide that she was disappointed with the size of the room. While it did have a balcony, it was only 231 square feet and that is tight by anyone's standards.

"Hey, baby, I know you would have liked a suite but the cost would have been too much for me to swing. Besides, how much do you intend to be in the room?"

"Much of the time but that will be in the bed, so I guess the size of the room is not the issue. At least the bed is queen size."

"Now you are thinking. Keep those thoughts. I like them."

The first thing they did was exactly the first thing all cruise goers do; they explored the ship. Finding anything seemed like a challenge and they were both wondering how they would find their way around to the various attractions and eating areas on the massive ship.

"Do you know someone said there are 3400 passengers on this thing."

"To me it looks like a city on the sea. I am amazed it can float," Vicki said as they passed the Theater under the stars, a massive screen above one of the pools. She thought this was an exciting attraction but little did she know it would become an irritation because of blaring noise that came from it all day and all night. The Crown Princess has four different pools and several hot tubs so it would be easy to escape the big screen noise. The restaurants, bars, shops and casino all added to Vicki's excitement as they explored the floating city that was going to be their home for the next seven days.

Vicki was determined to be noticed when she went to the pool on deck 15. After touring the ship, she realized that it was going to be easier than she had ever thought as the average age on the ship was middle sixty's and the average dress size was a plus. Most of the other passengers were retired people. Even so Vicki continued on her mission and when she first went to the pool on the first day, she was dressed in the smallest bikini which successfully showed off her breasts and firm ass. It was not long before the pool staff was all asking her if she needed anything. Todd found it all exciting and he had to keep a towel around his waist to hide his erection. He could hardly wait to get her back to the stateroom.

Throughout those first days of the cruise, Vicki remained totally attentive to Todd. They spent just about every minute together, drinking, swimming, going in the hot tub and, best of all, exploring each other in the stateroom. While Vicki flirted, she did not act on her advances and Todd was actually beginning to think this was the start of good things for them.

On day six, a day at sea, Vicki announced she really wanted to work her tan. Her plan for the day was to lie on a beach chair near the pool and let the sun bake into her skin.

"You know I always look best with a tan. Who knows it might even help me land a good job once we get back home."

"You know I do not have the patience to just lie there all day long and I really hate the sun," Todd replied.

"You can do your own thing then. That is up to you. We can reunite at the Spa in the afternoon for a couples massage and then I will give you a private massage."

"Sounds great; especially the private massage idea. Do you want to arrange to meet for lunch?"

"I am sure someone will be willing to get me something to eat. Really there is no reason for you to worry yourself about me. Go off and have some fun. You love the stinky casino and you know how much I hate the cigarette smoke."

"Okay- let's plan to meet at the Spa at four. I'll make the reservation for the massage."

"Great, see you then and have fun."

"You too."

With that Todd helped her pull a lounge chair into the desired position and took off leaving Vicki alone on the pool deck. He decided to go back to the cabin for his camera and to return to the top deck above the pool so he could take some pictures of her without her even knowing he was there.

Todd could not claim he was surprised when he returned to the pool area to see a crowd of the young pool staff circling about Vicki. He found it rather amusing that they were so obviously trying to get a close up look at her gorgeous boobs and tight ass. After all she did have a body that should be admired. Then one guy captured his attention. He was not an employee of the ship but rather a youngish guest wearing an expensive watch and large gold bracelet that just said money. The man had maneuvered his chair right up and close to Vicki and was actively engaging her in conversation. Todd could just tell that Vicki was really enjoying the attention and his inner self sensed trouble. Part of him really wanted to go down and barge right in but then he really needed to see how she would handle the situation. This could be a test of her conviction to keep her promises to remain faithful. Todd shot some pictures using the telephoto lens so that their faces were clear and then he just sat back to watch. Soon drinks were arriving and the man was signing for them. With the alcohol, Vicki was relaxing and enjoying the moment with increased pleasure. She was more animated and showing off her boobs in the most provocative ways.

The next thing Todd knew they were getting up together and walking away from the pool. Again he took pictures so he could prove what he was seeing should he ever have to do so. He knew he could not follow them as the likelihood of getting seen by Vicki was too great. Instead he went down to the pool deck and found the young man who brought them the drinks.

"You brought drinks to my friend and the woman he is with just a few minutes ago. He asked that I add to the tip he left you. Is it possible for you to bring me the check he signed?"

"Sure, sir, but he already left a nice tip on the check and I could get in trouble if I allowed you to add anything to Mr. Simpson's check."

"No problem. I'll speak to him later and if he still wants to add to the tip, he'll come up himself."

With that Todd went straight down to the ships photo gallery and asked for Mr. Simpson's room number.

"I am sorry, Sir, but it against ship's policy to give out room numbers of our guests."

"He just left his camera at the pool and I want to return it to him."

"You can leave the camera here and we will see that he receives it."

"Sorry, but I need to make sure he has it personally. He was talking about all the pictures he had and how much they meant to him."

"I do understand, Sir. Let me see what I can do to help you."

A few minutes later she was back with the room number written on a slip of paper.

"Please don't tell anyone I gave his cabin number. I could get in trouble for doing so."

"Worry not, no one will ever know."

Todd took the elevator up to Riviera Deck and promptly walked back to cabin R749, one of the mini suites on that floor. He was not at all surprised to see the privacy card in the card slot on the door. While he was tempted to knock and demand Vicki come out, he decided, instead, to walk to the pool area at the end of the corridor just a few doors down and to wait there for her to emerge. He stood where he was relatively sure she would not see him as she would be going back to the main pool and this was a smaller one in the stern of the ship. He knew he looked funny to the people sitting around the pool but he really did not care what they were thinking. He also knew he would not have to wait too long as they did have a four o'clock appointment at the spa and Vicki would be smart enough to make sure she was back where he left her long before that just in case he came by to pick her up.

An hour passed. It felt much longer to Todd who was thinking the whole time as to what he was going to do. One thing was becoming totally clear to him. He could not continue living this way. It disgusted him to think of her with another man and it was patently obvious that he would never be able to trust her. As he stood there waiting for the door to open, he decided it was time to end it with Vicki because his own sanity was at risk. Would he miss her? Desperately! Would he be able to start a new life without her? Probably. All that did not matter. What mattered was once they got off the ship, he needed to go home alone and close her out of his life once and for all. He was starting to see clearly why Stacey did not want her anywhere near the girls and he now believed she was right and he was totally wrong. He concluded she was the one who was right when she told him that men make bad judgments when they think with the wrong head. He had almost ruined his entire life thinking that way but now things would be different.

As the door to cabin 749 opened, Todd snapped pictures of Vicki and the guy leaving together. His hand was on her ass as they walked down the hallway. One very happy couple for all to see. Todd really felt as though a knife had gone through his heart but he also knew his resolve was strong. He was done with the lies, with chasing her, with bailing her out when she got in trouble and with loving her.

Vicki met him at the Spa at four just as they planned.

"I cancelled our reservation as I need to talk to you in private."

"Darling, I know it was hard to be apart for so long. Let's go back to our cabin and I'll give you that personal massage we discussed earlier."

"Okay, let's go," Todd replied not wanting to make a scene in the Spa.

Once back in their stateroom Todd said, "I have some pictures I want you to see," handing the camera to Vicki. Vicki was shocked and for once she did not know what to even say.

"It's over. I'm done. Once we get back I want you to go to your house and when I can, I'll make sure you get all your stuff out of my place. The locks will be changed, so don't even bother coming by. I told you before we left that I could no longer tolerate your promiscuity. Do you remember that conversation?"

"I was just having a little fun."

"Have that fun on someone else's expense. I am done; we are done! Don't you get it?"

"Where can I go? We're on ship and we will not be back to Lauderdale for a day."

"Find your lover boy and stay with him. I really don't care where you go or with whom you go; just get out of here. You disgust me."

"I need my stuff."

"Take whatever you need and I will pack the rest of the junk. You can pick up your suitcase at the terminal. I've even changed my flight so we don't have to return to New York together. Have a good life!"

"Todd, you can't do this to me. I love you. You love me and need me."

"Put all of that in the past tense. I don't need a common whore

235

and I cannot love a whore. You are a whore and you will never be someone who can be trusted. You will always be looking for the next rich guy who you can fuck to get whatever you want. I am done. Believe it or not; I do have some pride left."

"Why don't you go for a walk on the deck and cool down. I am sure once you come to your senses you will realize we belong together."

"That's just it. I've come to my senses. Be out of this cabin in one hour and I mean that."

"Where am I to go?"

"I am sure you will figure out something and I really don't give a damn where you go, just go." With that Todd turned his back on Vicki and stormed out of the cabin slamming the door behind him. He knew he needed all his strength to keep his resolve, but keep it he would. He was going to start a new life; one where his children would be centered. Maybe someday, he would even meet someone like Stacey and he would be able to have a real life again. But for now, he needed to get distance between himself and Vicki and that was going to be hard to do on the ship.

Vicki was blind with fury. She wanted to rip all of Todd's things as she threw them on floor but she managed to stop herself after just a few garments were destroyed. Throwing enough clothing into her bag to get through the night and to get on the plane the next day, she prepared to leave the cabin to try to find a place to stay. Jay Simpson was traveling with one of his buddies so he was a possible solution. Vicki called his cabin and was surprised when he answered.

"Hey what's up. I thought you had a massage appointment?"

"It's a long story but to make it short and sweet, I need a place to crash tonight."

"Do I detect trouble in paradise?"

"You could say that. Can I come up to your cabin?"

"Is lover boy going to make problems?"

"No, he's done and so am I. I need a real man. A man who can make me happy and not one that just wants me to service him."

"Well, baby, come on over and let me service you."

CHAPTER TWENTY SEVEN

Vicki was sure she would see Todd at the airport the following day, but he was nowhere to be found. She hadn't even seen him during the debarkation which was really strange as the ship had a schedule and it was pre-set. It was really strange flying home alone. This was something she had never done before and she was surprised to find the seat next to her was occupied. Somehow Todd had managed to change his flight and the airline had given his seat to someone else. At least that seemed to indicate he had purposely made the changes and he had not jumped off the ship while it was underway.

Once back on Long Island, Vicki was relatively comfortable in her old house. It was fun spending time with Joseph and she did insist that he sleep in the house with her instead of sleeping over with his father. George had not put up the expected argument and Vicki was beginning to suspect that he was involved with someone and he was actually glad not to have Joseph every night. When she tried to question Joseph, he was resistant to divulge any information and Vicki definitely felt he knew more than he was saying. It is amazing how smart the kid is when he feels it is best not to give out information. Only a child involved in a split marriage can be so cunning. It was his way of keeping the peace, she thought.

The real problem came the first night that Joseph was scheduled to be with his father. No way would the child give up his time with his "Buddy" but no way did Vicki want to spend the night alone in the house. She even thought about just going to Todd's house but her pride kept her from just doing that unannounced. Before she could stop herself, she was doing psycho dialing on the phone. First she called Todd and yelled at him that he could not just throw her away like garbage. When the first call went directly to voice mail, she rapidly called again and continued the tirade. Getting no satisfaction from the calls, the next call was to Donna who initially answered and even tried to reason with Vicki but she gave up and all calls went directly to voice mail. When Vicki called Evan, Roberta answered but promptly hung up. Next on her list was Jeff but something actually stopped her from making that call.

Alone and desperate, Vicki decided to do what she did the best. She took a shower and fixed herself up and left the house. Her first stop was the Roadside bar in Merrick. She was usually lucky there and she hoped tonight would be the same. A little action and not being alone would really help her frame of mind. When she walked into the bar she was surprised at how many people were at the bar. Usually on a Saturday night the place would not get busy this early as the music did not start until eleven. Vicki found a seat at the bar and quickly ordered a glass of red wine. One thing for sure, she did not want to drink heavily as she would have to drive home; the last thing she needed was a DWI.

It did not take her long to strike up a conversation with the guy sitting next to her. He was a large man and handsome in an interesting way. Their conversation was superficial at first and she was finding herself getting excited at the thought of getting to know him much better.

"What do you say we leave this place and find somewhere quieter and more private? She asked.

"Are you soliciting me?"

"If that is the way you want to think of it, think it. I think we could make some nice music together."

With that he got up and started walking out and Vicki followed at a discrete distance.

Once outside the bar, Vicki found herself surrounded.

"What the hell is going on here?" she screamed.

"You are being arrested for prostitution. You have the right to remain silent. Anything you say will be used against you."

"You, bastard, you don't have to read me my Miranda rights. I never asked you for a dime. I just offered you a good time. How can you accuse me of prostitution? I am totally lost on this one."

"You were asked if you were soliciting me. Solicitation is an act of prostitution according to the law."

"You are a real bastard; a real fucking bastard. I want to call my lawyer. You have to allow me to call him now."

"You can call him from the station house. Now let's go and stop making such a scene. You are making yourself into a real spectacle."

"You are the asshole here. I do not deserve this type of treatment and you know it. Why are you here bothering an innocent woman when you should be out there fighting real crimes not made up ones. You entrapped me and you know it, you fucking bastard."

"Let's put this piece of shit in the car and get her out of here. I've had enough of her."

With that the officers lead Vicki to the patrol car and forced her into the back seat. She was yelling profanities the whole time and some of the officers could not help but laugh at how pathetic she was. Once at the station house, the yelling seemed to escalate. It was obvious that Vicki was totally out of control and some of the police were wondering if they should call the psych division and have her committed. Instead one of the guys called her attorney whose number she continued to yell out in between her obscenities.

"Counselor, we have a woman here who keeps yelling your number. What do you want us to do with her?"

"What are the charges?"

"Solicitation."

"Do you have her name?"

"The only name we have so far is Vicki."

"That's enough. I know who she is. She can be really high strung but she is not dangerous. Just keep her and I will get to the station house as quickly as possible. Hopefully we can resolve this before it goes any further."

"You had better bring bail money because she is being arrested."

"I understand. Do you know how much the bail will be set at?"

"You know better than that. The judge will set the bail and it might be better for your client to spend the night here so she will not get into anymore trouble."

"We'll see about that. I'll be there shortly."

Larry was not happy to have to go to his wife and tell her why he was leaving with company in the house.

"You have to be kidding me. You are leaving our company for that nut job who doesn't even have the money to pay your fee. What hold does she have on you?"

"She is in trouble. You know there is nothing between her and me but I do need to help her. My guess is that there is no one else she can call and I really do not want the kid to find out his mother is in jail for prostitution. That child has had enough to deal with."

"You are a fool. Every time she gets herself in trouble she is on your doorstep. Every time you say this is the last time I am going to help her but that is an empty promise and we both know it. Luckily, I believe you when you say there is nothing going on between you and that nut case but you make it a hard pill to swallow and you know it."

"That's why I love you so much. You always understand. Please make my apology to everyone. I'll get back as quickly as possible. Hopefully, I can reach a judge and have bail set tonight."

"Will you be bringing the kid here if you do not get bail tonight?"

"My guess is that the boy is with his father and that she was all alone. Usually if she is alone, she goes crazy and does stupid things. So, no, I doubt I will have to bring Joseph here."

"She is one unfit mother."

"No doubt about that. She stands the chance that she will lose the kid for good if these charges stick. I know that will throw her over the edge. Despite everything, she really loves the boy. I have seen them together, and she is really good to him."

"Yeah, as good as a snake about to strike. It's all an act to get your sympathy and it obviously works. Someday, Larry you will stop feeling sorry for people like her. You know I do understand that by protecting her kid in a way you are protecting yourself when your mom used to mistreat you."

"Okay, let's stop the analysis. I've heard it all before. I have to do what I have to do and you know that."

"Yeah- I know it. Get home soon so we can cuddle together. I love you even when you are a fool."

"Thanks babe."

Larry was shocked when he arrived at the precinct. The woman brought into the interview room looked totally disheveled, haggard and crazy. This was not the sexy, vibrant person he was accustomed to seeing nor did she seem coherent.

"What the hell happened to you?"

"Larry, I give up. I can't do it any longer. It is as if there are demons in me and I cannot control them."

"What set you off this time?"

"I was alone. Todd left me while we were on the cruise. Joseph is with his father and there was no one for me. All I wanted was to have a little fun and now look at where I am. I was not soliciting as a prostitute and you know it. So do these dumb cops."

"What I know or what you know is not the issue here. The issue is the police report which states you admitted to soliciting the officer."

"When I said it, I did not mean it that way. All I meant was an invitation for him to leave with me and go someplace where we could be alone. I was picking him up, not soliciting him for payment."

"You do realize you have to stop this ridiculous behavior. You can't keep behaving like a whore and expect to keep Joseph. It just doesn't work that way."

"Are you here to help me or to lecture me?"

"Both. This will be the last time I leave my family to run to help you out of a jam of your own making. You have to change or accept the consequences."

"Yeah, yeah Ok."

"You are just yes-ing me I know when you have no intention of listening."

"I am listening. I just doubt that I am capable of changing everything. I need a man. Some people need food or alcohol or drugs, I need sex and right now I am not getting it."

"You need help to control yourself. You are on a path of self destruction. If you keep up with these one night stands, you are going to end up dead either from some awful disease or some crazy with whom you are. and then where will your son be?"

"Joseph is probably better off without me. If I were out of the picture he could have a more normal life with his father."

"Joseph needs you. I have seen how frightened he is when you leave him. That child really adores you and I know how he feels. I still remember how much I loved my mother regardless of what she did or did not do. Looking back, I realize what a terrible mother she was but at the time she was all I had and I loved her. That is where your son is and you have to be a better mother to him."

"Is the lecture over? Are you going to get me out of this fucking place or not?"

"I have to call the judge to get bail set so you can go home. Hopefully we will reach him and he will be willing to allow you to be released. We will then have to prepare your defense and, if we are lucky, I will get the charges dropped."

"If the charges are not dropped, what then?"

"Since this is your first offense, you will probably just get a fine and a warning. However, if George wants to use your arrest, he probably will have an easy custody battle."

"He wouldn't do that to me."

"This time, I am not so sure you are right. You appear to be a bad influence on your son and you are not in control of yourself. Vicki, no matter what, you need professional help to get your life under control and you need it now."

"What I need now is to get out of here."

"I hear you but I wish you would hear me. If you do not go for help, this is the last time I will respond to your calls. Am I making myself understood?"

"I pay you."

"Not enough for the disruption you cause in my life. Believe me, I don't need your money. I came this time because I feel sorry for Joseph. I still remember how I felt when my mother did things like this and continually got in trouble."

At that moment one of the officers came into the interview room to tell Larry that the judge was on the phone and wanted to speak to him. Judge Johnson was a personal friend of his and Larry was hopeful the outcome would be positive.

Away from Vicki's earshot, Larry explained what happened and told the judge he was convinced that the use of the word solicitation was being exaggerated in this case. Vicki only wanted to pick up the guy for a tryst. While she was morally deficient, she was not a prostitute.

"I will set bail at five thousand dollars and we will further explore this episode in court. Just make sure she does not go back on the street after she is released or I will hold you in contempt."

"Thank you, Your Honor, I will do my best to make sure she goes straight home and stays out of trouble. Personally, I think she is rather shaken by this whole mess and is in no shape to do anything else."

Larry wrote a personal check for the bail and got Vicki released. After driving her to pick up her car, he followed her to her house to make sure she went straight home.

"Do not leave the house under any circumstances or you will spend the night in jail. Am I making myself clear?"

"Worry not, I am too tired to do anything else."

"I'll see you Monday in the office."

"You mean you don't want to come in for some coffee."

"You never give up, do you? No, I am going home to my wife and family. See you Monday. Just remember, don't start with any of your crazy calling either. If you start that nonsense, you'll end up back in jail and my cell will be off for the rest of the weekend."

With that Larry turned his back and got into his car leaving Vicki to go into the house by herself. Once inside, she realized how exhausted she was but she feared being alone and knew she would not be able to sleep. She immediately went to the medicine cabinet and took an Ambien figuring that by the time she got out of the shower, it would start to work and she would be able to get that much needed sleep.

Neither the shower nor the Ambien worked. Vicki needed sex; it was as simple as that. Without a man, she felt crazy, agitated and self destructive. She did not know what to do with herself. One thing she knew for sure, she could not risk going out. If she were to be stopped, the police would surely arrest her for DWI. After all, the Ambien was having enough effect to make her reflexes slower and probably her judgment as well. With that she went to the phone and called Todd; maybe, just maybe, he would answer and come to her. Always, in the past, she could count on him. This time there was no answer on either his land line or his cell. George was her next try. Just as she was about to hang up, she heard his voice.

"There had better be a good reason for you calling at this hour."

"I am sorry, I did not realize the time. I need to see you."

"Don't give me that crap. You are alone and you think you can call old faithful and I will come running. Get with it. You made your choices and now you have to live with them. Joseph is here and I will not leave him in the middle of the night. That boy hates to wake up and not find me here. I can only guess where that insecurity comes from."

"Your mother is there so he is safe.'

"That is not the point. Besides, Vicki, I am not your sex toy. Get it through your head; I am finished. I have a new life and a good life with someone who cares about me. The only thing that would make my current life complete is if I have full custody of Joseph and you could be completely out of the picture. Going forward, you are only to call me if it pertains to Joseph. I no longer care if you are alone, in trouble, arrested, or whatever. I am done-finished-through. Am I making myself clear?"

"You bastard. I did so much for you. You would never be where you are if it were not for me. How dare you speak to me that way!"

"You did do a lot for me. You tried to wreck my life, take my son, destroy the family and who knows what horrible diseases you could have brought home from your encounters. I still have myself tested for sexually transmitted diseases. Yeah you did a lot for me. The only thing you did that was good was give me Joseph. Goodbye, Vicki, and don't try the psycho calling as the phone will be off the hook. You can vent your craziness somewhere else."

"You fucking bastard!"

Vicki was shaking when she finally hung up the phone. Even in her desperation, she knew not to call Larry as he would certainly cut her off and she did need his help. She, momentarily, thought about calling Jeff. That thought did not last long as she was sure he was with that bitch, Stacey, and they would enact the Order of Protection if she called. The only other person was Evan but she knew he would have nothing to do with her. That left Donna. At least if she could talk to her, she would not be so alone. Before she could stop herself, she was dialing Donna's number.

"Vicki, what's wrong?"

"I need someone to talk to. I am going nuts."

"Do you realize it is the middle of the night and you have just awoken the entire household?"

"I am sorry, I haven't looked at the time."

"Well, look at it. I am sick; I have cancer and my rest is very important if I am going to beat this thing. You cannot call here and disturb us just because you cannot be alone. Am I making myself clear?"

"It's your fault I am alone."

"It's not my fault that you are anything. If anyone should be furious, I should be. You were the one who meddled in my business. You are the one who caused all the trouble. Give me a break and just leave me alone. Don't try calling back. The phone will be off the hook for the rest of the night and I will never answer if I see your name. Am I making myself clear?'

"You fucking bitch; you will be sorry for that. I hope you die!" Vicki yelled into the dead line. There was nothing else left for her tonight. She finally went into her bedroom and turned the television on to channel 12 just in time to see a story about the vice squad and the crack down on prostitution right in Merrick.

"Good God, how bad could my luck possibly be?" she said out loud hoping that her picture was not included in the story. She knew she had to wait for the story to recycle. She just could not imagine what George would do if she was shown as part of that story and she knew he was an avid Channel 12 viewer.

"When life hits the shitter there is no end to the downward spiral." With that thought, Vicki started to think of suicide. If she ended her life right here and now, her problems would be over and the rest of them would feel guilty for how they treated her. She would have the ultimate revenge but what about Joseph? She got up and walked over to the frame holding his baby picture. She did love him and never wanted to hurt him. Her inner voice kept saying, "You will hurt that boy if you kill yourself. Remember, he is an innocent and has never done anything to hurt you." With that thought and still holding the picture, Vicki walked back to bed and fell asleep before the story recycled.

She did not get up early the next morning. The Ambien and the stress were enough to make her want to stay in bed long after her usual time. Besides there was nothing for her to do. Joseph would not be home until evening and Larry's words kept echoing in her head for her to "stay out of trouble." None of them understood her and they probably never would. When she finally decided to get up, she quickly made a strong pot of coffee and sat in front of the sunlit window in her somewhat outdated kitchen to read Newsday. Relief was the only thing she felt when she finished the paper and failed to see any mention of her arrest the night before. Of course, that relief would be short lived as the local papers always reported the current police blotters and she was sure there would be something in them.

Larry would have to help her defend her name. Hopefully no one who matters would see the local paper, but that was something she would deal with when and if she had to.

Somehow she managed to straighten up the house and even cook dinner so it was ready when Joseph came home. He was all excited about his time with his Buddy and kept talking about the hockey game, the movie and all the other things they did together. The only time he seemed to be resistant was when Vicki asked if anyone else was with them.

"It's ok Joseph. I know Daddy has someone new in his life and I am happy for him."

"Yeah, she is real cool and really likes to listen to me and to do things with us.."

"It's good that you like her. I really would be upset if Daddy were with someone you did not like."

"Yeah, like he is always upset when you are with Todd."

"That's different. Todd was his friend and Daddy always resents that he and I became a couple."

"Like Stacey resents that you two became a couple?"

"How does Stacey get into this conversation?"

"I just know. No one has to tell me things like that. I just know."

"I just know that her name is not one that is welcomed in this house. That woman has done everything possible to make my life miserable and I really dislike her. Am I making myself clear?"

"Just let it go. I really don't care about any of that stuff. It is all too complicated for me. I would love to have you and Buddy get back together but I know that is a dream and it is never going to happen."

"You are right about that. Sometimes adults make mistakes and he was my mistake. The only good thing that came from that relationship is you. You do know I love you desperately." With that she walked over to him and kissed him firmly on the mouth. His lips felt warm and sweet and she wished she could reach down and cuddle him like she used to do when he was a baby. But Joseph quickly changed the mood.

"Oh, Mom, I love you too but I have homework to do. You know you embarrass me when you kiss me that way. I would really appreciate it if you would stop that and just kiss me on the cheek like the other mothers do.

"Now you are telling me how I should kiss you! I don't get it."

"Mom, I am getting older."

"Who's talking now, you or your father?"

"Leave Buddy out of this. I am the one asking you not to embarrass me. Why can't you understand?"

"Next you will be telling me that you would rather not stay with me. Is that where this is going?"

"You are my mother. I love you but there is no way I want to be your sex toy."

"Sex Toy! Where the hell did that come from?"

"Buddy says you always need a sex toy and that it had better not be me."

"He's nuts and if he keeps filling your head with that type of nonsense, he'll find his ass in court before he can blink."

"Hey, Mom, let it go. I really don't want to start any trouble. I love you both and really want to be with the both of you. Give me a break here."

"Joseph you are growing up all too fast for my liking,"

"My counselor at school says that kids from split homes grow up faster because they have to. She says I'm ten going on thirty."

"I like it better when you're ten going on eleven."

With that Joseph left the kitchen to go to his room and Vicki was left shaking. She wanted to call George and yell at him for polluting the kid's mind but she stopped herself. Down deep she knew there was a lot of correctness in what was said and she feared that if she made an issue, it would work against her in any custody battle. There was no question that George was tapping her calls and if she were to call him right now, she would sound like a psycho.

"God, my whole life is falling apart," she said out loud. "Life sucks!"

CHAPTER TWENTY EIGHT

The next day a very subdued Vicki walked into Larry's office. He knew instantly that she had not had a good day, the day before and that she was very vulnerable emotionally.

"You guys just don't understand me. I need sex like other people need food or water. Sex keeps me alive."

"I have no solutions for you except to say what you really need is help, professional help, to get you to control yourself."

"Oh, now you are saying I am nuts."

"Don't put words in my mouth. What I am saying is that you need professional help. Without it you are on a path to self-destruction. You need to control your urges and your actions. Now they are controlling you."

"Well, I don't see it that way. I see that all I need is a good lay and a real man."

"In order for you to have a real relationship, you need to be in control of yourself. No self-respecting man is going to want to get involved with you. You are a nut case. Let's say it as it really is. Right now I would have a hell of a time defending you in a custody hearing. You will lose your son if you continue behaving as you have been. Am I making myself clear?"

"Clear as mud. Will you or will you not defend me with regards to this stupid arrest?"

"Part of me wants to tell you to find some other schmuck and part of me feels sorry for you. You are pathetic."

"So, now I am nuts and pathetic. Is there anything else?"

"That kinda sums it up."

"Where do I go from here?"

"Here is the name of a doctor whom I want you to see. Hopefully he will be willing to be a character witness should we need him. I also sincerely hope he can help you. I am preparing an answer to the charges against you and if we are lucky the judge will throw the entire thing out since there was no request for payment for services rendered. That is the major hole in the charges. You did solicit but not for monetary gain. I am going to claim you were the victim of an overzealous cop who encouraged you and entrapped you. How does that sound?"

"Like the truth. I really thought that bastard was interested in me."

"But, and this is the big but; you have to keep your nose clean going forward and you will need help doing so. I am not your safe keeper and I will not take calls from you at all hours of the night. I do have a family and you are not a part of that. If you psycho call people, and I know that is your modus operandi, you will only hurt your case. You must not go to bars to pick up guys. Am I making myself clear?"

"Clear as mud!"

With that Vicki broke down hysterically crying that she had ruined her life and no one cared about her. Even Larry felt sorry for the pathetic creature in front of him. There was no denying that she had ruined everything that was important to her and she stood a good chance of losing the last person who cared about her. He doubted she would be able to overcome losing her son and yet, deep in his heart, he felt that might be best for the boy,

"Make the appointment with Dr. Goodman and be honest with him. Hopefully he will be able to untangle your emotional mess."

"Is he single?"

"You are a nut!"

"Only joking."

Leaving Larry's office, Vicki felt that her entire life had hit the bottom and the only way was up. She knew Larry was right and that if she didn't change her ways, Joseph would be living with George and it was even possible that she would not be able to see him alone. It would be a complete bummer to have to have the law guardian present every time she spent time with the kid. Obviously, George had put weird ideas into Joseph's head or he would have never said what he did when she kissed him.

The next big question was how she would pay for any professional help. Psych docs were not cheap and they were not covered under her insurance. There was no way she could go to George and ask for money. No lie would cover her need for the money and the truth could only hurt her if there were to be a custody battle. Todd was totally useless when it comes to money and now he would not help her even if he had the dough. Evan had no interest in her or her problems. That left getting a job but since the Obama recession, jobs were hard to find, especially ones that pay well enough to meet her needs. "When life turns into a bummer, it just keeps sinking deeper and deeper." She said it as though she expected an answer. All the way home, all Vicki could do was to keep going over her options and to keep hitting the same dead end. If she weren't afraid of jail, she actually thought that selling herself could be the best answer to all her problems. Good money and good sex could satisfy everything.

Realistically, she had to give some thought to Larry's recommendations. The first thing was a job. Once she got home, she went right onto the computer to check jobs listed on Monster.com. Instead of looking for a position in Nassau, she decided to direct her attention to city jobs. A job within walking distance of Penn Station would be perfect and her reputation would less likely follow her there. There were receptionist positions listed in several legal offices, some financial institutions and even some medical offices. After a quick review of her CV, Vicki emailed it to the various offices. Hopefully interviews would materialize and she felt confident that if she were to interview with a guy, she would get the job. Just doing something made her feel better. She really did not think she needed the head doctor thing and decided that would have to wait until she felt really pressured to do something about it. Just because Larry said she needed help, did not mean she did.

The first request for an interview came from a law firm in Manhattan. The address was right in her target zone so only one fare would be necessary and, even though the LIRR was expensive, the current prices for gas outweighed the negatives. Vicki decided to respond and hoped that the she would actually be able to schedule additional interviews on the same day. Next on the agenda was choosing the right outfit. Nothing too sexy yet it had to show off her feminine side. The other requirement was that the outfit not be dated. She quickly discounted much of her wardrobe and decided a run to Foxes was indicated. After all there was nothing better than a new outfit to give a girl confidence.

The dark gray suit and matching shoes were perfect especially topped off by the pink silk blouse. Vicki was sure that her appearance would be just what the law firm wanted at its front desk. Unfortunately, she was not able to schedule more than one interview for the day but that's the way "shit happens" she thought to herself. Walking into the firm was totally different than the Long Island firms at which she had worked. It was more elegant and instantly told the clients that the services were expensive. To Vicki, that meant people with money came here and the opportunities could be interesting.

The interview went extremely well until the office manager inquired about the shortness of her last position.

"There was quite a bit of drama at Bergman and Bergman and I just did not want to have to deal with it."

"What kind of drama?"

"What happened at Bergman and Bergman stays with Bergman and Bergman. It is not my place to discuss the activities of that firm any more than you would want me to discuss the activities of your firm."

"That is a good answer. Actually this interview would be over if you had said anything else."

"I am prepared to sign any confidentiality agreement you would want me to sign. I want to do my job and leave my job here when the day is over. It is not my place to be involved with anything that does not pertain to reception and it definitely is not my place to discuss anything or anyone who comes here."

"I would like you to meet Mr. Fields, our managing partner. I think he may be in the office. Would you mind waiting to see him?"

"Of course not. I have no other plans for today."

Vicki returned to the reception area and watched the activity carefully. While the phones were busy, there were few people coming and going. Also in the reception area there was little indication of the workings behind the doors. This would be an easy job, but hopefully it would not be too boring for her. She really liked more buzz around her.

"Let's face it, sixty grand a year plus benefits looks good right now," her inner voice kept telling her.

About a half hour later the manager reappeared and told her that Mr. Fields would see her. Her first impression of the managing partner was that he was an older man who was extremely straight forward and set in his ways. Vicki's initial thought was "Why doesn't this guy retire?"

"Thank you for waiting Mrs...."

"Its Ms., I'm divorced. But, please call me Vicki."

"So you are a single mother?"

"Yes, I have a son but that does not impact my work. His father and grandmother live just around the corner so there is always someone to watch Joseph should I have to stay late at work or if he is home from school."

"That is a good thing as far as we are concerned. Sometimes this job requires overtime and we cannot have a clock watcher here."

"I am well aware of the working of a law firm and know there are times when it is necessary for me to stay and I am always more than willing to do so."

"If I were to call Jason or Evan would they tell me anything that would prohibit me from hiring you?"

"Please feel free to call them or to call Schwartz and Schwartz. I left both positions for personal reasons."

"Marjorie told me about your refusal to discuss the reasons for your leaving. I respect that and would expect the same loyalty should you get this job."

"That is not an issue. I believe strongly that it is unethical to discuss anything that happens at work with anyone including my fellow employees. I would be here to do a job as well as I can do it and to make sure you are getting your money's worth. I think my experience can be a benefit to your firm."

"I like you. Is there anything in your background check that I should know about?"

At that question, Vicki hesitated. There was no way she could effectively hide her recent problems with the police and she decided honesty was the best road to take. So she told Mr. Fields about the incident and the fact that her attorney was confident that there would be no record of her problems.

"You are an honest person. I have to tell you I already spoke with Larry and know all about the incident. He confirms everything you told me."

"May I ask you how did you know Larry was my attorney?"

"Lawyers have ways of finding things out. This was easy as it was part of the police records."

"And you were still willing to meet with me?"

"Larry said I would like you and that you were worth the opportunity. He is right. Had you not told me the truth, I would not have considered you at all."

"I am not a good liar."

"When would you be able to start?"

"Tomorrow or right now if you need me. All I would have to do is put a call in to Joseph's grandmother and I can be all yours."

"Why don't you do that! I think it would be in our best interests to start training you as soon as possible."

"Thank you, Mr. Fields, you will not regret giving me this opportunity."

"One more thing, Vicki. We have a strict policy at this firm that prohibits fraternization between employees or employees and clients. Can you live with that?"

"No need to worry. Right now I am not interesting in starting anything but a new job and I can and will do whatever it takes to make the job work for both of us. Thank you again for this opportunity." Vicki said getting up to follow Marjorie and wondering what the hell he knew that lead him to lay out that rule. What had that bastard, Larry, told him? "I could wring his neck," Vicki thought as she walked down the hall behind Marjorie.

"Don't let Mr. Fields scare you. His bark is worse than his bite. He runs this firm with a strong hand and he does expect all of us to respect each other and each other's privacy. That is why the position you are getting is vacant. Our last receptionist violated his rules and was dismissed immediately."

"Her loss is my gain. Can you tell me what it was that she did that violated his rules?"

"All I am prepared to say is that she was a lovely and beautiful person. She allowed herself to get involved with one of the clients and that was it in a nutshell."

"Well, you can rest easily. I have no intentions of getting involved with anyone. You could say I am off men."

"Ok, then I trust you will be here by nine tomorrow. Please wear a conservative suit. Mr. Fields does prefer the women to wear dresses instead of slacks."

"Marjorie, thank you for your time. I will be here promptly and I do look forward to working with you."

With that Marjorie showed Vicki the way out and watched her get into the elevator. There was no doubt on Vicki's mind that she was a lady to be contended with and Vicki was sure she would make it her business to stay under her radar. In many ways it was good that there was to be no inter-staff involvements. Vicki was sure that she could do the job and remain anonymous. After all New York was a big city and there could be any number of ways to meet new people of quality without screwing up the job.

As she waited for her train, she could not help herself but to call Larry to find out what he had told Mr. Fields.

"What the hell did you say to Mr. Fields about me?"

"Nothing of any importance except that you would be an excellent receptionist. Why are you asking?"

"He gave me the lecture about not getting involved with anyone who works or comes to the Firm. The way he said it made me think you had told him about my problems with the Bergmans."

"Vicki, let's understand each other. I would not do something like that as it would be a violation of the attorney/client relationship. I very much doubt if he has any information about your previous employment unless he called there and I also doubt they would say anything negative. After all it is in their best interest that you get a job and go off their unemployment insurance. My guess is that he is just a person who lays out his policies so there are no surprises going forward."

"That is for sure. I just had to know what you said to him."

"Good luck with the new job. When do you start?"

"Tomorrow. They fired the woman I am replacing and they do not have anyone to take her position. You would think she stole the family jewels or something."

"Whatever- at least you know what you are up against and I am sure you can do what you need to do to keep this job. It is best for your case to show that you are working."

"Fear not, I will keep this job and I will keep my personal life personal."

"Good girl. Just don't go out trying to pick up some strange guy and get yourself arrested again."

"I am trying to be celibate. Let me tell you it is really boring."

"Be bored- just stay out of trouble. I have to go."

With that the connection was broken and Vicki was left standing on the platform, thinking how her life could take so many turns without really going anywhere.

CHAPTER TWENTY NINE

The job proved to be extremely boring. While the phone kept ringing and there was a steady stream of visitors who had to be directed to the proper attorney, Vicki did not find any of it interesting. Everyone who came seemed so stiff and there was never any joking or laughter. She was seriously thinking of looking for another position but hesitated to do so because she needed all the legal matters settled and it was a positive that she was gainfully employed at a stuffy legal firm. Larry was actually beside himself with pleasure when she told him she had actually gotten the position.

Her boredom was only increased by the fact that the commute was taking up so much time that she had to rush home to make dinner for Joseph and then had to get him to his after school activities. There was no time for her to just go someplace and hangout especially since George was not as easily available these days. Vicki was getting the distinct feeling that he was actually trying to spend more time with the new person in his life than with Joseph. The flip side of it was that she was actually enjoying seeing Joseph and being a part of his life, something she had allowed to slip away. Of course, when she was with the boy, she played the part of the concerned mother and never even attempted to connect with any of the fathers who were there, not that she did not pick up on possible opportunities. It was just too close to home and she did not want to get into any more trouble. What she feared more than anything was that George would marry and then go for full custody. Her record needed to be cleared or she would not stand a chance in any court to retain custody. Losing Joseph would be the final blow for her and she knew she had to do everything in her power to prevent a custody battle.

In spite of herself, Vicki had to call Donna to find out how she was doing. She was totally surprised to learn that Donna's entire life was in an uproar. She could not work because of the cancer treatments; her appearance was awful, according to her, and her marriage was coming apart at the seams. Tommy wanted the kids and she was fighting him tooth and nail to prevent that. Since neither of them had any real money, she had a little advantage in that she knew several lawyers who were willing to help her while he had to pay as he went along. She owned the house and that was a good thing since he could not make her sell it and with the tenant in the basement, she was able to hold onto it despite the second mortgage they had taken out before all of this hit the fan. Tommy, on the other hand was deeply in debt from his gambling expenses, and all the money he put into his motorcycles.

Vicki could not help herself but to offer to take Donna into her house to allow her to rent out the rest of her place so she could have some money.

""I don't understand why you would do that for me" Donna replied.

"It's easy, I know what it feels like to be desperate and you sound desperate to me. Everyone needs a helping hand sometimes and you sure need it now. This is a big house and all the kids could get along until you can get back on your feet. Then we can both go on with our lives."

"I still don't understand why you would even think of such an arrangement. We were never friends."

"Let's just say we both helped each other screw up our lives and now it's time to help each other put them back together. I have a job and you could help keep the house running while I'm at work. That could be your contribution."

"You know I do not cook and I have always had a nanny to take care of the house. I don't know anything about being domestic."

"You could learn. Circumstance is the best teacher. Neither of us can afford a nanny nor can we afford to bring food in every night. Think about my offer. It is the best I can offer and who knows maybe Tommy will have second thoughts about ending your marriage if you do not appear so God-damned needy."

"Interesting point. I have never thought of myself as being needy before all of this."

"Well, now, you are very needy. Not that it is not justified. Having cancer is a bad break and until you are recovered and you can start your life over, you will remain needy. From what I know about it, and I only know things I have heard from other people, you will start feeling like yourself once the radiation and chemo is out of your system and you will be able to pick up your life and do things again."

"Wait till you see me. I am a total train wreck. No hair, puffy eyes with dark shadows under them and lopsided breasts. I scare myself when I look in a mirror."

"That will pass. Hair usually grows back, and your strength will return especially if you can minimize your stress."

"Since when are you Miss Know It All?"

"Think about my proposal and it you want to try it, let me know. That's the best I can do."

"Thanks, Vicki, you really made me feel better. No one has offered to really help. You really surprised me with your concern."

"Take it or leave it; it's up to you." With that Vicki hung up the phone feeling really sorry for Donna. No one deserved to be that alone and in so much trouble even someone who was as ruthless asDonna. Then the realization of what she said set in and Vicki could not help but wonder what possessed her to make such an offer. Normally she was not so carried away by another woman's plight. There was no doubt in her mind that Donna would never be as magnanimous had she been the one in trouble. After all Donna was ready to blame her for everything that happened at the firm.

"I have to be out of my fucking mind!" she said out loud in the empty house. It was almost like the words echoed back at her and her loneliness became even more evident to her. The days that Joseph was with his father were definitely the worse days for her. She had always solved everything by going on the prowl but now she feared doing anything like that so she just rattled around the house looking for projects and watching the minutes creep by. It is truly amazing how slowly time passes in an empty house.

Despite numerous advances, Todd still wanted nothing to do with her. She suspected that he had taken up with a new woman because no other explanation could justify his lack of interest or concern. In her heart, Vicki knew she really could not blame him. He had wanted to give her all he could and she was one who had cut him down. No guy wants his woman to flaunt her indiscretions right in front of him. She knew she had made him feel like shit when she took up with that guy on the cruise. She just never thought he would carry on for this long. He had always limped back to her no matter what she did or with whom she did it.

"Oh well, maybe all is not lost yet," she said as she dialed his number only to be disappointed again by the call being answered by his machine. Obviously he was not taking any private calls or he really was not home. With that thought in mind, she ran to her car and decided to drive by Todd's house and leave him a note. Hopefully she could stir up some interest if he thought she was really sincere this time.

Her heart fell into her feet as she drove by the house. Todd's car was there and so was another that she did not recognize at all. The girls were playing in the yard, so she could not even leave the note but the appearance of a family life really racked her soul and intensified her loneliness. Of course, Stacey would have no reason to prohibit the girls from being with Todd when he was with someone other than her but the hurt she was feeling was so intense that she did not know what to do with herself. Her first impulse was to call Todd but she knew he would not answer and leaving a psycho message would not do her any good. She also knew that if she called Stacey, she could be arrested for harassment and that was the last thing in world she needed right then. So she kept driving and before long she found herself at the beach. She parked at the lot and walked through the underpass onto Gilgo Beach, a spot that had always been a source of comfort to her. Walking up the deserted beach and feeling the wind in her hair and the sand beneath her feet, seemed to comfort her and calm her down. Normally during times like this she would consider suicide and she could remember on numerous occasions thinking how easy it would be for her to just walk into the ocean and disappear. During the off-season, Gilgo was so isolated and no one would see her. However, today was different. She did not want to end her life and never see Joseph again. She could not bear to know that if she did something like that, he would be forever scared. He was an innocent who loved her despite all of her craziness and he deserved to have a better mother than she was. She had to attempt to be a decent mother even if she failed everywhere else in her life. With that resolve, she walked back to her car and drove straight home to wait for Joseph.

Walking into her house Vicki never felt as proud of herself as she did at that moment. Not only had she resisted making a scene at Todd's house, she had resisted screaming into the phone and had realized the repercussions of her actions, something she had never given any thought to in the past. She was so proud of herself that she had to share it with the only person she knew who would appreciate what she had done. So she called Larry knowing that he would pick up if he saw her number which she had unblocked for this call.

"Don't tell me you are in jail and need me to come and bail you out."

"No, I am calling to let you know what just happened and to share with you the fact that maybe I am finally growing up." With that she recounted her actions.

'Whoa- I can't tell you how pleased I am. For once you actually thought about your actions and how they would impact on someone else."

"I am sorry to bother you at home but I just needed to let you know and I needed to hear that you are pleased with me. For some reason, your opinion is very important to me."

"Well, good going. Please continue to stay out of trouble and we will prevail in court and get all the charges dropped. Today is a good start for you, keep it that way."

With that he hung up and Vicki knew he was pleased with her. He was a funny man. Small talk was never one of his attributes but he was sincere in his caring and Vicki was proud that she finally did something that pleased him.

Vicki gave little thought to her conversation with Donna until the phone rang and she saw Donna's number on the caller ID.

"Holy Shit- don't tell me she is actually calling me!" she said out loud only to have her word echo back at her in the empty house.

"Hi, I hope I am not bothering you by calling."

"There is no one here but me and to tell you the truth, this place is starting to give me the willies. I am so not used to being alone."

"I know where you are coming from. It is really weird being home without the children. I hate it when Tom has the kids. At least when they are here there is noise and even if they bother me, it is better than the silence."

"I know what you mean. Before there was always a guy around to fill the time. Now it is a totally different story. Anyway, how are you doing?"

"I am finally done with the chemo and hopefully my strength will start to come back soon. Unfortunately, I am in no position to even look for a job. I look a mess and no one wants to hire a sick woman."

"Is Tom, at least, helping you financially?"

"He gives me what he can. Most of what he does give me goes for the kids. Believe it or not, Jason has been a big help. He has made sure I have health insurance and whenever things get really rocky, he deposits something into my account."

"I am shocked. I would never believe he would be so generous especially after all the turmoil you caused at the firm."

"Jason is a really good guy. He knows I am truly sorry for

everything. If I had it to do over, I would never have done what I did."

"Do-overs don't happen except in the movies. Believe me, there is a whole lot of stuff I would do differently now including screwing up my marriage for that no goodnick. I screwed over a really good guy and now here I am with nothing."

"Are things really over for you and Todd?"

"The bastard doesn't even answer the phone when I call. From what I hear on the grapevine, he is involved with someone new and I hear that bitch, Stacey, is cool with the new woman. Now Todd can get laid and still have his kids for the weekend so he is as happy as a pig in shit."

"Have you heard if Stacey is still with Jeff?"

"Yeah, they're a permanent number and they deserve each other. Jeff has been a real thorn in my side for years now. I know he put in a bad word about me when Evan hired him."

"That may be but from what I heard, you did a good job of screwing that up yourself."

"So, you are calling me to lecture me about the past!"

"Actually, I am hoping we can meet and have coffee or dinner together. I've been thinking about your suggestion and I think we can both benefit by combining our resources."

"I am willing to listen and since I have absolutely nothing else to do, let's meet at the East Bay Diner for a bite."

"It's four o'clock now. How about we meet in an hour."

"See you there." With that Vicki hung up and sat looking at the phone and wondering if she was about to make the biggest mistake of her life. Donna was never a person to do something that would help anyone but herself.

"Oh, hell, I guess there is no harm in listening," she told herself knowing she was bored out of her mind and any contact with another human would be comic relief.

The shock of actually seeing Donna was something that Vicki could not hide. While she was dressed well and wore a hat to cover her bald head, there was no hiding the grayness of her skin. Her face was sunken in and her cheek bones were exaggerated. Her eyes looked like they were in deep holes and all the sparkle was gone from them. She had always been thin but now she looked emaciated.

"Man, you look like hell."

"Thanks for the encouragement. Believe me I know how bad I look but it is better than it was a few weeks ago. Hopefully, now that the chemo is over, I will be able to eat like a normal person and the weight will come back on. Twenty pounds will make a world of difference and that is what they say I can expect to gain on Tamoxifen."

"You still have to take that stuff?"

"My tumor was estrogen sensitive and the Tamoxifen will suppress the estrogen in my body and hopefully, reduce the chances of a recurrence."

"I think it is amazing how everyone who has been sick becomes a medical expert."

"Today, the doctors discuss every single thing with you so you cannot say you did not understand and then sue them."

"My thought is that on a need to know basis, I do not need to know."

"You can say that because it is not you. If it were you, you would want to know. Believe me."

"Anyway, we did not come here to discuss your medical history."

"I wanted to talk to you in person about your suggestion that we combine our forces. We are both alone and we could help each other with the kids and the finances."

"What you really mean is that I could help you. I am the one with the job and house."

"Yes, but you are not good at being alone. If we were to combine forces, I would be there for you when Joseph is with George. We could do things together and you would be less likely to get in trouble."

"Oh, now you want to be my watchdog,"

"I am not saying that. It is just that I was thinking I could help you with dinner and stuff until I am able to get a job and I could watch Joseph until you get home from work. On the weekends, we could plan things so you would not feel so alone and neither would I."

"Once you get back together, you will be able to meet someone and where will that leave me?"

"That could go for you as well. Who is to say you will not meet some guy tomorrow and decide to take up with him?"

"It should only happen. Right now there is no meeting anyone at work and I cannot take the chance of going to a bar and meeting someone there. The last thing I need is to be arrested for solicitation."

"I heard."

"How did you hear?"

"Let's just say that what goes around comes around. It doesn't matter how I heard but I did hear about your little bout with the law. It really sucks."

"Did you talk to Larry?"

"No, he would never discuss a client with anyone. I am telling you it doesn't matter how I heard nor does it matter what I heard. I know you were not soliciting and I feel really bad about it."

"I just hate my life being an open book. George is a great guy but he would use this against me in a heartbeat. If you know, then he probably knows as well. That could really screw up my world."

"Think about us getting together under one roof and trying to provide a stable environment for all the kids. It can only help."

"The house only has four bedrooms. Joseph would not want to share a room with Tommy, so how would that work?"

"Patricia and Tommy can share a room. That is no big deal. That way Joseph can have his room just as he does now, you would have your bedroom and I would take the smaller remaining one for myself. I even have their furniture, so it would feel like home to them."

"The small bedroom has limited closet space."

"That should be our biggest problem. I could always put a rack up in the basement for clothes I am not wearing right now, and that is most of what I possess. You would really be helping me out. That is what this really is."

"And if it doesn't work, what then?"

"If it doesn't work, I am right back where I am now. I have no place to go and I cannot afford to keep the house I am in. Even my mother is not offering to take us in because she is pissed at me for what I did to Tom. My guess is that if she really sees that we are homeless, she will step up to the plate but I want to try everything else first."

"What does Tom say about all this?"

"He is willing to take the kids but that is the last thing I want. I do not want to lose my kids anymore that you would want to lose Joseph. Look, I know I have not been a great example of motherhood to those kids but I really want to make it up to them. This whole cancer thing has shown me there are more important things to living than what I considered important before and my kids are really important to me."

"Man, I get that. Look, I am willing to give this thing a chance. There are some practical matters that have to be considered. My expenses for running the house will be increased just because there are more people there. I am barely making ends meet now and I cannot encounter more expenses."

'I do get child support and that will all go to running the household. My kids are set for the near future with clothes and shoes and stuff. As for food, we will both save by making dinner at home instead of bringing in. I know I am not the greatest cook around but I can whip up something and have it ready for you when you get home from work."

"Now you are Miss domestic!"

"Have to do what has to be done. That would be my contribution to the deal. I will also be responsible for the cleaning and stuff and that should make your life easier. Once I get a real job, we would adjust things."

"Look- to be perfectly frank, I never even liked you when we worked at Bergman's. What makes you think we will get along now?"

"I am different and have different values now. I also will be beholding to you and somewhat at your mercy. If I cause you to want me and my children out, I will be the one in trouble. Look, I will even sign any papers you want stating just that and promising not to hold you responsible in any way for our welfare. If you want us out, we would be out and that's it."

"Let's think about this overnight. We can talk again tomorrow. At a minimum, I need Joseph to meet your kids to make sure they can all get along. It would be wrong of me to force two kids on him that he doesn't even know."

"That's reasonable. I am sure that no matter what there will be times when they will not get along. Kids will be kids and there will be fights and all that stuff. Let's be realistic here."

"Kids aren't the only ones who might have disagreements."

"We would both reserve the right to disagree. Just as we would both reserve the right to our own lives and being able to live the way we want. Neither of us would have to answer to the other. We will each be able to come and go as we wish. Hopefully, we would be able to schedule things so that the children will always have an adult at home."

"Let's talk tomorrow. I need some time to think about this. Truthfully, I never expected you to take me up on my offer."

"The decision is yours. Thank you for hearing me out and considering helping me. If I were not desperate, I would never be here right now."

With that Vicki got up and took the check. As she walked to her car, she could not help but wonder what she was getting herself into. Donna says she has changed but where the truth lies was an unknown, just as it was an unknown if they could ever get along under one roof. Of course, the time they would be together would be rather limited with her working in the City all week; so weekends would be the major issue. Then there was the shared custody. Would the kids be on the same custody schedule or would there always be kids in the house? While Vicki was unhappy when Joseph was not around, she knew she would be totally miserable if Donna's kids were home and he was with George. She could just imagine them whining at her and she could visualize herself losing it big time. The converse of that would be if all the brats were home together and she did not have any quality time alone with Joseph. That would be horrible.

As she did so many times in the past, Vicki drove to Gilgo Beach. Somehow being on the beach and watching the waves hit the shore always was a comfort to her and always helped her to make decisions when she needed to do so. Everything would be so much easier if there were a man in her life; especially one with dough. Keeping the house up and trying to make ends meet was getting harder and harder with all the increased expenses for heating oil and gasoline. George was a generous man but he shut her down now that he had a new woman in his life. She really could not blame him especially since he still was overly generous when it concerned Joseph. Her salary covered the food and most of the regular expenses but there was little left over for the unexpected which was a regular reality with an older house. Some of Donna's child support could go to cover those unexpected repairs and once Donna was able to get a job, her salary could put them on an easier path.

The solution she came up with was to have a trial weekend when all the kids could be together and they could see how everyone got along. It would give Joseph a chance to meet Donna's kids and after the weekend she and Joseph could discuss the merits of them moving in. It would also give her a chance to see if she could stand having them all in the house together. The next thing she knew she was calling Donna.

"Listen, I think we need a trial period. I have Joseph next weekend and if you have your kids, you could come on Friday and stay until Monday morning. We could see how everyone gets along."

"It is no problem for me to arrange to have the kids next weekend. Tom is very accommodating that way. I agree it would be a good idea to see how everyone mixes together."

"I understand that two or three days is a short time but it could be a start."

"Let's do it. And once again, thank you."

"I cannot say I do not have reservations."

"I understand your reservations but remember I am beholding to you. I have to make things work. I am the one up shits creek."

"If we decide to go forward with this, I will have one of the attorney's at my firm draw up papers for you to sign. It is important to me that we have a formal understanding that if I ask you to leave for any reason, you will leave immediately."

"Immediately has to have some time indication. I would need some time to find a place for myself and children. Let's be realistic here. If you were to ask me to leave, you would have to give me at least a week to find some place to go."

"That's reasonable. But I am not willing to give you more than a week, if things go really south."

"What do you think would be a reason for you to want us to leave?"

"It could simply be that I cannot stand to be around you. I remember feeling that way at the firm. You can be one selfish bitch and we both know that."

"You can also be difficult."

"Yeah, but it is my house."

"I get it."

"Let me know what time to expect you next weekend and we can go from there. Please understand, I am hoping things work out and I can help you and you, in turn, can help me. A little extra money would make life easier and if I do not have the pressure to get home by a certain time, that too would be helpful. I really do not like Joseph spending so much time with his grandmother. She cuddles him far too much and is not letting him grow up."

"I'll see you Friday at six. Is that enough time for you to get home from the city?"

"Yeah, on Fridays we leave at four, so I am usually here by five thirty."

"I'll bring pizza for dinner. See you then."

Going back to her car, Vicki had the strongest urge to go somewhere she could meet a man and get laid. It had been too long and she was really feeling the urge. She tried calling Todd, just for old time's sake, but he did not answer. She even called Jeff, just because, but he, too, did not answer. Then she called Larry who did answer and knew immediately what was on Vicki's mind.

"You listen and listen carefully. You are to go home from wherever you are and you are not to get into any trouble. Go home and amuse yourself but if you get into trouble don't call me. Am I making myself completely clear?"

"You don't understand. I need a man."

"I need a million dollars. So? Vicki I am not your keeper and you cannot always call me when I am with my family. Go home and stay out of trouble. That is my advice and if you do not follow it, don't call me." With that he hung up the phone and when she tried to call him back, he did not answer even when she started psycho dialing his number. Being so alone was horrible for her and she was literally beside herself. No one was responding to her repeated calls. She felt as though she was standing all alone on a planet full of people all of whom had someone and she had no one. Her life was a dismal hole and the only human with whom she had any contact was Joseph and even he could not respond to her now. Sitting in the parking lot at the beach, she just put her head on the steering wheel and started crying like a baby. She never gave it a thought that there were people on the boats in front of her who could see her and she was totally startled when a man tapped on her window.

"Lady, are you all right? I do not mean to interfere but I could not help but see that you are very upset."

"Thank you for your concern. I am all right. It is just that I feel terribly alone."

"Look, there is a group of us on the boat. Would you like to come aboard and have a drink with us?"

"That is really kind of you."

"Come on."

With that Vicki got out of her car and went on the boat where there were several people, just as the guy had said. They all seemed nice even though they were a little drunk. Vicki viewed the situation as a possibility to have some fun and she was glad she had accepted the invitation. After a few drinks, she too relaxed and before long the group started breaking off into couples. Some left the boat to go to other boats tied up at the marina and Vicki found herself with the guy who had asked her aboard. One thing led to another and before she could even think of stopping herself, she and he went at it. Vicki used all the tricks she knew to give him an experience he would never forget and she loved every minute of it. When the woman he was with came back on the boat, she joined them and it became an interesting threesome.

"You got over your depression rather well," he said when it was over.

"I don't know your name and I would prefer to leave it that way. I just want to say thanks for an interesting evening. You rescued me and I appreciated it."

"You fucked me as I have never been fucked before and I appreciate it."

"One good deed deserves another," she said as she put her clothes back on and gathered her things.

"Thanks again, maybe someday, we will meet again but don't count on it," she said as she left the boat knowing it would be a long time before she would return to the parking lot as it was always a good thing to never return to the scene. One thing was certain, she felt better and that guy had satisfied her need for a man. The only thing better than a casual fuck with no strings attached was a guy with lots of money.

Driving home Vicki kept going over the events of the evening. One thought kept coming into her mind; she was actually remembering the woman more than the man. The woman's touch had been exceptionally sensual. It was as though she knew exactly how to touch Vicki's breast and how to suck on them until she was almost brought to orgasm. When she spread her legs and used her tongue on Vicki's sweet spot, it was almost too much to bear. Vicki concluded that given the opportunity, she would love to be alone with the woman; a strange thought for someone who craved men as much as she did.

"Oh well, I'll not dwell on those thoughts. It is refreshing to feel satisfied after being so deprived for so long," she said out loud as though hearing the words gave them more meaning than just thinking them.

As she approached her house, she looked at her watch and realized she just had enough time for a long shower before Joseph was due home. She was excited about spending some quality time with him and knew she was more relaxed than she had been in a long time. Good sex always put her in a good mood.

Standing in the shower and feeling the warm water run onto her skin was one of the most pleasurable feelings to Vicki. She wished she could just stand there for as long as she wanted and just continue to relax. But that was not the situation this time. She had to get out and get dry before Joseph got home or there would be too many questions to answer and too many lies to tell. She knew he suspected her of seeing strangers when he was not home and he always feared her being away or disappearing for days on end. He definitely loved his father and his grandmother but there was no denying the special bond between them. There was no doubt in her mind that her former lifestyle had made him unsure and fearful but she was trying to change all of that now. She was always letting him know when she would be home and where she was; not that she had anyplace good to go. It was work and home, home and work. That was what made this evening so exciting. She had actually done something to make herself feel better and it was fun. Now it was back to saintly motherhood.

At exactly ten o'clock, Vicki heard the car some to a stop in front of her house. She ran out and was standing next to the door as Joseph emerged. It was exciting to see him after three days of being alone and she took his face into her hands and planted a big kiss directly on his lips.

"Joseph, please go inside while I talk to your mother," George said in a firm voice leaving no room for argument.

"I really want to see you before you go, Buddy,"

"Mother will let you know when I am ready to leave and you can come back out. There are some adult issues that we need to discuss for just a few minutes."

Joseph was used to them discussing adult issues which always centered around him, so he obediently walked into the house.

"If I ever see you kiss that boy like that again, I will make sure you only see him under direct supervision."

"What the hell are you talking about? He's my son and he was away with you for several days. I am excited to see him. There's nothing wrong with that."

"Look, Joseph is getting older and is approaching puberty. That was not a motherly kiss; it was sensual and it is horrible for a mother to try to sexually stimulate her son."

"I was not trying to sexually stimulate him. That is simply the way I kiss him."

"A kiss on the cheek and a hug is appropriate not a kiss directly on the mouth that looks like you are giving him tongue to boot."

"You are a nut. I was not giving him tongue or any other sexual stimulation. Your imagination is running away with your mind."

"Believe me when I tell you that if you continue to act that way in front of my son, I will take you to court and you can be sure you will lose. I know about the charges pending against you. You will lose and you will be charged with sexual misconduct with a minor. For the record, I took a picture of you kissing Joseph and any judge seeing it would find it as disgusting as I do. Vicki, I have looked the other way too many times and that boy's welfare is paramount to me. I will not have him sexually stimulated by his own mother."

"You are imagining things that will never happen."

"Remember I know you and all your tricks. I've chosen to look away because I believe that Joseph needs his mother. This is one issue I cannot disregard. Stop kissing our son as though he is your boyfriend or you will not be seeing him without a law guardian. This is not an idle threat."

"You bastard, you would hurt your own son just to punish me."

"You are the one hurting him not me. He tells me how he goes into your bed to snuggle and that you smell so nice and how he loves feeling your skin against his. That is not normal. I do not want to hear how you fondle him or anything like that. He is getting to an age that he can be sexually aroused and it had better not be by his mother."

"So, now I cannot kiss him or cuddle with him. What do you want me to do, shake his hand and say good night?"

"If you cuddle with him, make sure you are wearing proper pajamas not one of your sexy nightgowns and be respectful of physical contact."

"You are a sick person. I am just sorry that I have to have any contact with you on any level."

"Too fucking bad. Unfortunately, we share the same child and we will continue to share him until he is emancipated. I will stop at nothing to protect him. Remember that the next time you want to get your sexual jollies from exciting him. Do your whoring outside the house in the future.."

"Go to hell." With that Vicki turned her back on him and starting walking up the path to the front door. There was no way she wanted him to see that she was really upset by his threats.

"Just tell Joseph I am waiting here to say goodbye. And, by the way, I am planning on going to his hockey game on Tuesday. You don't need to rush home from work."

Without replying, Vicki opened the front door and yelled to Joseph that his father was leaving. She stood at the door watching them bid each other goodbye and she was jealous. She could see the special bond they had. She wanted to be the central person in her son's life. She was beginning to regret allowing George to have so much time with the boy. She definitely was going to make every effort to stop that practice going forward. Maybe, if Donna actually moved in, Donna could be there to watch Joseph until she got home. That would eliminate the need for George or his mother to watch him. Donna could actually be a witness, if she were to need one, to testify that she was not doing anything to sexually abuse Joseph. The idea of her moving in was becoming better and better with every passing thought.

"If he wants to fight, we will fight. I will make sure the cards will fall on my side if a fight were to develop. He is just stupid to think that I would just submit every time he makes a demand. After all, I do have an entire law firm where I can get help, if I have to do so," she mumbled half out loud and half to herself not wanting to allow Joseph to hear her mumbling.

George stood on the sidewalk watching mother and son turn their backs on him and walk into the house. He just hoped he had reached her and that she would stop what she was doing with the boy. He knew, all too well, that she was a sexual animal who uses sex to get whatever she wants. What he feared was that she would use sex to get Joseph's devotion. George knew for sure that he and Vicki were engaged in a competition to be the central figure in the boy's life. He also was aware that the next few years were paramount for the boy's future sexual health. He wanted his son to be able to have normal heterosexual relations and not be damaged by his mother. How he ever loved a woman like her was an enigma to him now. His own mother had begged him not to marry her but he was so crazy about her that he listened to no one. Now he was paying for his own infatuation.

That night Vicki tossed and turned. It was impossible to shut her mind to George's threat. Finally, she reached a conclusion. She would have Donna come and live in the house. That way she would have extra money to help support the house and George would be able to give her less than he was doing right now. That would eliminate one of the items he had to hold over her head. Secondly, she could be home to see the children when they came home from school. Joseph would no longer have to go to his grandmother's until she came home from work. That would reduce the time he spends with George and his family and would lessen their influence on him. The best of all, was that Donna could be her witness should he ever carry out his threat to charge her with child abuse. Vicki would make this a prerequisite for Donna moving in with her. She had to close all the doors to prevent George from ever taking Joseph away from her and she knew she would do whatever had to be done to close them. Before she left for work, she called Donna with her decision. They arranged to have dinner together that night so all the children could meet and hopefully get along.

CHAPTER THIRTY

Donna seemed extremely flustered when she arrived at Vicki's house. After making the necessary introductions, the children all went into the basement playroom to watch television.

"What's up with you? You do not seem to be yourself."

"It's been a tough day. I had to go for my MRI and they made me lie on a table face down for thirty minutes with that damn machine clanking away. You know they actually make you lie so that your boobs are in holes in the table."

"That does not sound like fun. But I guess you have to do what you have to do."

"It is always a little nerve racking to have any test done and not get the results immediately. I wonder if you ever get over the fear of them finding something bad."

"I can understand that but I guess it is better not to think about it until you have to. From the little I know, once you have had cancer, they never really let you go. That's probably a good thing because if there is something bad, they can catch it early."

"I know you are right. It's just that for me it is hard to even think about going through all this shit again. I truly don't know what I would do if they find something."

"You'll do what you have to do. You have two kids to think about and life is too precious to fool around."

"Anyway, the receptionist said they would call me tomorrow after the test is evaluated."

"That's nice of them. Most places just let the doctor know and you have to wait until he gets around to calling you."

"I guess they are used to dealing with women who have had cancer and understand the pressure. Anyway, let's not keep talking about this. What are your thoughts regarding the move?"

"I'm thinking that whenever it is good for you would work for me. I just need you to promise you will be available as a character witness if my ex does anything to claim I am sexually abusing Joseph. He wants full custody."

"That is nuts. What did you do to give him such an outrageous idea?"

"He didn't like the way I kissed Joseph hello. He said it was too sexually suggestive and on and on. He feels Joseph should not be allowed to sleep in my bed or to see me in any stage of undress etc."

"Have you considered that he may have some grounds there? Joseph is approaching his teenage years and boys at that age are easily sexually aroused. Vicki he is not your little boy anymore."

"So do I take it you agree with George?"

"What I just said is between you and me. If you ever need me to swear that you never do anything that is sexually arousing in front of your son, I will swear to it. But remember, Joseph will be able to tell his father if he is asked and that would carry more weight than anything I would say. My sincere advice to you is to be careful and not to do anything that could turn the kid on."

"That is going to be hard for me. I am a very sexually oriented person and that is how I behave with everyone."

"Everyone but your son. I know you can control yourself. You are doing a great job of that at your job. That firm you are working for is known to have very strict regulations and anyone who does not adhere to them is out on the street."

"The entire place is filled with old fuddy duddies who do not live in the real world. But the pay is good and there is no one there that even remotely interests me so it is easy to play by their rules."

"See, you can do it. I know you love your son and will do whatever you need to do. I think you get the picture."

"I get it but I don't like it; not one little bit. I feel like George is dictating how I should behave and he really does not have a right to do that."

"My guess is that he thinks he is protecting his son."

"He's my son too!"

"Vicki, remember your history would work against you if this were ever to go to court. You need to be careful."

With that the conversation ended as the kids came running up complaining that Tommy was bothering them. The two women proceeded to mediate the dispute and once peace was restored, they both realized that this was the way things would be going forward. Someone would always be bothering someone else, but so be it. The kids would just have to adjust to the new living arrangements. With that they settled on a move-in day a week away to give Donna time to get her stuff together. They also decided that since the school year was almost over, her children would finish out in their present school and that way they would not be disrupted. Since she was not working, it would not be a problem to take the kids to school or to pick them up. Since their day ended earlier than Joseph's, Donna was relatively sure she would be able to be back by the time Joseph gets off his bus and that way he would not have to go to his grandmother's. That being another major concern of Vicki's.

"Here's a key. Feel free to move your stuff in anytime you want to. I am really excited about the whole idea."

"Thanks. I just know we can make this work out for both of our benefits."

After Donna and the kids left, Vicki sat down with Joseph and discussed the situation with him. While he understood that Donna needed help, he was hesitant about having the children live with them.

"Look, your room is always going to be your room. If the other kids bother you, just go to your room. You have a TV and we will put your video games on it and that can be your cave."

"What if I don't want to spend all of my time in my room?"

"No one is telling you that you have to spend all of your time there. What I am saying is that if you are bothered or upset, you can use your room as an escape. Otherwise you do anything you want to do. This is still our house and if things don't work out, they will have to leave. It's that simple."

"I guess I could try. I do like Patricia, just Tommy; that is the problem."

"He is the youngest and there is no stopping him from doing things that will annoy you and everyone else. It goes with his age."

"Mom, he is not normal."

"I've heard that he has some problems. All the more reason to cut him some slack. Maybe if you act like his big brother, he will improve."

"I don't know but I guess I can try."

"Thanks, that is very mature," she said taking his face in her hands but stopping herself before kissing him on the lips. Instead, she gave him a big hug before telling him to get ready for bed since he did have school the following morning.

"Thanks for the hug, Mom. I liked it."

CHAPTER THIRTY ONE

nd so a new chapter in her life began. Donna and the kids were in the house and when she came home from work; dinner was ready. Vicki no longer had to worry what Joseph was doing after school and she no longer had to rely on her ex-mother-in-law to watch him. She viewed this as a good thing as she definitely preferred to limit his exposure to them and their influence on him. She still did allow him to walk over in the evening to visit with his grandparents; but he had to ask. There was no way she wanted to be accused of preventing him from seeing George or his parents.

Vicki was also relieved to learn that the charges against her were going to be dropped. The DA could not find anyone who would testify that she actually solicited anyone. As Larry explained, it was not against the law to give it away but it was a criminal offense to charge for it. Vicki found this rather amusing but she really did not care as long the charges were dropped and her record cleared. One less thing for George to use against her should he ever really challenge her custody of Joseph. Even George seemed to be more content lately. He seemed less aggressive during the time they saw each other when he either picked up or dropped off Joseph. At first Vicki was rather suspect of this altered behavior; but after talking to Joseph, she realized that he was probably not answering George's questions like he had formerly done. Also she was very careful not to kiss him in any way that could be construed as provocative and he no longer shared her bed at night. He was embarrassed to do so with the other kids in the house and though she missed having him there, she did understand that it was for the best. Her baby was getting older and soon he could be sexually active; a hard concept for her to grasp.

All of this left only one missing part in her life. She no longer had a man to satisfy her needs and she was still afraid to go out to find one. The trip to the beach had been fun but it was unlikely she would do that again. It was not her style to repeat with any strangers. Trying to meet anyone in the city was both difficult and dangerous. She would have to go to his place or some strange hotel and she knew that could leave her vulnerable. Somehow, going to the Gateway Motel had always been comfortable for her. Masturbation provided immediate relief but it did not satisfy her need for body contact and closeness. She had even tried to contact Todd to see what he was up to and to let him know she was sorry for everything that had happened. While he was courteous, he had no interest in restarting any type of relationship and told her so in so many words. Jeff was another call she made. He was very cool to her and basically told her that it would be better if she did not contact him in the future. Evan had a similar response to her call and he told her that he and Roberta were married and very happy. Something had to break with this aspect of her life. She just did not know what or when. One thing she knew for sure, she would figure it out just as she had always done in the past.

Donna, on the other hand, seemed perfectly content without being involved with a man. She always said she was enjoying being with her children something she never had the time to do in the past. She felt that she had had a wake-up call and now all she wanted to do was to enjoy life. She no longer wanted to be at the beck and call of anyone. She no longer wanted any man groping her and making her feel like his play thing. She was done with that and proud of her decision. The only item missing in her life was a job. She still did not have all her hair back and still looked somewhat ashen but in time she hoped to be able to get a job as an executive secretary and to be able to support herself. Until then, she often said, she was just happy to be alive and on the road to recovery.

Their unorthodox household fell into a pattern. The children often had disagreements but in general got along fairly well. Joseph and Patricia became good buddies and enjoyed playing video games and doing all the things children do. The only thorn was Tommy who still was a problem and even Donna was considering getting him some professional help. The stumbling block was that big Tom was unwilling to accept the idea that his son needed intervention and was unwilling to pay for the help. There was no getting him to understand, even the teachers at school tried to talk to him but it all fell on deaf ears. He refused to listen even when he was told that the child was behind in development and was definitely behind in his school work. The teachers even suggested holding him back a year in school to give him a chance to catch up. Still Tom refused to listen and Donna and he argued vehemently about holding Tommy back a year. Tom finally gave in on that as he felt that since the kid would change schools and all, he would not be too embarrassed by being held back as he really did not have a group of friends at the new school. However, that was all he would concede to. His son was perfect and everyone else was crazy.

Both Vicki and Donna had to deal with the other children on this issue. Joseph and Patricia were overheard calling Tommy a retard. This did not go over well with the two women.

"You can't be calling him names like that," Vicki told the older children. "It is not his fault that he is slower in school. You should try to help him not make fun of him."

"Yeah, you just don't understand. He is always in my way and he does things that are too stupid to deal with. He is a real pain," Joseph countered and Patricia readily agreed with him.

"Pain or not, he is here and you have to treat him properly. How would you like it if someone called you names?"

"Make him leave me alone," Patricia demanded of her mother. "He is always following me and interfering with me and my friends."

"That's because he wants to be part of your group. He doesn't have friends of his own."

"Get him some. Just make him leave us alone."

"I will try to do some things with him while you and Joseph are busy if you try to include him some of the time. I think that's a fair deal."

With that the children seemed to be satisfied for the moment. Donna and Vicki knew it would not last but were happy that a compromise was reached even if it was just a temporary one.

Donna got in the habit of planning an outing in the afternoon so she could take Tommy with her while the two other children were with their friends. She was shocked at how poorly behaved he was when they went into a store. He touched everything on the shelves and would not listen to her at all. One store owner even asked her to please leave because they were certain he would break things on display. That night she called Tom.

"Have you ever taken Tommy to a store?"

"Why would I do that?"

"I think you should and you should see how he misbehaves. The toy store in town actually asked us to leave because your son was such a monster."

"Now he's my son and I suppose you are Mother Superior."

"Knock it off. This kid needs help and you are the one refusing to give him what he needs."

"That boy needs quality time from his parents; something he never had from you. Maybe if you were not so interested in sucking your boss and you spent more time with your son, he would be better behaved. If anyone is to blame, it's you. You thought nothing about turning him over to a strange nanny so you could do your own thing."

"You forget, you were fine with the nanny as long as I was bringing home the big bucks."

"There is no point to this. I am more than willing to do things with Tommy and I am sure he will be just fine. There is nothing wrong with the boy."

"You are an ass and have always been an ass." With that Donna slammed down the phone. There was no point trying to reach that stubborn ass. Maybe it was time to consult with her attorney and have a petition submitted to the court. The school psychologist would probably be happy to submit papers delineating what type of help the child needs. Tom would have to comply if he is ordered to do so by the court. This was something she had reservations about doing. She never wanted the child labeled at school but it was clear that something had to be done and had to be done quickly.

When Vicki came home from work she was immediately aware that there was a problem. Donna was agitated and Tommy was even more hyperactive than usual. Joseph and Patricia were in the basement pretending to be busy on the computer. Neither was willing to make eye contact with her.

"Ok- what's up?"

"It's been a bad day and I am very upset."

"No kidding- that's obvious. Can we start somewhere so I can get a picture of what's going on? All the kids are really uptight and you are over the edge."

With that Donna poured her heart out and told Vicki all about the day and Tom's reaction.

"We all know that Tommy needs help. You do not even need an attorney to file a petition in family court here in Nassau County. You have enough legal experience to be able to write up the petition and present it with a statement from the school psychologist. It is hard to believe any judge would not recommend an evaluation, if nothing more."

"I know you are right. It's just that it hurts to have his father behave this way."

"Tom lives in never-never land. He did not see that you were having an affair and he cannot see that his son is less than perfect."

"But, you would think he would want to help the kid."

"If he doesn't see the problem, he doesn't see the need for help."

"I guess you are right. He's still an ass."

"Does that ass have the money for a shrink?"

"He has enough for that motorcycle of his and the boat and the new girlfriend."

"I got it. And you are just a little jealous."

"You are a tough crowd."

"I tell it like I see it. You forget I've been around the block a few times."

"George would never treat his son this way. If Joseph needed something, he would have it at any cost."

"Yeah- but if this were the case with Joseph, it would be my fault that he needs psych attention. Somehow, George would turn this around and make it a custody issue."

"Do you think Tom could do that?"

"Anything is possible. I think he is still hurting that you and Jason had it going for so long and he never suspected anything. You destroyed his perfect family and now you are saying his son is nuts."

"I see your point."

"If you open this can of worms, be prepared for them to all come out at you."

"What you are really saying, is to leave things alone."

"You could do what you can to try to help the kid. Maybe when things straighten out and you get a job, you could have him properly evaluated but my guess is that there is little anyone can do for him right now. He has to grow up some and then who knows what will be."

"It's easy for you to write the kid off. He's not your son."

"That's true but do you think he would be better off with his father than he is with you?"

"No, Tom is a direct line to drugs for the kid. He always used marijuana in the house and his friends are all big drinkers. I even worry when the kids stay at his place overnight. The only saving grace is that Patricia is a real tattle tale."

"Think about all sides of the situation before you take any action. That is my advice to you. Go take a ride to the beach or someplace.

I'll see to it that the kids have something to eat and get to bed at a reasonable time."

"Tommy is in a real bad mood. I doubt that you can handle him."

"I'll handle him better than you can. He knows he cannot play my fiddle the way he plays yours.

"Thanks, Vicki, I do need a break from all of this."

"Go!"

With that Vicki started yelling at the kids to get washed as they were all going for Pizza.

"Can I come too?" Tommy asked.

"Only if you know how to behave. No funny stuff or you come right home without dinner in your belly. Do you get it young man?"

"Promise-"

Vicki allowed Donna to leave by herself before she got all the kids into the car to head for Stella's Pizza, their favorite place. The guys there were wonderful and, somehow, they knew just how to help control the kids, even Tommy.

One could only imagine the shock Vicki had when they walked into the restaurant and saw George and his girlfriend sitting there having dinner. Of course, Joseph went over to his dad and Vicki had to control herself when the kid asked if he could sit with his dad for a while. There was no graceful way out for her, so Vicki went to a table at the opposite end of the restaurant with Tommy and Patricia.

"I wish my dad were here so I could sit with him," Tommy said, sounding almost pathetic.

"I know you miss being with your father and I am sure he misses you too. Now is the time to order and eat our dinner."

"I'm starving," Patricia piped in trying to help Vicki avoid a scene with her brother.

For Vicki, the stress was so thick she thought she could cut it with a knife. Leave it to George to make every situation worse for her, even if he wasn't trying to do so.

Joseph spent the whole time with his father while Vicki supervised the other children. The conversations were inane but through it all

Vicki kept a smile on her face. No way was she going to give George the impression that he had ruined her dinner nor was she going to acknowledge that Joseph appeared to prefer his father to her. Once back in the car, Vicki could not help but confront Joseph.

"You made me feel that you preferred you father to me at dinner and that made me very unhappy."

"You had Patricia and Tommy with you so I thought it was okay for me to be with Buddy."

"We wanted you with us as well."

"Sorry about that. I don't get as much time with Buddy now that Donna is at our house and I miss him."

"When you spend time with him, I do not interfere. His time is his time. Tonight was my time."

"Hey, Mom, it is not like I planned it. He was there. No biggie."

Vicki decided to drop the subject for now. Once she had Joseph alone, she would resume but something told her to let it go. That night when she again tried to talk to Joseph, he just exploded.

"I hate Donna and I hate living here. Sure, she is real nice when you are around but, let me tell you, when you are not here, it is very different. It's all about Patricia and Tommy. I just don't count. All she does is boss me around like I am their slave. I want to go back to being with my grandmother after school."

"That's not going to float my boat, young man. Maybe Donna is a little short tempered but you have to understand she has been very sick and probably does not feel well. I will talk to her."

"You are the one who doesn't understand. That bitch is using you."

"Watch your language."

"Watch my language, you ass. You watch what you are doing. Things were good before she came here and now everything sucks."

Vicki could feel that she was losing control of the entire situation. She decided it was time to end the conversation for now and give herself an opportunity to decide how she would proceed.

"Go to your room. You need to think about how you speak to

me before we continue. You will not and cannot curse at me. Am I making myself clear?"

"You cannot be arrested for prostitution and expect anyone to respect you. Am I making myself clear?"

"Where did you hear that?"

"You are really stupid. It was in the paper and everyone at school was talking about you. In what world do you live? Buddy has told me that if I am unhappy here, he will take the necessary steps to get the court to allow me to live with him."

"Now you are threatening me!"

"I just want to go back to the way things were before that bitch and her disgusting kids moved in here. Things were good then and now things are horrible and I hate it here."

"Joseph, please just go to your room. I cannot continue this right now," Vicki said as she stood there shaking. She knew she was losing control of the situation and of her son. He was all she had left and if she loses custody of him, she would have nothing to live for.

After Joseph left the room, she sank down into her bed and buried her face in her pillow. She did not want anyone to hear her sobs. She was not even aware that Donna had come into the room and was sitting next to her rubbing her back and trying to comfort her.

"All kids mouth off, it's part of growing up. You cannot take it so to heart."

"He hates you and he hates me. He is threatening to have George go for custody so he can get away from here."

"I am sorry if my being here is adding to the problem. I have sensed that he resents me and the kids. Believe me, I am trying to do everything possible to get him to like us," Donna said as she took Vicki into her arms and held her like a child. Normally, Vicki would have pulled away but in an odd way she liked the comfort and the physical contact. It had been too long since anyone had held her. That night the two women stayed together and Donna held Vicki all night. In the morning Vicki felt ready to confront Joseph and to try to establish a plan of action.

"I've thought about our conversation and I am very distressed over it."

"So am I. I am sorry I yelled at you. Just for the record, I do love you. I just want my life to go back to the way it was before. I want to spend time with Buddy and his parents when you are not home. When you are home, I want us to spend time alone together."

"I hear you loud and clear. I just don't want your father to think he can get custody of you because I have to be at work all day."

"That's not the issue and you know it. You are jealous of the time Buddy and I spend together. You cannot decide for me as to who I love and who I don't."

"No one is telling you not to love your father. I just want you to feel close to me. I want you to love me."

"I love you but I don't even like Donna and those brats of hers. Will you let me be with Grandma until you come home or not?"

"Do whatever you want. Just make sure you are here when I come home."

"Call me from the train and I will be here, no problem. Just one more thing. I want a lock for my room. I don't want Tommy touching and breaking my things. I am tired of hearing how sharing is important. I am sharing the house, I don't want to share my things."

"I get it and I do understand. We will lock your room when you are not here if that makes you feel better."

"Thanks, Mom, I am sorry that I yelled at you. Hopefully things will be better now."

"Hopefully," Vicki said without much conviction. She knew she had lost a major battle but at least she had not lost the entire war, so to speak.

"One more thing," she said as Joseph was turning his back on her, "those charges you talked about last night are totally false and are being dropped. I may have my faults, but I am not a prostitute and don't you ever call me that again."

With that Joseph grabbed his school backpack and started out the door.

"Remember, call me from the train and I will be here when you get home."

Vicki knew she had to hurry to make her train or she would be late for work, something that was frowned upon and, right now, she did not need any more confrontations. While she still hated the job, it was paying her expenses and there were not a lot of jobs out there, what with the bad economy and places cutting back on employees. Having a job was a good thing.

Vicki completed her morning routine in a robotic trance. She could not stop thinking about how Joseph had spoken to her. She had always refrained from speaking poorly about George and now it was obvious that he and/or his mother was not adhering to the same code. If she insisted that Joseph stop spending time with his grandmother, it would backfire on her and only make him turn more towards them and away from her. That much was clear to her but just how she would proceed was still an unanswered question. Clearly having Donna and her children in the house was adding to the stress. There, again, she did not know how to handle the situation. It would be hard to make Donna move until she could get a job.

Vicki did not realize how deep in thought she was until the man seating next to her on the train started speaking to her.

"I do not mean to intrude, but you do realize you are crying. Is there anything I can do to help you?"

"What?"

"You are sitting here with tears rolling down your checks. I, for one, am a sucker whenever a woman is crying. By the way, my name is Mort Green and I live here in Merrick. I usually see you on this train and I have always noticed what a beautiful woman you are."

"Thank you, Mr. Green, but obviously my mind is consumed at the present moment and I am not in the mood for idle talk."

"Sometimes idle talk helps a person to see more clearly. Why don't you tell me why you are so unhappy? I am a perfect stranger, so talking to me will have no impact on you."

Vicki could not help herself but to smile.

"See you feel better already."

"I guess I do. Thank you for trying to help."

"I don't know where you work but you cannot go to the office with those tear streaks running down your face."

With that, Vicki pulled out her compact and started adjusting her makeup. Mr. Green was absolutely right. She could not go to the office looking like she was and she needed to pull herself together.

"Thank you for your kindness. You are right I need to get it together and not let myself collapse.

"Here is my card. If you ever want to just get a cup of coffee and talk, I can rearrange my schedule and I will be happy to meet you wherever."

Vicki took the card and looked at it.

"Holy shit, you're a shrink."

"I am a professor of psychology, not a shrink, as you call it. However, I can see when a person needs some help. You, young lady, are crying out for help."

"I don't know if I am crying out for help or just crying because I am hurt."

"That could be determined."

With that the train passed through the tunnel entering Penn Station. Vicki gathered her things and put out her hand to Mr. Green.

"Thank you for talking to me. I owe you one."

"I would really like to meet you for coffee or dinner, whatever is your choice."

"Who knows, stranger things have happened."

"It's your call. I do hope the rest of your day is better than what has come before."

"It will be, thanks to you."

As Vicki left the train she watched as Mr. Green walked to the downtown exit before she turned to go uptown. He was an interesting man even if he looked somewhat geeky. There was a kindness about him that she was not accustomed to. She put his card in her wallet and decided to watch for him on future morning commutes; after all he did say he had seen her on the train before today. One thing was for sure; she was not about to rush into anything right now. The last thing she needed was to further complicate her life.

To her surprise her day went by smoothly. She found that she was able to concentrate on the tasks in front of her and not allow her mind to dwell on Joseph until she was on the train heading back to Massapequa. As she had promised, she called Joseph on his cell to tell him she would be at the Massapequa station at seven. Her plan was to take him to dinner so that they could have some quality time alone.

"Be ready to go to dinner," she said when he answered.

"I already ate. Grandma made some great meatballs and pasta. I figured that would be a marked improvement over the slop Donna makes."

"I am disappointed because I was planning to go out with you so we could have some time alone."

"I am sure there are some leftovers here. I will bring some home for you and we can sit together while you are eating."

"Please make sure you are home when I get there. I really do not want to call you again."

"I'll be there and just so you know, I had a really nice afternoon with Nona and Nono. They missed me as much I missed them and they said to tell you "thank you.""

"Is that them or you saying thank you?"

"No really, they told me to tell you that."

"See you soon and I love you."

"Love you too. Tomorrow we can plan to go out for dinner if you want to."

"I'd like that. Let's plan on it."

Joseph was at the house when she arrived and they went directly to Vicki's room where she did eat the leftovers and had to say, she really enjoyed them. They talked about his day at school and the upcoming hockey game but stayed away from the previous night though there was an underlying tension between them. Both of them feared the other was going to bring up the topic and neither wanted to pursue it. Finally it was ten o'clock and Joseph wanted to get to bed.

"All my homework is done. I did it at Nona's where it is much quieter than it is here, and I did it in half the time it would have taken me to do it here."

"Good but please understand, you can always use my room to do your homework. Just come in here and lock the door. No one will bother you here and if they do, I will take care of it. Do we understand each other? I just think it is nice if the homework is done before I get home, so we can have some time together."

"I do too, and I will try my best to do it as long as I do not have a big test the next day."

"Got you!"

With that Vicki walked over to him and gave him a big hug and kiss on the cheek. She really wanted to hold him forever and thought about how nice it would be to cuddle with him in her bed. Those days were done and she just had to get it through her head that her little boy was growing up and had a mind of his own.

"I'll come tuck you in, in a few minutes."

"That's alright, Mom, you don't have to do that."

"I know I don't have to do it, but I want to. No matter how old you are, you will always be my boy. Remember that, please."

"Got it."

When Joseph left the room, Vicki sat looking at the closed door. All she could think was that yesterday he had been a little boy and tonight, he seemed so grown up. It was incredible how fast it had all happened or was she so consumed with her own life, that she did not notice the changes before this? One thing she knew for sure; she was not going to waste whatever years were left. In four years he would be off to college and that definitely would be the beginning of the end.

As she walked down the hall to Joseph's room, she could hear Donna yelling at Tommy to get ready for bed. No matter what you wanted that child to do, it was always a fight. Hopefully, they would be able to end the living arrangements sooner rather than later.

She quietly entered Joseph's room and bent over his bed to give him a good-night kiss.

"Thanks, Mom. Just do me a favor and lock the door on the way out. I do not like it when Tommy barges in during the night."

"Can't say I blame you. Good night."

Vicki went down to the kitchen to take her dirty plates to the dishwasher, and was surprised to see Donna sitting at the kitchen table.

"I stayed away from you tonight. I thought you needed some alone time."

"You thought right. Joseph misses being alone with me and we have decided to carve out some quality time each night when I get home from work. I hope you understand."

"Of course I understand. I will leave your dinners on the stove and you can eat whenever you want."

"Thanks and by the way, we will be going out for dinner tomorrow; so don't prepare anything for us."

Donna could feel the coldness emanating from Vicki. Things were not working out well and there was no doubt about it. Unfortunately, there was little she could do about it right now. She still needed some time, a job and a way to get her own life back on track.

Once all the children were asleep, Donna decided to go into Vicki's room and to creep into her bed, just as she did the night before. She was sure the physical touching would be a comfort to both of them.

"What the hell are you doing here?" Vicki yelled as soon as she became aware of Donna's being.

"I thought it would be a comfort to you if we held each other like we did last night. You know another woman knows just how to please you. A woman's touch is gentle, slow and caring."

"Last night is a world away. Neither of us needs to be accused of being a lesbo. You stay in your room and I'll stay in mine and if that does not work for you, you had better get the hell out of this house."

"Don't get so excited. All the kids are sound asleep. I could make you feel really good; get it through your thick head."

"The walls have ears and the ears have tongues. I have no interest in what you are offering. Am I making myself perfectly clear?"

"I just thought that since neither of us has a man we could enjoy what is available now."

"Go enjoy by yourself! Leave me alone."

With that Donna walked out of the room. Once alone, Vicki could only think that maybe in a different time or place, she might have taken advantage of Donna's offer but now the stakes were too high. She could only imagine the horror Joseph would feel if he wandered into her room and found Donna in her bed.

CHAPTER THIRTY TWO

D onna spent a fitful night. She was extremely disappointed that Vicki refused her advances. That would have been her guarantee to keep herself and the children in the house. It did not take much to notice that Vicki and Joseph were getting disturbed by their presence and she really expected to be asked to leave. If that were to happen it would put her in a very difficult position. Her house was rented out and the people had insisted upon a year's lease. Her mother wanted no part of them and Tommy now had a new girlfriend. He would take the children but that would still leave her homeless and even more desperate. Had Vicki taken her up on her offer, she would have been able to blackmail her into allowing them to stay. There would have been no way that she would have wanted George to find out about their relationship because he certainly would go for full custody and probably would be able to insist that the living conditions had a negative influence on Joseph. Now she could not even fabricate a relationship as Vicki was locking her door, and Joseph knew it and would state that Vicki was indeed alone in her room.

Donna knew she had to do something immediately. Just what, was the question. She took a good look at herself and closely examined the stubble that was now her hair. Up to now she had only wet it down and plastered it to her head. Maybe it was long enough to be styled. That definitely would improve her appearance. With that decision made, she went into her file and looked for the number of the beauty salons that the cancer center had recommended and she called the closest one. She had enough of her child support money left to cover the expense; so she was good to go.

The afternoon at the salon was a life renewing experience. When Donna left there, she felt and looked like a new woman. The pixie style was surprisingly flattering and the salon even gave her a complimentary makeup session. The gray look and sunken eyes were gone. They even taught her how to do the makeup herself.

Next on her agenda was a job. A law firm was out of the question as the local community all knew about her and there would not be anyone willing to take the chance to hire her. She decided to look for a job as an office manager in the medical field. With some luck and some compassion she might be hired without checking her references too closely. Most of the offices she had been to as a patient had told her they often hired without checking as long as the vibes were there.

She decided to start by calling all of her doctors to see if any were looking for an office manager. After all, she now had the experience and compassion to deal with cancer patients and she could give them the encouragement to think they would recover as she had. She also decided to look on Monster.com and actually submitted her resume to several offices that had jobs posted. It was amazing how alive she felt for the first time in months.

Her next call was to Jason's private line.

"Look, I need a favor," she said when he answered. "I need you to give me a decent reference if a prospective employer calls you. You could say I left the firm because of illness or whatever."

"Donna, don't worry. I will give you an excellent reference but I strongly recommend not using the illness excuse. People are afraid to hire someone who has a history of cancer as they worry about a recurrence and having the person out of work."

"I get it. What do you recommend we say as to why I left the firm?"

"Just say personal reasons and I will say the same thing. If pressured, we can always say that you needed time to resolve your divorce issues, and that they are totally resolved now."

"You are so smart. Thanks for the help."

"You know I will always help you and care about you."

"I feel the same about you but we both know we cannot pick it up where we left off."

"Michelle would kill me, or worse divorce me and that would not leave me in a good financial place."

"Believe me; I get it. Add that to the fact that you would never completely trust me and we would have a recipe for disaster."

"Yeah; it's too bad we screwed up a good thing."

"Thanks for the help. I will keep in touch and let you know if I actually get a job."

"Good luck with that, and if you need anything in the meantime let me know."

"Thanks. You have been more than generous."

"Hey, before you hang up. Is it true that you are living with that bitch, Vicki?"

"Yeah- believe it or not, she offered to let us live in her house so I could rent out mine and use the money for living expenses. It has not been so bad since she is gone all day but I think her patience is wearing thin. Tommy is a real problem and he has annoyed her and Joseph. So, I am thinking that I had better get a job and a place of my own before she throws us out and we are homeless."

"I would never have given her credit to be so generous in the first place."

"She thought it would help her as well. I am actually doing the cooking and cleaning; so it does help her as well."

"I fail to picture you as Miss Domesticity."

"Me too. It's a real rip when you think about it.But you got to do what you got to do to survive."

"Keep me in the loop."

"Sure thing, and thanks again for the help."

Now, Donna was really excited. With Jason in her corner, she felt confident she would get a job and if not, he would help her if things really went south. Putting the phone down, Donna could not keep herself from going to the mirror in her bedroom. Looking at herself, she was amazed by the transformation. For years before getting sick, she had worn her hair blond and straight and very long. The pixi haircut looked whimsical and actually framed her face in such a way that her face looked fuller. Of course seeing her natural brown color was shocking especially since there was so much gray intermixed with the brown. The salon said her hair could not withstand a dye job at this time so grayish brown hair was better than none at all. The other major change was to her figure. She was really thin and since her implants were removed, she looked flat-chested. On the flip side, she thought that in a suit she would look very professional at a job interview which could work in her favor especially if the interviewer was a woman. She was excited to start the new chapter in her life and even more excited at the thought of being able to live on her own.

Donna knew she looked really good when Vicki came home. Her initial reaction was one of shock. Vicki just did not know what to say as the lady standing in front of her was nothing like the woman she left that morning. Even the children remarked at how nice she looked. Donna knew she was finally on the road to recovery and she was excited at the prospect. Now all she needed was a job, a home and a man and she just knew she would get all three.

The next morning there were several responses to her resume. She scheduled interviews for office manager positions at several medical offices on the island and at one legal firm in the city. She really did not want to have to commute but she figured there was no harm in interviewing, especially since the legal field was something she had experience in. She did not and would not apply for any job on the island in the legal field but the city was different as she knew because of Vicki's experience. It was totally shocking to her that most of the places were offering between fifty and sixty thousand a year when she was earning over a hundred grand at Gordons. That was depressing but she knew she would take it if only to get her resume updated. Besides fifty or sixty thousand was definitely better than nothing.

The interviews went well and most of the places seemed to ignore the gap in her employment history. Only the oncology office asked her if she had been ill and what her health status was. She answered honestly and added that her experience would actually be a benefit to their office as she understood how the patient feels and what the patient's needs were. She also said she would not mind discussing her condition as it could give others the hope of recovery and return to a full life after the cancer diagnosis. Her initial feeling was positive after the interview concluded and she knew she would accept the position should it be offered to her. The office was thirty to forty five minutes from Massapequa and it appeared to be busy with a very pleasant staff. The position was for a front desk manager who would work under the office manager but who would still have autonomy while not having to have the pressure of running the entire office with its large staff of women and five doctors. She viewed it as a good way to break into the medical field. The best was that the hours were from eight to four which meant she could be home in time for the children and not have to pay a sitter. After all Patricia was old enough to watch Tommy for a short time after school or she could have him in the latch key program which would keep him at school until four thirty which would mean the bus would drop him off close to five. This was a new experience for Donna as she never had to worry about who was with the children as the nanny was always there.

It took two weeks for the call to finally come and when it came, Donna could not hide her excitement. She told Pat, the office manager, that she was thrilled to take the job and she promised she would do everything in her power to make Pat know she had made the correct choice. It was Wednesday when the call came in and Pat asked her to report to work on Monday. That was great. It gave her some time to go shopping for a new wardrobe. Everything she had was too big on her. Luckily, she had been saving Macy's twenty per cent off coupons; so she decided that was as good a place to start as any. Formerly she bought her clothing at Ann Taylor but the prices there were more and she wanted to be able to pay off the credit card bill entirely once she received her first paycheck. No more partial payoffs and no more debt; that was her motto going forward.

She was excited to share her good news with the children and with Vicki who she knew would view the job as the first step toward liberation. There was no doubt in her mind that Vicki was anxious to have her move out, and lately, she too wanted a place of her own where she could be more relaxed when Tommy did something wrong. It was nerve racking always worrying that he would break something that Vicki or Joseph treasured. It seems as though whatever he damaged, was something they treasured. The reception to her news was exactly what she expected. Even Patricia was excited at the idea of them having their own home.

At ten the next morning, Donna was at Macy's prepared to complete her shopping. She bought three suits and six tops that all could be interchanged so she would be able to create different outfits. Shoes and a new handbag completed the outerwear. The underwear was a totally different challenge. The bras all looked like granny bras because she had been warned not to wear any with underwires. It was really hard to think of sexy panties with ugly bras.

"Oh well, nobody is going to see the underwear anyway," she said to herself as she put her selections on the cashier's table.

"Did you see the display over there with the uplifting bras?" the cashier asked as she prepared to scan Donna's selections.

"I did and I wish I could wear them but I have to stay away from the underwire."

"Oh, I understand. Please excuse me for interfering."

"It's okay. I am coming back and that's what's important."

"Good luck to you. We see too many women who have had a problem."

"I know that I am not alone but when it happens to you, the percentages go out the window and it is a hundred percent for you. But that is in the past. Thank you for your understanding and help," Donna said as she gathered her purchases.

It was a feel good moment as she exited the store. She had accomplished everything she set out to do. She had the new makeup routine down so she was confident that she would be able to look her best come Monday morning. She decided to make Friday a rest day for herself and then on Saturday and Sunday she could give the children some extra attention. It worked out really well that she had them this weekend and Tom would have them the next weekend when she probably would be tired after her first week at work.

Monday came and went in a blur. The office was really busy with the phones ringing and patients constantly asking questions. The time just flew by and Donna had to admit, she was tired when four o'clock rolled around.

"Don't worry, tomorrow will be easier and then it is all downhill from there," her co-worker told her. "When I first started, I thought I would quit at the end of the first day; but jobs are scarce out there and there is no denying that they pay well here."

"Thanks for the encouragement. The pace here is definitely more than a busy law firm. There most of the clients conduct their business over the phone. I am not used to having over one hundred people pass through an office in one day."

"Yeah- it's crazy. But it works with the five doctors working on the same day. Everyone actually gets good care here and they really help the people."

"I can see that. It must be hard when you lose the battle for someone."

"I try very hard not to get too personal with the patients. It's my wall of self-protection."

"But you are so nice to everyone."

"I can be nice but still keep some distance. If you noticed, my talk is always small talk and I never ask how anyone is feeling. I don't want to discuss their family or any personal details."

"Come to think about it, my doctor's staff was very similar. They never asked about my children or anything like that. I never gave that a thought before. Thanks for the advice. I will try to keep my distance as well. The only problem for me will be if it is a kid with cancer. That is very upsetting to me."

"Give that case to someone who has been here longer and who has developed a harder shell. You will not help the patient if you show you are upset. That says the patient is in real trouble. Get it?"

"Got it and thanks again."

On her way home, Donna kept running the conversation through her mind. There was no doubt that Susan was right. Hopefully, she would be able to mimic her when she had to deal with the patients.

It hit her as she was getting off the Southern State to go to the Seaford Oyster Bay Expressway; she felt totally different. All at once she felt empowered and confident much like she had felt when she was working at Jason's firm. Having a job meant her independence was returning and with that her life as she had always known it was possibly returning as well. Donna was confident she would be able to move to a place of her own; maybe she would actually be back in her own house in Oceanside as soon as the tenant's lease was over. She knew she would keep the one tenant in the smaller apartment and that would help defray her costs and still not interfere with her. It would be wonderful to be able to sit on the deck and overlook the canal. Thinking about it made her realize just how much she missed the house. Hopefully, the tenant would not leave it in shambles. She had always heard horror stories about rentals; but whatever it is going to be, it will be better than what she now has.

It proved to be an easy trip home from the office and Donna actually arrived just a few minutes after Tommy got home. Of course, he and Patricia were in a heated argument when she walked in the door but it was really over nothing and dissipated as soon as she said hello.

"How was school today?"

"I hate it," replied Tommy. "All my friends leave on the three o'clock bus and I have to stay until four. It's not fair!"

"Too bad! Get used to it. We have no choices in this matter. I have to go to work and I cannot get home any earlier than today. You cannot stay alone for two hours and Patricia cannot be responsible for you for that long a period of time. Maybe if you start to behave better, we can consider making a change."

"I promise I can behave."

"Yeah, I heard how well you were behaving when I came in the door."

"I promise."

"Promises have been made and broken in the past. You need to show me you know how to behave before I will consider changing anything. Now let's start getting dinner made."

With that Tommy ran from the kitchen and went to his room where Donna could hear him throwing things around. She considered going up there to yell at him but then decided not to acknowledge his rage. If he busted things that would be his problem and, just maybe, he would get the message if she did not replace anything.

"Now you see what I am up against with him," Patricia said as she entered the kitchen.

"I know and don't think for a moment I do not appreciate you watching him until I get home. Just keep thinking this is our ticket to get back in our own house."

"I don't mind for a short time like today but if he gets home at three thirty, it could be a real problem."

"Don't even think about it. He will have to stay on the late bus, but there is no point in telling him that at this moment in time. Maybe if he thinks things will change if he behaves, he might actually try to be good, though I doubt he can judging by what is going on right now."

"I just hope he is not breaking anything of mine or of Joseph's. Can you imagine how angry Joseph will be if he comes home and finds his stuff smashed?'

"Yeah- we could end up homeless. I guess I had better go and check on our demon."

With that Donna quietly went upstairs and looked in on Tommy. His entire room was a disaster zone but the damage was confined to his area. For once she was grateful that Joseph had insisted on a lock for his room.

"Now that you have made such a mess of things, I strongly suggest you start cleaning it up before dinner."

"You do it."

"Oh no, young man! I did not make the mess and I will not clean it up. If you want dinner you had better get started."

"I am calling my father and telling him what you are doing to me."

"I don't care who you call. You need to start to control yourself."

With that Donna turned her back on him and walked back downstairs leaving him standing in the middle of the mess he created with tears running down his face. There had been a time when she would have gone to him and hugged him to let him know she loved him no matter what; but not today. If big Tommy was unwilling to get professional help for his son, she had to do whatever she could to help him learn some self-control. Tough love could be a good thing.

Tommy was still in his room when Vicki came home with Joseph not far behind her. Vicki was appalled by the mess in Tommy's room where she saw him sleeping on a pile of broken toys.

"You know he is sound asleep on the floor," she said as she was about to sit down for dinner.

"I told him not to leave his room until he cleaned up the mess he made and I guess he exhausted himself with his temper tantrum."

"At least we can all have a quiet dinner." Joseph chimed in to the conversation.

Everyone contributed information about the day as they ate the pasta Donna had prepared. It was remarkable how pleasant the conversation was without Tommy interrupting and they all really enjoyed each other's company.

The next morning, Donna got Tommy up for school at the usual time. The room was still a mess and she decided to leave it that way.

"When you come home this afternoon, you are to go directly to your room and start the clean-up. You will have to stay in your room without television privileges or computer time until this room is cleaned up. Am I making myself perfectly clear?"

"What about when I am supposed to go to dad's?"

"You are grounded and that includes going to your father's house until this place is back in order. I already told him about your temper tantrum and he is in complete agreement."

"You're mean."

"You have no clue as to how mean I can be. Get your act together and get it together fast. Now get your butt out there for the school bus or you will have a long walk to school today."

Donna's second day at the office went extremely well. She found that the other ladies were all very receptive to suggestions and they all seemed friendly towards her. Even the doctors seemed to notice her and each gave her some encouragement. Compared to the turmoil at home, the office was offering her a zone of tranquility and the work was certainly not that complicated or demanding.

Donna was shocked when she got home. Tommy was actually in his room cleaning up.

"How did this happen?" she asked Patricia.

"He really wants to watch Survivor tonight and I told him to forget it unless the room was cleaned; just like you said to tell him. So, he went upstairs."

"Good job. He needs to know I mean business."

"Thanks, Mom."

That night when Tommy came down for dinner, everyone behaved as though nothing had happened. He sheepishly took his usual seat at the table and even tried to be a part of the conversations going on. For Donna this was a victory, and she savored the moment.

Vicki was the one to change the mood at dinner.

"Believe it or not, I have a date for Saturday night."

"A date with a man?" Joseph asked.

"Yep- a date with a very nice man whom I met on the train. He lives right in Merrick. I didn't think it was important to clear it with you as you are going to be with Buddy this weekend."

"When have you ever cleared your dates with me?"

"Come on, Joseph, it's been a long time since I've had a date with a really nice man. I thought you would be happy for me."

"Mom, just be careful. Things are good right now and we don't need any trouble."

"You are starting to sound like Larry. It's just a date. We are going to go for dinner and I will be home early. I promise to call you when I get home. Does that make you feel better?"

"How do I know where you are calling me from?"

"Now you sound like your father. Let's drop this topic."

After dinner it was Donna who came at Vicki with what seemed like a hundred questions. Vicki wanted to just let her know it was none of her business but decided to keep the conversation on a pleasant level. She told her how she had met Mort Green and how the guy had helped her when she was so upset about Joseph.

"This is a really nice guy and we are just going on a date without a motel reservation. Get it? Now let's drop it. I am sorry I shared my news with everyone. I should have just gone on the date and not said anything."

"Well, I guess I am on my own for Saturday night. Do you realize this is the first time since we moved in that you and I are not spending Saturday night together when the kids are gone?"

"Am I supposed to feel guilty about that?"

"No, not all. I would do the same thing if I had a date."

With that Vicki left the room to go up to spend some time with Joseph. This had become their nightly routine and they were both enjoying the time together.

"Sorry, Mom, I didn't mean to come down on you about your date. I am just afraid that things will change around here again. Every time you meet a new guy, things change and you are never here. I kind-a like having time alone with you."

"I like it too. Let's just take things as they come. I am just going on a date; I am not moving in with the guy or anything like that. I even planned the date for the weekend you are away. But, you can do me one favor. Please don't tell your father about my having a date. I really don't think it is his business and I don't need to be hassled by him."

"Okay! I don't get it; but okay."

All day Saturday, Vicki was surprised at how nervous she really was. She had her hair professionally blown out and even purchased a new dress. She wanted to look spectacular in a conservative way. No raw sex appeal; no flashy clothes. She actually had kept herself so busy all day that seven o'clock snuck up on her and she found herself rushing to be ready when Mort was supposed to pick her up at seven thirty.

He was prompt, just a she expected and she decided to meet him at his car instead of having him come into the house where he would have had to be introduced to Donna. In her mind, it was just better to avoid that. Donna had been a pain in the neck while she was getting dressed. She was hovering over her like a mother getting her daughter ready for her first date.

Once in the car, Mort told her that they would be going to Freeport for dinner on the Nautical Mile.

"One of my favorite restaurants is the Nautilus Café. It is amazing that no matter how many times I go there, the food is the same. I like that in a restaurant because if I reorder something it is because I liked it the first time and I want it to taste the same the second time."

"I have never eaten there. So this is going to be fun for me. I love going to new places and experiencing new things."

"Did you tell your son about our date?"

"I did and at first he was not happy about it. He desperately wants things to stay status quo. Unfortunately, in the past, I would neglect Joseph when I was in a relationship. Now he is still challenged by having Donna and her kids in the house and he does not want me to be an absentee mother."

"I can understand his feelings. How much longer do you expect Donna to have to remain?"

"Now she has a job so hopefully, she will be able to afford a place of her own really soon. I know she wants to move back into her house in Oceanside once the tenant's lease is up, but, I am hoping she will rent someplace until then. To be very honest, her moving into my house was a colossal mistake."

"Does she feel the same way?"

"I don't know nor do I care. I have made my feelings evident and hopefully she will move out before I need to tell her to. She and

Patricia have not been the real problems. It's Tommy who is driving everyone crazy. But now, I am getting tired of Donna as well. She is rather controlling and I hate to be controlled. Would you believe, she actually propositioned me to have a lesbian relationship with her?"

"She is probably a very lonely person and is looking for some physical contact to make herself feel better."

"Yeah, but it is really that she is afraid of a relationship with a guy who might be turned off by her scars and all that stuff."

With that being said, they pulled up to the restaurant where the valet was ready to take their car. Waking in, Vicki was totally surprised that the hostess actually knew Mort's name. This was a new experience for her as her dates usually made it a point to take her to places where they were not known.

"You look surprised. I told you this is one of my favorite places."

"Are you married?"

"I was for a long time. We divorced five years ago but we have a good relationship for the sake of the children. We share custody in a loose fashion since the kids are all teenagers and have lives of their own. I usually have dinner with them at least twice a week even if they are busy on the weekends."

"I had thought that George and I had a good relationship but lately we seem to constantly argue and challenge each other for Joseph's attention. He has really changed since he met his current girlfriend and I guess I didn't help matters with some of my relationships."

"I am sure that Joseph is well adapted to using that situation to get whatever he wants from both of you."

"This is beginning to sound like a therapy session. Please tell me more about you."

Mort was an easy talker who did not refrain from revealing details about his life. He had been married for twenty five years and had three children. During his marriage, he said, he devoted more of his time to his career and less toward keeping his marriage alive. He was shocked, never the less, when his ex told him she wanted out and that she had met someone else. That was five years ago and they both have managed to go on with their own lives; something he initially had thought would be impossible.

"Have you had many women during the past five years?"

"Not really. Some of my friends tried to set me up but nothing came of those dates."

"What is it that you want in a woman?"

"I am not sure I can put it into words. I think I want someone who is independent and fun to be with. I have learned that I can take care of myself and I really don't want to have to take care of another person."

"I can understand that. I always thought I needed a man to take care of me, but I am learning that is not the case."

Dinner came and went by so fast that Vicki could not even remember eating her food. She was intrigued by this man who loved boating and fishing and traveling. The theater, the movies and concerts were all part of his world and he really enjoyed telling her about his various trips and experiences.

As they left the restaurant, Mort's car was waiting for them. Once in the car, Vicki was surprised that there was no invitation to go back to his place or any other place for that matter. He drove her home and as he pulled up in front of her house, he made no move to kiss her or anything. Vicki immediately figured that the date had been a bust and she would never see him again. She was surprised at the level of her disappointment as she exited the car.

"Good night and thanks for the dinner," she said as she leaned into the open door.

"Thank you, I really enjoyed the company and I hope we can see each other again."

"Of course, just say when and I'll be there," Vicki replied trying to keep her excitement at bay.

"Can we aim for next Saturday or will that interfere with your time with Joseph?"

"Next Saturday it is. Joseph is always happy to be with his grandparents if his dad is busy. He and I can spend the day together and he will not mind my going out for dinner."

"Next Saturday at eight it is then. I'll pick you up."

"I'll look forward to it and thanks again for a fun evening," Vicki said as she turned to walk up the path to her front door. All she could think was that he was one very different guy. One minute she is thinking the date was a total bust and the next minute she is looking forward to seeing him in a week. No touching, no kiss, no nothing just talk; Vicki could not remember the last time she had a date like that.

Donna almost scared her as she entered the house. She never expected to find her watching from the window and she almost jumped as she opened the door and saw her standing there in the dark.

"What's going on with you? You know you are not my mother waiting for me to come home from a date."

"I'm sorry I startled you. I heard the car pull up and I was somewhat surprised to see you coming so early. I just wanted to make sure you were all right."

"I am fine. And, yes, I had a really nice time with a really nice man. There- does that answer your questions?"

With that, Vicki walked passed Donna and went directly to her own room. She wanted no more conversation. If Donna was jealous of her, too bad. She knew that Donna would never include her in anything if she were the one who had a date nor would she worry about what she would be doing. There is a time when it is every girl for herself and this was going to be Vicki's time. She just knew this was going to be a lasting relationship and she was not about to let Donna or anyone destroy it for her. She also decided that she would be the one to initiate a more physical relationship. Mort gave her the impression that he wanted to do everything the "right way" but she knew that if they were going to have a real relationship, she had to make him physically desire her. Men could be manipulated if the right head was properly manipulated and that was something she was definitely good at doing.

The week passed quickly and without any unnecessary drama at home. Things were improved since Donna had her job and everyone seemed to enjoy the relaxation of the tension in the house. Saturday night came and Vicki asked Joseph if he wanted to stay home with Donna and the kids or spend the night with his grandparents. It did not take but a moment for him to select being with his grandparents who were overjoyed to have him to themselves for the night. Vicki then selected a sexy black dress which showed off her boobs just enough to make it interesting to look at. Of course, she was ready before the eight o'clock time and she went out to meet Mort just as he pulled up to the house. There was no point in having him come to the door and having to introduce Donna and her children to him.

This time they went to the Sage Bistro in Bellmore, another of Mort's favorite restaurants. Again he was greeted like a long lost friend by the owner and staff and they were given a corner table where they could talk. It was a perfect dinner and when it was about to end, Vicki suggested that they were not far from the Gateway Motel where they could get a room and have a nightcap.

"We don't have to go to the motel. My house is not far from here, we can go there instead. I am much more comfortable doing that than going to the Gateway."

"Sounds like a call to me. I really don't want this night to end and I do not have to be home until the morning."

She was totally surprised by the house when they pulled into the driveway. He lived on the water and the house seemed enormous for just one man to live in.

"This was my house when I was married and my ex did not want to keep it, so I bought her out. It really is very comfortable and it's great when the children come because they view it as their home."

"All I can say is Whoa! This is a really cool house."

"Wait until you see the inside. It is a comfortable house not a show place. Everyone who comes here says it is a great place to kick off your shoes and relax."

"Let's see if I agree."

So began an interesting night. Mort had never been with anyone as sexually uninhibited as Vicki. She was amazing and knew just how to arouse him even when he thought he was totally finished. When he finally begged for mercy, they both fell soundly asleep; a sleep like none he had ever had before. The next morning he awoke to the smell of coffee and bacon.

"Why are you making breakfast? We could go out to eat."

"I thought it would be nice to have something together and then you can drive me home. I don't have time for the restaurant thing as Joseph will be coming home and then we are going to his hockey game. I hope you enjoyed last night as much as I did."

"That is putting it mildly. I can't wait for a repeat performance."

"Any time you want. I enjoyed it too."

With that she knew she had him and this relationship was going to be a good one.

Vicki was on a real high when she walked into her house only to be shocked by Donna's greeting.

"Where were you last night? Don't you think you should have called and let me know you were going to be out all night? I was worried sick."

"You are sick. Did you forget that you are not my mother and that I am an adult? I really don't get this, at all."

"We live together and people who live together need to keep each other informed as to their whereabouts."

"Hopefully, we will not be living together too much longer because I really can't take this nonsense. As long as you continue to live here, please don't worry about me. I can take care of myself and the last thing I need is another mother. Now if you will excuse me, I have to grab a fast shower and get ready to pick up Joseph so we can go to his hockey game."

"Joseph called before and I told him you were not home."

"What else did you tell him?"

"Nothing- only that I would tell you to call him as soon as you came home."

"Great! This is just the icing on the cake for me. In the future, please do not answer my home phone. You have your cell for your calls and I can deal with mine on my own terms. I don't need a secretary and I definitely don't need someone reporting to my son. Am I making myself clear?"

"Clear as mud!

With that Vicki stormed passed Donna and went directly to her room. She called Joseph on his cell and wasn't at all surprised that he had a list of questions for her. She explained, as gently as she could, that she had spent the night with a friend and that she was still planning on picking him up to go to the game.

'Great Mom, is it all starting all over again? Are you going to be away more than you are home?"

"Joseph, I don't intend to live a life of a nun but I do promise I will always be here for you; nothing is going to change for us."

"Yeah, yeah, I've heard that before and then everything changes."

"Let's talk about this later. I will pick you up in a half hour so you can be on time for your practice before the game."

"You don't have to rush. Buddy said he could pick me up."

"Please call your father and tell him I am taking you to the game. It's my time with you. See you soon and remember I love you."

In the shower, Vicki could only think that every bit of happiness had to have a black hole for her. She knew there would be all sorts of questions from Joseph and George and somehow they would try to ruin things for her. If they had their way, she would live the life of a nun and that was not going to happen.

It was amazing when she picked up Joseph. Instead of the steady stream of questions she expected, he was only talkative about the upcoming game and how it was of the utmost importance that his team would be victorious.

"I am really happy I can come to the game today, particularly since it is so important to you."

"Yeah, I am happy too. It is always fun to have you there rooting for me. I guess that's why I hate it when you have a new relationship with someone I don't know. Then it always seems like you don't have time for me."

"Let's get this straight right now. I will always have time for you.

You are the center of my universe and no matter whom I see, when it's time for you, especially if it is something important, I'll be there."

"I'm glad. It's just that Buddy says you will be off and running again."

"Oh, so it is ok that he has a new girlfriend but I can't see anyone? Don't give me that sh--. He is just saying that to stir the pot and get you upset. Don't even think about it now. There are much more important things for you to think about- like this big game. By the way, is he going to be there today?"

"He did say he would come by but didn't give me a time or anything since I told him you would be taking me."

"It would be nice if he were to come since the game is so important to you."

"Yeah, I would like him to be there too. I just hope you will not be upset."

"No reason for me to be upset. He's your father and just because he and I are no longer an item, it doesn't mean we don't want what's best for you."

Joseph just smiled at that. He silently wondered where this was going and where it was coming from. He had never heard Vicki so open to allowing his father to be wherever she was. Usually when she took him to a game, she expected Buddy not to be there. He could not help but think she was up to something and that something would definitely affect him. But for now, he decided to drop the subject and just use the time to think about the game.

Vicki also decided to drop the conversation. She felt she had made her point and that Joseph understood. He was amazingly mature and had developed skills to balance his two lives even when they came together. Mort had told her this was common for children of divorce and that it was better to allow times when both parents could be there than to fight it and make the child feel nervous. He told her that was the best way to win the child's respect and she could see that he was right. Joseph definitely seemed to appreciate that she was not going to fight having his father at the important game even though she did make it a point to let them all know it was her time with Joseph.

That evening Joseph actually came to her to thank her for a wonderful day.

"You know it was a great day all around and it was even better that we had the house to ourselves," he said. It was the first time that day that she actually realized that Donna had not been around at all.

"Do you have any idea as to where Donna might be?"

"I know she told the kids she was busy all weekend but she did not say where she would be."

With that Vicki came to the conclusion that Donna was up to her old tricks. Most likely she had connected with someone at the new office and was spending the weekend with him. In some ways she was delighted with the idea as that could expedite Donna's moving out of her house, something that could not happen soon enough. Of course, it would have been nice if Donna had said something to her. She could have used the house to introduce Mort to Joseph. Vicki was sure Joseph would like Mort and it would be great if they could have a relationship. She decided to call him after Joseph went to bed and set up breakfast together for the morning. She would not tell Joseph about her plan as she was sure he would stress out over it.

Once Joseph was sound asleep, she called Mort. She was really excited to tell him how well the day went and how she had taken his advice. He readily accepted her invitation for breakfast, as he too, was anxious to meet Joseph. If he could win the boy's favor, it would go a long way in helping the relationship between him and Vicki. From what Vicki had told him, Joseph had met several of the men with whom she had been involved and had developed a protective armor when dealing with them. No one could blame the child. It sounded like men came and left and Vicki probably never explained what was happening to the boy. It also sounded as though every time one of Vicki's relationships ended, the boy was driven closer to his dad and his grandparents who offered greater stability for him. It had made Mort shudder when Vicki told him how Joseph would panic if she disappeared from his sight, even if she was in the same house as he.

The next morning Mort came with fresh bagels and all the

trimmings. He introduced himself to Joseph telling the boy he was a friend of his mother's.

"My mother has lots of friends but none of them stay for long."

"I understand your reserve. I would like to be more than just a friend, but I feel that is something that has to take time to develop and definitely needs your cooperation."

"Well, I guess I will be spending more time with Buddy and my grandparents."

"Not if I can have my way. I would really like it if the three of us could spend time together and get to know each other."

"That's what they all say. The next thing I know is that I am excess baggage and I am shipped off. Don't worry, I get it. I understand that Buddy wants to spend time with his new love and that I am in their way as well."

"Let's take this whole thing slowly and let's just try to get along; all three of us together. It might work and it might not. We have nothing but time to lose."

"Yeah! Can I have the cream cheese?"

"Do you have practice today?" Vicki asked to change the topic.

"I have to be at the rink at two. Are you going to able to take me?"

"I am planning on it. Do you want me to stay and see practice?"

"That would bore you out of your mind.It should be over by four and you can pick me up then."

"Let's plan on going out for dinner after your practice," Mort said.

"Okay- sure- whatever."

"Sure- I really do not have anything special to do and it might be fun. Your son is very speculative about your bringing a man home."

"He has been that way since the separation. He really wants his father and me to reunite and now that George has a girlfriend, Joseph is even more withdrawn. He has to resolve his issues himself. There is nothing I can do about it unless I want to live like a nun, and that is not going to happen."

"You are definitely nothing like a nun."

"Keep that thought and after Joseph goes to bed, I can really show how unlike a nun I really am."

"Don't you think it would be better if I went back to my house tonight? I get the feeling that your son does not look kindly about a man spending the night here."

"I can't leave him alone."

"I realize that. There will be many other nights we can spend together. I would like to try win Joseph over before I challenge his morality."

"I hate having to answer to a kid."

"What time is that practice?"

"Two-"

"Let's go to the beach for a walk."

The rest of the day went smoothly enough. Joseph seemed to enjoy being with Mort and they talked sports and stuff, often leaving Vicki completely out of the conversation. After practice, they went to Mort's house so that Joseph could fish off the dock, an experience Joseph really enjoyed and one that he had not had since Vicki and Todd broke up. Topping off the day was dinner at McDonalds before Mort dropped them back at Vicki's house.

"That guy is pretty cool," was Joseph's only comment as Mort drove away.

"Hopefully, we can all spend more time together."

"Yeah, if he sticks around."

"What the hell does that mean?"

"People come and go; that's all I mean."

Joseph went to bed and it was around eleven o'clock when Vicki decided to call Donna's cell phone.

"Where the hell are you, and are you coming home tonight?"

"I thought you made it a point that we did not have to touch base with each other when it comes to our personal lives."

"It just would be nice if you let me know when I have my house to myself."

"To answer your question, I am not planning on coming back

there tonight and the kids are with Tommy. Where I am and what I am doing is none of your business."

"It certainly did not take you long to hook up and return to your charming ways."

"Don't get it wrong! I appreciate what you did for me and kids when we needed your help and I would like to remain friends. It's just that life takes strange turns and I am liking the turn my life just took."

With that the connection was broken and Vicki could only guess the guy had come into the room.

"Poor schmuck. He doesn't realize what he is getting into," she said out loud.

CHAPTER THIRTY THREE

Within days, Donna had packed her stuff and moved herself and the kids out of Vicki's house. They moved into a house on the North Shore owned by one of the doctors in the practice where she worked. All Donna would share was that he had left his wife and kids and had planned on the move before she and he hooked up. Patricia and Tommy would finish the school year in Massapequa since it was only two months before summer vacation. She arranged to pick them up at Vicki's house after school but they would only be there a short time.

While Vicki did not like the arrangement, she agreed as long as the kids would be picked up before she came home from work. Joseph would continue going to his grandparents' house right after school, so he would not have to be with the kids.

"You do realize that if this does not work out for you, you will have to make other living arrangements."

"I think we all know this is it. We both need to live our own life. I will always appreciate you taking us in and if you ever need anything, I will be there for you."

"Thanks. I'll remember that."

Having the house to themselves proved a wonderful thing for both Joseph and Vicki. The friction was gone and so was the whispering and complaining. Joseph still locked his room whenever he left the house since he knew Tommy was there for an hour or so after school, but other than that, he was much more relaxed. He even began to accept Mort coming for dinner during the week and the two of them started to talk using sports and fishing as the jumping off point for most conversations. Gradually, Mort started to stay later and later at night and eventually he began staying over. Vicki made sure she made the nights he stayed memorable even though they had to keep the noise level down. The biggest step was when Joseph agreed to stay over at Mort's house. The weather was beautiful and they could use Mort's boat to go fishing in the bay; something Joseph was really enjoying. Mort made one of the bedrooms into Joseph's room and Vicki was loving every minute of the situation. She was having a wonderful time being a family and while Mort was still not sexually exciting, his many other attributes made him someone she wanted to be with. She was even allowing herself to think that she might be able to stop working in the City; Mort certainly had the money to support them.

Everything abruptly changed when Vicki accidentally bumped into Todd while she was at the Sunrise Mall. He was alone, as she was, and the magnetic appeal that had existed between them seemed just as strong as it originally was. He no longer had his girlfriend and before Vicki knew what was happening she was at his house and in his bed. He had not lost anything when it came to satisfying her and she completely gave into it without thinking of anything or anyone else. Before she knew it, her cell was ringing and it was Mort asking her when he could expect her home.

"I have to go. Joseph is coming home and I don't want him to come back to an empty house."

"When can I see you again?"

"Let's go slowly. You were great and I definitely missed you; but we have both hurt each other."

"The past is the past. We have to go forward and you know we are right for each other."

"I need some time."

"Is there someone else?"

"No, that is not the issue. The main issue is Joseph and then, of course, it is you and your kids and that witch Stacey. I am just not sure I can take it all again."

"I am making enough money now to keep you happy."

"Please, I need some time."

With that, Vicki gathered her clothing and ran to the bathroom where she showered and dressed. There was no way she could go back to Mort's house smelling of another man. He was much too smart for that. She decided she would just tell him that she met an old friend while at the Mall and they lost the sense of time catching up on each other's life.

Driving back to Merrick, Vicki knew she really did not want to risk losing Mort and all he offered. Going back to Todd was sexually wonderful but the baggage he carried was too complicated and she just knew it would not be long before all the old problems and fighting would be back. Maybe, just maybe, she could have them both. She could find a way to have the sex with Todd and still keep her life with Mort together. She knew she could always use Joseph as an excuse. Mort would understand her having to leave if she had to pick up Joseph or spend time with him alone. On the other hand, there was no way Todd would believe her. She had done this in the past and he would be on alert if she said she had to leave. If she just saw Mort when Todd had his girls, that could work but the time was too limited and she feared Mort would lose interest or become suspicious.

"Money talks- bull shit walks," she said out loud. "Mort is the future and Todd is the past." Hearing her own voice say it made the decision seem that much more binding. Mort had the money and the connections to make her life better. She could see being able to stay home and not work. She and Joseph could live in that beautiful house and have the social advantages Mort could offer while if she went back to Todd, she would still be living with an electrician who has child support payments and visitation that she could not be a part of.

"It's time to grow up and take the better path," she said with resolve as she pulled into the driveway at Mort's house to see him open the door for her. Obviously he had been waiting for her to return and she immediately wondered what excuse she could give for being away so long.

"Great to have you home!

"Thanks. Sorry I am so late but my errands took longer than I expected and I kinda lost track of time."

"No problem. I took it upon myself to order dinner for us. Will Joseph be here?"

"Joseph is with his father tonight, so we have the place to ourselves. Do you have any plans for after dinner?"

Mort chuckled as he put his arm around her waist and drew her to him.

"I think we can think of some entertaining idea. Don't you?"

"I can only imagine what you are thinking of. Let's have dinner first. I'm starving."

He is such a nice man; Vicki thought as they walked into the house. He never makes demands and never questions her. It could be too easy, she thought as her resolve weakened.

That evening, Vicki pulled out all her tricks to excite Mort. She repeatedly brought him to the peak of excitement only to make him wait so she could do it all again. When he finally cried out for mercy, she allowed him to climax and then to sleep. For her there was no real climax only the faked one that she staged to make Mort believe that he had satisfied her as well. There were worlds of separation between sex with Mort and with Todd. Todd knew how to push her button and bring her to that magical point but Mort just didn't get it or have it. Vicki finally got up and went into the bathroom where she played with herself until she climaxed and felt relieved. It was not the same but it would do for now.

In the morning as they got ready for work, Vicki told Mort that she would have to go to her house after work.

"I am thinking that Donna will be moving out and I am concerned that Tommy does not take any of Joseph's things. He would be really upset if that were to happen."

"You're absolutely right. Do you want me to come over and be with you?"

"No, I think it is best if I am there alone. I don't want to make ending the arrangement with her any more unpleasant than it needs to be."

"I don't see it needing to be unpleasant. You did a really nice thing for her when she needed help. Now it is time for her to move forward. You can still be friends."

"That is the ironic part of this. We were never friends and there is no reason for us to be friends. Donna does things to help herself and she is the paramount user. She has been very close-mouthed about her new relationship, but I think she is involved with one of the doctors in her office. My guess is that she will not let the relationship go along like it did with Jason where she never became the wife with the benefits. If I were to predict, I would say she is forcing him to leave his wife and to marry her."

"Is marriage what you want as well?"

"I am still not divorced. George and I never completed the divorce package though now that he has a permanent girlfriend, he may want to remarry. I just never wanted the attorney fees and all that crap."

"You know I could pay the attorney fees for you and even get you a good attorney who would be willing to represent you."

"Thanks but let's just give it some time. Joseph needs to be comfortable with any arrangements I make for my life and he definitely needs time to adjust."

"I agree with that. Call me if you need any help tonight."

With that they left the house and went to the train station in two cars. Before Vicki got to the station, she called Todd on his cell and arranged to meet him at his house after work.

"I can't stay long as Donna is planning to move out of the house tonight, and I want to be there to make sure Tommy does not take any of Joseph's things."

"I'll take whatever I can. Do you want to go out for dinner?"

"No, let's just take something in. If we go to a restaurant, it will eat up all of my time."

"I promise to make that a wise decision. What time do you expect to be at my place?"

"See you at six," she said as she disconnected the phone and got out of the car. All she could think was that one night was not going to hurt anyone.

That night after work, Vicki called Mort on her way to Todd's house.

"Just wanted to check in and tell you that I love you. I'll call you once things settle down at my place."

"I'm sure it will go smoothly. I just wish I could be there to help you, should you need it."

"Thanks, but I really think it is better if I handle this alone. I'll call you later."

There was that old comfort level that came upon Vicki as she got out of the car in front of Todd's house. The house itself was nothing special but it was on a large canal. Being able to see the water was always comforting to her.

The front door was unlocked, as it usually was when Todd was expecting her. She walked in only to find him stark naked on the couch.

"You said we had limited time to be together; so I figured why waste any of it."

"You are a real panic. I guess that is part of why I love you."

"Come; show me how much you love me."

With that Vicki knelt down and wrapped her lips around his erect penis. She knew she could make him come just like that; but this was not to be about him being satisfied. So she just brought him to the edge and then got undressed. Like always, he knew just what to do to excite her. He touched her with a gentleness that very few other men ever exhibited and she came numerous times, each with more intensity. When it was finally over, Vicki could not believe how wonderful she felt and how comfortable she was with Todd.

"Sorry to have to fuck and run but I really have to get home to supervise Donna's departure."

"If she wanted to take things from your place, she could have done it before now."

"I know, but I still want to be there. I want this to end on a positive note."

"That's my girl; never burn your bridges. Will I see you tomorrow?"

"I have Joseph tomorrow night so I don't think it is a good idea to see each other. I need to prepare him to have you back in his life."

"That complicates things as I have the girls for the rest of this week."

"That is usual for us. We both have to accept it. How are the girls anyway?"

"Getting bigger by the day, and more demanding to boot."

"Let's hope they don't become their mother."

With that Vicki quickly dressed and kissed Todd goodbye as she ran to her car. No need to shower, so she could continue to feel the wetness all the way home. It was a feeling she really liked.

Donna was alone at the house when Vicki got there

"Gee, I am sorry Lester is not here. I was looking forward to meeting him."

"He'll be back. It was shocking to see how much stuff we accumulated. We filled the car completely so Les took it to his house and he'll dump it there."

"Do you really think you are going to marry this guy?"

"If I am going to suck dick, I want something for it. No more giving it away for free! I learned my lesson with Jason; he was never going to divorce Michelle and I was always going to be his plaything. That is not happening again. Lester has actually left his wife and once the divorce is final, we'll marry. The big house, country club and all that shit will be mine and this guy does not have a problem paying child support or any of that shit."

"Is he cool with the cancer thing?"

"He's an oncologist. He keeps telling me it is a done deal and that I have nothing to worry about going forward. Working at his office has taught me to put the cancer thing in the background and to enjoy my life. I plan on living life to the fullest and Les promises to help me do so."

"Sounds like you scored a winner. Will you be able to continue working at the office after you marry?"

"That is something Les and his partners have to decide. I am cool with whatever decision they make as I will not need the money once we marry though I would like to have my own dough. Whatever."

"Maybe keep me in mind should you need a receptionist. I hate the commute and the law firm where I am is boring as hell."

"I wouldn't forget that I owe you one. What's the story with you and Mort?"

"He's a really great guy but lacking in some divisions."

"Money talks, bullshit walks. Don't be shortsighted. I still remember how unhappy you were with that electrician guy. He was great in bed but poor in everything else."

"You have a point there. It's just that Todd is a magnet for me. I have real trouble avoiding his pull."

"Don't tell me you are involved with that bastard again. You are hopeless! You are going to screw it all up again."

"I didn't say I was involved with him."

"The words didn't say anything but your face does. I still remember the balancing act you did when you were seeing Evan. You wrecked it for yourself-big time."

"Evan would never have married me. He wanted the status of a Roberta. To him I was a plaything just like you were to Jason."

"I think you are wrong about that. I just know that Todd scared him off big time and that psycho will do it again, if you are nuts enough to be involved with him. Mort may be boring but he is quality and you could use some quality in your life."

"Thanks, mom."

"Here comes my quality. Believe me, I am looking forward to the boredom."

"Hopefully he wouldn't chicken out once Tommy is living with you guys."

"He has two kids of his own and understands having a hyperactive kid. He really thinks he will be able to help Tommy."

"I hope so for Tommy's sake. That kid is out of control."

"On that topic; thanks for allowing him to be dropped off after school. I really don't want to make him and Patricia start a new school this late in the year. I will get here about a half hour after the kids are dropped off."

"I agree with you and we'll do whatever is necessary. Joseph usually goes to his grandparents' house right after school so he will not be here with the kids. Just do me a favor and stress to Tommy that he is not to touch Joseph's things."

"I'll do my best and I'll tell Patricia to keep an eye on him. I am sure Joseph will continue to lock his door."

"Yeah- that goes without saying."

With that Lester was standing in front of Vicki. He was a relatively tall man who despite his receding hairline, he looked younger than his years. Donna transformed herself into the adoring woman and kept staring into his eyes as he spoke. The act was almost too much for Vicki to take.

"I'll let you two continue with what you have to do. It's nice to meet you, Lester."

"Nice to meet you, too. Donna has told me so much about you and how grateful she is to you for helping her when she needed it."

"Let me know if I can help."

"No problem."

With that Vicki excused herself and went to her room to call Joseph and Mort. Mort again offered to come over to help but Vicki begged off saying she was too tired and wanted to get a good night's sleep as she did have to go to work early the following morning.

"The creeps are having a meeting at eight-fifteen in the morning; so they asked me to come in at eight. The only good thing about it is that I can leave at four. How about we plan on having a home-cooked dinner? I can arrange to have Joseph eat with us or have George have him for dinner. Whatever, you prefer."

"Let's include him. I really want to establish a relationship with the boy."

"I like that. See you tomorrow at my place."

"See you then. Have a good night."

The next call was to Joseph who was all excited about his hockey game and went on and on about his day at school.

"I'll tell you what, tomorrow we will have dinner, you, me and Mort, and you can tell us all about the game and everything else."

"Can't we just have dinner together; just you and me?"

"I really want you to get to know Mort. He is a really nice man who is very interested in you."

"Yeah, sure. He is interested in you; not me."

"Don't be so cynical."

"Mom, I can't help it. There have been too many people in my life who are interested in me. I feel like a pawn who is used to get to you."

"I am sorry about that. Hopefully, you will learn that Mort is different. All I am asking is for you to give him a chance."

"What time do you want me to be home?"

"I am leaving work at four so I should be on the four thirty train. I plan on coming straight home."

"That works out. I have hockey practice after school until five and I am sure the coach will drive me home after practice."

"How are you getting to practice?"

"Coach is picking a bunch of us up at school. I'm not the only kid with working parents."

"Great! See you tomorrow and remember I love you."

"Love you too."

Vicki just couldn't get over how old Joseph sounded. He was no longer the little boy and she hated the thought of him growing up and growing away from her control. Now it was almost as though she was answering to him. Everyone had told her that once elementary school was over, it was a blink of the eye before the kids were off to college. Between friends and after school activities, there really was not a great deal of time left for parents. In her case, the little time was even less, what with her having to share time with George. Separating from him just continues to bite her in the ass. She should have stayed married to George and having Todd on the side. But who knew!

CHAPTER THIRTY FOUR

Dinner with Mort was spectacular. He made Joseph the center of attention and seemed genuinely interested in everything the boy had to say. All Vicki could think was that this is how family life should be and that this was the life she really wanted.

After dinner the three of them settled in the den to watch television. Mort and Joseph quickly decided to watch the Islander game. Both were ardent Islander fans and it wasn't long before they were both shouting at the referees and the players. Vicki was surprised at how much Mort knew about hockey and even more surprised to learn that he still had great seats at the Coliseum. She thought everyone gave up their seats after the glory years. Mort even offered to take Joseph to the next game.

"You and I can have a guys' night out. I only have two seats so your Mom is not invited."

"Sounds like fun. I love seeing the game in person. What will you do, Mom?"

"I'll sit home and pout. Really don't worry about me. I think it will be great for the two of you."

'When is the next game?"

"Let me check my schedule and I'll let you know. Obviously, I do not keep all the games; so I have to check when I have the next game. I'll let you know tomorrow so we can make our plans. Hopefully it will not interfere with your time with your dad."

"Don't worry about that. He will be happy for me to get the chance to go to the game even if it is on his time. He's really understanding about things like that."

"Okay, then-done deal."

All Vicki could think while this conversation was going on was that it was as if the two of them had known each other for years. They seemed so natural together. This was so atypical for Joseph who always looked at the men Vicki had brought home as a challenge to his getting attention. He would never talk to them, let alone make arrangements to go someplace with one of them.

After the game was over, the three of them drove to the Yogurt Place in Bellmore. It was Joseph's favorite place as he loved to make his own sundaes. All the way over, Joseph kept trying to decide exactly what he was going to put on his yogurt. Neither Mort nor Vicki tried to persuade him one way or the other; they just enjoyed him being a child.

On the way back home Joseph casually asked Mort if he was going to be at the house in the morning. It came out so casually that Mort was somewhat taken back by the question knowing this was not the first time a man had stayed over; nor was it the second time.

"I think that is up to your mother."

"I would really like you to stay," Vicki chimed in before Joseph could say anything more.

"So it's settled, Mort, you're staying over, and Joseph you are going to bed as soon as we get home. You have school tomorrow and a game after school."

"Will you be able to come to my game?"

"I have to work. Will your father be there?"

"He has to work, too. Maybe I'll ask Grandpa if he can come. He gets all excited at the games."

"Good idea. That way he can drive you home as well."

When they got back to Vicki's house, Mort was amazed at how Joseph just went to call his grandfather and then went right up to his room. His own children would have stalled and found a whole lot of things to do before going to bed.

"That is one nice boy, you have."

"Yeah, I am lucky to have him. He is the only good thing that came out of my marriage to George."

With that, Mort decided to drop the conversation. He really did not want to discuss George or any of the men Vicki could have brought home previously. Somehow, not talking about it made him feel better. In some ways he was surprised that he even cared; but he had to admit to himself, he did care and he didn't even know why. This woman was no shy violet.

All negative thoughts quickly went out of his head once he and Vicki retired to her bedroom. She knew just how to touch him to make him want to yell for mercy but he controlled himself so as not to wake up the kid. Vicki was definitely the most uninhibited woman he had ever known. Nothing was taboo to her whether it be taking him into her mouth after they had just consummated the sex act or having anal sex; something he had never experienced before. When she was finally finished with him, he felt as though he was unconscious and he was shocked when the radio went on in the morning.

The morning activity was hectic just like in any other house where three people had to get ready for the new day. Vicki was up before the radio went off and she was finished with her shower when Mort was first getting out of bed. Joseph was already in the kitchen getting his breakfast and preparing his lunch. He was very self-sufficient and when Mort came down, the coffee was poured and his cereal was waiting for him.

"I hope you like Cheerios, as that's all we have," Joseph said as Mort was sitting down to the kitchen table.

"That's fine. Do you make breakfast every morning?"

"Yeah- my mother is not what you would call a morning person. So I make her coffee and this stuff. It works for us. When I am here on the weekends, she makes breakfast or we go to IHOP. They have the best strawberry pancakes."

"If you like IHOP's pancakes, you have to try John's pancakes out in Montauk. They are the best ever. They put blueberries, strawberries and bananas on theirs."

"I've never been to Montauk."

"I love it out there. The fishing is great."

"I used to fish off the dock at Mom's friend, Todd's house. That is the only fishing I've ever done."

"You can fish off the dock at my house or we can take my boat out and fish in the bay."

"I'd like that."

"We'll plan on it as soon as the weather gets a little warmer."

With that Vicki came into the kitchen. She looked absolutely radiant even in her conservative business suit.

"What are you two up to?"

"Mort invited me to go fishing on his boat as soon as the weather is warmer."

"Sounds like fun. Am I included in the plan?"

"Only if you want to be included," Mort responded. "I would never picture you sitting in a boat holding a fishing pole."

"Picture it; I would love to do it."

"As long as she doesn't have to bait the hook," Joseph chimed in making everyone laugh. "I have to run to catch my bus. Love you, Mom. Will I be here tonight?"

"I will come home right after work and we can have dinner together after your game."

"Sounds great! Thanks for a fun night, Mort."

"Thank you. We'll talk tonight about that hockey game."

With that Joseph was out the door on the run. Mort sat for a few minutes in silence but then could not help himself but to bring up his thoughts to Vicki.

"That boy is wise beyond his years. He obviously has seen several men come and go and he easily accepts you having company here. Not all kids can do that."

"Look, Mort, I have not lived like a nun since my separation and I will not discuss what I have done and with whom I have done it. There have not been that many men in my life and there have only been a few whom I have brought home to meet Joseph. Don't forget his father also has a life and has had company when Joseph has been there. Joseph is a child of divorce and as such he has grown up more quickly than other kids."

"I guess my kids are lucky our divorce happened after they were grown and off on their own. To change the topic; are you free on Saturday to have dinner with a couple of my friends?"

"Sure, that would be great. Joseph is scheduled to be with his father this weekend; so, I am free as a bird."

"Great- then after dinner we can go back to my place. I'll call you and let you know if we're on and where we will be having dinner once I get the plans firmed up."

"Are we taking the train into the City together?"

"No, I have to go home first and get some fresh clothes so I am going to take a later train. Thanks for a wonderful night."

"No sweat, speak to you later."

With that they both left the house and Vicki could not help but have a strange feeling as she got into her car. Mort may be a push over in most ways but he definitely was not comfortable with her having had multiple sexual partners. It could be a problem if he were ever to find out about Todd. Could she be monogamous? Maybe, she thought, if she could ever get him to the point where he could satisfy her or if there was enough money there so she could be satisfied in other ways. The guy definitely was showing that he could give her the type of family life she craved and Joseph wanted and needed.

"No point in putting the carriage before the horse," she said out loud as she parked her car at the train station and ran to catch her train.

That day, at work, both Todd and Mort called. Todd called earlier and Vicki could not resist the magnetic pull he had on her.

"Let's do dinner tonight and then we can go back to my place," Todd suggested.

"Let's do take-out sushi," Vicki replied suddenly afraid to be out with Todd. One never knows who sees what in the relatively small community in which they all lived. There may be over one million people living in Nassau County but somehow, everyone seems to know everyone's business.

"Sounds great to me. What time will you be coming?"

"I'll call you from the train. Right now I have no idea as to the time I will be able to leave this place."

"Great! Looking forward to seeing you and touching you."

With that, Vicki hung up on Todd as there was no appropriate response since others were within earshot.

When Mort called, the call was much more formal as Vicki pretended to be very busy with other people standing around her. She decided the less said the better as that way she would not have to remember a series of lies in the future.

"Hi, I am glad you called. I was going to call you. Unfortunately, I have to work late tonight and there is no getting out of it since they allowed me to leave early yesterday."

"Why don't I meet you for a late supper? I know you will be really tired when you finally get home."

"I think it would be better if I go straight home. Joseph really wants some alone time with me and hopefully I will get home before he has to go to sleep. Let me call you in the morning and we can make plans for tomorrow night."

"Call me tonight after Joseph goes to sleep."

"I'll try, if I am still awake. You really tired me out last night and I feel like I need toothpicks in my eyes to keep them open. I really have to go. There are all types of people standing here wanting something."

"No problem. Speak to you later."

As she hung up, Vicki made a mental note to turn off her phone before she got to Todd's house. That way all her calls would go directly to voice mail and she could always tell Mort that alone time with Joseph included no phone calls.

The last personal call Vicki had to field was from Joseph.

"Do you remember I have a hockey game after school today?"

"Yeah, I remember, but I unfortunately have to work late. I tried to get out of it but they basically said tough. In fact they are insisting that all cell phones be turned off as they do not want their meetings interrupted by calls coming in. Can you call your father and see if he can pick you up? It would be best if you were to spend the night with him since I have no clue as to what time I will be home."

"I am sure Dad will be happy to come to my game and spend the night with me. He's always there for me."

"Is that a dig?"

"I didn't mean it that way."

"You do realize we need this job."

"Yeah, Mom, I know. Really, it's no problem."

"I love you. Have a great game and you can tell me all about it later."

"So you will call me."

"I'll call you when I can. Just have fun."

Once she hung up the phone, she could not help but realize that Joseph's antennae were up. He always knows when she is being sneaky. He could be the one to blow up her cover.

Vicki was ready to leave the office at five. The brisk walk to Penn Station was invigorating. She could feel herself getting excited as she thought about the upcoming evening and decided to save some time by having Todd pick her up at the Amityville station; that way her car would remain at the Massapequa station should anyone decide to check on her story that she was in the city and she could be with Todd sooner. There was definitely something to say about the excitement he stirred in her, an excitement that Mort could not and probably would never be able to create. If only Todd had the money to sweeten things, then it would be closer to perfect. His kids and ex-wife would always be a problem but she could deal with that; if the money was there.

She quickly put those thoughts out of her mind and concentrated on planning the sex for the evening. Todd was open to anything just as she was; so she knew it was going to be an exciting time. She could actually feel herself getting wet just thinking about it. By the time she saw Todd's car, she was in a sexual frenzy and she could not help but notice his erection as she got into the front seat. It took all her will power not to take him into her mouth right there and then; but there were too many eyes around. Instead she ceremonially turned off her phone and pulled her bra off through her shirt sleeves. Her nipples were hard and when Todd reached over to touch her she could feel herself tingle.

As soon as they got to his place, it was a mad rush to get their clothes off. It was after ten before Vicki returned to the real world. She quickly grabbed her phone to call Joseph.

"How are you Butch?"

"I was really getting worried about you. I even tried to call the work number but it went directly to the answering machine."

"I told you I had to shut my phone during the meetings and the switch board closes at five. Is there anything wrong?"

"I just wanted to tell you I was declared the best player at the hockey game. It was really exciting and it's too bad you were not there."

"I am so happy for you. Did your father get to see the game?"

"He was there and he is really proud of me.'

"Well, I'm finally on my way home. Do you want me to pick you up?"

"Dad said he would drop me off in the morning so I can shower and get ready for school. I am really tired right now and I think I will just go to sleep here."

"I'll have breakfast ready for you in the morning and you can tell me all about the game in graphic detail. I love you."

"Love you too."

With that, Vicki started pushing Todd to get up.

"I need you to drive me to my car. Joseph will be at my place for breakfast in the morning and I really need to get some sleep."

"You're a real kill joy. It would be nice if you stayed the night and we could do it again in the morning."

"That's a weekend activity. I have to get to work tomorrow; so don't be ridiculous. Just get up and drive me to my car."

On the drive back to Massapequa, Todd was really quiet at first.

"It was just like old times tonight, wasn't it? You know, Vicki, we have something very special and you could move back in with me. There is plenty of room for Joseph and we could be a family."

"But, if I did that, our sex would have to be completely restrained. Joseph is old enough now to understand what we are doing and when we are doing it. Besides, there are still other issues that we cannot resolve; namely your kids. If I were to move in with you, I would have to leave every other weekend. That means keeping my house as well. Do you remember how much I hated going into exile?"

"I guess if we were to marry, I might be able to get things changed."

"One little problem with that. I am still not divorced and George still refuses to give me a divorce as it is against his religion. There is no talking to him about it. My only hope is that when his folks die, he might change his mind, but who knows when that will happen."

"You mean they are cool with him living with another woman? That is not against their religion? Give me a break!"

"There are some things that are just not worth discussing. His folks have always controlled him and will always do so even if it is from the grave. Anyway, let's let this go for now. We had a wonderful evening and I just want to enjoy the afterglow."

"Will I see you tomorrow?"

"My guess is that tomorrow, I will be with Joseph. He was really bummed that I missed his game today.'

"You can bring him to my place and we could all have dinner together."

"I need to prepare him for that. He still thinks we broke up forever and I need to help him along to accept the idea that you are back in our lives."

"Start preparing him as I am back and I intend to stay this time. I was miserable without you and I hope you were equally miserable without me. We are meant to be together and don't you forget that."

"Let's just go slowly. My kid needs to have security and he is not really ready to share me with anyone. I have to work on him. Thanks again for a perfect evening. I loved every minute of it."

"Am I going to hear that you love me as well as the sex?"

"Don't be stupid, of course, I love you or I wouldn't be here at all."

As Vicki got out of the car, she still could hear him saying,

"Don't screw it up this time. I can't stand it when you screw around and come back to me expecting me to be the puppy dog who loves you without hesitation."

"I got it. Don't worry. Somehow we will work this out. I know you're the guy for me."

Once safely in her car, all Vicki could think about was the intensity of Todd's feelings. He would definitely have a shit fit if he were to find out about Mort, just as Mort would probably leave her if he found out about Todd. Things were definitely getting complicated, and in the past when things got complicated, she always ended up the big loser.

It was rather nice walking into her quiet home. She took a long shower before getting into her pajamas and putting on the television in her bedroom. Somehow, she never got to see any of the show she had on as she was fast asleep before the first commercial. When the alarm went off in the morning, the television was still on and Vicki was surprised at how refreshed she felt. It was easy to get up, dress and have breakfast ready for Joseph when he arrived. She listened with total attention as he went through the entire game and explained each play in detail.

"I promise to be there for the next game even if it means losing this stupid job."

"I don't want you to lose your job but I really would love you to see me play next time. I doubt I can be as good as I was this time but I'll try. I really want you to be proud of me."

"I am always proud of you. You don't have to be the best player in the game for me to be proud of you. Now get your books together and let me drive you to school. I do have a train to make.'

"Can we have dinner together; just the two of us?"

"Sure, I will do my best to get out by five and you and I can go to the diner if you want."

"Let's go to Applebee's. I like it there much better than the diner where all the old people go."

"Applebee's it is then. Make sure you are home by six thirty."

"Great!"

As the train pulled into the Merrick station, Vicki could see Mort wait to board. She got up and waved at him so he would come to her car.

"Whoa- you got home late last night," he said as he bent down to kiss her hello.

"I told you they were going to keep me there really late; but how do you know what time I got home?"

"I don't but I passed the Massapequa station on my way home from dinner with friends and saw that your car was still there at ten o'clock,"

Vicki could feel her blood boiling and was trying her best to control herself.

"Were you checking on me?"

"No, I just passed by the station and thought that if your car was not still there, I would call you. Why are you being so touchy?"

"I don't like it when people check on me- pure and simple."

"That almost sounds like someone with something to hide."

"That almost sounds like you are accusing me of something."

"Let's stop this ridiculous conversation. I wasn't checking on you nor am I accusing you of anything. I have no reason but to believe that you were stuck at work last night and all I am saying is that I feel sorry for you to have to work such long hours. Secondly, what you do is none of my business; I have no ties on you."

"I am sorry. It's just that I am super sensitive about people checking up on me. In my world everyone always wants to know where I am and what I am doing. Joseph tries to keep tabs on me; George does the same even if it is through Joseph and I always feel like I have to answer to someone. It is nerve racking to say the least."

"Would I be able to see you tonight?"

"I promised Joseph dinner out tonight. He was not particularly happy that I got home so late last night and he had to spend the night at his grandparents' house."

"I understand. Let's let it go until Saturday. I made plans with my friends and I will confirm with them on Friday and let you know where we are meeting."

"It doesn't matter to me where we go. Why don't you come to my place first and then we can go to the restaurant together?"

"Sounds like a plan to me. What time would like me to pick you up?"

"Joseph will be with his dad on Saturday and I have the house to myself which is a beautiful thing. Why don't you come over for lunch and we can have some adult time together before we go to dinner?"

"Sounds like a plan to me. I'll even bring lunch so you don't have to fuss with anything."

"Great! You have no idea how much I appreciate having my house to myself now that Donna and the kids have moved out. It's like a burden was lifted from my shoulders. It really wasn't her fault as much as it was having another person to whom I had to answer and we could never be able to enjoy an afternoon delight if they were around."

"We could use my place if that was the case."

"I know. I was just thinking out loud."

They both fell silent, each absorbed in private thoughts. Mort was thinking about the excitement of spending the afternoon with Vicki while she was thinking it would all work out perfectly. Todd had his kids for the weekend so he was not going to spoil anything for her and she could still get her sex fix on Thursday night without any complications. With that thought, she reached over and touched Mort's leg. The smile on his face said it all to her; he was hers.

Once inside Penn Station, they gave each other the usual kiss on the cheek goodbye and promised to speak that evening.

"Call me after Joseph goes to bed as I don't want to interfere with his time with you."

"Great, we'll talk at about ten, if that is not too late for me to call."

"I'll look forward to it. Have a great day and don't let them keep you overtime tonight."

"Fear not; I had enough last night to last a long time. Besides, I have a dinner date tonight with a very important man in my life."

"As it should be. Have fun."

With that, Vicki turned and started walking to her office. All she could think was this was a little too easy. She was afraid that she raised suspicions with her reaction to hearing that he saw her car. Now his antenna could be alerted; that has happened in the past.

"It's a bitch having two guys at one time," she said out loud but to herself. She could even hear her inner consciousness lecturing her on the merits of giving up Todd and just staying with Mort. After all, he has the money, status and everything that goes with it to make her life better. "So what if he isn't the greatest fuck in the world! I can do this, I know I can," she again muttered to herself as she walked to work reiterating the merits of Mort; no baggage, no young children, no orders of protection, money, position in the community, nice house and the ability to allow her to give up this shitty job. Todd can do none of these; all he is good for is a great fuck and who is to say she could not continue to meet him occasionally.

Her day seemed extremely long and boring. She knew it was because she was still tired from the previous night but she was also bored to death by the job. Half way through the day she decided to call Donna at her job and inquire about any possible opening there.

"Hi Donna, how's it going."

"Everything is going really well. Tommy and Patricia are settling in and I could not be happier. Next year they will be going to school here. That will make life easier for me. How's it going for you?"

"I really do not have time to get into everything, but I wanted to ask you if there is any possibility of my getting a job at your place. This commuting thing is really getting to me and the job is boring as hell."

"Gosh, I wish I had something. Right now this place is overstaffed and until someone leaves there is nothing. Lester and his partners have put a hiring freeze in place."

'Thanks anyway. I know I can always count on you."

'Let's leave your sarcasm out of this. You know as well as I do that this is a bad economy and people are not hiring. I promise I will keep you in mind should anything open or if I hear of anything in another office."

"Thanks anyway. I just thought I would try." With that Vicki hung up and knew she would never hear from Donna. Donna was probably right, it would be a disaster for them to work together.

Dinner that night with Joseph was like having dinner with a motor mouth. He never stopped talking about his day, his games and how happy he was to have his house back. The end result was that Vicki was completely exhausted by ten and when she called Mort it was short and sweet.

The next day she decided to take an earlier train into the City. That way she would not have to sit with Mort and she would have the hour to allow her mind to just recuperate. Having no one to talk to can be wonderful, especially if one's mind is cluttered and she felt that hers was over cluttered. She knew she was at a crossroads and she needed to make a decision before the decision would be made for her. She could lose both Mort and Todd in a heartbeat if they found out about each other. There was even a part of her that was jealous about Donna's relationship. Somehow, she always manages to come up on her feet. Now she had the rich guy with the big house and was even looking forward to marriage. Vicki wondered if she even liked the poor bastard but that would not matter to Donna as long as she gets what she wants. Money, security and position, that was what mattered and Vicki knew in her heart that was what she wanted as well. Mort could provide all of the above and all she needed to do was to give up on the sex. Decisions, decisions: it was never easy for her to make decisions and this was no exception. Todd had a draw that kept pulling her to him. She knew this when she first got involved with him. She was willing to leave George for him even though George was the better provider and now she had to decide between him and Mort. Again, was she willing to give up the security for someone she knew would never have the funds to give her the life she really wanted. With Todd, working was a necessity and she would never be able to stop and just stay at home.

"Life is a bitch!" she said half out loud and half to herself. No one around her seemed to notice or to react to her words. They all probably felt exactly the same way as they were all caught up in the commuter rat race; all eking out a living doing something they probably hated. Her inner voice seemed to be yelling at her.

"Mort could save you from all of this shit if only you would give him the chance."

She wanted to yell back;

"Yeah, I know but he could also bore me to death. If I commit to him, I could end up a dried up old woman. He just doesn't get my juices flowing."

"You fool!' yelled her inner voice. "You are going to screw this up just as you have screwed up everything else in your life."

Friday passed as Fridays always do with a boring cadence. No one wanted to start anything new and the minutes passed so slowly that they felt like hours. There were very few calls on Fridays so Vicki was even more bored than usual. She could hardly wait for five o'clock so she could leave. On the way home she called Todd and told him she was going to stay with Joseph and that she would see him Sunday night after he returned his girls. Then she called Mort and told him basically the same thing except that she would see him Saturday afternoon for an afternoon delight before they were to go out with his friends. The third call was to Joseph.

"Hey guy. I had so much fun last night; let's do it again tonight."

"I thought you wanted me to go to Dad's tonight."

"You will be with your father Saturday and Sunday. Let's spend tonight together. I can rent a movie on my way home and we could just snuggle down with some popcorn."

"Sounds like old times. I'll call dad and tell him I will see him tomorrow. Do you think he'll understand?"

"He will. He knows tonight is my time with you and I am not willing to give it up. He gets lots of extra time with you. Meet me at the house at six. I'll bring dinner and popcorn."

"Don't forget the movie."

"Would I do that?"

As she disconnected the call, all she could think was he was getting so old and so grown up. At times he sounded more like the parent than she did.

That evening Vicki and Joseph really got a chance to sit together and talk.

"You know I really like that guy, Mort."

"Why? What makes him special to you?"

"I like the things he offers for us to do together and the fact that he really seems to enjoy including me. It is so much fun to fish off the dock at his house. It would be great if we could all go to Montauk and fish on a party boat. My friends tell me there is a boat named Lazy Bones and the guy is a really good fisherman."

"I am surprised that you would like to do that. I would be afraid you would get seasick."

"I'm not a baby anymore. I think it would be great fun and I hear that Montauk is a fun place to go. The beach is supposed to be really nice."

"I've been there and it is a real fun place. I would love to share that with you."

"Yeah- Buddy is too busy to go out there and his girlfriend does not like fishing or boats."

"Your Dad is not too big on fishing either."

"Buddy says I should not expect this thing with Mort to last. He says you are addicted to Todd and you will always run back to him even if it is not in your best interest."

"Really! Now he is an expert on human behavior."

"Let's not let this become something that is angry. I am only saying what he said and I guess I am hoping he is wrong."

"Am I to take it that you do not like Todd?"

"If you want the truth; yeah, I don't like him. He always makes me feel like it's a big deal that he allows me to be there. I do not feel he likes me and I still remember that he is the reason you and Buddy broke up."

"We broke up because we stopped communicating. Your father

had his life and he never really included me in it. That is beside the point. Grownups often grow apart from each other and it does not have to be anyone's fault."

"Would you and Buddy ever get back together?"

"That's not going to happen. I know that children in families where there is a divorce always want their parents to go back to one another. It just can't happen here. Your father has moved on to a new life with a new lady. He and I could never see eye to eye or live together no matter what."

"That's too bad. I love you both so much."

"We love you too."

"I still hope you and Mort can stay together. He is the nicest guy you have had."

"I'll tell him that you said that. I am sure he will be pleased. I know he really likes you too. Now let's watch that movie before it gets too late and you have to go to bed."

"Yeah- I have a game tomorrow. Are you coming?"

"I can't make it as I am having dinner with Mort and some of his friends and I have to get ready and all that girl stuff."

"Man, am I glad I am not a girl."

After Joseph went to bed, Vicki could not help but keep reviewing her conversation with him. It was obvious that he noticed the different men that came and went from her life. It really bothered her that he did not like Todd and she could not get out of her mind his comment about Todd being an addiction. If she were to be honest with herself, she would have to agree with him and George. Todd was an addiction for her. He could satisfy her like no other man; but there really was no future with him. His girls would always come first and she would always be pushed away when they were with him. That bitch, Stacey, will never relinquish that Order of Protection and allow her to be a part of the girls' lives so she and Todd could be like a real family. The bigger question was what to do with Mort? He is a really nice man, but there is no excitement there for her. Could he ever be enough? Mort is security, status, independence from George and a healthier life for Joseph. In the end, Vicki fell asleep without resolving any of her questions. This, like all other aspects of her life, would have to resolve itself.

CHAPTER THIRTY FIVE

S aturday started out early. Joseph was very excited about his hockey game and wanted to make sure he had everything he needed. He was downstairs for breakfast at seven with his bag packed.

"Your father said he would be picking you up at nine."

"I know but I just want to make sure I have everything I need. Sometimes after I finish packing I realize I forgot something."

"What do you want for breakfast?"

"I am thinking eggs and pancakes, if that is ok with you."

"Whatever is your fancy, sir."

Time passed very quickly and before Vicki knew it, George was outside beeping his horn and Joseph was out the door.

"Just a minute, young man. You forgot something."

"Oh, Mom, you do know I am not a baby any longer."

"You will always be my baby. Give me a kiss goodbye."

"Oh, Mom."

"Have a great game and give me a call to fill me in."

"Will do! Love you."

"Love you, too. Have fun."

Right after Joseph left, Vicki made a beeline for the shower. She wanted to smell just right when Mort arrived so she used her special soap from Fragonard in France. While she allowed the hot water to run off her body, all she could think about was Joseph's request to go to Montauk. She had flashbacks to her times out there and suddenly was anxious to share seeing the deer feeding on the shrubs right next to the road, walking on the beach at sunset and picturing how excited he would be catching a fish. Yes, it would be fun to go there with Mort and Joseph. They could even go fishing on Lazy Bones. That way if the weather were bad they would not lose anything as Lazy Bones does not require reservations. Drying off and using her moisturizer, she was convinced that she could arrange the trip. Again, this was something that would be impossible with Todd. He would just complain the whole time about the cost, it being ridiculous to go fishing on an open boat when they could just fish off his backyard or on his skiff. His only interest was having her on her back and he certainly had no interest in doing anything with Joseph whom he saw as an impediment. After all, when Joseph was with them, despite how infrequently that may be, sex was a no-no.

Vicki quickly pushed her thoughts away as she continued to prepare for Mort's arrival. She chose a flimsy see-through gown to wear and let her hair down and curly, just the way Mort always said he liked it. Her makeup was simple as well; just a little eyeliner and mascara and of course lipstick. When she was finished she was pleased as she looked into the mirror. She looked sexy but not slutty. She actually laughed out loud as she remembered the time she went to Evan's house wearing a trench coat with nothing under it. That was slutty, no doubt about it. Today was going to be different. She wanted to give Mort an afternoon he would never forget as she wanted to be the center of his universe when they had dinner with his friends. She wanted the world to know that she made him happier than he ever was before.

At exactly twelve noon, the doorbell rang. There was Mort standing holding a big bouquet of flowers. He really was a nice man, a considerate man and a very punctual person. If you told him to be there at twelve he was there at exactly twelve; not five minutes early or five minutes late. As she opened the door, she could hear him actually gasp as he saw her.

"My God, you are beautiful," he said as he held out the flowers for her to take.

"Why, thank you sir. You're not bad yourself. In fact, I have been anxiously awaiting your arrival. Do you want to eat food or me?"

"Say no more, my lady. I am on a strictly Vicki diet at the present time."

With that she led him to the couch in the den and straddled his lap as she started taking off his shirt and working her way down his body discarding the clothing as she got there.

"Shouldn't we go to the bedroom?" Mort asked as she was about to help him remove his undershorts.

"We have the whole house so we can start here and work our way through all the rooms. When I am finished with you, you can tell me your favorite room."

"Sounds interesting, but what makes you think I will be in any shape to remember my favorite room?"

"I am betting you will," she said as she wrapped her lips around his penis and heard the air be expelled from his lungs. And so the afternoon passed with Vicki driving Mort so crazy, he finally begged for mercy. She knew just how to bring him to the brink of satisfaction only to stop before he could come. It wasn't until they reached the bedroom that Vicki allowed him to come and then she smiled as he lay limp on the bed with sweat pouring out of his body.

"This time it was all for you but next time, I expect you to return the favor."

"I doubt I could ever do for you what you do for me."

"I need you to try," she said as she lied down next to him and started playing with herself. Mort quickly got the idea and started touching her. He played with her breasts and her clit and felt it harden under his touch. Before long her body tightened and while he could not enter her, he knew he would, at least, pleasure her this way.

"Thanks."

"No, thank you. Next time I am going to make sure you are satisfied before you make me totally crazy and leave me like a limp nothing. You know, you are amazing."

"Glad you think so. Now why don't you rest for a few minutes while I take a quick shower? I need to put myself back together before we go to dinner with your friends. By the way, should I leave my hair curly or should I blow it out straight?"

"It doesn't matter how you wear your hair. You are beautiful either way. Just do whatever is easier for you. Let me know when you are out of the shower and I will shower too, after I figure out which room has which article of my clothing."

Vicki laughed as she left the bedroom. She was sure Mort would never forget this afternoon but for her it did point out why she needed Todd. Todd knew how to make her feel good and how to hold back enough to really do her. He was a real stud while Mort was more like a choir boy. For her, the question remained, could she live with the choir boy and give up the stud permanently? She had to stop herself from answering her own question out loud. She wanted to say that it all depended on the total package.

She dressed with extra care. Wanting to appear sophisticated and not trampy, she chose a simple black dress, black pumps and small earrings. She chose a necklace with one diamond that though simple, still said success. Looking at herself in the full-length mirror, she was pleased with everything including the leather clutch bag she was holding.

"How do I look?" she asked Mort as she came down the stairs.

"You look so beautiful and if I weren't so satisfied, I would tell you we are skipping dinner and going straight to bed."

"Now, now- a man does not live by sex alone. There is plenty more where this afternoon came from. I think it is going to be fun to meet your friends. Hopefully, they will think I am worthy of you."

"The question is if I am worthy of you? I am sure they will like you, and hopefully you will like them as well. Maybe we should get going. You know I hate to be late."

"Let's do the two car thing. That way if Joseph needs me, I do not have to drag you around."

"I really do not like the two car thing. It would be so much nicer to go and come together."

"I get it, and hopefully next time I will know for sure that George will be there for Joseph. Unfortunately, when George picked him up this morning, he did say there was a possibility that he would be called into work, and asked that I pick up Joseph if that were to happen."

"Okay, just follow me but in case we get separated, we are going to Bella Notte on Merrick Road in Bellmore. It is a small restaurant right after a 7-11 and there is parking on the side and in the back."

"No sweat. I've seen it in passing so I know where it is."

On the way to the restaurant, Vicki did all she could do not to call Todd. It would have been awkward to have to explain to whom she was talking if she were to be asked and, if she did call, there was no way she could promise to be there tonight. After all, Mort might expect her to either go to his house or for him to come back to her place.

They arrive at the restaurant together and were able to go in together. Vicki could not believe the reception Mort received from Teddy, the owner. It was like they were long lost friends or something. She knew she was looking good by Teddy's reaction when Mort introduced her and this pleased her immensely.

"I gather you come here frequently," she said once they were seated at what was supposed to be Mort's favorite table in the corner.

"This is a good place to come even you only want a light dinner. The food is good and the people are friendly. When I come here alone, I do not feel alone and when I come with friends, we are never rushed out.'

"So, tell me a little about these friends of yours."

"I have been friends with Jeff for many years and he is my go-to person when I have legal questions."

"Am I meeting him for a go-to opinion?"

"Stop being so self-conscious. I hope you will like him as he is someone I see rather frequently. I did not arrange this as a meeting to judge you. I just want you to be comfortable with my friends. Would you like a glass of wine while we wait for them?"

"I'll have a glass of merlot if you are having a drink too. Otherwise, I can wait."

With that two glasses of wine arrived at the table without Vicki ever hearing Mort order them.

"How did they know what we wanted?"

"I told you, I come here frequently and they know I enjoy the merlot."

Vicki laughed and asked, "What if I had wanted something different?"

"They would have taken the merlot back and brought you whatever you asked for."

The wine tasted good and Vicki felt herself relax as she sipped it. The good feeling vanished in an instant the moment she saw Jeff and Stacey enter the restaurant. She felt her jaw drop but no words came out of her mouth as Stacey quickly turned and left the restaurant.

"What happened?" Mort asked as Jeff stood in front of him.

"We have to leave. Stacey has an order of protection against Vicki and I think it is best if I let her explain this to you. If you want any clarification, call me later. Better yet; just call me as I doubt you will get the full story."

With that Jeff left as well. Mort just sat there in silence as Vicki tried to get her thoughts in order. She could not help but wonder what the chances were that they would be Mort's friends and she knew that no matter what she would or could tell him, Jeff would point out the lies and the hidden facts. Jeff would portray her as a tramp and a liar and for sure he would tell Mort about Todd and all her habits. There was no point in saying anything; this was over. With that thought crossing her mind, Vicki got up and walked out of the restaurant without saying a word to Mort.

Once in the car she tried to call Jeff but only got his voice mail. Her message was simple as she yelled, "You crazy bastard, you ruined my life once again. I hope you and your whore feel good about that!"

Next she called Donna who answered but who was not prepared for the psycho call. "You have to help me. That bastard Jeff just ruined my life and now all I have left is my cheap electrician. You have to introduce me to a rich doctor like you have!"

"Listen, Vicki, you have to calm down. Stop yelling into the phone. I don't need this."

"I need your help. When you needed help, I was there for you or have you forgotten that?"

"We can talk when you calm down. Right now you are irrational." With that Donna ended the call. This made Vicki even more furious and she immediately called Donna back only to have the call go directly to voice mail. Vicki's message was, "I know you don't want your rich lover boy to know your past and you are afraid he will overhear us. I will make sure he knows everything and then you will know how I am feeling right now. You are a user, you bitch!"

Vicki then repeatedly called Jeff and Donna and kept screaming into their voice mail with each message getting more hateful and vile. She was so desperate and so upset that rational thought was not a part of her being. She even called Mort and screamed at him.

"You used me and now you will throw me away like garbage. Your friends are more important to you than I am so go fuck your friends."

Mort was astonished and could not even think of a reply and when he tried to get a word in, his attempt was met with more profanity and more yelling, so he too ended the call only to immediately receive another with more yelling and more cursing. Finally he too turned off his phone as he needed time to get his thoughts in order. Obviously, Vicki was not who she portrayed herself to be and her calls just pointed out that she was crazy. What he needed was to speak to Jeff and to try to understand what actually happened; but when he called Jeff from his private number, he got voice mail immediately and he knew that Jeff had turned off his phone. Mort knew he would have to wait for Jeff to call him and for the moment there was nothing he could or would do. Jeff had his private number so even with his phone off, Jeff could reach him. Mort just hoped that Vicki would get home safely without hurting herself or someone else.

Mort had barely walked into the house when the private phone rang, seeing it was Jeff, he answered it.

"Well you really had yourself one hot wire. I am betting you never had sex like that before."

"You could say that. Just tell me what is going on and how you are in the middle of this."

"To make it short and sweet, Vicki broke up Stacey's marriage and took up with her ex. When money got tight, she blamed Stacey and would psycho call her and threaten her until Stacey had to get an order of protection for herself and for the girls. That's the short story and all of that happened before I met Stacey. I knew Vicki when she worked at the Schwartz firm and she was the receptionist. Vicki was always on the make and any successful guy was her target. She even went after one of theBergman brothers and tried to break up his relationship with his now wife. All the time she was involved with Eric, she was still seeing Stacey's ex. I am sure you heard that she has to work late, or she has to be with her son, or she has to pick up the kid. The excuses probably sounded viable but she was most likely with Todd. I am surprised that you did not get a visit from Todd suggesting you stop seeing her because I know that other guys who were involved with her had such visits and they were all unnerved by it. Vicki is addicted to sex. She was even arrested for prostitution. What saved her was that she did it for nothing.

Please believe me. This is a woman who brings havoc wherever she goes. Men become slaves to her because of the sex but she is incapable of really caring for anyone. A guy like you, with money and position and who is lonely is prime prey for her and all she will give you is heartache and unhappiness and take your money. I know you have been lonely since your marriage ended but, please, think with the right head and stay away from that woman. She is trouble with a capital T."

"I would never have thought that what you are saying is possible. She seems like a dedicated mother and really seemed to care about me."

"It's an act. Just remember that dedicated mother is fucking some other guy when you think she is with her son. The poor kid is so insecure that if he is with her and she is not in his sight for a moment, he panics. He is lucky his grandparents live close by as he spends most of his time at their house when he is not with his father."

"How come the father does not have residential custody?"

"It is too expensive and I know he does not feel he needs it since he spends more time with the boy than she does. He is not a bad guy and he is just starting to get his life together after they split. The poor guy never saw it coming and he was addicted to her at the time."

"You keep using the word addicted and I understand its meaning. She is addictive."

"Just stay away from her. She even had one poor schmuck arrested because he went to her house begging her to resume their relationship. She actually accused him of domestic abuse and you and I know the trouble that can bring. She is just a sick puppy and you should think of her as having rabies."

"Thanks for the warning. I feel sorry for her."

"I feel sorry for a rabid dog but that does not mean I want to extend my hand to it."

"Wow! I am getting it. Thanks for the call and for caring."

"Just stay away from her. I really do not want to have to bail you out of jail."

After hanging up, Mort again tried to call Vicki but again the call went directly to voice mail. He just could not stop himself. He had to get in the car and drive past her house all the way telling himself he was doing it just to see that she made it home. As he drove past, he could not deny the shock of not seeing her car in the driveway. If he were to believe Jeff, and he had no reason not to do so, she was at that guy Todd's house. He had to know for sure.

"Sorry to bother you again, Jeff. I just need to know that guy Todd's address."

"Don't tell me, you are outside her house and her car is not there?"

"I just had to see if she made it home."

"Now you just have to see if she is fucking Todd's brains out. Believe me, I get it and believe me that is exactly where she is. It is probably what she was planning before you went to dinner and that is why she took her own car there instead of going with you. I know she is there because the girls are back home with us and she cannot go there if the girls are there because of the order."

"What is his address?"

"I really hesitate to give that information to you. You can only get in trouble if you go there. Confronting her is pointless. This is her behavior and it will always be that way. Accept it; it is over for you, if you have any self-respect."

"I just want to see it for myself. Can't you understand that?"

"His address is 10 Hewlett Court in Amityville. It's a real quiet street and his place is at the end. Your car will definitely be seen."

"Thanks for the info. I promise I will not make a scene and I will not get out of the car or confront them in anyway, form or matter. I just need to see for myself that she is there. It is truly hard to believe she can put on such a good act as to be extremely upset one minute and then go to another man's arms the next."

"That's Vicki. I am telling you that she planned to go there tonight before we walked into the restaurant. She would have told you she had to pick up Joseph."

"Come to think about it; that is why she said she had to take her own car in the first place."

"Go home and forget about her. She is not worth a minute of your time or thoughts."

"Thanks for caring."

With that Mort turned his car toward Amityville. He just had to see for himself and when he passed the house all he could do was shake his head in disbelief. There in front of the house was Vicki's car, just as Jeff said it would be. He could not believe how stupid he had been. He was ready to give her anything she wanted. He was a fool; there was no way to deny that. He had always heard that a man would do anything for good sex but he never thought he would or could be a victim of that. Vicki had him under her spell; there was no doubt about that. He wanted to trust her and to believe she had really changed but in reality, all that she did was to lie to him and to try to use him.

"Thank God for Jeff," he said out loud. Had he not scheduled a dinner with Jeff and Stacey, he would have dug an even deeper hole for himself. People always say there are only six degrees of separation but he could not help but wonder at the coincidence of Jeff knowing Vicki and of Vicki having been the person who destroyed Stacey's first marriage.

As Mort entered his house, he was keenly aware of the silence. The house, all of a sudden, seemed empty, cold and even a little hostile. It had been nice thinking of filling the place with a ready-made family. He had to admit to himself that he would miss Joseph. He was such a nice kid, and looking at that from his current perspective, he had to wonder how the boy was turning out to be so nice. One thing that was evident was that Joseph's insecurity probably had its roots in Vicki's behavior. Obviously, she lied to the kid just as she lied to him.

"Stop yourself," Mort said to himself. He had to stop analyzing her and her child. What she did or did not do with the boy was none of his business.

"I have to get my own life back on track!" With that remark, the phone rang. Mort could see that it was Vicki calling and this surprised him enough that he actually answered the call.

"I am so sorry I ran out of the restaurant and just left you there."

"Look, Vicki, it is time to stop the lies. I know you went directly to your boyfriend's house."

"You followed me!"

"No, I did not follow you. Jeff told me where Todd lives and predicted that you would be there. I drove by and saw your car."

"We're just friends and I went there because I was too upset to just go home. I knew Jeff would tell you all sorts of lies about me and Todd. It's all lies because he is jealous. Todd and I are just good friends and that is all there is to the relationship."

"Stop yourself. I know all about you and Todd and I am sure that if I were to call him right now, he would confirm what I know is the truth."

With that Vicki started yelling into the phone. She called

everyone involved vile names and Mort could sense that she was becoming more and more irrational. His professionalism kicked in and he did exactly what he would recommend a client to do; he hung up the phone. What followed was another round of psycho calling with her yelling and him hanging up until he could take it no more and he just took his receiver off the hook to busy it out.

Mort sat in the dark room knowing his message center was getting a workout. He could not help but wonder how he allowed himself to get involved with someone like Vicki. He rationalized that the sex was so wonderful and exciting, it clouded his judgment and prevented him from seeing that the sex was a symptom of greater mental problems. No one is that uninhibited without underlying mental problems. He now also realized that he was extremely lonely, and his loneliness made him more vulnerable than he had ever been in his life. He wanted the family that came with Vicki and he really enjoyed the time he spent with Joseph.

"That poor boy does not stand a chance with her as his mother," he said as though hearing the words helped him to accept what he could not and would not change. Any relationship with Vicki was doomed and all that would result from it was further pain. She was as addicted to her boyfriend as she was to sex. Jeff was right, she would always need Todd.

While Mort was sitting in the dark at his house, Vicki continued screaming into the phone. She called everyone she could think of, and as soon as the other person heard her voice, the call was disconnected. Even Todd hung up on her and left his phone off the hook. He knew that when she was like that, there was no point in trying to rationalize with her. He also knew that eventually she would calm down and crawl into his bed like a wounded puppy. He had been there before and knew that she probably had had another affair that went bad. It did not matter; she always came back to him and things would be even better for a while as she tried to make amends for her errant behavior. He laughed out loud at the thought that this time he did not even have to pay a visit to the poor schmuck; the guy got scared off all by himself.

CHAPTER THIRTY SIX

J eff sat in the car and wondered where the years had gone. Everyone he knew had moved on after knowing Vicki, and the only reason he still had any knowledge about her was because of his and Stacey's connection with Todd. Todd was always careful to maintain the restrictions of the Order of Protection and the girls were never exposed to Vicki nor were they told about her whereabouts when they were with Todd. The time the girls were with Todd was greatly reduced since they were busy in high school with their own after school activities. Janet was the busiest as she was actually preparing to go to Cornell and the whole family was excited to begin a new chapter in life. Then, of course, there was Gregory, who at five was the star of the family. He had four mothers to fawn over him since the day he was born. Jeff laughed out loud as he thought about how brilliant and handsome his son was and what a gift he was to the whole family. There were no shared weekends for Gregory and that was the best ever.

Seeing Vicki lying on the workout bench had triggered so many memories. Their lives had crossed more times than Jeff cared to remember, and each time there was a junction in their paths, chaos had followed. He could not help but wonder how many more lives she had turned upside down since his last involvement with her when she and Mort were seeing each other. He knew for sure that her patterns had not changed and, in fact, the girls had told him that Joseph had decided to live with his father right after his sixteenth birthday. That had to have had a horrible effect on Vicki but Jeff could understand the decision and he was happy for the boy. George was always the one who gave stability to Joseph's life.

Just as those thoughts crossed Jeff's mind, his phone rang with an unknown number being flashed on the screen.

"Good seeing you again after all these years. Are you still with that boring bitch you married?"

"You haven't changed a bit, have you?"

"You were always the one I really wanted. Are you ready for a real woman? I could meet you and show you what real sex is like."

"Vicki, you are crazy. The last thing I want is to be involved with you in any way or form. I know you want to hurt Stacey and that is probably why you are saying the things you are saying. It is not going to happen; now or ever."

"I hadn't thought about Stacey; but now that you bring her up, it would be a real kick to take two men away from her."

"As I said, it is not going to happen! I am not going to be another notch on your sex belt. Go back to Todd and stay there. You deserve one another."

"You deserve that frumpy, boring woman you married. If you ever had a real woman, you wouldn't know what to do with her. You don't understand; I am alone and I need your help. I hate being alone. Even Joseph has deserted me! You crazy bastard; you've ruined my life many times. I am offering you a trip to paradise and all you say is 'go back to Todd.' I need your help; you fucking bastard! You owe me!"

"Vicki, you never understand. I do feel sorry for you. I know it is hard on you having Joseph live with George and I know you are probably bored with Todd. I cannot and will not help you. Call Todd! He is the only one who is always willing to help you. You deserve one another."

With that Jeff disconnected the call and he knew psycho calling could start at any moment; so before she had another chance to call him, he called Stacey.

"Hi, I need a favor."

"Sure, what's up?"

"I need you to meet me at field seven at the beach. I need to go for a walk with someone I love more than life itself."

"I'm on my way. Kristine is here to watch Greg so I can leave him home. Let me call you from my car so we can talk while I drive."

"No, I'll call you.'

"Give me five minutes."

As soon as Jeff disconnected the call, the phone rang with the unknown number flashing on the screen. He had to laugh because he knew her so well and knew the calls would continue for hours. There was absolutely no point in answering and telling her not to continue calling, though it might be fun just to infuriate her more. Maybe he would even let Stacey answer as that would really make Vicki crazy.

Jeff put Stacey's number into his phone and hit send just as he saw Vicki's call disconnected.

"Tell me you saw Vicki and she is calling you."

"How could you possibly know that?"

'I know you better than anyone and that wicked bitch is the only person who could make you need to call me like you did."

"You are right, as always. I ran into her at the gym. I was there to see a client and decided to workout. Seeing her opened a flood gate of memories none of which were good. She had not changed at all."

"Plastic surgery is a wonderful thing."

"I don't mean just her looks. She is as crazy as ever."

"She is someone who uses her body to try to get what she wants. I am sure she would love to have a relationship with you as that would hurt me. In her crazy way, she thinks I ruined her life.'

"I actually told her that."

"I am coming down Ocean Parkway right now and I will be at the field in just a few minutes. A good walk on the beach will clear your head."

"I love you. I promise, once you get here, we will not talk about her."

'She is poison but I have a lot for which I am grateful to her.

Without her, I would still be married to Todd and you and I would never have met. Greg would never have been born and the wonderful life we have would never have been."

"You are right. From evil good can come." With that they both disconnected the call, and Jeff promptly turned off his phone as he saw Stacey's car enter the parking lot. They ran to each other like the lovers they were and both inhaled the ocean air and felt the cleansing it brought to their minds and bodies.